VOLUME SEVEN
The Ozark Mountains Historical Fiction Series

MISSISSIPPI CENTRAL

THISTLES IN THE WIND

JOANN KLUSMEYER

innovo
PUBLISHING

Published by Innovo Publishing, LLC
www.innovopublishing.com
1-888-546-2111

Providing Full-Service Publishing Services for Christian Authors, Artists &
Ministries: Books, eBooks, Audiobooks, Music, Screenplays, Film & Curricula

**THE OZARK MOUNTAINS
HISTORICAL FICTION SERIES
FOR ADULTS**

VOLUME 7

**MISSISSIPPI CENTRAL
&
THISTLES IN THE WIND:**
An Anthology of Southern Historical Fiction

ISBN: 978-1-61314-702-3

Cover Design & Interior Layout: Innovo Publishing, LLC

Printed in the United States of America
U.S. Printing History
First Edition: 2021

Has God called you to create a Christian book, ebook, audiobook, music album,
screenplay, film, or curricula? If so, visit the ChristianPublishingPortal.com to learn
how to accomplish your calling with excellence. Learn to do everything yourself, or
hire trusted Christian Experts from our Marketplace to help.

CONTENTS

Josephine Findley, almost 18, had the poison selected and handy in the event she couldn't handle another day, or even another minute. Rat poison was easy to get. The thing was, though, she had seven strong chains tying her to old terra firma, and they were called 'siblings.' And there was another thing. If she solved the problem this way, there was no way back, and whatever way her life turned out to be, it was the only one she had. Something to think on while washing overalls and digging potatoes.

Is it possible for the wind to blow a couple of seeds across several states to be planted where they were needed? Or would it require Help from somewhere else?

MISSISSIPPI CENTRAL

1

The Findley family was in direct line of the right-of-way for the locomotive tracks for the Mississippi Central railway. Their sparse farm was located on the flat plain leading to the Tuscalera River. They would have to be moved. Trouble was, the owner of the land and the father of seven children was hard to deal with. It seemed an injury (or something) had happened, and his thoughts came out a bit twisted. It was pathetic and unfortunate, but the railroad was going to take the land, and there was that family to consider.

The oldest girl, Josephine, seemed to be the one to deal with, but her father wouldn't permit it. He was a wood cutter by trade, but there were no trees on his land that could be cut. He worked pitifully hard on land belonging to others who wanted it cleared, and his oldest son was drafted to help,

There were the children to consider, so what was to be done? They had no recourse but to avail themselves of the skill on a negotiator. The land would be taken, but the owner could not understand how the railroad got access to his land. It didn't make sense to him. Perhaps the negotiator could help.

It all started with the Mississippi Central, a busy little locomotive that plowed through Mississippi until it reached the big river. There it stopped suddenly, and any movement west was done by ferry, and then by horse drawn wagons and motor lorries.

Obviously, not much business happened that way. Now, if that track was made to pick up on the other side of the river, they could do away with the wagons and have contact the capital city of Arkansas, called Little Rock, and also a lot of lesser towns on the way.

Of course everyone knew that northern Arkansas was quite mountainous and unwieldy for building a railroad, but the southern part of the state was relatively flat and ideal for rice production.

Also, the Rock Island Line came down from Kansas straight to Texas, but there was a spur line over to a small town called Jacksonville. If the rail line left the river and went as far as it could on the flat land, perhaps, somehow, a connection could be made for the Mississippi Central to hook onto the Jacksonville spur.

A lot of the mountainous portion was practically uninhabited, as there were rock ledges and bluffs to contend with. But now the wise heads got together and decided it was possible. A lot of the land could be gotten practically free, and the owners of the rest of the land would just have to contend with it. Either take the price offered, or be evicted, and evictions were really bad press for the railroad owners.

A wide strip of trees must be taken from the railway right of way, and that made a lot of wood that was downed and must be cleared, but usually there were homeowners who came and cut it up for their home use.

The decision was made and the connection began in Jacksonville heading southeast to be met by the extension of the Mississippi Central.

This event made a lot of conversation in the small towns along the way, as to whether it would be good or bad, but it would make changes all along the right-of-way. In time, the small town of River Bend came into their sights. There the usual mountains to contend with, but there was also a very wide and rushing river to cross, and to get a permit from the state, they must install a wide, four lane bridge of steel with treated wood pilings to hold it up.

They had circled the end of one mountain range, being required to buy an eighty farm hanging on the side of the mountain. That farm was made up of bluffs and ledges of old rotting lava and solid gray boulders the size of a small house. If they bought that farm, they could use a narrow valley and escape a much worse section.

After that, the next land to be acquired was owned by a family with seven children and a man who cut wood for a living. He sold the wood to the residents of the little town, and seemed, somehow, to eke out a living.

The owner was a hard headed fellow, and didn't seem to see the value of the money paid, and insisted it was his land, and he was staying on it. Of course that was not going to happen, but the railroad hated evictions. They left such bad feelings, but they had a negotiator named Jonathan Snowden, a clever Scotsman from a family that was acquainted with mountains and volcanic hills.

Jonathan would be sent to iron out this little problem before the loggers who were cutting the right-of-way got close. Maybe a deal could be worked out for wood to sell, but that would be Jonathan's problem.

Mr. Jonathan Snowden, 25 years old, arrived unceremoniously on horseback. He tied his horse to the rickety hitching post and knocked on the door. Pa answered. Not good.

Josephine, age 17, was bent over the washboard with the stomper beating the dirt from the overalls of the wood cutter father and brother. Her ma, Ettie, was turning the handle of the wringer that transferred the washed clothes from the soapy water to the rinse tubs.

Ettie, in a concerned hoarse whisper, said, "Josie, get on in there and get where you can listen. You know Pa can't put two and two together nomore."

Josie nodded, dried her hands, and left. Her ma was a little bit wrong. Pa could put two and two together, but he could never understand a transaction, and ever since the accident, he thought everyone was 'out to get him.'

Josie eased into the room with a dust cloth. She wished to avoid an introduction, so she crossed the room and wiped the cloth on the glass of the window. It could stand a bit of cleaning, anyway, but who had time… and energy?

Mr. Snowden must have been clued in on pa, because he was using a soft voice and starting with reason. Yes, it was a raw deal, and a lot of people were upset about having to move. The railway made it as easy as possible, and even helped to find a place for them, and also provided help in moving their livestock and household possessions.

Pa wasn't having any of it. The fact was, he wasn't understanding what was said, or realizing the inevitability of it. Josephine and her ma couldn't see how they could lose on any deal made, as what they had was next to nothing. Wouldn't even grow a good garden. Winter rains on the mountain overflowed from the tributary and kept the ground soggy. Couldn't even leave turnips in the ground the way they should be kept, they rotted. Couldn't have a root cellar, it filled up with water.

Finally Mr. Snowdon gave up and walked back out to his horse. Josephine slipped out the back of the house and signaled to the negotiator, "Sir, are you permitted to talk with me?"

Jonathan looked toward the voice. "I can talk with anyone who'll talk with me. Would that be you?"

"Yes, sir. "My name is Josephine. I listened while you talked. Where would you find a place for us?"

"Josephine, my name is Jonathan. Do you have an idea of where he would consent to go? It would be dreadful to have the sheriff have to physically move him, but it will happen if we can't come to an agreement. The railroad line is coming right though where your house stands. I could have showed him the schematic, but I didn't think he'd look at it."

The girl nodded. "Yeah, and likely wouldn't understand it if he did. He didn't used to be this way, and he knows he ain't what he used to be and it makes 'im mad at everyone. I don't hardly think he could stand it to live in a town, and he couldn't cut wood, and that's all he can do now." She stared helplessly at the negotiator who stared helplessly back.

"Tell you what, Miss Josephine. I'll do some thinking. You've helped a lot in tellin' me about 'im, and I'll do some thinkin' and get back to you. Would there be a way to see you, without him along?"

"Sure could. Him and my brother go cut wood of a mornin' and get back for dinner about 2 o'clock. Till then it's just me and ma, and the little'ns. If you can give us an idea, maybe ma and me... well, we can try."

Jonathan nodded. "I can surely do that. Would tomorrow be good?"

"Any time you can come."

"Look for me tomorrow about mid morning." And he took the reins from the hitching post and swung aboard the horse. Josephine watched until he was just a spot on the horizon.

She went back to the laundry, and ma was wringing clothes out of the rinse water. It was a hard job alone, so Josephine took the wheel and turned while her ma fed the clothing into the rollers of the wringer.

Her ma looked her with a question in her eyes, and Josephine told her, "He's gonna come back tomorrow when it's just you and me. He's gonna see what he can do,"

"What'd that be...?"

"Don't know, ma. We'll see tomorrow."

TOMORROW MORNING

Jonathan was apprehensive as he entered the shack on the flood plain of the Tuscalusa. He was not particularly fond of this duty, but he knew it had to be done, and his success told him he was likely the best for the job.

He came in a buggy this time, as, if he was successful with his negotiation, he might need it.

Josephine and her ma were in the kitchen, which had a window toward the front of the shack, and they were glancing every minute or so, mentally crossing their fingers. This problem could get messy. Years ago there'd be no trouble with pa, and he'd see what had to be done and make the best of it, but his injury made him apprehensive, and extremely paranoid.

And when the buggy approached, they decided that must be him. Drying their hands and brushing down their dresses in an attempt to be presentable, they met him at the door.

Jonathan carried a roll of paper, and Josephine was immediately uplifted. He had something. A cross of fingers helped her to be hopeful.

He began, "I know you must be wondering if I had an idea, so I'll start right in. I did have one thing, and I hope it will be good for Mr. Findley."

He spread out what seemed like a hand-drawn map of the immediate area. There was the river and the marked out area of the right-of-way. There was a block representing the shack and an outline of a fence just on the other side of the river.

"What we have here is a Schematic, showing the projected path of the Mississippi Central and the surrounding area. Here where the marker is we have an abandoned farm. Your neighbor across the river could have just deeded a slice of land to the railroad, but he stubbornly held out for a total sale. He was getting older and wanted a place in town that was flat because he was tired of climbing.

"We arranged that for him, and the place is empty. It originally contained 100 acres, but 13 acres are in the right-of-way, leaving 87 acres, mostly up and down. It's impossible to show that on this drawing, but there is a bluff here and also up here, but the land is not soggy and has an excellent turf of grass. The former owner dynamited an edge of the bluffs to create a way to climb to the top.

"The whole area is fenced with the exception of that bordering the right-of-way. The place has a house in good condition, somewhat larger than this one, and it has a garden space that seemed to be productive. There is an all-weather spring and a roomy cellar. The shed could use some repair but is usable and quite roomy."

He paused to let the ladies try to imagine what he had said, and then he added, addressing Josephine, "There is now a number of goats in the top enclosure that the former owner used for food, and they go with the place. If you think this might be a possibility for your family, I am ready to take you there. Would there be someone to stay with the children.

Josephine gave a look at her ma, who looked back and nodded. "Mister, them youngen can take care'a themselves."

Then Jonathan, "So you are ready to go look at it?"

Josephine answered for her. "Yes, sir, Mr. Jonathan. We'd like to go right now."

While the ladies sat on the back seat of the buggy, Jonathan drove across the rickety bridge that the railroad would turn into a wider bridge, braced with iron girders. He urged the horses to climb the hill to the first flat area. There, behind a grove of oaks and a few catalpas, was the house.

It stood tall and solid against the mountainside. It could use a coat of paint, but still looked strong and attractive. A rosebush was blooming in the yard, and a part-collie dog came out to meet them, wagging his bushy tail.

Jonathan said, "That dog refused to leave, so they just left him here. I imaging he is friends with the goats, and he seems well fed, so he must take care of himself."

He pulled up to the front porch and tied the horses to the hitching post prepared for that purpose. He could almost feel the anticipation of the ladies. Even from the outside, they could see it was miles better than the one down on the flood plain.

He produced a key, and they entered. Josephine turned and looked at all sides of the front room. "Look, ma, at these windows. I can see the river and the road and when the leaves turn colors, it's gonna be like a bouquet!"

Ma was silent, but nodded. They passed through the house and out to the shed. It had a southern exposure, against the north wind, and had a fenced corral. Josephine added, "Our cow'd really like this… and the horses, too, and look at all that grass!"

Jonathan smiled inwardly. It seemed all was well. "Would you like to climb up to the next level?"

They would, and also to top level. On top there were a lot of trees, and all were neatly trimmed to a height of about 6 feet. There were six long-haired white goats and several kids, bouncing around in their play. Jonathan wondered if he should say something, or should he let the goats do the selling. He paused and watched ma's face.

"You say them goats go along with the deal?"

"Sure do. There's room here for cows and horses, and I was told the goats take care of themselves, along with the dog, and I think they called the dog, Bowser. Sometimes animals form friendships like that. He may think he's protecting the goats"

Josephine stood on the edge of the top bluff and looked out over the land. She breathed in a deep breath of the breeze that was flowing up from the river.

"Mr. Jonathan, if we was to agree to the trade, how much money would it take to have this place?" That was important to know before she let herself get her hopes up.

Jonathan could never have heard words he liked better. "Miss Findley, there would be no money required. It would be an even trade. In addition to that, the railroad would move you free. They would send a van with fellows to do it. And they'd bring your animals, as well.

"You can plainly see the value of this place, and the railroad is willing to make an except in this case, and not put this place up for sale. The thing is, the decision must be made quickly. If Mr. Findley insisted on money, the value would not be nearly enough to buy this place, you can see, but the railroad is willing to do this for your family, so this difficulty can be over in a short time."

Josephine wanted assurance. "You sayin' we wouldn't need to pay any money, and we could just move in?"

"That's what I'm saying, but I might remind you. The state taxes on this place will be more than your house on the flood plain, thought I don't know how much. If you decide to do this, you'll know what the taxes will be. If you've seen everything you want to see, we'll go down and let you ladies talk about it."

They were silent on the down hill trip. Jonathan knew they were thinging what would be best with pa. He mustn't be let to say 'no' too quick, as he would not be likely to change his mind.

When Jonathan was driving away, ma turned to her daughter. "Josie, honey, you set your head to how to tell you pa. I couldn't do it. He'd see how much I liked it and he'd say 'no' thinkin' there was a trick in there somewheres."

Josephine was not surprised at the assignment. She was already thinking. She'd need to approach the subject round about so he'd not say 'no' until he listened to everything.

Ma had Josephine kill a chicken, and she had made huge kettle dumplings. There wasn't much meat, with so many diners, but there was fat from the chickens scratching on the wet soil for insects. The fat helped with the flavor, and pa liked dumplings... so warm and filling, and reminded him of his ma.

He was resting on the porch when Josephine brought him a cup of peppermint tea. While the tea had steeped, she thought, "I'll have to lift up them peppermints plants and take 'em to the hill." In her mind, she had already moved.

She gave him the tea and sat on the edge of the porch leaning back on a pillar, just like she had nothing better to do. Actually, she didn't, because this was the most important thing she ever did in her life, and she had to do it right.

"Pa, do you like goats?"

Pa thought a bit. "Used to," he finally said. "Your grandmum had a way'a fixin' 'em that us boys really liked. Thought one time I'd like to have 'em, but there weren't no place for 'em here."

Josephine waited a minute. "Today I saw some that were right pretty. Had long hair and the little fella's bouncin' around like rubber balls."

"What was you doin' out where you'd see goats?"

Josephine was ready. "Ma needed something from the Mercantile." True, as ma always needed something from the Merantile. That didn't mean she was going to get it.

"Fella that had the goats was givin' um away. Course, they had to stay with the place, and it was really good for goats. It was all up and down, and the goats were up top. Right pretty they were."

That had Pa attention. "He was givin' 'em away free?"

"Yeah, but they had to stay with the property. He wasn't lettin' em be took off, because they liked it there so much. You know what, Pa? Goats can trim trees. They stand up on their hind legs and reach up as far as they can for leaves. Can you beat that!"

"Yep. Seen that myself. Why'd the fella with the goats want to sell his place?"

"Getting' old, he was. Bad knees… at least that's what I heard. Didn't see 'im, myself."

"Who's takin'care'a the goats?"

This was going good. Pa was interested.

Josephine answered, "Nobody, I reckon. Seemed there was a part-collie dog that was left with 'em, and the dog thought he was in charge."

Pa nodded. "Seen that, too. Them collie's… their good to have."

"Could be he'll not be alone very long. It's a good place with a house and shed, and it's up for sale or trade. I sure did like it." She stood and straightened her dress. "If you're through, I'll take you cup. I gotta get busy."

He handed the cup to her, and asked, "When you get time, you could bring me another cup'a that tea."

"I'll do it now." And she was gone. She smiled at the walls and doorway. The conversation was going better than if she had scripted it. Pa could still think, it just took him longer, and he was inclined to mix up the important parts of it. He must not be told too much.

Ma was waiting in the kitchen with a question in her face. Josephine told her, "Looks good, Ma. I didn't tell him about the railroad. He'll think about it, and I'll say more tomorrow."

Ma sat down heavily. She was in the last months of pregnancy, and it had been a hard, discouraging time. She was not up to it, physically, and they certainly couldn't afford another mouth to feed, but the mouth was coming, and the baby was certainly not to blame.

Josephine and Ma spent an anxious day, and Pa was again on the porch, relaxing from a hard day, and was preparing to go to bed.

Josephine brought the tea, and turned to go, and he stopped her. "You said them goats was up for trade?" Not that he had anything to trade, but the existence of the animals intrigued him.

Josephine drew in a concerned breath. It was dangerous to tell Pa what he could and couldn't do, but it was necessary this time. "No, Pa. It was the land with the nice house that was for trade. You wouldn't want a place that was so up and down."

She made a move to go, and he told her, "Sit down here, girl. You don't know what I'd want!"

She sat, practically at his feet. "That's right, Pa. I shouldn't'a been talkin'. It was just somethin' that I saw, them bein' so pretty and white against the grass and trees."

"Where at is this place?"

"Not far. A body could almost see it if they had a telescope."

"You think that fellow'd want to trade for somethin' like we got?'

"I don't know, Pa. I didn't talk with 'im, but I heard he didn't want no hills to climb on bad knees."

The silence hung heavily, disturbed only by a flock of gulls headed for the river. Should she... or shouldn't she. But she might have risk it. "Pa, I didn't ask much, not knowin' how you felt, or if you even liked goats. I think some folks don't like 'im. Wisht I knew how your Ma fixed 'im."

"Why would you care? We ain't got goats"

"I know, Pa. I just thought I might have goats some day. If I did, I'd like white long hair like them I saw on the bluff."

"Well, I gotta work, but if you'd locate that fella and asked, I might be interested. Couldn't handle much in the difference, if he wanted what we got. I'm thinkin' maybe mountain air'd be good for your Ma."

Josephine forced herself to not ruin this by being in a hurry. "Sure, Pa. I can find some time. Could be a while to track 'im down, and maybe it'd be gone by then." She knew perfectly well that Mr. Jonathan was expected tomorrow, hoping for an answer. This looked good, but there was another dangerous thing she must say.

"I don't know, Pa. That land bein' part'a the right-a-way, it'll be the railroad that has to ok the deal. That fella that was here, I don't know, Pa. Maybe he'd help, but he didn't say he would. I didn't get to talk to 'im that evenin' he was here. Maybe the fellas workin' on the right-a-way'll know how to reach 'im."

"Well, tell your Ma you gotta check it out. I'm done in. I got'a hit the hay." He handed her the tea cup and left through the door. She sat still for a moment savoring the success. Maybe it could get done before Ma's time came.

As she lay awake, she mulled over in her mind the shape of the hillside house. There seemed to be five rooms, and they were big rooms. There's be one for the boys and another for the girls, and one for Pa and Ma.

After that there would be a room for the kitchen and one for the parlor. What does a person do with a parlor? Not that they had furniture for a parlor! But it would nice to have an empty room on rainy days that the little ones were home from school. The school would be a little farther, but that could be taken care of later.

The thing, now, was to get the move done before Ma... Well, it was going to be a hassle but well worth the effort, if it worked. If this fell through, she thought she just couldn't stand it.

Spring water, it had, and it came flowing down inside a pipe all the way to the back door. Pure luxury. For sure!

She finally went to sleep. With a family of seven children, soon to be eight, life was nothing but work and problems. Some nights she was too tired to sleep. Maybe they could put a big tub in the shed and heat water for a bath. It seemed like a bath in a tum would help her sleep, and the wash cloth and wash pan just didn't get it.

JONATHAN CAME

His was apprehensive. He would have made the trip in a saddle, but the ladies might want to see the place again... hopefully the pa would be at work. He was.

Josephine listened as he told what the next steps would be. Her eyes shone with anticipation. She told him, "Even if the trade was even-steven, Pa'll likely want to make some change just to show he was in charge. I thought maybe you could put up a fence along the right-a-way between the goats and the train."

"Uh, the goats are fenced in, but I can to tell you this. We would be putting up a fence anyway. It's in the contract."

Josephine frowned, "But don't let him know. He'll want to think he got sometin' extra. I didn't tell 'im that there's be help movin' in. That'll mean a lot to'im."

Jonathan nodded. Understandable, from one in the shape of her father. There is often that paranoia when one is disabled.

He suggested, "I think I have a way to work this out. If you are sure of his answer, you and I can make the trip into town to make the transfer. Considering the health of your mother and the number of your siblings, I feel that the property should be in your father's name, and your name. It might be you taking care of your mother, if I don't miss my guess."

Josephine agreed. "Yeah, she had too many of us. Most of her life has been pregnant. Oh, I didn't mean to say that to you!"

"Think nothing of it. We'll take care of this. Shall we wait for your father for his signature? I will be signing for the railway, and believe me, you're doing the right thing. It was just a lucky chance that place was available. It is worth twice the price of this one, but the railway is glad to avoid the delay."

"Mr. Jonathan, you saw him. My pa won't even know his name was required. My ma needs to know what I'm doin'. I can tell my ma, and we can go now." Josephine's heart beat so hard it hurt her chest. The whote deal could be completed today! Then ma can be comforted that it's done.

At the bank where the transfer was made, there was no problem with Josephine signing for her father. The entire town knew the shape he was in.

THE MOVE

Pa came in exhausted as usual. Duncan, sixteen years old, worked with him and said he worked like a demon that was tryin' to escape the flames of perdition. He even had to be made to stop for lunch.

Duncan said, one time, that it seemed that Pa had been assigned a certain amount of work to do, and he was afraid he wouldn't get it done. He and Josephine were to think of that, later.

And he came home with hardly the energy to wash up for supper. Then he always sat on the front porch for a while. No matter how cold or wet, he sat on the porch a while before he went to bed. Said he really loved a porch, and never had one as a boy. So today he settled himself in the chair.

Josephine sat herself at his feet and leaned against his knees. "Pa, a wonderful thing happened today."

"Today…?"

"Yes, and you're gonna be glad. The house is all taken care of, and I knew you'd want somethin' extra, so I said we'd have to have a fence 'tween us and train track on account'a the little 'ens. They agreed to it 'cause they really want this place. And another thing you're gonna like. They'll do all the movin'. Strong fellas'll be her to load on the furniture, and they'll take the extra horses and the cow.

Hard as you work, you shouldn't have to do that, and I fixed it all up for you. the same way you did things for me when I was little."

Josephine had practiced her speech carefully, moving from one item to the next without giving him time to consider it, and she'd be explaining how everything was good. And she finished with the memory of him as a little girl. All of it was true, and the only omission was that she had signed for his signature.

Pa looked down at her head, her brown hair parted straight and combed straight. She was such a beautiful girl, he was lucky to have her to take care of the details for him.

Josephine looked up at him, love in her eyes, and he patted her head. "You're a good girl."

She caught his hand and kissed it. Her memory dated back to when he had a whole mind… and she wanted to comfort him now, in his misery. "Ma has fried chicken. She thought that'd make two less hens to catch to move. We need to set another hen for babies. Ma and Lola have got supper on. Let's go eat."

He followed her to the kitchen, and the younger children chatted about this and that, saying nothing about the move. Josephine had threatened bodily harm if they did. It was her plan that everything should be moved tomorrow, and she would wait at the old house with the buggy, and Duncan could drive the wagon load of cut firewood up to the house. They'd need it all, anyway.

It was at the end of summer, and there had been a round of birthdays. Josephine had planned the move practically down to the last item. Pa couldn't do it… and neither could ma, so who else was there to do it?

1. Josephine, age 18

2. Duncan, age 16

3. Lolita, age 14

4. Eldon, age 12

5. Darlene, age 9

6. Jeffery, age 6

7. Sammie, age 3

Darlene and Jeffery, who wished sincerely to stay home from school for the moving, did not get their wish. They were sent off to school, and instructed to stop over to the Mercantile in town and pick up two loaves of white bread, and two pounds of rat-trap cheese. Moving day would be a treat day, as toasted cheese sandwiches were a treat to everyone.

Duncan, of course, went with pa to work. Cutting wood brought in the only money, so that was essential. Josephine saw the two moving wagons pull into the yard of the old house, and she was ready. Ma was in such pain she could hardly stand, and it was not from the beginning labor. Josephine was greatly worried, but the move had to go on.

Lolita would ride up to the new house with the first load and direct the movers on placement. That was just rudimentary, as there would be changes later. The first load had beds, and she would see that they got in the proper room.

The next load would have Eldon and Ma, and Lolita and Eldon would see that Ma was put in bed. It was the best Josephine could do at that moment. Eldon would build a fire in the cook stove and make tea for ma with a sprinkling of her pain-relieving powder. He was also instructed to put on the bean kettle and keep a blaze under it. Beans were a staple for every meal, and some meals at the Findley house were quite skimpy. Cornbread and beans could fill in the empty spots.

On the third load, she and Sammie would go, and it would be loaded with tools such as the corn grinder, shovels and hoes, spare wagon wheels and such, and would be loaded in the barn.

She would leave Sammie and bring back Lolita, Together they would scour the house and shed for any missed item, and the extra team of horses would be tethered to the wagon. Lolita would return to the house with that load and direct the off-loading.

On the last load, there would be the plow and harrow for gardening, and the bushel baskets containing the potatoes, both white and sweet, the fresh pulled turnips from the garden, along with tomatoes and cucumbers. Some of the garden products would not be ripe, and a trip could be made later for them, No one would be living in the house, and it would be torn down immediately.

Josephine was told that she could have the torn-down lumber from the house for firewood or whatever she wanted, but it had to be done soon, or it would be burned in place. It would be brought up later, as it had to be hauled off anyway.

The operation went essentially as planned. Ma was put to bed, but something was certainly wrong. The other babies did not cause this pain, and Josephine could worry tomorrow… she did not have time, today.

She arranged as much as possible, but made a late trip down to the empty house and waited for Pa and Duncan. She wanted to be with Pa when he first saw the house. He would be comforted for his wonderfully wise choice for his family and assured that everything was going to be better. If he could make it through that first night, he would be fine… or at least as fine as could be expected.

Ma was not able to come to the table, but she managed to consume a cheese sandwich. Pa was restless and left the table twice to look in on her. The children studiously avoided mention of the happenings, as talking about them made them more real.

There were enough 'real' things happened in their lives, so why create more. Ma would surely be up tomorrow. She always got up, so why would this be different… but Josephine knew it WAS different.

After the meal, Jeffery (age 6) made his trip to the outhouse and came back wide eyed. "We got us two new horses in the yard."

Duncan responded, "Horses…?

"Yep! New ones. One is fat!"

Lolita wondered, "Did we leave the gate open after milkin'?"

Jeffery insisted, "New horses. There two of 'em tied together with a chain."

Josephine looked at Duncan, who decided, "I'll go look. Maybe a hole in the fence…?"

Eldon went along. Jeffery had said new ones, and he was not one to make up stories. Also, he would have recognized any of their four.

In minutes the boys were back. "Jeffery was right. There's a stallion and a mare chained on a six foot chain, like a tandem."

Jeffery stuck out his small chin and told them, "I said we had two new horses, and one was fat."

Josephine comforted him, "You sure did. You did right to come and tell us."

Eldon put in, "Not only that... tell 'em, Duncan."

"You tell 'em."

"I will. That mare is about to foal. She's in last stages, foal looks to be way back."

Pa sat watching the wall. Not good! He was no doubt worried about Ma and not knowing what to do.

Then Josephine. "Eldon, can you make a sign to put on the road. Like maybe 'two horses found'? Somebody'll come lookin' for 'em."

Horses having the importance they had, for transportation also farming, it was natural that there were a lot of them around, and that some would get out of their pens, occasionally. The way to find lost horses was to go down Main Street and look for signs until they were found. The hillside house was up on the first bluff not close to Main Street, but there was a frontage, perfect for a sign.

The immediate problem was that there was likely to be three horses before they were found, and if there was anything the Findley family needed, it was not something to disturb the routine. It was time for Pa to intervene and give orders, but he was silent.

Duncan decided, "Well, that chain needs to come off them, and we got lots of pasture. That'll take care of 'em for the moment. Pa and I gotta go to work tomorrow. Eldon can keep an eye on her. She appears to have foaled before, so there should be no trouble."

That settled it for the moment.

Lolita began to pick up the dishes for washing. There weren't many. Why not have sandwiches every supper... so much easier.

Eldon looked around the kitchen, and no one seemed to be interested in the chains. "I'll go put those horses in the pasture and take off that chain."

Duncan decided to investigate the new house. He walked down the short hall and, back at the rear porch. a narrow stairway arose to the attic. *Hmmm,* he thought. *I gotta see this.*

He climbed about half way and looked around with his eyes level with the attic floor. There was wonderful space for at least thirty feet. The sides were sloped down from the roof, giving it a tent-like appearance.

He announced in a loud voice, "I know where my bedroom is!"

Eldon echoed, "Mine, too."

Duncan objected. "Nope. Yours is with Jeff and Sam. This is my bedroom. I'm too big to be crowded in like I've been. I want to be alone up here with the mice and spiders."

The matter seemed to be settled, and Eldon left for the barn.

Darlene, age 6, went to re-examine her bedroom. Two beds. Lots of room. It was easy to walk all the way around the beds. She sorted her doll from among the miscellaneous items and hung it on a convenient nail on the wall. Dollies belonged on the wall when not being played with. Otherwise they might get crushed.

Duncan sorted out a quilt and pillow and took them upstairs. Oh, how wonderful it was going to be. All alone. No one else in the bed to kick him when they turned over. Sammie was a rough sleeper and couldn't lay still.

The sun went down, and Pa made his way back to be with Ma. He spent most of the night gazing wide eyed at the dark ceiling.

ANOTHER DAY

Jeffery ate hid scrambled egg sandwich and thought about the new horses. He'd just slip out to the shed and see if they were still there, or if someone came and got them in the night.

One of them was in the corral. So it was still here, but where was the fat one? He found it in one of the stalls licking another horse. Standing beside the new horse was another one. Pa and Duncan were gone, so he'd better go and tell Josie about the new horses.

He went in the house and found her in the kitchen making biscuit and butter sandwiches for lunches. He told her, "We got two new horses."

Josephine nodded agreeably, "Right, and you were the one who noticed them."

He shook his head. "No. Two new horses, again."

Now he had her attention, also Eldon's. "Two more horses in the yard?"

"No. Two new horses in the shed."

"In the shed...?"

"I said 'yes.' I can show you."

"Good. I want to see two more new horses."

"No, there not two more horses. They're little horses."

"Do you mean donkey horses?"

"No. I'll show you."

Eldon followed and looked through the slats where Jeffery was looking and pointing. "See beside the big horse? The big horse was licking the little horse."

It wasn't easy to see in the dimness of the shed, but there were, indeed, two more horses. Babies!

"You were right!"

"Of course I was right. I know what horses look like."

"Let's go to the house. You can tell Josie we have two new baby horses."

Josie was amazed. "Twins? I never heard of horses havin' twins. 'Course that doesn't mean anything. There's lots of things I've never heard of."

Eldon agreed. "Me, too. I couldn't see plainly, but I think they're girls. Two little filly's."

Josie added, "Yeah, and whoever they belong to is gonna be surprised."

Jeffery looked at those two people like they were out of their minds. "The little horses are ours. They were born in our yard, and that makes them ours."

Josie winked at Eldon. "Let 'im have it. He'll know sooner or later."

Jeffery was getting out of patience. "I know now they're ours."

Josie told him, "Fine. Now get ready for school."

He and Darlene left with their lunch pail, and Eldon went back to the barn. The new mother allowed him to enter the stall, and he patted her face and then he patted the babies. She grumbled contentedly down in her throat and gave the nearest baby, another swipe with her tongue. The baby rocked on wobbly legs, but braced herself against the force, and remained standing.

'Two foals,' he told himself. 'How soon could we advertise them to sell?' He climbed up and sat on the edge of the stall and gazed out over the new house and grounds.

Through the trees he saw a bit of silver. The river! Rivers have fish! Fish can be eaten! He slid off the railing of the stall and hurried to the house.

"Josie…?" No sister answered. He peeked in Ma's room, and she was there. Eldon did not step inside the room. It might make Ma worse, or whatever she has might be catching, and he didn't want any. He'd wait till Josie came out. He had plans to make.

When she came out, he asked, "Is she better…?"

Josie shook her head. "Worse, I think, and I don't know what to do."

"No more pain powder?"

"Yes, but it doesn't seem to be working."

Eldon thought about his question, should he bother Josie? But then he thought, 'I'm just tryin' to help.' He'd ask.

"Josie, I just thought'a somethin'. Close to the river like we are now, I could maybe catch some fish…?"

Josie's answer was instantaneous. "No. That river current is too dangerous."

"But I'm twelve years old. I'll be careful."

"No. Grown men with seines get swept away when they slide in."

"I don't have a seine. I'll use and pole and a hook."

"Still… I don't like it."

"But what if I catch some fish?"

Josie thought a minute, but was unshakeable. "No. You are too valuable to the family to risk losing you."

Hmmm. Too valuable. He'd never heard before that he was valuable. He'd have to think about that. While thinking, he had an idea.

"What if I tie a rope around myself, and then around a tree. Then if I slipped in, I could pull myself out with the rope."

Josie thought again. "You know there's a tree close by?"

"There's bound to be a tree somewhere. Oh, I know. There's them pilings under the bridge. I could tie to one'a them."

Josie re-considered. Twelve years old. The restless age for boys. "Well, if you tie the rope in a grannie knot…."

"I will! I'll be careful." He disappeared like a puff of smoke on a windy day.

Josephine watched him leave with great excitement. Maybe fishing would be good for him. And we could use the fish if he should be lucky. Then she went back to worrying about Ma. What could she do to ease her pain?

Eldon left her, with his heart singing. He could go fishing! He knew where to get worms. The rich soil around an animal shed always had them, and the first spade full of dirt produced a half a dozen. That'd be enough for today.

He had found a couple of old cane poles in the shed, and he took the rope he promised to use to tie himself to the bridge piling. He put the rope in the metal bucket which he hopefully wished to carry back the fish he'd catch.

So with a straw hat, pail, pole, and worms, he set out, hopefully. He'd never caught a fish in his life, but how difficult could it be. You offered the worm, and the fish either took it or didn't.

The fast rushing river was about a quarter of a mile away, and that was nothing to a country boy. He tied the rope to his waist, remembering how Josie had said he was too valuable to lose. He anchored it to the mossy pole and seated himself under the bridge. He threaded a worm on the hook and tossed it in the water, then leaned back against the wooden piling and prepared to wait.

If there was anything to the saying, 'beginner's luck,' it appeared it was Eldon's day for it to happen. In the space of an hour, he had landed four large catfish. He wasn't too clear about catfish, but thought he remembered they were mostly head and not much meat. There were nine people in the family, and it would be nice if everyone got a piece.

The next throw into the river, a big bass (it looked like) grabbed at the worm and pulled it off the hook. Eldon stared with hatred at the fish. The rascal had obviously done that before, and that was his last worm.

"Shucks!" he pronounced, vehemently. "All I wanted was one more."

The river didn't care what he wanted and just rolled on. He looked at the catfish lying quietly in the bucket and contemplated his next move. The fish were dead, so why couldn't he bait a hook with part of the catfish.

With his knife, he removed a fin (not much fin like on a perch) and threaded it on the hook. "All right, river," he told the rushing water, "give me one more fish, and I'll leave you alone."

The river did its best. Here came a bigger fish, not a catfish, and it appeared, down in the reflections in the water, to be the one that had had stolen his worm. The big fellow attacked and grabbed the chunk of catfish fin and tried to swim off, but was stopped by the end of the rope.

Eldon stood up, for better control, and held to the pole with a white-knuckled grip. The fish was headed out into deep water and was pulling on that pole like a headstrong horse pulls on a lead rope. He stepped closer and reached for the piling to hold on, holding to the pole with his right hand. That strong fish was twisting and flipping, and Eldon had to let go of the piling and grab the pole with both hands.

At that moment the ground below his feet gave away, and he started to slide. What now? Grab the piling and lose the fish? Hold to the fish and trust the rope! Which…? He must decide in an instant. He had tied ropes since he was a toddler, so he held to the pole and the fish and slid into the water up to his waist. Then his foot caught against the next piling and stopped the slide.

He braced the pole against the piling and pulled the fishing line with both hands. He felt the smart of pain as the line cut into his skin, but he held on. As a general rule, a boy of twelve has more strength than a fish that was a foot and a half long, and he eventually pulled fish and hook back close enough to reach.

He found that a fish has no handle to hold it by, and it was slippery as greased glass. It took a mighty effort, and pulled him down into the water, but he managed to sling the fish, line and pole to the bank. There was a lot of flopping, but Eldon pulled himself back on the rope and climbed the slippery bank.

He stepped up out of the water, dripping a stream on the river bank, and tossed the fish farther up on the bank. He was determined not to lose it. He'd earned it, and he was going to take it to Josie. He'd show her he had not wasted an afternoon.

With his knife, he cut the fishing line and left the hook in the fish's mouth. He didn't want to risk losing it, as he didn't know where he would get more hooks.

His clothes were soggy, and his shoes were muddy, but he sloshed his way up the hill swinging the bucket with five fish in it. Heavy bucket! Wonderfully heavy! Even if the catfish were mostly head, there was that big one he was sure was a bass.

He was no longer dripping, but was still soggy when he reached the house. He stepped inside the kitchen door, and said, "Sis? Come look what I brought us."

Josie stared in horror at her soggy brother, but he was standing there, safe. She walked over to the bucket, and it was half full of fish. "Eldon! You wonderful brother! You're safe, and you have fish! I've been too worried about Ma to worry about you, and here you are!"

Eldon grinned, "If you'd had time to worry, would that have kept me from sliding in?"

"You stinker!" she shouted at him, and hugged him, soggy clothes and all. He couldn't remember when he was last hugged. It had been a long time, and it felt good.

"If you'll let me go, I'll clean these fellows. I don't know how, but I ain't gonna learn no younger." She released him, and spatted him in the rear. He could actually remember the last time she had done that.

He took the butcher knife and left for the shed. He made a dreadful mess, but he learned a lot. Next time, he would do better, and the pieces that he had skinned and divided would look like fish fillets, but this time they were scraps. He'd bet the farm that Josie could make them taste good.

It was after 3 o'clock when Pa and Duncan came straggling in, hungry and exhausted. Josie slipped a pan of cornbread into the oven. Twenty minutes and they could have something to hold them over until supper.

Eldon, the fisherman, morphed into Eldon, the waggoneer. This load of cut stove wood had been sold about a mile down the road. He changed out the horses, hitching the two rested mares on to the wagon and left, whistling merrily to himself.

Duncan moved close to Josie. "How's Ma?"

"Worse, I'm afraid, and I don't know what to do. How's Pa?"

"Silent as a ghost and workin' like a demon. He didn't even talk, sayin' nothin' sensible, like usual. It was like workin' with a machine all day."

"I'm makin' tea for him. Could be it'll help," she added hopefully.

She rinsed the fish pieces and cut them into pieces of reasonably similar size. There was really a lot of fish. With the hush puppies she would make, everyone would be full, and that was always the goal.

Eldon delivered the wood, assisting in removing it off the wagon and into the rick for the buyer. He pulled back out onto the road just in time to pick up Darlene and Jeffery. They settled into the wagon, and Eldon entertained himself by thinking how excited they would be with all the fish for supper.

When he climbed back up the bluff, he turned his attention to the stallion who had wandered in. He was a beautiful beast, and obviously well taken care of. He was friendly, and when Eldon patted him, he grumbled companionable as though he was accustomed to being stroked.

He patted the muscular neck, and on a whim, swung himself up onto the broad back. The stallion didn't flinch. Evidently he'd been a saddle horse. Some other day he'd try that saddle if no one came for him. It had been several days now, and they were right there on the edge of town, handy for someone looking for lost animals. It looked good for keeping them.

He tried not to think they'd get to keep him. At the other place, there'd be the thought of feeding him (because he would eat like a horse!), but here there was grass aplenty for twenty horses... or maybe thirty horses.

His nimble brain projected a few years and a few horses later. They really could raise horses for sale if they just had a good start. And the four horses they had were all mares, as Pa said they were more manageable. What if???

'Forget it, Eldon,' he told himself. 'That fellow you're sittin' on is not yours!' But he just couldn't believe it. He named him King, and King certainly felt like he belonged right where he ws. And how did he and the mare just wander in when they would have had to leave Main Street and climb up the lane. It just didn't make sense.

He dismounted and patted the beautiful red-brown pelt of his face. He hugged the neck, and King bent his head around to touch Eldon's shoulder. He wanted that horse like he never remembered wanting something in his whole twelve years.

He'd have liked to share the attic with Duncan, but that did not compare to this. He was surely looking for disappointment, because someone would come for him. They had to. He was a valuable animal.

The aroma of fried fish whiffed out from the kitchen. He sighed and gave King a final pat, than followed his nose to the kitchen.

The family gathered around the table, and there were hush puppies at both ends of the table. Josephine came with the fish. The seldom used turkey platter was full to running over with crisply battered fish. It was hard to tell what was catfish or what was bass, but who cared?

She piled several pieces on the plates for Sammie and Darlene, as a signal that there was enough for everyone to have all they wanted. Pa looked at the crusty pieces, helped himself, and said nothing.

Eldon bowed his head to hide his sadness. There should have been some word for him about catching the fish, but his Pa was not in this body that resembled Pa. It was like there was no Ma or Pa, and he might just as well get used to it.

And there was the mare. No one told him about the horses and the foals… why would they? And Pa was not gonna be no help.

Duncan, on the other hand said, "Eldon, old man, I'll say this for you. This is the first time I ever had all the fried fish I wanted at one time. This is wonderful!"

That helped a lot, but where was Pa's words?

Sammie lifted a piece and said, "This here doesn't look like a fish, but I like it."

Darlene told him, "It's just a piece of fish. The whole fish would be too big to fry in the skillet."

Darlene just burst with information.

ARRIVAL OF AMY FINDLEY

Pa went to bed as usual, but Josephine did not trust him to react if Ma took a turn for the worst. She made a pallet bed beside her mother and tried to sleep.

It was about midnight that Ma reached down to her, patting her arm. Josephine bolted upright, "What is it, Ma?"

The weak voice answered, "I think, come daylight, you might send for the midwife. The pains are beginnin' to feel right."

"Sure, Ma. Can I get you anything?"

"No, darling girl. Get sleep if you can."

There was no way that Josephine would get any sleep. She looked at the clock. It was barely past 2:00. It would be 4:00 hours before daylight, and anything could happen by then.

She slipped out of bed and went to kitchen. She poked up coals to warm the tea. Duncan had worked through a hard day, and he was all the way up into the attic. She tiptoed into the boys' room and felt for Eldon.

She put her hand over his mouth and whispered, "It's Ma. I need you to slip out quietly. I want to ask you something."

Eldon rolled his sleepy twelve-year-old body from the bed and felt his way after his sister. At the table, she poured two cups of tea. "I need to get word to the midwife, and you are all I have. Duncan has to take care'a pa, and it seems Ma's time has come. Could you get a horse ready to go as soon as it's light? I hate to ask, but we may need her."

Eldon sipped the tea that was almost hot. "I can go, Sis. I made friends with King, and he could use exercise. I'll go saddle him now, and I can go on. There is moonlight."

"But, you...?"

"Don't worry. I'll get dressed and be ready. Is there any fish left?" It had been a long time since there had been leftovers of any kind.

"Yes, there is fish and hush puppies. I'll warm them up."

Eldon slipped away. He moved as though he was made of wood, but he would loosen up. The tussle with the fish had called into action a different set of muscles.

He lit the lantern and took the saddle off the saddle tree. King snorted a soft greeting, and Eldon told him, "We got to make a trip, you and me. Are you up to three miles there and back?"

King grumbled a reply and stood still for the saddle. Eldon led him to the kitchen door and twisted the reins around the pump handle. He needed to make a hitching post. He needed to do a lot of things.

He went into the house and sat down to the plate with two pieces of fish and a hush puppy. He wasn't really hungry, but he would be later. He knew exactly where the midwife lived, and it was a good mile and a half.

Josephine was doubtful. "I hate to see you start out in the dark."

"Don't worry," he told her. "There is a moon, and it ain't really dark. And it's Main Street all the way up to Rock Creek Road. I can make it. That'll let her get here in time. Then maybe Ma'll be better."

"We can hope," his sister said, doubtfully. She had a very bad feeling about this. There was that pain that was not caused by the baby. Either way, the baby was obviously coming, and she did not want to be alone when it happened. Sometime ago they had set aside the $5.00 for the midwife.

Eldon set out. King made his way down the rocky driveway and on to the road like he had provided a midnight ride every night of his life. Eldon felt wonderful. There was a feeling of power beneath him, like that horse could just lift off into the air and ride into a cloud.

The midwife was always ready. She quickly lit the headlights on her buggy and was rolling down her driveway, and then on to Main street. King wanted to gallop, and Eldon let him. He could look behind him and see the pair of lights following.

Streaks of light were appearing in the east when King thundered across the rickety old wooden bridge, and then turned into the driveway. Eldon pulled him to a stop while he waited for the midwife. He wasn't sure she'd see the driveway in the semi-dark.

He led her to the house, and hurried ahead to open the back door for her. Going through the kitchen would be the quickest way. Within minutes, she was in the room with Ma.

"Josephine," she said. "you'll have to move your Pa out of the room, I can't have him in her while this in goin' on."

Josephine nodded. She went to his bedside. "Pa, you'll have to come to the other room for a while."

"Sure, honey. I'll just go on to work."

"Not yet, Pa. I have to make your tea. You just lay down in my bed for a while, and I'll come for you when the tea is ready." Maybe he'd just go to sleep again.

She stood by the door, to be ready if needed. The commotion brought Duncan down from his lair. "You sent Eldon? I could'a…?"

"No, you couldn't'a. Eldon can sleep all day if he wants, but you have to take care'a Pa. To do that, you need your sleep."

Duncan nodded. He could see the truth in that. Seeing tea was hot, he helped himself to a cup and sat down at the table. Josephine joined and remembered with a start that she had not moved the peppermint plants from the old place. That meant a final trip to the shack. How does one get along without peppermint plants? She would have thought there'd be plants at the new house, and maybe there is, but who had time to look?

She'd make time for that plant, but that was a chore for later. Ma had come about long enough to insist she leave the bed for a pallet. "It's gonna be messy," she insisted. "Can't mess up the bed."

The midwife didn't like it much, but it wasn't the first time that had been requested. There were some who thought it helped labor to be on the hard floor. Maybe it did, but this delivery was not going to go well. Too much blood and she couldn't tell where it was coming from. In all her years, she'd never had a case like this one.

It was after 6:00 when they heard the plaintive cry of a newborn. The baby made it. Josephine was called to come and take the baby away. She almost fainted at the amount of blood, but squared her shoulders and firmed her jaw. She could do this. She forced herself by sheer will power to walk out with the tiny baby girl, clearly needing to have stayed where she was for another month.

Josephine cleaned her and wrapped her in a blanket, worn to softness by previous babies. The baby girl whimpered and would have been put to the breast, but there was no breast.

Eldon was going to have to make another trip. By the time he got to the Mercantile, it would be open, and they had the bottles and nipples in stock.

King was still in good shape, having had a couple hours rest. By 8:00 o'clock, milk was poured into the bottle, and dripped slowly in the baby's mouth.

Pa aroused and came into the kitchen. His comment was, "Oh, the baby. Name her Amelia."

"But Pa, that's Ma's name."

Pa was adamant. "Do it anyway."

Josephine nodded and told him, "Sure, Pa."

Then she instructed the midwife. Her name is to be "Amy Joyce. Ma said so before she got bad off." Pa'd never know the difference, and she could tell him Amy was short for Amelia, without admitting what she did.

She turned the tiny girl over to 14-year-old Lolita, and went back to Ma. She didn't need the midwife to tell her that Ma was never going to be up again. It might be hours or maybe days, but she would not last for weeks, and her pain was almost unbearable, the midwife said. She was given pain powder, and if it got too bad, and her Ma begged for it, there was something more to give her, but only at the very last. She didn't tell Josephine what it was. She didn't have to.

The midwife said nothing was to be gained by prolonged suffering. But that was not her concern, now. The baby appeared to be all right, but who could know what such a difficult birth would do to a baby?

She was paid her $5.00 for her labor, and she rode away.

THE NEXT DAY

The tiny girl should never have drawn a breath. The problem was, she did. When she should have been put to the breast, there was no breast for her. Her mother struggle each moment, with the pain.

Pa finally pulled himself together, not wondering why he was in Eldon's bed and not his own. He ate breakfast and climbed aboard the wagon that Duncan had hitched and never asked about Ma. He would never have done that! Pa has took a turn for the worse.

It was a clear indication of his deterioration. The interesting thing was, his work with the saw was not affected, unless one would say it was increased. He bowed his back to the work, and the chunks of wood fell in rapid succession.

Duncan loaded them on the wagon and chopped and sawed when he could. By mid afternoon the load was filled to overflowing, and no more could be loaded on top. Duncan pulled the wagon across the rough ground of the right-of-way to reach the graveled road. The weary horses pulled it up the hill to the houses.

Inside the house another problem reared its head. It was 8 o'clock AM, and Josephine reluctantly woke Eldon. He sat bolt upright in a startle. What was the problem?

Josephine began, "I'm so sorry, but I need another trip."

"Sure thing. What do you need?"

"I need a trip to the Mercantile for a baby nursing bottle with a nipple."

"Ma can't...?"

"Ma is out'a her mind with pain on the inside. Her body don't know she had a baby, and the baby's hungry."

"I'll be ready in a minute. I left King saddled."

"King...?

"The new stallion. I love to ride him. I named him King. I'll bet he was the sire of those little fillies in the shed."

"Eldon, those horses are not ours."

"They are if nobody comes for them. We have a good sign out on Main Street, and we're takin' care'a them. I'll ride King to the Mercantile. He likes to gallop."

Indeed, King was ready. Eldon had to rein him back from running down the rocky driveway. On Main Street he was turned loose. His hooves beat a jazz rhythm on the hard-packed, oiled gravel.

By 8:45 baby Amy was offered nutrition. She was not particularly happy with it, but she adapted. She really needed that last month inside, but she didn't get it. Josephine had turned her over to her aunt Lolita, who had a lot of patience.

As Eldon had galloped off, Lolita had mentioned to Josephine. "Eldon's gonna have other things to do. I need to learn to ride a horse."

"But, Lola... you're..."

"I know I'm a girl. I've known it for years, but I'd bet a shilling that Duncan's outgrown overalls won't know it, and they would fit me."

"But I thought we..."

"I love your thoughts, but all of us are gonna bein' doin' things we wasn't made to do. Duncan wasn't meant to see after his Pa, but he's doin' it. You wasn't meant to take on a family, but you got one. You wasn't trained in nursin', but you'er doin' it. Darlene hasn't learn kitchen jobs, but she's gonna have to.Just like me ridin' a horse. Eldon'll help me learn."

Josephine thought about it. Lolita was exactly right. Eldon might be somewhere else, and she would need something.

And that was the day that another horse found its way up the driveway to the lush green grass. And it was also Jeffrey who discovered it. He came to Josephine and said, "We got another fat horse."

Josephine assumed he was missing the attention he got from discovering the stray horses. "Wasn't it two horses."

"No. If it was two horses I would have said two horses. This in one fat horse, and it's eatin' our grass. Do you want me to chase it away?"

"No! no! no! Leave it there. It must be hungry."

The little boy nodded. "It's hungry, but it won't be hungry long. It's eatin' its supper. When are we havin' supper? I wish I could eat grass."

"You can. We have a lot of it."

"I can't. I tried it and it won't go down. That's when I saw the fat horse."

"Why didn't you go tell Eldon about the fat horse?"

"I tried, but he's busy looking at the little horses."

"No matter. You can tell him later."

A vote was taken, and everyone agreed. Amy was a fussy baby. Maybe she had a right to be, as she was robbed of a whole ninth of her pre-life.

The thing was, she didn't sleep. Not only that, no one else could sleep except Pa who had turned the world off, and Duncan, who occupied the attic.

Ma held out for nine days and asked Josephine for the 'other medicine.' Josephine's breath caught in her throat. This was it, and Ma had all she could take. "Ma, I can't do that. I know what it does."

"Yes, and I would like to live, but I can't. Just leave it here on the stand, and I'll take care of it."

"No, Ma. I can't do that. I need you here."

Ma nodded. "I know, darling girl. It won't be long, anyway. I wish I could tell my children how I love them. I tried but so much went wrong. When you remember me, think about how I loved you."

Josephine hugged her, and tears dropped on her face. It was the best profession of love that she had, and ma decided she would go on without the help of the 'medicine.'

Morning arrived, and Josephine came with tea and the pain killer, and saw that her Ma had no pain. She had passed on in the night, and Josephine was certain it was from sheer will power.

She called her siblings and told them. Duncan voiced their combined opinion. "It's better this way, Sis. She couldn't get well, so she left. I wish I could make it easier for you, but I have Pa to take care of. We also have customers. Don't you try to go tell the preacher. Send Eldon."

Which she did. He came back saying the grave would be ready in two days, and he would send someone tomorrow mornin' to pick her up. The church shed always had a box ready for such times as this.

If she had neighbors, they might have helped, but Josephine considered it a last act of love to prepare her. Lolita took over on Amy, and that was a big help.

Lolita also stayed home from the funeral, keeping Amy, Jeffery, Sammie and Darlene. Josephine rode with Duncan and Eldon, with Pa not knowing where he was going. He was not able to visit the grave and drop in the handful of dirt, signifying consent to close the grave. Nor did they expect him to.

There was no funeral, just a Bible reading at the grave, and a couple of neighbors that stood with them, in addition to the grave diggers. It didn't last long.

Josephine cleaned the bed and assigned Eldon to sleep there as Pa had taken over Eldon's bed. It was easier that way.

She was tired… all the way inside her bones, tired.

Eldon made another trip to the river, and he went better prepared. He took more worms. He also decided to stay closer to the piling so if he snagged a bigger fish, he could step around the piling and let the fish pull on the piling instead of himself.

Catfish were plentiful, and Bass were occasional. He had to count on the loss of an afternoon, but it made a big meal for the family. Maybe he'd count on going once a week, unless something special happened.

He loved to watch the young goats playing on the third bluff, the very high one. They bounced around like their feet were padded with rubber. He also noted that they were made of meat. It was meat that was maybe better than fish. There had to be a way to butcher them, but he hesitated to mention it to Duncan.

Pa was being a big concern to Duncan, but nothing could be done. Pa was going to do what Pa wanted to do, and he let reasoning flow over his head. It couldn't be on purpose, but that didn't make it any easier on Duncan.

And there was that other horse. She was beautifully patterned tri-color Paint. Her black, brown and tan (almost dull orange) seemed to have been applied by a painter. And, like Jeffrey said, she was fat. She was well fleshed, but the 'fat' was clearly a foal. He couldn't tell how soon she might drop the foal, but it had to be soon. She was really fat!

She was eating her head off, so to speak. Where she came from, there must not have been good grass… and maybe that's why she wandered away. She might just be looking for greener pastures… well, she found one.

The 'found' sign was still on the road, so Eldon just let her into the pasture and watched her. She seemed to like the other horses, the four mares Pa had selected for hauling the wood wagon. He had never bred them as he had no use for foals, and the little fellows took a couple of years to grow up and be useful.

Also, sometime someone was going to have to break the fillies to the harness. Eldon had no doubt who that would be. No matter. He really liked to fool with horses. That was good because there were six adults and two babies when the Paint appeared. That made another adult and another baby. Horses sort of took care of themselves if there was plenty of grass, and the Findley's had acres of it.

Then Duncan came in with the wagon at 10:00 o'clock in the morning. Not only that, someone was with him, and a saddle horse was tied behind the wagon. They pulled up into the yard, and the other person waited in the wagon while Duncan came in the house.

Duncan called Josephine and Lolita together. His sober face showed not one shred of emotion. He started with, "Pa did it."

Josephine was tongue-tied but Lolita said, "Pa did what?"

"He was cuttin' down a tree, and when it started to fall, he just stood there, lookin at it. I yelled 'TIMBER!' but he didn't move. Some'a them big trees take a while to start fallin' and this'n did. I yelled at him to get out'a the way, and he just stood there and watch it fall right on top'a him." He paused, still expressionless.

Lolita pressed him. "Did it hurt 'im?"

Duncan nodded. "Yeah, it did. It killed 'im."

"You mean Pa's dead?"

"It was a big tree. He wouldn't move. He watched it all the way till it knocked 'im down."

Josephine swallowed hard. "Where is he?"

Duncan pointed with his elbow. "Out in the wagon. I'll put a blanket over him to bring 'im in. His face is all right. The boss'a the right-a-way thought I ought'a needed someone with me, to help get 'im in. He was right. That fellain Matthew. Pa's gotta be covered to carry in and the little 'em gotta be somewhere else.

"That bad, huh."

Duncan nodded. "Worse."

Josephine turned to Lolita. "Could you…?"

"Sure could. I'll take 'im to look at the baby horses. Tell me when it's safe to come back."

Duncan explained further. "The fella out in the wagon is a friend, and we got to be friends durin' lunch and talked when we could. His boss was the one that picked 'im to come with me. I sure did appreciate it."

Josephine nodded. Things had to be said no matter how hard it was to listen. This was hitting Duncan hard. The littler ones couldn't really remember the real Pa, but Duncan and Eldon did.

She said, "Bring 'im in to Ma's bedroom. I'll get a canvas to protect the bed."

"No, sis. We'll put 'im on the floor. He won't care, now."

Made sense, when a body thought of it.

ANOTHER FUNERAL

Eldon and King made another trip into the village. He reined up at the preacher's house that was snugged up beside the church. He tapped on the door, and the preacher answered.

"Sir, I hate to bother you again, but it's my Pa."

"Sick? An accident…?"

"Accident, sir. He was hit by a tree over in the right-a-way for the Mississippi Central. He's in need of a funeral. My sister wondered if there would be a space for him by our mother?"

"There certainly would be, and I'll send a wagon with a box to your house right away. Are you living on the river flat down by the right-of-way?"

"No, sir. We're on the bluff by the river. The driveway is a little bit hard to find. I could…"

"Son, I know exactly where it is. It's the place with the bluffs on three levels."

"That's it, sir."

"Beautiful place. The former owner has knee problems and had to move. I'm so glad you were able to pick it up. I'll contact someone, and we'll be out there sometime before noon."

"I thank you so much, sir."

Eldon left, and the preacher turned to his wife. "Jane Ann, that is one polite young man. Had good raisin', apparently. The damaged pa seems to be goin' to be with their mother. That leaves a house full of children alone. The oldest girl isn't quite twenty, if my memory is right."

Jane Ann agreed. "Have you noticed how when trouble starts to happen to some folks it just don't know when to stop? I wish there was something we could do without seemin' to be buttin' in. Folks need to get to keep their pride."

Keeping pride was the last thing on the mind of the 'almost twenty year old' who now lived on the bluff. She had the sensation of having the earth fall out from under her feet, and she was plummeting downward.

When Pa, even though damaged, and Ma, over-worked with duties and child-bearing, were still alive, it was different. Even though a major part of the duties had been shifted to her slim shoulders, her parents were there as a buffer from the knocks of life. There was someone to make a final decision (except Pa who couldn't be trusted to sign his own name... if he even remembered what his name was).

She cleaned the room where Pa and Ma had slept and gathered the bottle of pain medicine and the other prescription to put in the special drawer. That other medicine really should be tossed... but she hesitated. It was against her nature to destroy anything that might be of value later.

She looked thoughtfully at the bottle and then stood on a chair and placed it on top of the cabinet beside the rat poison. She had counted the pills, and the correct number of them remained. Ma had not taken one. Somehow Josephine took comfort from that.

She stood, lost in thought, and stared around the room at the kitchen that was so roomy, and how their massive round table had fit so well, just like the colored set in a ring.

Then a plaintive whiny cry came from the bedroom. Amy was awake. Didn't babies ever sleep? It seemed impossible that anything so tiny could have the strength to cry... or even live. She resembled a baby bird, just hatched, with pinkish skin and thin arms and legs. Is that the way a baby looks a month before it's born?

The cry was smothered by back pats. She could mentally see Lolita holding her against her chest and hugging her trying to make her feel like she was where she had been supposed to be. Josephine felt a wave of guilt that she had so thoughtlessly tossed the responsibility onto Lolita.

But then, Lolita had offered. And Duncan went on to work as there were customers to supply, as well as their own woodstove. He should have been allowed a day off, but that meant no money. Pa, as bad off as he was, had seemed to make just enough money to get by… and he was gone.

Duncan could not go on alone, and Eldon, only twelve, was needed in a dozen places. If he was not given a chore, he would be with the horses. He had started taking them to the second level of the bluff to save the lower grass for winter. Horses could manage on dry grass if they had no hay, and how could they manage tocut hay for six horses… no it was seven. The new 'fat' mare had not been a figment of Jeffery's imagination.

Eldon had put her in the corral to await the event. Jeffery had been right. She was vary 'fat'. There could be a problem birth, and Eldon, thought he knew nothing about it, thought there might be something he could do to help. That foal needed to live, and not kill it mam while being born.

Somehow Eldon could not seem to realize the new animals were not his, and when the owner came, it was going to pull his heart out to let them go… especially that red-brown stallion he had named King.

Not only that, a spotted horse wandered in. What made the rocky, uphill driveway so attractive to stray horses? And that crazy thing he said when she chided him about becoming too fond of the lost animals. He told her, "Maybe they ain't lost. Didn't there happen to be a story in the Bible about cookies coming down to the people when they were on a long trip?"

"It wasn't cookies, it was manna*, and it don't hardly seem the same as a pair of pregnant mares would just climb up the rocky driveway."

*Exodus, 16:15

"Oh, I don't know about that. They got good eyes, and that green grass is plain to see, even from the road. Did you know it was easy to see goats up top? They look like tiny toys that are Christmas presents for rich kids."

Josephine kept forgetting about the goats. They minded their own business and took care of themselves, without requiring the help of one of her brothers. So why think about them?

Eldon had more to say. "You know something? Goats are made out of meat, and I'll bet those babies have real tinder meat. Come winter, we could maybe butcher one. Another thing, we have a lot of squirrels. Didn't Pa have a gun put away somewhere?"

Josephine was not particularly interested. "Maybe. I don't really know what was in his tools."

"I know where they are. I think I'll look."

His sister made no reply. She was really down in the dumps. Sure, they'd lost both parents, but they didn't have to go with them. They were still alive and breathing, and every day the sun came up. Sometimes behind a cloud, but it was always there.

While he had it in his mind, he went to the wooden tool box that had been relegated to the shed. Inside he found several things like a form for nailing soles back on shoes. Now, that might come in handy. There was an auger for drilling holes in boards and set of rusty screw drivers.

Hmmm, interesting…. There at the bottom was a large canvass wrapped bundle. He worked it out of the jumble of items and put it on the ground. Laying back the cover he uncovered the rifle. It was clean and smelling of gun oil. Lying beside it was a hand gun that said Colt on the side. He grinned spontaneously, maybe his new spotted horse, that he had named Daisy, would product a big, healthy colt.

Thinking of Daisy, he needed to check on her. He'd heard that big foals sometimes caused trouble… though what he'd do about it, he hadn't a clue.

He closed the tool box and rewrapped the guns for later. Climbing the ladder to the empty hay loft, and laid the package in the edge of the hay. He'd tend to that later when he had time. Right now he needed to see to Daisy. He'd'a liked to have gone to the river. That fried fish just seemed to hit the spot, and it was free, but Daisy had priorty.

It was a good thing, too. She was in a stall and was restlessly stomping around. She even made mouth noises, though not quite a 'whinny.' The sounds were more like horse conversation.

He let himself into the stall and closed the gate. She must not be let to wander off. He patted her face and talked to her. She was definitely not happy. Maybe she was hungry. There was no hay in the manger.

He let himself out and gathered a double handful of the lush greenery. He offered it to her, but she turned away. She twisted and humped, and tossed her head. He decided to stand on the other side of her so he could step up on the paneling and not be stepped on.

While passing behind her, he saw the pair of little hoofs protruding from her body. HOOVES! The BABY! She strained but no soggy lump followed the hoofs. He grabbed up a rag hanging on a nail and wrapped it around the slippery hooves. How hard should he pull? Was there a danger of hurting Daisy? But Daisy was already hurting, so he pulled as hard as he could, and the little legs twisted in his hand. Daisy relaxed and the soggy bundle followed the little legs and landed on the straw on the floor at Eldon's feet. Daisy tried to turn, but the stall was a bit narrow. She was determined, so Eldon scurried up the boards of the ladder to get out of the way, and another soggy bundle dropped.

Daisy got turned, and Eldon hung onto the top boards of the stall and watched as the experienced mother released the babies and began to clean them… first one and then the other.

The amazed twelve year old stared in disbelief at the two babies trying to stand and Daisy trying to encourage their attempts. Twins again! And when Jeffrey had tried to tell the teacher and the class that they had twin baby horses at his house, they told he was just imagining them because that would be fun.

The classmates were not so kind. They said he was lying. Jeffrey retorted that they couldn't say that until they came to his house and saw there were no twins because there were twins. While at that moment, there was another set of twins joining the animals at the bluff house.

Eldon sat on the top of the partition and watched, himself being unable to take it all in. One of the little fellows must have been pushed into being crooked, and the hooves were like a cork in the bottle. Pulling straightened them and out came the little fellow.

He was fighting curiosity as to whether they were colts or fillies, but Daisy was now contentedly absorbed, and he didn't want to bother her. Time would tell, however even in the dimness of the stall he could tell that one of the babies was a Paint, like Daisy, and other appeared to be black.

His heart fairly pounded with excitement. Four babies, and even if the owners came for the strays, those babies should be his, wouldn't they? They HAD to be his! Their appearance would remain a secret for a few hours. No one but Jeffrey would be interested. Toomany problems.

A pang of nervous hunger attacked him, and there were usually biscuits left over. He entered the kitchen to the aroma of peppermint tea. Josephine offered, "Got fresh tea. Want some?"

"Don't care if I do," he answered, and poured the steaming liquid in a mug. "Believe I'll have a biscuit, too."

Josephine did not respond, but just sat with the tea mug in both hands, like she was warming them. The tea was cooling, and she just sat there.

"What's the matter, sis?"

She startled as though her thoughts had been in another world. "Nothing," was her untruthful answer.

Eldon was persistent. "I know there is. Can I help?"

"Nobody can help."

"But I could listen. Maybe that'd help."

"It wouldn't." She left her tea on the table and retreated to her room.

Lolita appeared, with a finger to her lips. "Got the baby to sleep, and I don't want no noise. I need to see you about somethin' I need from you."

"What'd that be."

"I want you to help me learn to ride horseback."

"Horseback...? But you're a..."

"Girl? I noticed that a few years ago. The thing is, we need another driver here because you can't be two places at once. I can fit in Duncan's outgrown overalls if I have to."

Eldon processed this problem. She was right. "I think you'd fit better in mine. They're pretty ragged, but I manage."

New clothing was an impossibility, but there was a second-hand store in Jacksonville that specialized in used clothing. If a body had time to look, there were bargains that were affordable. Ma used to make a trip every so often.

"Could be. When can I learn?"

"Anytime, I guess. Josephine could take over with Amy while you're gone."

"Josephine? Right. Eldon, she ain't doin' to good."

"What's wrong? Ma and Pa gone…?"

"Maybe. And she's tired. She don't sleep for worryin', and bein' the oldest of us makes her think she's gotta have all the answers."

"Yeah, well, Duncan's gonna be the same way. Him thinkin' he's gotta take Pa's place on the saw. He can't do it. I'm thinkin' we may have to sell a pair of the wagon mares. Sure would hate to do that, now that we got grass, and we got King. I don't think you need to learn to ride, usin' King. He's got fire in his belly, and not good for a beginner. Maybe one of the wagon mares? They'll not be doin' much."

"How about the spotted one?"

"I named her Daisy, and she shouldn't be used for a couple'a weeks."

"Why not?"

"Come and I'll show you."

At the stall, Daisy had managed to lift the latch wither nose, and she was outside the stall, and inside were two tiny fillies, their legs spread the better to stand alone.

Lolita looked at the babies, then at Eldon. She held up two fingers and raised her eyebrows in question."

"Yep. Twins, again. I don't really believe it myself. I don't think someone is going to come for them. Sometimes good things happen, and the powers above may have thought we were ready for some good things. I don't know how Daisy rides, but she might be good for you… maybe on short trips."

"Thanks. I told Josephine, and she don't want me to, but I know she ain't right on that. Duncan's gonna have to find somethin' else to do, and not be here. We might need somethin' from the Mercantile, or maybe we needed help. When I get good, I can go to the store in Jacksonville and get us some new clothes. The church sent a present for Amy, but she'd gonna have to have more."

Eldon nodded. "Well thought out, actually," he told himself. "Daisy seems good tempered, especially for the shape she was in.

She was sent to us, for certain, and I was told to be there when those hooves broke through."

Something seemed to be trying to help the Findley siblings, and he wanted to help that 'something' as much as he could, but there was only one of him.

One thing certain, he was going to butcher one of those young goats from up top. He'd already found the butcherin' tree, with its block and tackle pulleys and everything still in place.

MATHEW WARLEY

He'd worked around Duncan Findley for a few weeks as the cutting crew had neared the town of River Bend. They'd had lunch together on a few occasions. He knew there was something different about Duncan's pa, but it was not discussed. Then he was chosen as the one to accompany the body of old Mr. Findley after the accident.

They were calling it an accident, but Matthew new differently. Duncan had been very vocal on the way home, rather like he was full to running over with words that he couldn't share with family, and it was safe to talk with Matthew. Certainly Matthew was safe to talk with. He was no stranger to trouble.

When he was hired by Mississippi Central to bring down trees in the right-of-way it had been part of the answer, but not all. And Matthew knew that cutting trees was not a job for all his life, only to help him get a better one, and there was a chance he would be taken on permanently when the rails were being put down.

That job would last longer, but it would all be a long way from Jacksonville and his family. Not that it was a problem. Maybe he could stay on until the railroad hooked up with the rails coming from the big river. That would last through winter, and maybe a whole year. That would give him time to think.

He knew, because Duncan told him, but also he sensed that Mr. Findley was sick, they used to call it. He was clearly not of a whole mind, and Duncan had explained the accident, and how it changed him from a dad to a stranger.

He had helped carry the body into the bedroom and had seen several of the family members. He saw Josephine and did a double take. What a lovely girl, even with red, tear-wet eyes.

He was past twenty, and it was time he was giving girls a second look… maybe also a third look… and one like Duncan's sister would be high on his list of desirability. Of course he saw her for minutes, only, but there was something about the 'caring' way she moved like she thought she might be able to do something for her pa, and him already dead.

Another thing. As they were approaching Duncan's home, he had pointed out that the hill with the three grassy flats was their new place, swapped with Mississippi Central for the one they took. It looked like a very good place, and he could see the goats on top, looking like little toys a boy would play with.

Goats had been a favorite of his mother's while she was still with them, and about two times each winter she'd arrange to have one butchered for them. She canned and dried the meat, and she could do magic with the cooking. He'd like to have her dumplings on times when he ate a dry sandwich for his working lunch.

She had a way of cutting the meat into thin strips and simmering it in spices. Then when she dropped in the dumplings, the magic happened. Little lumps of dough turned into small, fluffy clouds of flavor, laced with bits of the spicy meat.

But his mother was gone, and so were the wonderful goat-meat dumplings. Also gone was his big brother, back near Jacksonville hauling gravel to make a railroad bed. He didn't like the job, either, but he had to get away. He hoped for a better one soon.

Pa's new wife made living impossible to stay at home when she installed her own selfish demons into the house. He and his brother had tried, but there was no way to stay, and even Pa didn't stand up to them. His brother, Harold, had wanted to take over the farm and grow hay, but it wasn't going to work.

Harold's girlfriend didn't like it either. He was living in a tent on the grounds in the right-of-way, just as he, Matthew, was in another tent. It was cold and the ground was hard and rough. Breakfast had hot coffee but everything else was cold. Eggs had been boiled yesterday. Breakfast sausages came from a can, and were cold. White bread had nothing to it to keep a working fellow going.

There on the bluff Matthew was given a meal of the most delicious beans he had ever had, and huge slabs of rich cornbread (with butter!) when he accompanied the body of Duncan's Pa. He could still taste those delectable hunks of cornbread when soaked in the juice of the beans. Duncan's life was tough, but he had a family and a house to come home to.

And when he saw those goats on the top of the bluff, he almost produced tears of nostalgia for the life he once had.

Not only that, he really liked Duncan. They had been friends (for the few minutes of lunch) and had seemingly been kindred souls, at least able to understand each other.

The way the wood cutting was going, he would only in the vicinity of River Bend for a couple of months. Then the house of the bluff would be far behind, and Duncan, who was not such a good wood cutter, would be out of a job.

It was while they were eating a cold lunch, Matthew commented, "I'd give a shiny dime for a bowl of beans like I had at your house." Duncan had been surprised. He hadn't thought of that.

Matthew had more to say. "My Ma was a good cook, but her beans didn't taste like those at your house. Is your older sister the cook?"

"Yeah, well, Lolita helps, but Josephine is the boss in the kitchen."

"I have a question."

"Fire away…"

"Is your sister seein' anyone?"

"Seein'…?"

"Does she have a boyfriend?"

"Not that I know of. She'd too busy. Why?"

"Just wondered. She sure is a pretty lady."

"Really? I never thought of it."

"Yeah, for you she's just the cook, huh?"

"I guess."

Then it was on another day that Matthew shared that he would really like another job. "This job pays pretty good, but we're always on the move, and we get charged a dollar a day for their tent at night and cold food three times a day."

"They charge you a dollar a day? I can't believe it!"

"Believe it! And we get a pillow, a canvas pad and one quilt."

"I sleep in the attic on a pallet."

"Lucky fellow. I wouldn't mind payin' a dollar a day for a pallet in an attic, and a bowl of hot oatmeal for breakfast."

Duncan thought that over. Hmmm, he'd have to check with Josephine, and he'd only be here for two months, but, hey, a dollar is a dollar.

And then Matthew said something very interesting. "You know somethin'? That day I was in the wagon with you, and you pointed out where you lived, I looked up and saw those sheep on the high bluff. That's when I remembered something my mother cooked with a butchered goat.

"It had spices and dumplings and a lot of pieces of shredded meat. I'll bet if a fellow had a bucket'a somethin' like that and pulled up to the cuttin' crew about noon time, he could sell a big bowl of something hot with meat in it for a nickel a cup... maybe more if he also had hot coffee. It could be kept hot on the site, maybe from a tripod over a bonfire. There'd be plenty of sticks laying around to burn."

Duncan listened. This fellow was just full of ideas, and he really liked this one. Fact was, in a couple of months his own job would also be gone. Then it would be a few weeks before the track laying happened. That would take a lot longer than the cutting. They might be close for several months. Hauling all that gravel to make a mound took a while. The beans could be made at home, and just heated on the bonfire.

Maybe that would do till he located something else. The pressure of money was getting him down. Bad dreams and restless sleep. But he certainly did like his attic bed. Matthew could sleep there, easily.

Josephine was in no mood to argue. "Do what you want. The food wouldn't be a problem. Lots of bed space in the attic."

So Matthew moved his gear into the attic, and slept wonderfully on the pallet. He watched Josephine when she wasn't looking, and that was also a pleasure. The thing was, something bad was bothering her, and she had good reason for feeling bad.

It was Lolita who asked about the goat dumplings. "You don't remember the spices?"

"I remember Basil, because I knew a fellow with that name, and I recognized garlic and onion. Nothin' else, and she cooked that meat twice. Once in a big chunk and again as slivers as thin as she could slice 'em."

Josephine passed the food, and ate a few bites, and looked out a window, her mind far away. Occasionally. she glanced toward the top of the cupboard. The poison was not visible from the floor, but she knew it was there… that and the final medicine that had been left for Ma.

JOSEPHINE FINDLEY

Josephine knew that something was going to happen to her. It would not be enough to lose Ma, and then Pa, and not have something happen to her. She was next in line, and she was in charge.

It wasn't that she asked to be, but most of her siblings checked with her on this and that, and she seemed to be the clearing house for all ideas… it being her job to make a decision, one way or the other.

Lolita was the lone person who did what she did, and let the consequences take care of themselves. Eldon coached her horseback lessons on one of the wagon horses who was stodgy and patient and had to be urged to go. She was an apt pupil, and after a couple of weeks, and found that Daisy was easily handling her twins, he put Lolita on her back. Daisy must have been a saddle horse, because she obeyed like she understood English. Lolita fell in love. She insisted her rear end fitted well on Daisy, and she didn't need a saddle, just the pad that went under the saddle.

Daisy didn't mind pulling the double shaft buggy that was rigged for one horse, rather than a pair. Lolita began to think of Jacksonville and the clothing store, but she would need to talk with Josephine, and that was like talking with a zombie, whatever that was.

Josephine answered Amy's cries when Lolita was out of the house, but otherwise ignored her. It was almost like she thought she was to blame for Ma's death. It was untrue, she knew, and she knew it was too much work that was too heavy and too many pregnancies too close together that took her Ma. By the time she had Sammie and Amy, she was getting old enough to be past all that, but Amy came anyway.

She knew Duncan was about to go out of his mind with worry and the loss of Pa, though he had nothing to do with his death. She worried when Eldon caught fish, though he assured her he always tied himself tightly. She felt guilty that Lolita was mostly caring for Amy, doing the night feeding and diaper changing.

She knew she should instruct nine-year-old Darlene in household duties, but she had no strength, and anyway, their whole world was going to fall apart, so why bother? Then she felt guilty for feeling guilty about Amy. She should have died with Ma, but she didn't. Why is she alive and Ma isn't?

The more she thought about it, the more often she glanced to the top of the cabinet. No, she told herself. There were her siblings to think on... and that reminded her that the quantity of siblings was the reason she was so tired. Cooking came naturally to her, and she disliked having Lolita help, but it was mostly that she hated needing Lolita. Lolita's fried fish and hush puppies did not turn out like hers. She felt guilty about that, too.

Her three older siblings had tried to talk about what was bothering her, but she would have none of it. There was nothing bothering her, she told them.

Then there was the night that she took Ma's final medicine to bed with her, sliding the bottle under her pillow. She was sleeping in the room with Darlene, so Lolita and Amy could have Ma and Pa's room. The noise of Amy's crying was less noticeable that way.

Darlene was a bit fussy about her room in the new house, and she always made up her bed and adjusted the curtain so the sunshine could come in, and she regularly swept the floor and shook her braided bedside rug. She was irritated that Josephine carelessly left her bed unmade until after breakfast.

She began spreading up the covers to make it look better, and she fluffed the pillow and accidentally put her hand on the final medicine bottle. She pulled it out and puzzled over it, then went to the kitchen with the bottle and asked Josephine what it was.

What could she say? "Oh, that's some… here, give it to me and I'll put it up. I was saving it."

She handed the bottle to Josephine and went back into her wonderful room. She sat down on the bed and asked herself, 'saving it for what?' And why should it be under her pillow? Should she tell Lolita? Maybe she'd just wait a while, Lolita seemed busy with the baby.

Josephine took the bottle of final medicine and slipped it in her pocket. Now why did she take it to bed with her? What if she had taken a pill? One thing that would happen would be that she wouldn't hurt anymore! Maybe if she took two of the pills, she would be very sure that she didn't hurt anymore.

She was so very tired, and couldn't seem to get rested. She opened the bottle and poured several pills out in her hand. The outside door opened, and Eldon came in looking for tea. He poked the coals it the stove, and set the teapot over the blaze.

Josephine dropped the pills and the bottle into her apron pocket. She thought, Eldon. Dear, sweet and helpful Eldon. Duncan just as worried as she was… Lolita doing night duty on their little sister, and never complaining, and making herself ready for errands, at the expense of her modesty. Darlene making her bed and finding… oh, Josephine, you have got to do something about yourself!

Eldon filled his tea mug and sat down. He'd like to have taken Josephine to see the foals, but was afraid to say anything. He just drank his tea and left. Curiosity was getting the best of him about those goats that belonged to them and were just up there consuming grass, getting fat and having babies. There were quite a lot of them, and some were getting shaggy with loose hair hanging in wads. What was wrong with them?

Maybe he'd have to find out where the former owner lived and see him? Could there be something in their shed. He checked the building that was made for them, and it looked good. It could afford to be raked but that wouldn't make them sick.. In fact, they didn't act sick. Maybe the preacher would know where the former owner moved to.

Then Josephine made a decision. She was going to do something, and she was going to do it as soon as she could manage. When Eldon was a baby and it was just Duncan and herself, Ma used to take them to the church. It was quite a hassle with the three of them as Pa didn't go and then she got pregnant with Lolita, and it was just too much.

Josephine had really missed going. The old preacher at the time told stories while he talked, and some of them were interesting and puzzling, but she made herself remember them all so she could think about them later.

She was good at numbers, and she learned to count. The preacher said that God had told people that if they needed something, they could ask for it, and if there were two people, or maybe three people, it was even better, because God (who seemed to be invisible) was right there with them. Now what made her remember that?

She certainly needed something, but really couldn't put her finger on what it was. They were getting along well, but it seemed like it wouldn't happen very long. Mostly, she was afraid of the future and felt it was her duty to see that it worked out all right. But how was she supposed to do that?

The old preacher was gone, but the current pastor and his wife were very kind to her at the funerals. Whatever that story was, the young preacher would know the story, and maybe if she heard it again… Well, maybe she just needed to go talk with them.

Tomorrow she would ask Eldon to hitch up the buggy for her, and she would go after her peppermint plants that she had forgotten in the move. And then she would just go on into the town and talk with that preacher, or maybe his wife.

Eldon put one of the wagon horses in the shafts for her, and offered to take her, but he insisted she wanted to go alone. It was just a little chore to go get her plants that would be destroyed by the railway.

He watched her go, and then went to the goats to look for ideas. He was there when he saw, in the distance that she was coming back from the old place. Good. She'd made it, and now she might feel better. But, no, she drove right on past the driveway.

He forgot about the goats and went back to the house. Lolita met him with 'shhh' fingers at her lips. She sat down to the table, and Eldon joined her. No, she had no idea why Josephine would go on into town. She should have asked one of them. She had told Josephine that she could hop onto Daisy, and take care of trips, but Josephine didn't ask.

Eldon nodded, decision made. He put a saddle on King, and made him walk to town. King did not want to walk. He wanted to gallop, but that would make him catch up with the buggy. He realized he should have chosen one of the other horses, but King was such fun!

He followed as she reached the church, and walked next door. She knocked, and was let into the house. Hmmm, well, she had a right… but the way she had been feeling, maybe he'd just wait around.

Jane Ann, the preacher's wife, listened and decided this was a job for the preacher. She told Josephine, "I am so glad you came. The preacher will help you on anything ask, and that is his job. I'll take you there."

Eldon saw them go from the house to the church, and he dismounted and allowed King to snort and toss his head. If she just came to ask about something, that was her business, and he'd just take King and go home. He'd wait for her, and if she didn't come, well… he'd go look for her.

Actually, she'd seemed better today. Oh, well….

Josephine was taken to the church where the pastor was in his little office. She was told to sit and ask anything she wanted to. Jane Ann left, but stayed in the church. Joe always wanted her to stick around when he had a lady in conference. It looked better that way.

Josephine asked about the two or three together story, and if it was true that they were permitted to ask, if they needed anything.

He asked if there was something she needed to ask for, and she said it was just how she was feeling. He asked if she was ill, and if there was something she needed, but she shook her head. No, it was just…

And then she told him about the final pills, and tears were streaming when she told of seeing that bottle in Darlene's hand, and what might have happened if Sammie had found it. Everything went into his mouth. She put her arms on the desk and buried her head, and she wept like she had not wept for years, even at the funeral.

Jane Ann could not help but hear, and she peeked through the door. He motioned her inside. "I think I'll need you. Could you get a napkin for her, and just sit down?"

She left, and Josephine still cried her heart out. Jane Ann returned with a soft cloth that she pressed in Josephine's hand. When the weeping quieted down to snubs and hiccoughs, she looked up to the two people in the room.

She wailed, "I'm sorry! I'm so sorry! I don't know what made me do that."

Jane Ann extended an arm around her shoulders. "Don't worry, you did nothin' wrong. You cried 'cause you just came to the end of your rope, and needed help. You came to the right place."

The pastor agreed. He placed a Bible on his desk and asked, "Can you put your hand on this book?"

"Just put my…?"

"Right. Just spread your fingers. That's right, now Jane Ann."

Jane Ann placed her hand on Josephine's and the pastor put his hand on top. "Now, we are going to request the help promised in this book. There is one promise from God that 'where two or three are gathered together, there am I in the midst.'

"And there is another promise that is just as important for you. It is '… your (Heavenly) Father knoweth what things ye have need of before ye ask'.*

"And there is one more promise that says …ask and it shall be given you, seek, and ye shall find.*

"Now, Miss Josephine, you see there are three of us, we know that God is in our midst, and we have a request and we may not know what to call it, but God knows more about us that we know about ourselves. Then there is the other promise that God will answer, and He may be answering already, because many times the answer is on the way even before we know what to ask for.

"I will express our desire in words, though God already knows what it is.

"Dear Heavenly Father, the three of us have come with a request that your daughter, Miss Josephine Findley be given an answer to her problems and comfort from her distress. We know that she carries a great burden since her parents have been taken, but You promised help with burdens too heavy to carry. So now we are thanking you for the answer, and Miss Josephine will have peace and strength to do what she must do for her family.

"We ask this in the name of Jesus. Amen.

"Now, Miss Josephine, you may take this Bible home with you along with a list that has been placed in the Book containing other great promises."

He picked up the Bible and handed it to her.

"Oh, thank you so very much. I'll be careful with it. When should I return it?"

The preacher reassured her. "You will never have to return it. It is yours. May I see it a minute?"

She handed the Book to him, and he opened to the fly leaf. He took the lid from his ink bottle and lifted the pen, then he wrote, 'This Book is a gift to Miss Josephine Findley from God and from her church.'

"Now, this is yours forever. You may return to you home, knowing there will be answers to your questions and help with your problems.* Come back and see us at any time, and when you can come, we will enjoy you in our Sunday services."

*Matthew 7:7, Matthew 18:20 & Matthew 6:8

At the door, he shook her hand, and Jane Ann gave her a shoulder hug and a smile. With that, Josephine thanked them and went to her buggy and her green peppermint plants that she must set in the garden.

Eldon was wandering around on the top of the bluff with his own problems. He was watching the road for the return of his sister, and now that happened, so he turned his attention to the other problem.

What was happening to his goats? Their hair was growing longer, and the poor animals must be smothering. Some of was falling out. He had to find the people who had lived there to tell him what to do for them. That took another trip into River Bend to the preacher's house.

The question was quickly answered. "Certainly I know who lived there before you. I try to keep up with everyone in town. You need to see Mr. Wilbur Beasley, and I can sketch a map on where he lives now. That railroad came along just in time for him because he had to move anyway because of his knees, and he had to leave the goats. They were more trouble than he wanted at his age."

"Trouble? I didn't know they were a trouble. They seem all right except for their hair. It doesn't stop growing."

"Growing? Oh, you don't know! Certainly you must see Wilbur so he can tell you how to sheer them. It should have been already done, and it must have slipped his mind."

"Shear them…? You mean I need to cut off their hair?"

"Absolutely. That hair is valuable, but Wilbur will tell you all about it."

Eldon left the preacher, his head whirling. Hair valuable? That can't be. It's long and dirty, but it would be wonderful if it was valuable.

The old man chuckled, and apologized. "I'm old and I plum forgot that the new owner of the goats might not know about them."

Eldon left with a lot more knowledge than he knew what to do with. He also knew where the shears were, and if he, Eldon, would come and get him, Wilbur would make one more trip to the top bluff with shearing instructions.

It was also this time that Matthew, who had become a temporary resident of the attic bedroom asked Duncan, "Could you take me to see your goats? I saw a picture of them one time, the different way they look, and I think they may have hair that can be cut and sold."

Duncan passed it off. "Huh! Surely not! I haven't been up there. No time, with Pa like he was. Eldon's been everywhere, though, and he'll take you."

Matthew was one happy fellow. He had a room with a solid warm floor and no fear of a snake wanting to share his sleeping bag. He had real quilts to cover with and plenty of room for his feet. When he looked up, it was not to ascertain what weather might descend on the leaky tent but to see solid wooden rafters holding up a solid asphalt roof.

He had a roommate who didn't snore. He could go to sleep with the knowledge that he would wake up to hot tea, hot oatmeal, and biscuits, and maybe bacon or sausage, and he could have more oatmeal if he wanted it.

He had a civilized chair (bench, actually) and a table to rest his elbows. He had people who treated him as a person equal to themselves, and he might even find a way to be a permanent part of this happiness. He was working on that!

His first choice would be to win the favor of Josephine, who now seemed to be a different, and even better, person than a few days ago. She could smile and join in the conversation. When one looked at her there seemed to be something behind her eyes. (No more looking into emptiness!)

He began to think further. Was there a tangible way to reward this object of his intended affection? There really might be.

When he was essentially booted out of his home, he left certain items as he had no place for them. There was the bureau of drawers, deep and roomy, and a carved frame with a mirror that attached to it. He had a rocker that was a bit small for a full grown man, and he had it because there needed to be a place to store it… along with a roomy quilt chest that seemed to match it.

These items, along with the metal bed rails and carved headboard had been relegated to the shed and were likely doomed to deteriorate from exposure to temperature changes. Then, there were his animals.

He had the mare that was given him on his last birthday that Ma was there… being four years ago. She was (is) a beautiful Paint mare, with a large white patch with a black pillar inside. Atop the pillar was a small brownish patch that made him think of a candle. So Candle became her name. Candle produced a filly with a lot of orange-ish brown, and he named her Flame.

Chances were good that Candle was again pregnant.

He would go to Josephine with his request. If he was turned down, then he would make other plans for his life. He would say to her, 'Would you be open to storing some items for a while? My home was taken over by tyrannical strangers, and I need to find a place to put them for a while. If they would of use to your family, I would be happy. If not, I would gladly pay storage.', then he would relate to her what they were.

He needed to do it quickly, because he could not let himself become attached to these people. Even baby Amy could crawl up to him and grasp the leg of his trousers. Now, who could resist that?

Also, there was his mother's buggy. Small, like she was, and it would most certainly be left to ruin. No one else would want it.

He managed to catch Josephine sitting at the table with tea, and he decided he would not get a better time. As he related the bed, he noted a look of interest in her eyes. They could use another bed… Amy was coming on, and Sammie still slept with Eldon.

It was when he said rocker and chest that he received assurance that the items would be welcome… and the chest of drawers with the mirror sealed the deal. It would take two trips, he told her, but the chest and rocker could come first, and if he could borrow their wagon, there might be other things when he brought the bedsteads and rails.

She asked, when could he do it, and he told her 'the very next week end which in in two days'

Matthew was one happy fellow. It was like birthday, Christmas and the last day of school tossed into the air and raining down on him like the confetti at the circus! Bright colored flakes and all flowing down on him!

Now if he could just go slow and feel things out, he could be the winner of the whole pot… the pot being a family, a beautiful girl, a friend he liked already and seemed to like him… and a place to live where he would make himself indispensable.

GOATS AND HORSES

Within a week, Matthew arrived with his Sunday clothes, along with the rocker, chest and bureau (with mirror) somehow worked into the charming little buggy that was only marred by chicken droppings as it had been stored in the chicken house. The smooth linoleum top cleaned well, and the droppings left no stain. He had oiled the bearings in the wheels, and they rolled silent as a whisper. Pa had gotten the best for Ma, but now she was gone.

Matthew told Josephine, "It would be my great pleasure if you would use the buggy any time you could. Being stored was hard on it, and it was made to be used." He could see that once more he had said the right thing. The little buggy was light and snug, almost like wearing a well-made garment, and the family buggy she had been using was large, unwieldy and with much too much room inside.

The next load brought the bed, a grain grinder, a few plow points and a whole plow. He picked up other items, like metal buckets, knives and a spade. He also loaded on the box that contained the settin' hen over a dozen half hatched eggs. The hen gave him a bit of an argument, but Matthew was bigger, so he won out in the end. Someone was likely to be unhappy to see the hen gone... but so be it!

At the bluff, the bed used by Pa and Ma was taken down and moved to the shed until other moves were made. The headboard and foot of the bed were carved to match the back panel of the rocker, and the drawers of the chest. They could use a bit of oil polish, but that was easy. Josephine moved her personal possessions into the chest of drawers, and the extra quilts fitted perfectly in the matching quilt chest.

The room looked beautiful, and a new curtain at the window would make it perfect. She'd have to think about that.

Along with the bed and sundry other items, he had tethered behind the wagon, a pair of beautiful paint animals, Candle and Flame, and also the one carried inside Candle which was likely to also be a Paint. In another year, Flame could be bred. Eldon was going to like that.

He also brought a tripod his family had used on occasion with bonfires and camping, and it might also be missed when it was discovered gone... but so be it, as well.

Eldon took a look at the horses tethered behind the wagon, and was instantly smitten. Just picture Candle and Daisy prancing along, pulling a single tonged wagon... or maybe a better buggy. It was so easy to get one's hopes up!

Matthew explained, with all his other plunder, he should pay a dollar and a half a day for all the room and board, and the care of the animals. He warned that it was only temporary, as when the railroad blasted its way through the next mountain, he would be too far away to stay with it, and they would be hiring other cutters in the little town of Piney.

When that came, he would surely be hired on where his brother worked, and would be close again, for a while. During that time, he would be looking for a better job, and he would like it to be in River Bend.

Duncan found himself a sheet of paper and began arranging a way to take care of the animals. He also estimated the value of taking hot food to the workers on the right-of-way, though, as Matthew said, it would have moved on in a couple of months.

But soon after that, the laying of the tracks would be coming by. If serving the food worked for the right-of-way, it would work for the rails, and that would last several months, through the winter. During that time he would look for something better.

And it was now that Wilbur Beasley had a good week of hot, dry weather and his knees felt better. He arrived in his own buggy, ready to take Eldon to the top of the bluffs for an education.

He looked at the goats and gasped. Oh, the poor, unfortunate beasts, and he, Wilbur, was to blame. He had been so glad to get off the bluffs that he had entirely forgotten the animals that were mostly no trouble, but when they were trouble... they were a great lot of trouble.

He looked sadly at Eldon. "I did you a great disservice. These goats should have been sheered three months ago. I can see you have a busy week ahead of you. This hair will not be first class, and the weather will be stinkin' hot up here, but then next year they can be sheared on time.

"I think there are sacks in the loft to the shed, and I know there is a book that shows how to butcher a young goat. You got too many animals. Those little fellow should'a been eaten. That book on the butcherin' has ways to cook the meat, 'cause those baby rams can't be let to grow up, unless you are ready to change out the breedin' rams, and that'll happen about every five years.

"What I gonna tell you now is that you DO NOT EVER SELL A GOAT. You can sell a dressed out animal, but never a goat as these are special, and you don't want the neighbors growing them. Remember that, and you can't even be nice to someone and give them a baby. This here is a business, and it's a payin' business. It's took care of my family for years, but my youngens all went to Jacksonville to work, leavin' me with 'em.

"You're either gonna like 'em or hate 'em, but they'll make money and food, and nature feeds 'em. It ain't like up north where a fellow has to buy square bales. They will need a little grain in mid-winter, but that hair pays for it. And there's another thing. Anything you butcher, you do it a certain way and save the skin. You can sell that, too, or the big ram skins will make good throw rugs. They're warm and last forever. There's fellows that even made bags outta them skins, like puttin' two together and stitchin' with cord. Just punch holes and thread the cord."

Eldon had listened, first looking at Wilbur's wonderfully wrinkled face, and then at the pitifully un-sheared animals, roasting in the summer sun. He could see his life stretched out before him, and it looked wonderful!

Lovely horses! Matthew's Candle was fully as attractive as Daisy, and their color patterns blended. There were the four foals growing like weeds, and he took a deep breath and let it out slowly and enjoyably.

How could he, who had been rotting and going crazy down on the flat, now have this wealth?

He brought Mr. Wilber in the kitchen for a cup of tea before he left home, and they chatted about the work and the pay, and when things should be done. He stressed the care of the wool, and don't try to wash it. They do a better job where they make sweaters, shawls and fancy rugs."

Josephine was working around, and listening to Eldon's animated, excited voice. He was going to have something important to do that could create money... and they'd had those goats for months, not knowing. Imagine that!

Then it came to her that Someone 'knows what you have need of, before ye ask Him". It worked! She asked for help, and it was already hers! Not only that, it seemed that the energetic Eldon was even happier than he usually was. It looked an answer for him, too.

Then, when it was said that those young rams had to be butchered soon, like last week, there was Duncan planning soup and beans, both needing meat, and Matthew was helping. Matthew seemed to fit into the family like a hand in a glove. She really wasn't thinking when she said he could board with them, but now she noticed him. He really seemed to like Duncan and Eldon, and he was letting her use the lovely bed and rocker (so nice for putting Amy to sleep). And there was that grain grinder… so much nicer and more efficient that the one she used. Maybe he'd leave it here a while.

It seemed there were recipes in the book Mr. Wilbur left in the goat shed. She needed to see that, too.

The words drummed in her head, 'Before ye ask Him.' 'Before ye ask Him.' It was wonderful not so be so worried all the time.

The darling little buggy would work nicely on Sundays, for church. She, Lolita, and Amy would just fit, and the fellows could come in the other one. Sunday church was a necessity, if only to be thankful for what had been waiting for them before she'd asked.

Another thing. They needed new clothes… at least different clothes. The little buggy that would be at their house for several months, maybe a year, would be just perfect for her and Lolita (to drive), and Amy was now old enough to be taken.

Josephine even had thoughts about the garden. The peppermint plant did not even die back through the winter. When she found a place to plant it, she found one was already there, but not doing well. No matter. Josephine knew what to do with peppermint plants. They were highly important to her family. While she was there she inspected the rest of the garden. Looked good. It even smelled good, with the aroma of rich soil… not soggy, staleness.

It was late now, but still time for potatoes. Maybe a few beans, if there was a late frost, but certainly there would be turnips. She was feeling good, maybe even optimistic. With Duncan's plans with the soup bucket, and maybe even coffee as suggested by Matthew, he was even experimenting with beans, first, and asked Eldon when there would be meat.

Eldon said, "How about tomorrow? I'll get started, and you can help when you get home. With neither of us knowing what we're doing, we should be finished by dark, and you can simmer your meat all night. Start the beans this morning, and you'll be that much ahead." That was Eldon… give him an idea, and he ran away with it.

Duncan looked at the supply of dry beans in the barrel and saw, right off, more would have to be ordered. A trip to the Mercantile, for sure, though not today or tomorrow. Might also order 50 pounds of corn.

Eldon strung up the body of the little half-grown ram and looked at the instruction book. 'First: Take off the skin carefully. Cut straight down the belly, then out to each hoof. Slide knife carefully just under skin. Remove and tack in place on a solid surface to avoid shrinking and buckling.' (What was buckling?) No matter, he could do that.

Lolita wandered up to watch. She looked at the book. First remove usable meat from legs. She picked up a knife and began, tossing small pieces in the bucket. When it was half full, she took it down to the stove and poked up the coals. She stoked them with wood for a blaze, and took the pail back up the hill.

Josephine looked in the large cooker. Hmmm. well, it appears there will be goat meat for supper. What was the spice Matthew's Ma used? She could only remember Basil, and she had that. Then she'd wait until the aroma of the meat came out, and she might get a clue on what to use… oh yes, the onions and at the end, the garlic.

These chunks might lend themselves to hash. She'd give it some thought. That would stretch out the potatoes that were getting low.

Those pails Mathew brought were coming in handy. Lolita brought down another half pail of meat pieces and put them on the burner, bucket and all, because that was what Duncan would be using. If it decided to leak, best he find out now.

Josephine watched the simmering pail, sniffed the aroma, and thought of the spices she had put in the fish. Why not? If it was going to be ruined, best it happen now.

Duncan cutting wood, trying to work with the chunks of wood and keep his mind on it. The trouble with temporary jobs, they had no future. Duncan needed to think far out. Matthew thought they'be both be taken on permanent when the track laying reached Calhoun, because it was becoming too far for the wagon haulers to get home to Jacksonville for the week end.

Matthew's brother was a permanent worker, planning to go all the way across the state until they reached those coming on from the river. It might take a year, altogether, but he said hiring would begin, and he would put in a word for the both of them.

The work was a killer, but the pay was good and by then he'd maybe have an idea for what was next. Right now he was learning to make cornbread. Josephine had Matthew's corn grinder brought to the kitchen, and corn was being ground. Good grinder. Blade was sharp.

She mentioned to Duncan that if a field was plowed, they could grow corn in this rich ground instead of buying it... and remember all the horses that would need corn. Duncan stirred the batter and poked the pan into the oven. They'd have this for supper, and after tomorrow, he would try serving lunches to a work crew.

Matthew was sitting on the edge of the front porch looking out over the road. Lolita watched him with an idea. She had the feeling she was like a broom, or maybe a mop, working around other people's lives. Whoever needed help, there was Lolita, but she couldn't seem to help it. When she had ideas, she had to do something with them... didn't she?

She was observant, seeing the way Matthew looked at her sister, and she approved. He might be just what she needed, but maybe he could use a little push. She was not concerned with being subtle with her suggestions. What did subtlety get you but a loss of time?

She sat herself down on the porch the way he was sitting, and when he turned to look at her, she said, "Would you like to know what Josephine would like?"

Matthew brightened quickly. He'd like nothing better.

Lolita didn't wait for an answer. "She would like to have a bench swing here on the porch so she could sit in the cool of the breeze blowing up from the road."

Matthew considered that. "You really think so? Did she say she wanted a swing?"

"No. She didn't have to. I just know things, and that is what I know, but you don't need to do anything about it. You're gonna be gone, anyway. I've got to go bring the clean clothes off the line. See you later," and she was gone. That was the say to do it… toss an idea and leave, so the person didn't have to use it or reject it.

Matthew pulled his legs up from swinging on the edge of the porch and looked up. There were solid rafters in just about the right places. For making the swing, slats would be nice, but they had no slats. Boards would have to do temporarily, and there were some lying around.

He sorted through the tools he had brought… that he had decided he had earned, and took out the drill, a hammer, and saw. Surely there was a chain somewhere around here, but if not, there were ropes until he could get a chain. The thing about Matthew, when he got started, he was a whiz at building.

Before dark he had a board seat, board back and armrests. It would seat two (maybe the exact right two!), and there was plenty of room for it to swing gently.

He drilled the rafters, and threaded a rope. The swing was usable before he went to bed. It worked, but if she liked a swing, he would make it a lot better, later.

FELLOWS AT THE LIVERY STABLE

Horses, being the most used instrument for getting around in small towns, required such services as a livery stable. The establishment boarded and rented out horses, and it also offered medication for horses. Harnesses and saddles were on display, and usually there was a blacksmith nearby for the replacement of iron shoes on horses.

The small town was one of the places for an establishment such as this. Autos were highly used in the towns, but they were subject to breakdowns, and there were very few repair shops in small towns as there were not enough automobiles to make it profitable… hence, the livery stable. A disabled auto had no choice other than being hauled in by mules or horses, and they were acquired from the livery stable.

The small town of River Bend was one of those small towns, being about 12 miles from a larger town of Jacksonville, had a livery stable, and it was a wonderful hangout for men of all ages between other duties, or those just looking for a bit of company of other men.

It was a place for sale or rent notices to be tacked on the wall. It was a place for a stranger to ask directions, have emergency help on a horseshoe.

The livery stable in River Bend was managed by Ed, who was good at his job, and a likeable fellow who liked to have others hanging around. When they talked, they exchanged news, and that way Ed had an idea of what was going on.

He asked, "Have any of you fellows seen what's goin' on down on the bluff by the river?"

"You mean the old Beasley place? That's been took over by the Findly children what lost both parents nigh onto a year ago."

Others joined in when a conversation opened. "Just children…" No grown up takin' care of 'em?"

"There was till we buried 'em. The Ma didn't get over the last birth, and Pa was the one who got the sense outta 'im. Both of 'em, not a month apart."

"Yeah, and they were fast funerals, not much advertised.

"I heard that oldest girl took it real hard."

"A body wouldn't be surprised at tha, and her barely eighteen."

"With no grownup, what's keepin' 'em?"

"Keepin' their selves, seems like."

"Yeah, and didn't they make a swap with Beasley's, the fellow woith the goats?

"You should'a seen what they had to swap. House deemed to be held together by dirt dobbers. The Pa cut wood for sale. He's been missed. He was good at and somehow kept body and soul together."

"How many yougens were there?"

"A passel of "em. Six or Seven… maybe eight with the newborn baby that got throwed in on 'em."

"Shame the kid didn't go with the Ma. What chance does it have being raised by chidren?"

"Oh, I don't know. That girl was eighteen. That's old enough to have one of 'er own."

"But they got that piece'a bluff property. How can they make a livin' there? Ain't no land to farm, hardly."

"Had a good house, though. It looks down on the road there by the bridge. Good lookin' house."

"But no farm land. They ain't gonna make it there."

"Seem to. Nobody's been askin' around for help."

And the Tuesday Sewing Circle tried to figure it out. Should someone go down and see if they needed help. They got that newborn baby, sometime back."

Jane Ann felt it was time to head off any speculation. "Oh, they're doin' fine, and that newborn is crawlin' on all fours, Josephine said. Lately they been comin' for the Sunday preachin' but you may not'a seen 'em, they leave out early on account'a the baby."

"Didn't they get lift with no Ma or Pa?"

"Sure did, and it was terrible for them, but they're fighters. They'll do fine, and never asked for help for anything. That place of theirs is really good for horses, and they have several. If they were hurtin' for money, they'd sell a horse, but they haven't done it."

Jane Ann left the quilting and stirred up the fire under the teapot. It was not good to let some conversations get started, and let someone say something that shouldn't be said. Josephine's temporary problem was nobody's business.

And Josephine dipped a spoon into the steel bucket that had the goat meat. Not bad. Not bad at all. That variety of spice she used for the fish was just right. Now the proof will be how does it go with beans.

She sampled the beans that had been on the stove all day. About right. Just tender. She scooped out pieces of the meat and let them cool enough to cut. With her sharpest knife, she divided the meat into the smallest pieces she could and scooped it all into the deep dutch oven. She tossed in bacon grease and several cups of the beans. Who knows what it'll taste like, but its time find out. She popped it in the oven with the cornbread.

They seated themselves on the benches, and passed around the… what would one call it… Maybe bean casserole? That was as good a name as any.

Accidents happen, and this was one. Everyone prounced it perfect, except Amy, and she couldn't talk. She did like the bites they gave her, though.

Duncan loaded on the tripod and some oil fire starter. He'd need to make coals in a hurry. He had counted the bowls, and if he took all they had, there'd be none at home, and it would not be enough.

He'd taken the horse to the Mercantile and bought twenty seven bowls the big bowls, and that was all they had. He'd like to have had thirty five, but this was a start. He really didn't want to do this, but he had to do something.

Lolita watched and listened, her active brain sorting and planning. There was an idea in there somewhere, and she was going to find it.

BIRTHDAYS AGAIN

Another round of birthdays brought Josephine to age twenty and Matthew to twenty four. Amy turned one, and Sammie was now eight.

Lolita became a lovely sixteen. She had taken over the setting hen that Matthew had smuggled away from his former home. She fed it and watched as the dozen chicks popped their shells and preceded to feed themselves on the insects in the grass. Almost immediately the mother hen got broody again. Almost seemed like she was a chick factory all by herself. All new chickens were welcome, and roosters eventually got to the table.

Duncan drove his wagon down to the worksite of the workers and built a fire. The aroma of the beans and meat just about drove the cutters nuts until lunch, and he sold all he had at five cents a bowl, and cornbread came with it, also tea if they had their own cup and most of them did. Tin cups hooked nicely on belts.

Duncan made a $1.35 on the venture, and that was not bad. His load of sawed stove would have sold for $3.00 if he had any, and that would have taken a lot of work. Tomorrow he'd have more food. Of this continued until the cutters moved on over to Piney, he could do a lot better than he would cutting by himself to sell.

On the way home he stopped by the old home site. The railroad had pulled the house down, and the old lumber was stacked ready to create a massive bonfire. Duncan loaded all he could on the wagon and took it to the bluff. Old boards would burn beautifully in the cook stove. A body had to do what he could, but it would be nice to have a job he didn't hate.

Lolita helped Eldon tack the goat skin onto the wall at the back of the shed. Seemed like a good place, and by the time it was dry, another one would be ready. This was rather fun, actually. It was something different, and that was what she was looking for... but this was Eldon's project.

She examined the furry hide and decided it really would make a good bedside rug, rather than the braided ones. A body might even find a way to sell them, but later they would not have a number of goats that had to be butchered. This could be fun, but it was not going to satisfy her search, besides, it was Eldon's project, not hers.

She put the bucket of beans that Duncan would need onto the burner and poked up the fire. It seemed she was forever picking up the pieces of someone else's project.

The porch swing got made, and it made Josephine happy... and made Matthew happy that Josephine was happy. His dreams were clearly getting better and better if he could just figure something that didn't require him to leave River Bend. He knew that Josephine would never leave that house on the bluff, so what he did would have to be there, also.

One thing he could so right now was to plow that field that was so grown up with grass. She had been adamant about the corn patch. It was too late to plant corn, which took a long time to mature, but he could plant wheat, and it would come up in time to make winter grazing for horses. He remembered a few things from his father's teachings.

Besides, there was Candle and Flame and the little filly, Star, to consider. They were here and they ate corn, and he had no place to take them if he could not stay on the bluffs. One little problem he kept running into... there was no one in charge, and the siblings didn't seem to need a central clearing house for plans.

As it was Josephine's wish for the plowed field, and it didn't seem it was going to get done, (certainly Eldon did not have time) he'd just ask her. No, he'd just do it. He chose one of the wagon horses and used his own plow that he took from his father... should be his, anyway.

The summer evenings were long, and it was light till after 9 o'clock. He was tired from working all day, but the horse was fresh and seemed to have done that before, though he noticed that she was a bit expanded in her belly. Hmmm, as animals were Eldon's project, he pointed it out. At supper he mentioned it.

"Getting' big, huh? I hadn't... you know what? I plum forgot about King! Here he was, with all those mares, what else was he to do? I'll bet the other three are pregnant, too, and Duncan hasn't noticed. He don't notice much these days for bein' worried. Well, there ain't no reason not to use her. Bein' pregnant ain't bein' sick, and that ground shouldn't be too tight, like down by the river."

So Matthew put his plow point in the ground urged her forward. It took two evenings to do the good job he wanted to do. He was bone-tired when he climbed the stairs to his bed, but it had almost been a pleasure. Just himself and the horse and the plow, and no other concern.

When the ground was turned deeply over, and the grassy surface was eight inches down, he leveled the rows with the harrow and viewed it with great satisfaction. He thought it might be well to thank someone, and from what the preacher said, that Someone might be above, so he looked up just as though their might be Someone up there who had noticed him. Felt good, actually.

The next day was Sunday, and not a work day, he decided that the next day he'd run up into town and bring back the wheat seeds. Wouldn't take more'n and hour to seed the whole thing.

Eldon reported, smiling, that the other three wagon horses were also creating foals. For that matter, Daisy might be the same way. It had reached the point of deciding what to do young ones. Maybe another fenced in area. The goats had kept him so busy he had let the horses to their own devices, and they did what horses do... they reproduced.

Lolita watched and wondered and did a little planning. What she finally did would depend entirely on what was currently on the bluff, and what she could do with her own two hands. Her hands were rather busy, but so was her mind, and when a neighbor stopped by with a request, she made a snap decision that would change her life, though she didn't know it.

The neighbor, Mrs. Tullis, had a father who took a lifesaving preparation of some sort, and it only came from Jacksonville. Ordinarily she ordered the medicine by the mail hack that came once a week with the mail, but the old man had let the medicine run completely out. He was old, and forgot, it was understandable but that did not make more medicine.

She climbed up the driveway and knocked on the door.

She wondered, as there seemed to be young men and horses around at the house on the bluff, could one of them run into Jacksonville and pick up the prescription. She knew it was a great imposition, and she was eager to pay for his time. She presented a $5.00 dollar bill as proof, and if he could start right now, he could be back by dark.

It was Josephine who took the request, and she sadly shook her head. The fellows were either gone or too busy. She was sorry.

Lolita butted in, "No, Mrs. Tullis, my sister forgot. We do have someone, and we'll do it right now. Let me have the address of the pharmacy and the person to see, and I'll see that it's done."

Josephine stared… speechless! Sammie was only barely nine and was not let out of the yard on a horse. What was Lolita thinking of?

But the harried woman had given the information to Lolita, and hurried back to her father. The sisters faced each other. Lolita said, "Sorry, sis. But this is an emergency, and I will go to Jacksonville and get the medicine. That pharmacy in on Main Street is the one, and I'll go straight to it. I'll get my overalls, and take Daisy."

As always, with Lolita, there was no room for doubts or conversation. This time it seemed there was no room for sense.. Josephine stared after her as she rushed to her room and reappeared in her overalls, shirt and straw hat. She practically ran out the back door and yellow for Eldon.

He was not sure what was going on, but harnessed Daisy in minutes. He hoisted her aboard and yelled after her. "Don't let 'er gallop, she'll get to tired."

Lolita appreciated that advice, she was planning to start off on a gallop, but now held her down to a trot. Daisy seemed to detect the urgency. Horses are smarter than a lot of folks think, Eldon had told her. He said they spent time looking at faces and actions to read humans the way they read each other and communicate.

So Lolita tried to communicate the problem to Daisy who swiveled her ears to listen and obeyed heels poking softly into her sides. Lolita bounced comfortably in the saddle, but knew before nightfall her rear end was going to be anything but comfortable. She had never ridden for almost four hours straight, and that was what it was going to take.

Josephine saw Daisy pick her way down the driveway, then strike a rhythm on the hard gravel of the road. She went to the shed to find Eldon. She had to talk to someone. Lolita was clearly out of her mind, and someone needed to go with her.

Eldon disagreed. "Don't worry, sis. She knows what she'd doin', and she was prepared for it. Remember, she's sixteen. She ain't wantin' to be treated like she ain't her own person. She'll be back before dark, wait and see."

Josephine sighed, highly uncomfortable. She guessed she had no option but to wait and see. The other fellows were at work, so she went to her kitchen and stirred the beans and added more water to the simmering meat. It seemed her stove always had buckets of something boiling or simmering, or frying.

She had to quit thinking of Lolita out there on the road alone. What if...? Stop it, she yelled at herself. There's some things you can't no nothin' about. Find somethin' else to do. But then she began to think.

There was that trip to the preacher when she embarrassed herself so badly, but she'd learned something. Answers can come before questions are asked. And her own nimble brain told her that answers for some persons are still questions for others and vice versa.

Lolita was always a different person, and she was old enough now to know what she wants. She wanted to be ready if another rider was needed, but this was all the way to Jacksonville? She'd be fine in town. They'd gone to the clothing store, and the town was set out simple to find one's way around. It was just the trip that was a concern.

Stop it! Josephine. Think about something else. Let's see... hey, there was that thing Mathew's ma cooked that was meat, spices, and dumplings, and the meat was shredded, not in chunks. Now was the time to try it while there was so much meat available that it could be tossed out if it was inedible.

So, let's see. He said she simmered the shredded meat with the flavorings before adding the dumplings. And they were 'little' globs of dough that expanded into 'clouds.' Of course, that was a 'little boy' memory and might not be accurate. Maybe more baking powder.

She fished out chunks of the meat to cool. And while she did that, she remembered, now, that they had a good grinder, maybe she could grind some of the meat and add sage to make sausage. Hmmm, well it would give her something to do to keep her mind off Lolita, out there unprotected and alone, and anything could happen to her!

No, Josephine. Stop it! She's sixteen, and she's going to do what she wants to do. What if it was Pa who could have been helped with medicine?

All right. Let's see. Salt, pepper, baking powder. Oh, well, she'd try it and the day was early enough to start something else. She needed new ideas. Next week Eldon was going to butcher another one, and it would have to be canned so the meat wouldn't spoil. Maybe she'd wash up the jars right now.

Lolita and Daisy were trotting right along on an easy gait that was good for the horse but rather hard on Lolita's back side. No matter. The familiar scenery passed by her gaze, and Daisy was a dream to ride. She stayed right there in the hard tire tread where there was no way to stumble or step in a gopher hole.

It always seemed that Jacksonville was so far away that trips had to be planned carefully. Maybe it wasn't the distance, but the amount of time it took away from working? That might be it. There were a lot of ladies who might be wanting a trip into the city, but there was no one to take them.

She needed something to think on and that seemed as good as anything. How would it be to be stuck out in a tiny place like River Bend? It might even seem like a prison... maybe a prison with no walls, but there was nowhere to go if the person escaped.

Escape was the best word. They had heaven to thank about the railroad needing their land down by the river. That had been a blessing like a good tomato or potato crop when they planted on land that was either soggy or rock hard.

She had walked over to where Matthew was plowing, and the turned over dirt had earthworms, alive, and squirming. At the other place the earthworms would have been drowned or broke apart when the clods dried out and shrunk.

Broke apart. That described their pa. He was all right, they said, and then he wasn't and then every day seemed a little worse. Pa's mind was still in his head, but it wouldn't think straight, and maybe it thought it would be better if he didn't have to think at all. Poor Pa.

Daisy trotted right along, her iron shoes clicking on the packed gravel. Ma had said that the gravel had been a blessing, and before that, it was impossible to get to Jacksonville except to ride on the grass beside the road. Now that also might seem like a prison.

Maybe their pa felt like he was in a prison, and standing under that tree was the way to get out? Well, he was right. Now he's out.

It looks like that old Mississippi Central track might also have been a blessing. It let Mr. Wilbur escape to the city and let us have a place we could never afford. It gave us goats and Eldon was going to get money for their hair? Imagine that!

And the meat. Duncan was doing the best he could, and making more money than if he cut trees, but he was not happy. Also, this was temporary.

Another thing the Mississippi Central gave them was Matthew. One might say they didn't need another person, but they needed him. Eventually, he would marry Josephine. He brought furniture and animals, and he was not any trouble. He keeps looking for things to do for us… or maybe for himself, because he, also, escaped from the prison of his home.

Hey, right up ahead was Jacksonville! The trip half over and the sun was still high in the sky. She guided Daisy to the pharmacy which had a hitching post beside a water trough. Wonderful. She hadn't thought to take her to water before she left home, and maybe she wasn't thirst yet… but she is now.

Lolita slid down from the saddle and hurried into the pharmacy with the note. In minutes she was back. There was the convenient rock placed for short people to mount, and she used it. Daisy was still dripping water from her mouth, so she was ready.

She turned back to the road to River Bend, and the sun was on her back, and a clear road was ahead. A couple of miles down the way she met a long rider coming fast. He was a big strong man, and he was in a hurry. He lifted a hand in greeting, and was gone in seconds, but he left Lolita with a thought.

That fellow could make two of me, and Daisy is a valuable animal. What if he decided to steal her and leave me stranded... or maybe dead? Josephine might have been right about danger. She'd have to see if Matthew knew how to shoot a gun? There was that one wrapped in the canvas with the rifle, and if she had it, she could shoot into the trees or the ground, and maybe discourage a robber. That was a thought.

Daisy was getting tired, she could tell, and there was still about four miles to go. She pulled her over in a deep shade and let her get a few good breaths. She lowered her head, and Lolita could feel the ribs heaving. Maybe she should have stopped sooner, but that was too late to remember hat now.

Sometimes she had more courage than sense, and possibly Daisy was the same. She'd have to watch that. Couldn't ruin a good horse. In about ten minutes Daisy was breathing normally and was tossing her head. She was saying she was ready to go, so they went.

She trotted across the rickety bridge that the Mississippi Central was going to replace with steel, and passed her house. She kept going as the neighbor lived about a quarter of a mile farther, down by Bascom's boarding house.

She pulled Daisy to a stop, slid off and hurried to the door. She tapped rapidly and it opened. Mrs. Tullis stared at Lolita, then hugged her.

"Oh darling, you don't know how much I thank you. I paid you, didn't I? Good. I'll talk with you later," and she was gone, leaving Lolita at the door.

Satisfied and smiling, Lolita returned to Daisy and stepped upon the mounting stone, then into the saddle. It was quite possible she had a blister, but, no matter. She had helped someone who had no other choice but to beg for help.

She tried to slow Daisy to a walk, but the animal knew she was near her home, and she came on. Just like when she came up the driveway tempted by the lovely grass. She walked on to the shed, and Lolita slid off and faced Eldon's relieved and smiling face.

"I knew you could make it."

She nodded and patted his shoulder, then went to through the kitchen door. Josephine was bent over the kettle on the stove, dropping bits of dough in a bubbling pot. Quietly, Lolita moved to the table and sat down. She squirmed a bit to relieve a sore spot. Tomorrow she might not even be able to get out of bed!

Josephine was still concentrating on her cooking, but Amy saw her and called out, "..Ita! Ita!'Josephine turned and saw Lolita. She gasped and came and hugged her, "You're back! I tried not to be worried, but I couldn't stop. You're fine, aren't you?"

Lolita hugged her back. It was good to have someone so concerned, even it if was unnecessary. "I'm fine everywhere, except what touched the saddle. I may have a blister. Next time I'll be better prepared with heavier clothing."

Next time! Of course there would be a next time, and a next time. Josephine and her own rear end had just as well expect it. She took the five dollar bill from her pocket, tucked it into an envelope, and slipped it under her underwear in the bureau. This was going to be the start of something big. She didn't know what it was, yet, but she knew it would be big.

There was the simmering kettle behind her, and duty called to Josephine. You couldn't leave dumplings on their own. They could go flat, or they could boil over, and these were an important experiment. If they were impossible to eat, then plain hunks of spiced meat would work for supper. It seemed suitable, so it appeared on the table along with two dozen perfect biscuits.

Darlene and Sammie eyed the new food with concern, but everyone else was eager for the taste test. Matthew held his breath. The aroma was about what he remembered, though it had been several years ago. He dipped the cushiony clouds, laced with shreds of brown meat, onto his plate. He felt Josephine's eyes on him. He took a bite, and then another.

"I just thought about something. If my Ma was alive, she would have been pleased if her dumplin's were this good. These make me remember being eight, nine, and ten, and comin' home thinkin' I was starvin' to death. These dumplin's had a way of fillin' every little crack in my stomach. I remember likein' 'em even cold and left over. I think it's that rich broth that does it."

Josephine sighed a long, relieved breath. The others were busy with their spoons and didn't comment. There were no leftovers this time, but there would be next time.

Matthew had been to the lumber yard and requested slats for the porch swing, and they had to be ordered. They were now in, and he wanted to go and get them. This might be a good time to take another step toward Josephine.

"I have to run up town to pick up the swing slats, and I'm takin' the little buggy. I thought you might want to ride along, and stop at the Mercantile if you wanted to."

"Well, I couldn't… Yes, I could. I believe I will. Just let me change my dress and fix my hair and…"

Matthew became brave. "You look fine. In fact, you look wonderful! Just take off the apron, and you're ready."

"Are you sure…?

"Absolutely certain. Positively sure. You are perfect just the way you are."

Lolita was in the room and heard. Under her breath she said, "Yeah, Matthew! That's the way!"

He disappeared to get the buggy and horse, and Lolita told her. "Why don't you stop off at the Mercantile just to see what they got. They get in new things along, and you don't ever to anywhere but to church. It won't hurt you to look around."

Josephine listened, but said, "Well, maybe…"

Matthew appeared at the front porch with Candle in the shafts. He stepped down to offer her an arm, just as if she was royalty. He kept Candle in a walk to make the trip last longer. "If it's all right, we'll get the slats and chain first, then we can spend all the time you want in the Mercantile. Is that all right?"

He didn't wait for an answer. He was being very careful. She waited in the buggy while he entered the lumber yard door, and in minutes he was back and stowed the bundle of slats and the length of chain in the boot of the buggy.

"Now, the Mercantile..." He received no objection, so he stopped Candle at the hitching post, and offered an arm for the first step down. Lady's skirts could be dangerous on that long first step down.

She took full advantage of this visit, and examined a lot of things. All she bought was a pound of rat trap cheese. She'd had an idea of something else to do with the goat meat, using pickles, peppers and cheese, along with a quart of canned tomatoes. It would either be delicious or horrible. Nothing ventured, nothing gained, they said, and a lot of times, 'they' were right.

Back at the bluff it didn't take more than an hour for the new swing with the new precut slats to be put together. He invited her to test it, and it was perfect for the two of them. They both knew they had stepped into another section of their lives, but neither said anything. Some things need to be thought about before then can seem real.

Lolita now had a bed to herself. Josephine had moved into their parents' room, and Amy chose to sleep with Darlene, a tiny eleven year old. They snuggled in the bed like two birds in a nest.

It was a good thing Amy was not in her bed, or she might have been injured. Lolita had a dream she would never forget, and could remember clearly when she woke up, though she usually did not remember details.

She woke up after thrashing around in the bed, pushing her pillow onto the floor, and winding her sheet into a wad. She had perspired so much she was forced to change her gown, then she went to the kitchen and poured a mug of cold tea. This took some thought, and it involved that five dollar bill that Mrs. Tullis paid for the trip for the medicine.

She sat, holding the mug in both hands, and she played the dream through her mind. She was standing in an unknown area of land with a lot of brush and trees, and a wide river, near in size to the Tuscalara.

She didn't know why she was there, but it seemed she had come for something, and she couldn't remember what. It seemed she must cross the swift current, and she didn't know how or why. Across the river she could see a row of small buildings like so many outhouses side by side. The doors were closed and locked with a chain and padlock.

She looked around to see if there was something that would help her across the river, but all sticks of wood were too small. Then she found herself fingering the five dollar bill she had hid in her underwear drawer. She was trying to make it bigger so she could make a raft out of it. (Now, wasn't that silly? Like she could make a raft that would cross the current, out of a sheet of paper, no matter how big she stretched it?)

She sipped the cold liquid and considered that. She needed a raft, but she wasn't going to get one. While she was thinking, she remembered the five dollar bill in her fingers, and it was growing bigger, but it was still flimsy and would never make a raft.

While she held it, it lifted up and the ends became wings. It tried to blow away, but she held tight, and it lifted her up and over the river, landing her on the other side and then becoming small again with no wings.

So that now she was on the other side, she realized she had a key attached to a chain around her neck. She went to the first of the little outhouse-shaped buildings and tried the key in the lock. It fit, and the lock fell off onto the ground.

The door opened, and outstepped Mrs. Tullis, and she hugged Lolita and went away. Puzzled, she went to the next little building and the key fit that lock as well. Out stepped a lady she did not know, but thought she might have seen somewhere... maybe at the church. The lady thanked her and left.

Lolita tried the next lock, and like the others, it dropped and disappeared. Another lady came out.

One by one she unlocked all the doors, and the ladies were now gone, and Lolita felt very good and ran after them to see why they were locked in the buildings, and the only one she could find was Mrs. Tullis.

Mrs. Tullis shrugged and told her she was locked in the building because she had no way to get out. Lolita asked her how she got in there, and was told that Mrs. Tullis went in there by herself, and the door locked behind her.

Now, for ridiculous dreams, that one surely took the cake as being the worst! Or best! Lolita couldn't think how she had the key to all those locks, and why one key fit them all. Also, she couldn't have helped them if her five dollar bill had not developed wings and flown her across the river. Why would she have a key?

She had been told that dreams didn't come out of nowhere, even when it seemed they did, but how could anyone put all that together into one dream, and it was interesting that the only lady she recognized was Mrs. Tullis.

There were a few time that she remembered stupid or silly parts of dreams, and she told them to her siblings for a laugh, but this was one dream she would tell no one. There was something weird about this dream, and it seemed she should know more about it than she did. Maybe it just took more thinking. Something was going to happen.

She had a deep-down feeling that the five dollar bill was part of it, but she had decided she would not spend that money. She had never had that much that was her own, and there was no reliable way to earn another one. That made it special.

Eldon had contacted the goat hair market and told them, in a letter, the whole tale of not knowing he should have sheared them. The company said to send the hay on to them, and they'd check it to see if they could use it. They said that after this, he must shear them in the early spring. He knew that! He didn't let it spoil on purpose. Now was the problem of shipping it. Mr. Wilbur had said he had a choice of going to Calhoun, seven miles away, or Jacksonville, twelve miles away.

It he had to make a trip, it might as well be Jacksonville. It was a bit of a pain, but the trip would need to be made only once a year. He hated paying to send something that he was not sure of, but it was part of learning. He marked the sacks with the little tags in the box with them and loaded them on a wagon. He was back by mid-afternoon, so it wasn't all that bad.

Now. he'd see what happens. In the mean, time he had four more of the bigger rams that had to be butchered. Not only that, he had to make a pen for the young fillies that nature had given him. It was driving him crazy, and he dearly loved every minute of it.

Josephine had mentioned to her siblings that God was able to answer requests for his people before they asked the question, and she had mentioned that she was sure that the route of the Mississippi Central was an answer to them in their need caused by losing their parents.

It made sense when she explained it, and she showed it to them in the Book the church had given her.

Eldon had not known he wanted horses and goats, but now he had them, and he loved taking care of them, so that may have been what happened, the answer coming before the question. This would never have happened if the railroad had not chosen to take their land. It was like a puzzle, and the pieces fit if they were turned just right.

He was going to have to figure a way to put some hay in the shed, because horses could not graze all winter like the goats, but they also needed hay in their shed. He'd need a cutter that was pulled by a horse, that was like a lot of knives. It could cut the hay, and with some changes, it could rake it up. He really needed it, but this year he would just cut it with the scythe.

It would be hard work, but nobody told him life was easy. He had been given animals and it was his duty to care for them. He certainly had grass he could cut. The flat top of every bluff had wonderful grass. Mr. Beasley thought it was because the mountain was once a volcano, and was made out of fertilizer, or something. That sounded believable and Eldon had no reason to question it. He just took the scythe from the shed and headed for the tall grass.

Duncan took his buckets of soup and tea to the cutters of the right-of-way every day, and he was highly welcomed. Matthew's idea had been a good one, but the only thing Duncan liked about the job was that it was temporary.

It wasn't the serving of food that was so discouraging, it was the waiting. Waiting until time too effer the food, for the food to get hot, for the fellows to eat, for gathering the dishes… for bringing the dishes back to the buff.

While he was cutting wood, he was doing something, and at the end of the day there were sticks of wood. On this job, at the end of the day there was dirty dishes, cornbread crumbs, empty kettles and a trip home. There was money, of course, but there was no energy put into it. His sisters took over a lot of the work, making of the food... likely they didn't trust him, and they were likely right not to trust him. The way he felt, he might use pepper instead of salt.

But there was that hope. There was deep-down hope based on a favor from a person he had never met. Matthew insisted that his brother was well liked by the railroad people, and he would have a say in hiring them both. Now if that could happen... well, it would be a job of doing something. It didn't matter much what, it would be something that he could look at when the sun went down, and say to himself 'I did that!'

According to the Book the church gave Josephine, an answer could be on the way, and he just didn't know about it. She was convinced, because she had asked for the better job for him, so it was being taken care of. She said that believing the answer was coming was called 'faith,'* and God was pleased when a person had faith.

*Hebrews 11:6

Duncan wasn't sure about it all. He'd believe it when he heard that he was hired by Mississippi Central... but, of course, that wasn't faith.

Someone else discovered the Book. Darlene became a bright little star of eleven years old. The pitifully small library at her school had a few books and she had read them all... most of them twice.

Then she learned from Lolita that Josephine's book had a different kind of stories. Some of the words were different, like 'you' was called 'thee.' It was like a puzzle game to figure out what the words meant when they were sometimes backward to the way school books were written.

Not only that, but Josephine's book had a guide on where to find stories like Adam and Eve*, the first people, and Noah**, the fellow with the rainstorm. Another person knew how to use a slingshot,*** but from the picture, it looked like the sling shot was not like boys at school played with.

*Genesis chapter 2
**Genesis chapters 6,7&8
***1Samuel,chapter 17

A really nice thing about the Book was that the pages were thin like tissue paper so there could be a lot of them in the book. Josie would only let her use read the book when the table had been wiped off clean, and she had washed her hands. She couldn't look at it when it was not on the table laying flat. She said Darlene was too small to look at it in her lap. That made the Book even more special.

There was even a story about a man who went up into the sky in a whirlwind*, and heaven was up there. She hadn't read it yet, but Lola said it was there. Darlene rationed her reading so the stories would last longer, though Lolita said she didn't need to because there were so many.

*II Kings, Chapter 2

That Book really helped during the long summer when there was no school. Sometimes she read a story that she thought Sammie would like and she read it to him, stories like the fellow who spent the night in a den of lions* and another one about a bunch of people who build up a city wall while an enemy shot arrows at them.** Sammie didn't like to read, but he liked to listen.

*Daniel, chapter 6

**Nehemiah, chapter 4

WORKING ON THE ROADBED

Duncan worked through October, which is usually one of Arkansas' better months, and the cutting crew made very good time, with Duncan meeting them at their new daily location. He built the fires and filled the bowls and dreamed of hearing from Matthew's brother.

By the time the cutting crew reached the mountain, half of them were laid off until spring, when they would be too far away to commute. Matthew was among those laid off, and he was glad. Duncan put away the kettles and cups as there were not enough workers left to make it profitable, also they were too far away.

Mathew's wheat field (that would be the eventual corn patch) was green with nutritious plants eight to ten inches high. He suggested to Eldon that he put the herd of young fillies in on it. Their tromping around on plowed ground would be a benefit, also their droppings would make a good addition, come spring.

He surveyed the green field with satisfied pride, realizing he was just a farmer at heart. This field was going to make a lot of corn, and it would have wide leafy stocks good for chopping and offering to the horses during the winter. Horses need roughage like folks needed bread.

The number of the fillies had reached eight, and most were the same size. There were a number of pregnant mares coming on, but that was not his problem… it was Eldon's.

Just before Christmas, the brother sent word. Matthew and his friend were to report to Mississippi Central terminal in Calhoun, about seven miles away. They were to report on the second Monday in January.

Matthew was relieved, as he had need of something to do that created money, and Duncan was thrilled that he would have no cups and bowls to mess with.

On the designated day, the two started early following the clear-cut right-of-way as it led directly into the terminal, and the path of the right-of-way was the absolute closest distance between two points. They would go to work the first of February and would be operating a dirt scoop to build up the roadbed for the rails, or driving a wagon to bring in the gravel for the surface. Then the gravel would be packed with a sheep-foot roller pulled by horses. Then came the cross ties made from Arkansas oak trees and oiled generously.

The sections of metal pipe would come on the hand cars, and would be nailed in place on the cross ties. It was a slow job of building up the roadbed to the desired height and creating enough drainage to keep the weather from causing erosion.

The two newly hired persons would be doing any of these operations, and would work wherever they were placed. Duncan was to be handling the team of horses that hauled gravel. He was wondrously pleased, happy, and relieved. Horses, he knew, and he would be good at that job.

Matthew was operating a dirt scoop, and he was dreadfully morose about leaving the farm and Josephine. Also he was back in the big tent sleeping on the rough ground in a sleeping bag, and he was consuming cold food while remembering Josephine's tasty cooking.

When the crew reached a point two miles from River Bend, the fellows exchanged the tent for the attic pallet, as they were close enough to commute.

When they were one mile away, it was March, and Lolita set out the bowls and mugs. If she was to put wings on her five dollar bill, this would be a way. Josie's book had said 'whatsoever thy hand findeth to do, do it with thy might'.* And Lolita's hand easily found the bowls, the mugs, and the buckets.

*Ecclesiastes 9:10

She requested Eldon to butcher a little ram for her, which he was glad to do. Little rams became big rams and were quite rambunctious within the herd. The family had been obliged to buy beans and also corn in 50 pound sacks, so there were a lot of beans.

Instead of tea, she would offer coffee and instead of five cents, her price would be ten cents, but there would be all the cornbread the diner wanted, and there would be seconds on the beans or soup, as long as it lasted.

Duncan questioned the price, but Lolita pointed out that these workers were making more money than the cutters, and if they didn't want to pay her price, they could do without her food. If she didn't ask it, she wouldn't get it, and each day she must create 'feathers' for the wings of her five dollar bill, though she didn't mention her need for wings.

She prepared her buckets (two of them as food was cheap) and coffee caldrons (coffee was expensive), and she cleaned out the wagon and selected the horses. She requested that Eldon teach her to harness the horses, but he said he'd do it. She had held the heads of the goats while being sheered, so turnabout was fair.

She dressed in her overalls and shirt (the work site was chilly), and she wore a stocking cap (it was not necessary to appear to be a boy). She was safer, she decided, with twenty fellows than she would be with one or two.

By the time the roadbed was within a mile, she was ready. Duncan and Matthew would be part of the crew by then. There were some who did not participate and ate the cold food that was free, but the chilly wind of March encouraged a line of hungry fellows to hand over the dime for the food. Besides, there were seconds, and the beans were wonderfully meaty. Her coffee was strong and bracing.

Lolita gathered the bowls and mugs and loaded on the buckets and caldrons on the wagon. She seated herself on the buckboard and headed home.

She was tired. Of course she was tired… what had she expected? A bed of roses? She had supposed that she would be able to reach the work site all during March and April, and by then they would have reached the mountain.

The blasting crew were already working on that mountain, breaking apart huge boulders and flattened the top of the mountain by dragging the debris to the edges of the site to make the climb of the locomotive more gradual. It was impossible to remove the mountain, but it must not be let to climb a steep enough grade to give trouble to a loaded locomotive.

All day the valley echoed with the blasts. It must have been frightful for the close residents and babies trying to nap.

Lolita released her weary horses and carried her bucket and caldrons full of bowls and mugs to the kitchen to be washed. She cut the meat into chunks for the next day, and set it to simmering. This cooking took more wood, so she carried in an armload of the lumber rescued from the old house. It burned fast and hot.

Then she sat down at the table with a cup of tea and counted her dimes (feathers). She had earned two dollars and twenty cents. That sounded like more than ten dollars a week possible. She would require a good number of feathers if her five dollar bill was going to fly, and this job would not last long.

What she was going to do when the roadbed crew passed by the bluff and reached the mountain, she hadn't a clue, and was too tired to think about it.

Eldon received a check for his goat hair and with it came a letter. It stated, in part, "We were able to use parts of the product you sent, but we will be glad to once more receiving clean hair, as we did from the last supplier from River Bend." Eldon divided the amount of the check and gave half to Josephine to run the house.

Also with check was a supply of the sacks they wanted used, and a box of the mailing tickets printed with his number as a supplier. How handy! And his animals had spent the year growing more money for him... and all of this came from the Mississippi Central wanting to run on land under his house. It was really interesting, if one thought about it. One little decision in the office of the railroad had made such a difference in so many lives.

Darlene finished with the school which went to the sixth grade, but her teacher gave her the address of the place to get books for the seventh and eighth grades that there necessary for receiving a teaching certificate. She had no immediate plans for the certificate, but she wanted it, anyway. One couldn't have too many books.

There was a very good library in Jacksonville, and when she had an opportunity, she checked out as many as they would let her have.

Matthew managed to survive the scraper, pulling dirt up from the surrounding sites and piling it in heaps to be packed into a solid roadbed. It was a day to day job, no change and no challenge. He mentally counted the weeks until they would reach the blasting crew, and then it would be too far to travel daily so it would be back in the cold tents and rough ground.

What he would do then, he hadn't decided and was too tired to think as he climbed to his attic pallet.

Duncan was joyously happy. His days were filled with activity, shouts, directions from someone, guiding the horses and watching the lift dig gravel from the river and pile it on his wagon. The pay was good. He handed half to Josephine and put the rest in a safe place.

What he would do with it, he hadn't a clue, but that was not today's concern. He knew he could do a good job, and he did. He was noticed. He was cheerful, well-liked, took orders well, kept his team moving and was never late. He what the kind of person Mississippi Central needed, and a fellow who could do one job well would be able to do other jobs just as well. They would remember Duncan Findley for later use.

When they reached the foot of the mountain, Duncan was asked to stay on as there was a lot to do while crossing the mountain. There were rocks to drag away, and he would be good at that. Duncan did not even take a moment to think. He would be glad to stay on and live in the tent.

Matthew was also asked but only because his brother requested it. He tried, but when he was operating the scoop on the mountain above the town of Piney, he thought of the bluff and its comforts, also Josephine. He had accumulated a bit of money, and surely there was something else to he could do. When the crew reached the top of the mountain and could look down and see Piney, Matthew became physically ill. His head hurt, and his guts hurt, and he drew his pay and headed for the bluff and 'home.'

He walked all night, and the April sun was shining when he reached the old bridge. The bridge builders for the future metal bridge were measuring and digging. He stopped and wearily watched them. "You fellows weren't puttin' on extra crew, were you?"

He was told to ask Buzz Temple. Buzz said, "For a fact, yes. Do you live close?"

"Yes, sir, right up top of that hill," and he pointed with his elbow.

"Good. We can use someone for odd jobs for a month, maybe six weeks. You got access to drinkin' water?"

"Positively the best!"

"Then that'll be one of your jobs, bringing water. That all right with you?"

"Absolutely, sir!"

"Then report in the morning ready to stay the day. Bring your own lunch,"

"Thank you, sir. I'll be here." It was a strange thing, but he did not notice until later, after breakfast and a nap in the attic, that his headache and belly ache had disappeared. Then, why wouldn't it? He was home where he belonged!

Eldon came and told him, "I took care of your horse."

"My horse…?"

"Yeah, that Paint stallion you brought it. When I saw you down on the road, I wondered why you wasn't ridin' 'im, and then I saw that limp. I looked at 'is foot and found a flint rock stuck in under the shoe. I treated 'im and he'll be fine. He shore is a fine lookin' animal."

Matthew looked at Eldon with a puzzled frown. "I don't know what you're talkin' about?"

Eldon repeated, "That big Paint stallion. Didn't you bring home a horse?"

Matthew shook his head. "I don't know nothin' about it."

Eldon sighed, "Then we've got another stray that wants to stay here. For some reason, stray horses come up the driveway. We thought it might be the good grass, but we don't know. We tried to advertise to their owners, but there wasn't no one who came by.

"I'll put the sign back out there but I sure hate to. That horse is a beauty, his spot pattern is spaced even, just like Daisy and Candle. You'd think he was a full brother to them."

He left, shaking his head in puzzlement, but he was ready to 'bet the farm' that no one would come to collect him. He just as well think up a name and see if Matthew agrees. That horse was purposely following Matthew. He saw it with his own eyes. And why couldn't Matthew hear him walking on the gravels. That has got to mean something… but what?

HORSES AND MORE HORSES

Now that Matthew was permanent, Eldon had a question. "When you feel like it I'd like to ask you somethin'."

"How about right now?"

"Good. It's about all our horses. Treatin' that hoof on the Paint, brought up what I been thinkin'. We've got all this land, but it's so open with no cross-fencin'. Maybe we could separate the Paint mares away from King and have them together. With all those fillies, we got more horses than we know what to do with. (Matthew love the sound of "we"!)

"We could put out a sign on the road sayin', 'HORSES FOR SALE' and maybe make some money on 'em. Those fillies'll be the age to breed, and they came from twins. I wonder if they'll tend to have twins. Likely not, but the time'll come when we have to decide what to do with "em.

"Those four wagon mares we brought up are all carryin' foals now. I was thinkin' if you wanted to mess with it and watch out for the foals, we could raise a lot of animals, and maybe take 'em in to Jacksonville to the animal action.

"If we'd breed those paint fillies with the new stallion I'm callin' Buster, less'n you want to call 'em somethin' else."

Matthew told him, "Buster's' fine with me, but what if someone comes for 'im?"

"I'm bettin' they won't. There's a funny thing about this place and horses. I gettin' to think this is like the preacher said about answers comin' before the question's been asked. Could be that you and me ought'a be askin' what do we do to make money to live on. Horses might be the answer.

"I got pretty well all I can do with the goats, and I'm thinkin' you like farmin', and that'd be good. There's things Josephine wants raised. But there'd be time for tendin' to the horses along with it. That is if you want to."

"Eldon, I'd like nothin' better, but this is your place, not mine."

"Sure it's yours, if you want it. It needs more'n me, and Duncan ain't comin' back to it."

"You sure about that...?"

"Absolutely certain and positive. He never was interested any more than he had to be, and didn't have any idea's on what to do next past wood cuttin'. I don't think he's ever been up top with the goats. I was thinkin' how we'd need a grass cutter to make hay for the barns, and fencin' to keep King and Buster in the right pens."

He just couldn't keep his mind off Buster. "Them Paint horses are sure a picture, and we might keep that goin' if we do the separatin' now. I'm thinkin' maybe Buster was sent to us for a reason. I'll keep the sign out for a couple's months to make sure, but I think he belongs to us. Like a gift from somewhere."

Matthew knew he was now officially part of the family as clear as Eldon could make it, and at eighteen, going on nineteen, he had the right.

"I'd like nothin' better than to be in business with you. I know I'm a disappointment to my brother. I would have made a lot of money, but I couldn't stand the work. Dead machinery. Moving dirt. Then later it would be travelin' from 'nowhere' to another 'nowhere' and then back again, and me wantin' to be somewhere to stay, permanent like."

It was on the evening of that day that Matthew was resting in the porch swing with Josephine, and he said to her, "Josie, I got a question for you. I think you knew me pretty well by now, don't you?"

She answered, "I think so."

Matthew nodded pleasantly and continued, "Then do you think you could stand me for the rest of my life?"

Josephine turned and looked him over from head to scuffed work shoes, and answered, "I think so."

She wanted no wedding. In the presence of her siblings and the preacher's wife, the pair said the proper words. The only real change in the family was that he abandoned the pallet in the attic and returned to the bed of his childhood from another life. Somehow, the bed seemed a lot better than when it was in his father's house.

FEATHERS ON THE WINGS

Lolita was perched on the fence of what was to be the new garden. It was now a lovely green from the wheat stalks. The herd of fillies had been moved to another pen, and Matthew had planted the point of his plow into the soft ground and was turning the green of the wheat stalks into a rich brown of the soil. His pa had called it 'green manure,' and the green plants would now be fertilizer for the stalks of corn.

It was while she watched Candle pulling the plow that an idea struck her. Remembering the wild trip to Jacksonville on Daisy and the payment of a five dollar bill, and adding in the fact that they had a two wagons, and could hardly use more than one for the hauling they did.

She stirred the idea around and added in the fact that a lot of the ladies in River Bend did not get regular trips to the city where they could shop by themselves, and add the fact that when they were taken to the city by a family member, that family member lost time taking her where she wanted to go. This mixture made an interesting batter, but it was not yet ready for the oven.

The fire of a good idea had to be lighted under it, and the attractive spots on Candle lighted the flame.

She needed a wagon with comfortable seats that would be a rest to bones of older ladies. It needed rubber wheels and not the iron or wooden ones. The wagon needed to ride like a pillow.

The wagon needed a cover, like the pictures some of the auto, with a fancy top and a fringe around the edge. She wouldn't need the fringe. Just the top that would shield from the sun and rain, and it needed flaps on the sides that could be rolled up or down, to protect from cold or wind, or maybe flying dust or rain.

When she got that wagon, which would be the wings that the five dollar bill grew in her dream, she could schedule a trip maybe once a week when she would pick up the ladies in town and take them to Jacksonville. They would be hiring her for the day for a set figure. Twenty five dollars was a figure that stick in her head.

That amount seemed large, but could be shared by however many ladies wanted to go that day, and she would make the wagon hold eight ladies... that is if most of them were not extra wide creating a wide bench space. The fare for the trip could be split however the ladies decided, as long as she got the total in one lump sum.

She would fix up the wagon with paint and cushions, and it would be like they came over for a visit and could sit and talk all the way there and back. There would be rules and a lot of details, but that could be figured out while she painted the wagon.

She would prefer to use Daisy and Candle, but there were beautiful paint fillies coming on. That would be no problem. The wagon would be painted with orange, brown, and black spots arranged like the colors on a Paint horse. The side panels could also be painted on the fabric to match the wagon.

The patterned paint would assure the riders that this was a party, or an outing like a picnic, for visiting and shopping on their day out. The church had a quilting party every Tuesday, and the ladies met and gossiped, but they did not go shopping. Her wagon would go to the city and park for several hours, just so she could get them back home in time to fix supper. It could all be arranged. She would abide by the joint decision of the ladies.

This would be more fun than hauling buckets and bowls to the right-of-way, and it would take only one day out of her week, and require no cooking the day before.

She could see the dream now, her puzzle over having the key that gave freedom to Mrs. Tullis and any other resident who wanted to go. They might have to schedule it among themselves, but a day of visiting and shopping would be a treat. Of course they might go only once in a month or six weeks, but River Bend had a lot of ladies who were 'locked' in their houses because of lack of transportation.

As she sat on the fence and watched the look of satisfaction on Matthews face as he plowed furrow after furrow, she saw the whole picture. It would take work, and the rubber tired wheels would have to be ordered, but she had time. She had the rest of her life.

She let herself down from the fence and went to look at the wagon that was not used. Slightly beat up, but not bad for having been used to haul wood. It would work. About four coats of white paint on the old wood, and then the black, brown and orangeish colors.

It was at the summer table that she made the announcement. During a pause in the conversation she announced, "I'm going to have a transport service for ladies. Once a week I will make a trip to Jacksonville and let the ladies shop for two or three hours. I'm going to paint up the un-used wagon, and use a couple of the paint horses... maybe Daisy and Candle."

She paused and continued eating. No one said, "Oh, honey, you can't do that!" or "Why would you do a thing like that?", or "It'll never work."

The people at the table all knew this was Lolita. She did not ask permission, she informed. Matthew was first to comment, "How soon can you get it going?"

Lolita had the answer. "Maybe two months. I need to locate rubber tires for the wagon."

Nobody said, "Rubber tires? What for?" and no one said, "You can't get rubber tires for a wagon." They knew this was Lolita. They could just wait around and see it get done.

Sammie, now a boisterous seven also had an announcement. "I'm gonna work on the Mississippi Central like Duncan."

Eldon offered, "It'll take a lot of bowls of beans before you get big enough for that."

Sammie nodded, agreeably. "By then Duncan'ill be so smart, he can get me a good job."

What does a body say to that? It really could happen that way. Brothers helped brothers, even if some of them didn't stay 'helped.' Matthew concentrated on his food. Good for Sammie. A body couldn't start too early on thinking about the rest of their life.

RUBBER TIRES AND PAINT

Lolita had money and that removed the problems from many projects. The money earned by ladling soup and pouring coffee had a purpose, and now she knew what it always was.

She went to the livery stable up town on a Saturday that there would be a lot of fellows in to 'shoot the bull' as they referred to it. When she appeared at the front, in dress and straw hat, she had all eyes.

"Fellows, I have a question. Where would I find tires for a wagon that are like the ones on an automobile?"

The shed of the sable became pin-drop quiet. Allen Upchurch, the local maker of fancy saddles spoke up. "I just happen to have the answer. There is a tire shop over in Jacksonville that is experimenting with wagon tires. I understand they are quite expensive, but some fellows are buying them."

Lolita set their minds at rest on the cost. "I have money. I just need to know where they are."

Allen told her, "It's the Ready Rubber Tires and Hoses Company and it's right by the animal auction."

Lolita smiled and thanked him, and then turned to go. One of the men called to her, "Hey, you might get the lumber yard to bring 'em out to you. 'Course, it'll cost ya."

"Thank you for the suggestion. I have money."

Lolita returned to the tiny buggy and stepped solidly in and sat on the bench. Lifting a hand in farewell to the audience at the stable, she urged Daisy onward toward the lumber yard.

Sure enough, the advice was good. They could do that. They knew about those tires and considered stocking them. They'd bring her a set at four dollars and a quarter per tire. She did not flinch. "Do you want the money now or later?"

"Later will be fine. It will take a week."

"That's good. I'll be back. Don't let anyone else have them."

As the buggy passed by the livery stable, the talk began.

"I wonder what in the tarnation she wants with rubber tires."

Allen Upchurch, a fellow who made it his job to know, told them, "I would bet a pretty penny we find out, likely before the summer's over."

"Waste'a money… rubber tires!"

"Not if you got creaky old bones, it ain't. Wisht I had 'em."

"Me, too. I want'a see what she'd doin' with 'em."

"Her? I figger one'a her brothers sent her in."

"Nope. That young lady has something in mind. Ain't she one'a the Findley family that lost a ma and pa?"

"Shore is. She's likely be the second girl. That first boy went to the Mississippi Central and has a good job. Can't come home every Sunday on account'a bein' busy."

"We don't see much'a them youngens. The town thought they'd have to chip in and help themget on, but it don't seem to be."

"The next younger girl went to school with my youngens. They say she is really smart in her lessons."

"I hope that Findley girl does what she's gonna do pretty soon. I'm in a rash to see what it is. A body don't need rubber tires to haul hay."

"That bluff house where they live has a sign out for horses for sale. I speck they'd be in good shape, too, with the grass that bluff grows.

"Why'd anyone suppose she'd need a rubber tired wagon?"

"Reckon we'll see when she wants us to see."

But Lolita was far down the road at that time, and her mind was not on whether the fellows were curious or not. She was thinking how she was going to put a solid top on the wagon, and her mind kept going back to Matthew. If he could build a porch swing, he could make a surrey top for a wagon.

When she went back to the lumber yard for the tires, she'd get the paint and the boards. Matthew would tell her what boards to get, also nails and other stuff.

What would she call her service? She needed to decide on a name, because it would need to be painted on the side. She could be thinking on how to use goat skin fur on the inside benches. Maybe she'd put a carpet on the floor. It must be made special, so the ladies would feel special. For this job she would not have to wear overalls for, but she would take them along, just in case.

And there was the gun. She had the gun from the canvas bag, but had never shot it. How hard could it be? One pulled the trigger, but it was so far from the handle her fingers did not reach. Was it possible to shoot a gun with both hands? She'd ask Matthew.

She did, and Matthew said, "Oh, my, no! You can't use this. You'd have better luck throwin' it at a robber than shootin' at 'im. But I got just what you need. My Pa got it for me when I was eight. It'll just about fit your hand."

It did. Lolita would never be a marksman, but she didn't have to be. A gun in the hand of a female was, in itself, a scary thing. She learned to hit a fence post, and that was good enough. Robbers were larger than fence posts.

Josephine heard the racket of the target practice and said nothing. She just poked cotton in her ears so she couldn't hear that her little sister was shooting a gun.

PAINTED WAGON

Lolita brought home her four wagon tires, and the boards Mathew had told her she needed. In addition, she brought home the paint. She picked a bright, sunshiny day and the weathered boards of the wagon slurped up all the paint and still remained gray. It was not a surprise… it was expected. The next day another coat of paint was applied, and the wagon became a lighter shade of gray.

It was the fourth day that it turned white. The seats (benches, actually) were extended out over the edge of the wagon making more room in the aisle for the ladies knees. Four braces attached at the corners of the wagon bed held up the frame for the overhead cover.

Boards would have been good, but they were too heavy. Heavily oiled canvas became the protection.

The benches were covered with goat skin, hair side up, and the floor was covered by linoleum, a new product offered by the lumber yard. It would be easy to clean with a soapy water swipe.

It took five weeks to finish and for the final coat of paint to dry. The patches of uneven shapes mimicked the 'paint' spots on the horses. She started with Daisy and Candle, but would have younger animals as soon as they were broke to the harness.

Lolita printed up a notice to take to the Livery Stable, as she thought that might be the quickest way to spread the news.

> *NOW OERATING*
> *LADY'S DAY OUT VEHICLE*
> *Offering a trip to Jacksonville,*
> *each week, weather permitting.*
> *The stay in the city will be at least two hours,*
> *That way permitting the vehicle to be back to*
> *River Bend in time to prepare the evening meal.*
> *The price for the trip would be $25.00 per trip whether*
> *Carrying one passenger or six. Maximum number*
> *Of riders will be eight, and they would need*
> *To be small persons, or children.*
> *There will be no exceptions.*
> *Trip price will be paid before vehicle*
> *leaves River Bend. Visiting while*
> *going either way will be greatly encouraged.*
> *Those interested should be at the Livery Stable*
> *No later than 8:00 am on Friday.*

She had written in script a note to be thumbtacked to the bottom of the note and to be removed later. It advised:

"First trip will be in two weeks, being 16th of September"

It was a dreadful lot of printing on the sheet of cardboard, but she wanted to be perfectly clear on every point from price to seating capacity. When the paint was totally dry, she attached Daisy and Candle on either side of the central tongue and they pranced grandly up Main Street from the Mercantile back to the livery stable.

She requested permission to post the notice, and it was given. If fact, it was insisted! The fellows currently in the stable were permitted time to thoroughly examine the wagon, from its rubber tires to its protective roof. This would be the most effective way to advertise to more persons than if she had driven up and down Main Street with a bull horn speaker.

Men could be more effective than women on an interesting subject and this one was extremely interesting. Putting the first trip two weeks away gave the ladies time to prepare for it. Ladies couldn't do things on the spur of the moment just because they might want to.

She took her Ladies' Day Out Vehicle home, and Matthew would have given a half a week's wages (and that would be a fair among of money paid by the Metal Bridge Builders) just to be in the stable and hear the comments made after she left. He couldn't do it, of course, as his presence would put a damper on their opinions, but he would have bet the same amount of money on the fact of ladies waiting on the date, eager for their day out.

She was not even out of sight, and someone in the livery said, "Did you look at that!"

"Sure did. That girl'll make a killin'."

"A one day a week job. Can you believe it!"

"I know that if I had a youngen the right age, I'd be sendin' him over to check her out!"

"Who'd'a thought of that… and her such a good lookin' girl?"

"Yeah, but that don't make no difference. You'll see how long that lasts. She'll take up with some fellow, and he'll put a stop to that travelin'."

"If he does, it'll show that he'd stupid."

And the remarks went on and on. It wasn't often they got a chance at conversation like this one.

If Matthew had made that bet, he would have won. Five ladies were waiting and each had their money ready. It was a huge price to pay for a trip, but two hours in Jacksonville along with four hours of gossip was worth a lot. They might even plan on a trip like this every month!

Lolita appeared in a neat dress and jacket, the inside pocket of which garment held the toy gun that shot real ammunition. The ladies didn't need to know about the gun, but it would not be kept secret. Eventually, the whole town would know.

Duncan came home when he could, which was most weekends. He boarded a horse in the stable in Calhoun, and rode it the seven miles to the bluff.

He was sitting at the table eating supper when a neighbor, Charlotte Cole. dropped in to borrow sugar. She lived across the road and was a potter who made fancy things out of clay to go on the wall. It took most of her time to create things and keep the fire burning under the kiln. Couldn't remember to buy groceries.

She took one look at Duncan, and he looked back. They were made for each other. She really didn't need a full time husband. Weekends were fine. She was a busy lady.

Duncan could make it home only on weekend. That was enough for Charlotte, she was a busy lady.

Consequence? The two pallets in the attic were left to the mice and the crickets.

The Ladies Day Out Vehicle left Riverbend in a beautiful sunrise with happy ladies, almost in a giggling mood. How wonderful was this?

The first topic of conversation was that new church that arose on the land just across the new silver bridge. "Look at that! It'll sure be handy for the folks livin' over here. New church right on their doorstep."

The state was a bit lax on furnishing schools to new areas where the population was growing, and it was of great interest when another sign went up on the church property that a school was soon to be added. Things take time, and the addition of the school was slow coming.

Darlene finished with the local public school, and went on her own to study as did several other students of the era. Books were available for the next two grades, but had to be purchased. Darlene insisted they be bought, and she plodded on alone, managing to easily pass the test for teacher's certification.

The Lady's Day Out trips continued. They were a bit spotty during the winter months because of inclement weather, but the ladies were troupers, and if it took more clothing and a quilt over their knees, so be it. The regularity of the trips matched the weekend sales in the city, and their existence gave hope to cabin-bound ladies. It was something to look forward to.

When Lolita started something, she persevered. This project seemed to be one of those 'answers' that were being arranged before the question was made, and it fitted comfortably within her strange dream.

When the widow, Mrs. Essie Walker, had made a couple of trips, she had an idea. Though her twenty year old son, Clifton, kept offering to take her to Jacksonville and didn't get around to it, she made trips on her own, and it was very satisfying. Now she must go a step farther.

When Clifton took her to the Livery Stable to wait for the wagon, she insisted (demanded!) that he wait with her. He pointed out that there were other ladies, and she could wait with them.

She said 'no' and was quite firm. She might need help getting into the wagon, and he should be there to give a hand. He said, were there not others to help… and wouldn't someone from the livery help her?

She said why should they help her when she had a grown son with a strong arm. Besides, it was almost 8:00, and it wouldn't hold him up very long to wait. She won the argument as she usually did, though she tried not be a pain to him, but this time was different. It was necessary that he wait.

He sat with her in the buggy until the unusual wagon appeared behind the two beautiful Paint mares. The driver of the wagon climbed down from the bench and arranged the box which served as a step stool.

Essie took her time leaving the buggy and was last reaching the step stool. The driver stood by as she always did, carefully watching as each lady found her place.

Mrs. Essie Walker (and son) approached the wagon, and Lolita watched. Clifton spied Lolita in her modest blue dress with the dainty white jacket she always wore. The slight weight in the jacket pocket could not be anything else than a gun.

Clifton looked into the face of the gun-carrying young lady and could not look away. The young lady looked back and smiled welcome. Mrs. Essie took her time with her entry into the wagon while being assisted by the strong arm of her handsome son.

She settled herself comfortably with her friends and smiled with intense satisfaction. Mission accomplished.

The driver and her son took a final, appreciative look at each other, and both knew it would not be the last. Clifton was soon seen guiding his horse up the rocky driveway to the bluff house.

When Lolita was nineteen, the pair exchanged promises at the church. Then later, he asked her if she would miss her Friday trips into Jacksonville, and she told him, why would she miss them just because she was a married lady? They would continue as usual.

They chose a spot of land over past the cornfield and built their home. Lolita's savings bought the furniture she wanted... sturdy and no-nonsense oak, never minding the exorbitant price. The ladies of River Bend, freed from the chains of their kitchens, paid for it.

It was a year later that the sign in the church yard was changed to,

School Teacher Wanted
State Certification Required

Lolita could hardly wait for the day to be over so she could tell Darlene. Here was this wonderful opportunity to use her new Certification, and it was less than a mile from the bluff house!

Who would have thought the association would send out a young preacher, just finished at the seminary. He would occupy the small parsonage by himself. He saw Darlene, and within a year, he was no longer alone in the parsonage.

If the school had been operated by the state, she would have had to quit teaching to be married, but it was a private school without that restriction. In fact, in this case, it would be encouraged by the association. Otherwise, the pulpit at Brookside Church might be difficult to keep filled.

Marrying a 'local' tied him firmly to the post. Sometimes things turned out right.

Lolita produced a charming little replica of herself, and she continued the trips to Jacksonville up to the last two weeks. Some of the ladies hoped the 'grand entrance' would happen at Jacksonville, but it didn't.

Little Cicily stuck to the rules and appeared when expected. Lolita took off two weeks, then resumed her one-day-a-week job. Papa Clifton took Cicily to his mom for the day.

At two, Cicily came along a lot of the time, and took her nap in the floorboard of the Vehicle. She was her mama's girl, in many ways. She knew what she wanted and was ready to deal by the age of three.

She said to her Ma, "If I take a nap, can I have ice cream?"

Her Ma said, "If you don't take your nap, you will get a spat on the back side."

She decided, "I'll just take a nap." Obviously, Ma won… she was the biggest.

Ma said, "Get you pillow and lay down where I can keep the flies off you."

Cicily did so, then sat up with a question. "If we take River Bend flies to Jacksonville, will they like it there?"

Ma answered, "I don't know. When you wake up, you can ask them."

The ladies riding behind looked at each other and winked. The world was turning the right way. The driver of the Vehicle would not raise a brat. The world had enough of them already.

THISTLES
IN THE WIND

1

The two children rode silently, simply because there was nothing left to say. Their words had been used up hours ago. The loaded wagon bumped and slewed its way around the stones and stumps and a few fallen logs, the horses straining to keep it moving. There had to be a road somewhere.

The boy, twelve, held the reins that guided the bay who had had a limp on his near hind leg for most of the afternoon. A patch of the steep trails were covered with a lot of small, rolling rocks, and it was certain the animal had a sprain. The blue roan mare was doing most of the pulling.

The girl, ten, sat beside the boy, lips firm and eyes straight ahead, the snake gun lying across her lap. A shot from the small 22 caliber hand gun would chase away most unwanted varmints. The shotgun lay on the floor behind the buckboard seat where they rode.

The trail they followed was the right-of-way for the new Mississippi Central Railway. The trees had been cut, but the stumps still remained, and the weary animals were attempting to avoid them.

They had cleared the small hill that would be cut down when the tracks were actually laid, and they were now approaching a valley. The roar of the Tuscalara River could be heard straight ahead, and a new iron bridge was in sight. A bridge over the river meant a road, and a road should go somewhere. Sure to.

At this point, it was necessary that they go somewhere… so they must find a road to take them.

The blue roan mare struggled to pull the wagon up the grade to the road, while the bay was still unable to find a footing to help her pull. His pain was increasing by the minute.

The twisting wagon screeched on its axels as the wheels dug into the dirt, but the strong mare finally pulled all four wheels onto the smoother roadway.

"Theo, the sign says RIVER BEND. Could that be the town pa said?" Lavinia spoke softly, hoping to be guessing correctly.

The boy shook his head. "No. I don't remember because I wasn't really listening. I knew Pa knew, so I didn't need to. But I think that town had a 'ville' on it instead of a 'bend.' But that don't matter. We gotta go that a'way. Old Buck ain't gonna pull no more for a while."

The truth was that 'old Buck' had done an extraordinarily good job for the two children. For the last day and a half, the pair of animals had pulled the wagon through creek beds, around stumps and over rocky hills with absolutely no road.

Closer to the town, a Livery Stable became obvious. Theodore knew the livery to be the best place for answers, especially about animals.

Buck did better on the roadbed, and the loaded wagon rolled successfully across the bridge, passed Bascom's Boarding House and the Land Office. Next was the Livery Stable beside a Hat shop.

The boy guided the horses to the Livery and halted them with a resounding "Whoa!" The animals were very glad to oblige. Theo stepped down and approached the group of men.

"You knowin' this kid?" Ed whispered to the group in the shed.

"Never seen 'im before. Never saw that team, neither."

When he reached them, the boy asked, "Sir, I come askin' for help. My horse, he's got a sprain, and I'm needin' a liniment rag for 'im. And then I wonder where I could put up a tent for us to spend the night."

"Where ya headin', Son? That horse needs a couple'a days 'afore he gets on the road again."

Theo nodded agreement. "The thing is, we ain't hardly got two days. We…" He seemed not to be able to finish the sentence.

Allen Upchurch stepped up and repeated the question. "Where at you headed, Son? There's not any place close to here that you could'a come from, and it almost sundown."

Theo sniffed nervously. "Don't really know, Sir. My sister and me, we run into a bad patch, day before yesterday. Pa was the one to know were we was goin', and he ain't here no more." The boy swallowed hard and drew in a deep breath.

"Where is your Pa? You're going to need some place to stay till he gets here."

"He won't be getting' here, Sir. It was a painter in the tree. Pa… he was sightin' on a young buck deer for us to eat, and I saw that painter right over 'im. They was two of 'em in the tree. I'd'a shot one of 'em but Pa had the shot gun. Then it jumped right on 'im and…"

Here, he sniffed and buried his face in his sleeve, struggling for control but loosing. Sobs and shaking shoulders took over.

The man reached for him, circling the heaving shoulders. He looked at the other men. "Painter? Is that what he said? A painter in the tree?"

"Uh… I think he's a'sayin' 'panther.' I recall bein' in Kentucky and that's what they called 'em. Like our black mountain lions, I'd suspect. Evil critters they are, and climb trees like a squirrel. Best it could hope for was a man stopped still under his limb."

"Son, your Pa hurt bad? Where is he?"

Lavinia had been listening. Putting her gun aside, she climbed down from her seat. "Mister, our pa, he ain't hurt bad, he's gone. The painters drug 'im off and we didn't hear nothin' from 'im so we was knowin' he wasn't livin' no more."

The boy regained a small control. "Could'a shot 'em both, but Pa had the shotgun. That 22 wouldn't'a done nothin' but make 'im turn on us. I had her hidin' back'a the wagon, and they'd'a had her in a minute. I sneaked off and brought up the horses. Got'em hitched and had us turned around 'afore we saw 'im again."

The girl added, "Never heard a sound out'a Pa. We heard tell a painter breaks a neck first if he can. We reckon that's what he did."

The children stood side by side and looked at the men with red eyes and tear-wet faces. The men glanced at each other. "Reckon we ought'a see the preacher? Likely he'd…"

Theo took over. "Fellows, we wasn't beggin' nothin'. We just needed a liniment rag for Buck, and we can pay for that. Need to rest the horses and think about…"

Allen Upchurch again, "After the horses get better, what do you plan? Do you have family… or someone…?"

Silence. The two looked at each other and seemed to get an answer. Theo looked at the helpful man. "I was a'thinkin' on the way over here. I'm twelve years old and real strong. I could get a job and we could live in the tent till somethin' else… Well, if'n you could help, I could work. Maybe someone's got a field or a place we could be? Or a shed they ain't usin'? We ain't bein' particular. And we can fish in that river for food, can't we?"

This was going to take some thought. Obviously the responsibility was going to fall on the town, and these few men were its best group of its representatives. They could call on Preacher McCrey. Then again there might be a closer answer.

Philip Flanders had been silent, looking around for an inspiration. There had to be one somewhere. His eyes fell on a tiny cabin in the back of Markham's Pharmacy. Markham, now, was a… idea!

"Listen up, fellows. I'm lookin' over across the street, and I see that little cabin where Markham put his old ma till she died. To my thinkin', there wouldn't be nothin' in there but spiderwebs and maybe a field mouse. If he…"

"…that's there's a good idea. For a few days till we get this here thing settled. Ain't no way we can let…."

"…Naw, that's a fact. It'd be up to us. Now Ed, here, he can pull these here horses in under the roof and treat that bay. And…"

"…I'm gonna talk with Markham." Allen Upchurch announced. "Pull the wagon with these youngen's plunder on into the shed. There'll be a way to pay later." With that, he headed out across the hard-packed gravel road toward the pharmacy.

There were no complaints in the Livery. If Allen couldn't take care of it, well, it couldn't be took care of. Fact was, something would have to happen, and it couldn't be Bascom's Boarding House. Fellows were crammed in there like sardines in a can, and they would be that way until the Mississippi Central got itself going.

In less than ten minutes, Allen was coming back with the pharmacist in tow. Looking from one to the other of the children with a critical, assessing look. "Couple'a children looking for a place to stay? Well, there's a good chance I could be of help."

Turning his eyes on Theodore, he sized him up and down. "How old are you, Son?"

"I'm twelve, Sir."

"Good size for twelve. Could you happen to be lookin' for a job?" It would be impossible to tell from his face that he had been tipped off. It wouldn't hurt to save this young fellow's pride."

"Yes, Sir. I'm really strong. We was over on the big river, and Pa was workin' on loadin' barges. Said one more year and I'd be took on part time. Good money."

"Hmmm, and then your Pa left and headed west?"

"Yes, Sir. It was ma. She took a cough, and it didn't get better. When she was gone, Pa... well, he couldn't stay there no longer. Got upset and restless, and then Viney, my sister there, she took to coughin'. Pa, he said he wasn't stayin' there to lose any more'a his family." He stopped for breath, and Lavinia picked it up.

"We was headin' for some town with a 'ville' in it, and it wasn't this one. We didn't hardly think about it on account'a we thought...."

Theo again. "We didn't have no thought Pa was gonna..."

Mr. Markham nodded, knowingly. "I see the problem. Well, if you'd consider a job working for me, well, that little house back there by the bluff? It goes with part'a the pay. So does food. 'Course the job is hard and long, and you might be able to find something better. What do you think?"

Theo stared, somewhat stunned and speechless.

His sister found words quickly. "You say that little toy house is for him? If he couldn't do everything for you that you wanted, I'd help. I can do a lot of things. Could we really live in that little house? ...maybe for a while...?"

The pharmacist could readily see who was the decision maker. Turning to her, he asked, "Do you think it would be big enough?

Two people have never lived in there. It only has three tiny rooms. One of you would have to sleep in the little upstairs. Would that be all right?"

"Mister, whatever size it is, it's a heap sight bigger'n the tent we been for that last month. And there was three of us."

He smothered a smile. Good point she made. Mrs. Markham should get a kick out of her. Clear thinking and practical. Just about the kind of girl she would like to have had, if the Good Lord had seen fit to let them have one. Nothing wrong with that boy, either. It shows that he's been under a considerable strain… loss of their Pa… strange country… younger sister… injured animal…All in all…

John Markham looked at the group of listening men. "Fellows, I didn't mean to just push in and take over, but I've been needin' to take on a helper, and I thought I'd nab this strong fellow before someone else did. Ed, I see you got his animals under cover. Go ahead and take care of 'em, and we'll settle up later."

Another smile, as he thought of the surprise Mrs. Markham was going to have! Tough lady she was, and she could roll with the punch. Whatever needed to be done, she'd take care of it.

Two pairs of anxious, expectant eyes were trained on John Markham. He looked at each of them individually, and nodded his head, approvingly.

Then, "Come along. I have a good idea."

They followed as he crossed the street and turned left to the building that said MAIN STREET CAFÉ. Holding the door for them, he escorted them to a table with two chairs. There was no one else in the restaurant at that moment.

He held the chair for Lavinia, and Theodore seated himself. About that time a young lady came their way. She wore a cute little blue trimmed hat, and her apron was snowy white with blue trim. Also she wore a smile.

"Miss June," he began. "I have a couple of friends here who have had a long trip, and they're a little tired. I'd like you to bring them a cup of your delicious hot chocolate. Marshmallows if you have them. Then, after they rest a while, they might want something to eat. Maybe your venison stew… or a sandwich. They'll decide which."

With a nod, Miss June was gone.

"Now. I want you two to sit here with hot chocolate for a while and rest. If you want more, you just tell Miss June. Then she has all kinds of other things to eat, and I think you should choose what you like."

At their nods, he continued. "I have a couple of little chores to do, but I'll be back. You just wait right here and rest." And he was gone.

The wonderful aroma of chocolate teased their noses, and the lovely steam made circles and swirls as it lifted up from the liquid in the cup. Two marshmallows floated on top of each mug like turtles on a pond.

Spoons. Shiny silver. They hadn't seen silver spoons since they left the big river. Packed away in their special chest, their silverware rested in its special wrapping cloth. The one supposed to keep it from tarnishing, but didn't... really. They hadn't opened the chest since they left the big river.

Tantalizing click on the cups as the spoons stirred up the flavor that had sunk to the bottom of the cup. Postponing the wonderful moment... the first delicious sip.

Then they set down the cups and looked at each other. Lavinia studied her brother's face. He seemed to be anxious... about something? Weren't things going right?

"What're you thinkin' on?"

"Nothin, really."

"Don't say that to me. I been knowin' you too long for that."

Another sip, to prolong the answer. "Well, it was just that the man called us friends."

"What'd be wrong with that?"

"Two things. He ain't been knowin' us long enough to know if we was friends. The other thing, did you ever think Pa's boss was his friend?"

A hesitant agreement. "I reckon not. Leastwise not that I remember."

"See? He said I was gonna work for him, and that makes him a boss and not a friend. It don't hardly sound right, somehow."

Lavinia sighed and wrapped her weary fingers around her delightfully warm chocolate mug. Things looked too good, huh? Couldn't let false hope get up. That's what Pa'd say.

"Viney, I could'a shot that old painter right 'tween the eyes."

"I know you could'a. Just didn't get no chance."

Then Miss June was back. She brought two bowls of steaming venison stew and two slabs of buttered cornbread. Without even asking them. With a smile, she was gone again.

The ten year old girl was concerned with the trouble ahead that her brother saw, but just now she was attracted to the cornbread. She liked her's hot and steaming, that meant she needed to get strared eating.

2

Lily Markham set down the tea pot the better to stare with amazement at her husband. "We have what? What're you sayin'…?"

With his tormentingly expressive smile, he answered. "Just doin' our Christian duty, like it says in the Good Book. Remember what the preacher said about entertaining angels unawares? Well, it could be that there are a couple of them over at the Café having lunch at our expense."

She frowned slightly and tipped her head to get a better view of her life mate who had obviously taken leave of his senses.

He continued. "Boy, twelve and girl, ten. Not tramps or ragamuffins. Seems to'a lost both parents in the last few months. Losin' Pa was just a couple of days ago. Our local black panther seems to have attacked."

"So they're not angels, actually."

"We don't know that for a fact. Remember that family that came up river… that the town took in? And then they weren't here with no sign of 'em ever bein' here. That don't matter, though. I'm wantin to see you take a look at that little girl… and it's a fact that I was thinkin' on lookin' for a local boy to do chores. Time I get busy in the back, there's no one to look after the front."

A pause. "I sort'a promised they could stay in the back cabin, at least for a while."

"Your mother's cabin?"

"Uh, well, so to speak. But the fact is, she's been gone for almost three years, and I don't expect her back. She's likely to be right happy where she is now. In the meantime, we have a couple of children who are victims of bad luck and were preparing to move into their tent. No way the town'd let that happen."

The two in the café couldn't hold another bite. Lavinia couldn't get her mind off the little toy house, and her brother couldn't get it out of his mind that he had been called 'friend' instead of maybe, "boy"? His sister was not particularly concerned, as she knew her brother to be a worrier. Even Ma had said that a time or two. If there was worrying to be done, he did it well. Came in handy, though, sometimes… like when he had shoved her down behind the wagon when he saw the painter. That way, she didn't have to see Pa being dragged off by the pair of beasts. Seeing Ma covered over with dirt had been bad enough.

Then Theo had made her stay hidden while he went to where Pa had dropped the shotgun. Too late to help Pa, but they needed the gun, the same way they needed her snake gun.

Then the man was back.

"First off, we'll go look at the house to see if it is going to be all right. Then we'll go see the lady of my house.

The door swung back quietly, revealing a colorful braided rug that almost covered the whole room. That must be the parlor. Kitchen? It wasn't there. Only a tiny stove, a cupboard, a table the size of a small washtub, and two darling chairs with padded seats. Lavinia looked around with her mother's eyes and thought, *Ma'd just love to see this. It really is a toy doll house… just like I thought.*

The door off the parlor opened into a room that had held a slender bed, a tiny wardrobe closet and a small chest of drawers. There wasn't room for another thing, except the slipper stool that was padded like the chairs.

Also up from the parlor was the narrow stairway… almost just a ladder but very easy to climb. Lavinia made her way up and Theo followed. Bare floor… window at the end.

"I can take this room," she offered, kneeling to peek out the window.

"Do you really like this one better?"

"Well, I… You need to take the room you like. You are the one who has the job."

"Then I want this room. I don't want a bed here, just a feather pad like we have on the wagon. Then, I can open the little window and get a good breeze in my face."

John Markham stood below the stairway listening. A pleased smile crept across his face. They were obviously settling in and could use a little privacy. Fact was, they had not had a chance to cry, properly, and certainly had no funeral for Pa. One minute he was there, and then he wasn't. Decisions followed. That boy had a way to go to get back to normal, again.

He called up the stairway. "You two just go ahead and look around. I'm going to have your team and wagon moved over to my barn, and then you can bring what you want into the house. Take your time."

Two hours later, they sat together at the tiny table. It hadn't taken long to bring in their belongings. Living on the road pares one's duties down to a minimum, and possessions even further. The silverware was valuable and could be sold if necessary. The food box replenished only as necessary. Minimum clothing changes.

Lavinia picked up a few of the sticks outside the door, and the tiny stove had quickly warmed the parlor and the miniature kitchen. The traveling mattress pad had been worked up the narrow stairway and stretched by the window. Clean case on the pillow.

Now they sat in the kitchen and looked at each other. Theo was first to bury his head in his arms and sob. Events had demanded that he stay tensed and ready, and try to make decisions, but now his arms were empty. No immediate decisions to be made. There seemed far too much to be frightened about because answers had come too easy… if they really were answers.

Lavinia tried to busy herself with the little cupboard, but was soon back at the table adding her tears.

John Markham had come by the toy house and looked through the window. So tears had finally won out. He went to the Pharmacy where Lily was watching over it until he could get back.

"Gonna need to wait a bit," he told her. "They're shedding tears together, and they don't sound like angels at all. They sound like two frightened children. We have to give them a little while."

Sniffles and hiccoughs fading away, Theo Brownfield stood, squared his shoulders, and announced to his sister, "Thinkin' I better get on over there and get to work."

Summoning no immediate reply, she watched him go and continued to sit at the little table and look around. Suddenly it seemed that everything she knew was just out of reach, and there was nothing left to hold to…? No Ma and no Pa…

There was a gentle knock on the door to the tiny kitchen, and the door was pushed open. In stepped a lady with a smile and a tall cookie jar. Putting the jar on the table, she sat down.

"Lavinia, is it? I'm very glad to see you. I'm Lily Markham, and maybe, after a while, we can think of something easier to call me. I brought this cookie jar over because I thought there would be times you needed something to nibble, and it would be right here. When it gets empty, you and I can make more. What kind of cookies do you like?"

The lady looked kind. Maybe like she wanted to be a friend. She might not be hard to work for. Maybe she was going to say right now what work she would want done… to let them live in the toy house. About the cookies…

"I like most kinds. My Ma mostly had sugar cookies, and we put jelly or butter on them."

"Mmmm, that sounds good. When I knew you would be staying for a while with us, I thought of something. I know that if I had been traveling for a few weeks, I would have an itchy head. I have nice warm water, and I wondered if you'd like to come over to the big house and maybe rinse your hair. How would that sound?"

Lily Markham knew that was a brave thing to say to a total stranger, but if they were ever to be friends, they'd find out with a tub of soapy water.

The girl looked up, somewhat startled, but recovered nicely. "I can if you want me to. I never did like tryin' to be clean in cold water."

A relieved sigh. The girl's hair was a sticky tangle of oily black strands. A washing was bound to make her feel better.

Theo had gone to the Pharmacy and presented himself for work. "Mister, I can work hard. I can plow and pull weeds and feed horses. I'm really good at milkin' cows or goats, either one. I'm good with horses, and old Buck, with the sore leg, he'll take me on errands or anything you want."

"That sounds good. I have some other things in mind, but as you mentioned your horse, I think you'll want to go see about him. That leg'll need to be re-wrapped. You can do that?"

"Sure can, Mister. Done it a lot." And he left through the back door. When he was finished, he faced his benefactor with his question.

"Mister... Sir... uh, I was wonderin' when it'd be that you'd tell me what work I'd be doin'? Not to hurry you, nor nothin', just that I was gettin' anxious to get at it."

After a small hesitation, the man suggested. "First off, you need something better to call me. We're going to be working partners for a while, maybe a long while, so we need to settle that. I have an opinion that your Pa wouldn't have let you call a man by his first name, but if he was someone you knew well and liked, how would it be if you called me, 'Uncle John'? Now, that is not a commandment," he tried for a friendly smile, "but just if you feel comfortable. Maybe tomorrow or next week you will feel more comfortable about it. We'll talk again.

"So, about the job? I promise that it will start tomorrow, and after you milk the cow, I will expect you to be in the pharmacy in your best clothes with your hair combed. How does that sound?"

"I can do whatever you want... uh..."

"Sure, son. We'll start in the morning."

While in the kitchen of the Markham's spacious house, tubs of warm water were prepared, and Lily Markham removed the wrapper from a fresh bar of lavender scented soap and placed it by the wash basin.

Lavinia watched her, then looked up at her with her black-unblinking eyes. "I mostly use lye soap for my hair. My Ma said it was healthy."

"Why, honey, I have lye soap if you prefer. Look in the drawer on the stand. I just didn't know yet about what your mother said."

The girl gently opened the drawer, selected a bar of the gray lye soap. Dipping it in the water, she began to scrub her hair. Lily busied herself in the kitchen after placing a fluffy towel near the rinse water.

Thoroughly soaped and rinsed, the girl expertly made a turban of the towel and stated, "I mostly suds out my underthings in my wash water. I'll go get them." And she did, bringing along her brother's underwear as well.

After a through scrubbing between her small fists and a twist to wring out the water, she asked, "Could I use some clothes pegs, please?"

Lily handed her the bag, and the girl proceed to the clothesline to hang out the garments. Lily watched through the window, "Dear Lord… how do I treat this lovely child. Her pain is showing through clear as a pane of glass, and I don't know how to help." She sighed and looked up, but no answer seemed to be painted on the ceiling.

The girl returned with her comb and hair brush which she thoroughly cleaned in the wash water, her wet hair still in the turban. Removing the turban, she dried the comb and lifted it to begin on the tangles.

In another rush of bravery, Lily asked, "Honey, would you let me help you comb out your lovely hair?"

Startled, Lavinia turned to face her. "If you was wantin' to, I don't mind."

Pleased, Lily suggested, "Let's sit right here, and see how we get on. You tell me if I do something wrong, or pull a tangle too hard."

Lavinia sat, held her head up straight and responded. "My Ma says I got a tough head. Mostly it don't hurt with tangles bein' combed out."

Small relieved sigh, and a mental, Thank you. Lord. Carefully she removed the snarls from lock after lock. Poor little thing had likely not gotten to brush her hair for two or three days, tangled as it was. It took a while, but she sat still as a stone statue.

Interesting hair. With snarls removed, it hung in strands smooth and shiny as satin ribbons. Sure enough, that lye soap seemed to be healthy. As it began to dry, it twisted into small waves and turned up curled on the end. Fantastic! Just look at that hair! So black it seemed to have a blue shine. Bangs hung low onto her heavy black brows. Did she dare?

"Honey, did your mother trim your bangs when she was there? Such lovely hair you have. I don't know if you want your bangs really long, or shorter. Either way is pretty."

Immediate reply. "I mostly liked 'em short like Ma cut 'em. The thing was, Pa tried, and it looked so messed up he wouldn't do it no more. Then Theo tried and he did better. He taped my hair to my forehead and cut above the tape. He sorta scratched my forehead with the scissors and felt bad, so he wouldn't do it no more. I said it didn't hurt, but he didn't believe me 'cause there was blood. I was thinkin' when we got to where we was goin', I'd find a mirror and sharp scissors and learn to do it myself."

Surprise! What a speech from this taciturn child. Reply quickly! "Honey, would it be alright for me to try? It's been a long time since I got to cut a little girl's bangs but I think I remember."

"What little girl?" Lavinia demanded.

"It was my sister, and she was five years younger than I. Her hair was not such a beautiful color as yours, but I loved her very much."

"Where is she?"

Hesitation. "She got sick and died. Diphtheria. It was a long time ago."

Lavinia nodded. "It's not good when folks die. If you was to want to cut my bangs, I'd not mind."

Lily caught her breath from excitement. "I'll be right back."

Bangs trimmed fashionably short, and sides evened up where they touch her shoulders, she was stunning. She could have just stepped off one of the colored pictures in the Montgomery Ward Catalog. Dress attractive and well made, though soiled and wrinkled, but that would change. Be patient, Lily, she reminded herself.

Next was the evening meal, and Lavinia watched closely enough to be taking instruction… committing it memory. How should she act with these strangers? Lily found courage to ask, "Do you and your brother like milk with your meal?"

"We always used to when there was enough. Pa bought milk at farms sometimes, but it was for our oatmeal. Times he could, Theo used to drink two glasses, if they weren't too big."

Good enough. The quantity of milk was never a problem. And not surprising that her brother could drink two glasses. He had the appearance of becoming a tall, broad shouldered man in about ten years. Maybe less.

When they had eaten, the girl excused herself and dipped the wash pans full of warm water from the stove reservoir. Taking the plates and silver from the table, she washed, rinsed, and dried them while the boy finished his milk, and the adults drank coffee.

Lily refrained from mentioning that she didn't need to hurry with the cleaning up... because it might seem like a criticism. Getting acquainted might be like walking a circus tight rope for a while, but Lily could do it. If this girl would only consent to stay with them, she might go a little way toward filling a vacancy within Lily caused by the child she never had.

Or was that too much to ask, Lord?

Later, "Theodore, would you carry this lamp out to the toy house? I know you two are exhausted from everything that's happened today, so we'll let you go get some sleep and see you tomorrow."

The children nodded, gratefully, and left.

3

Theo climbed the narrow stairs and not another sound came from the small attic. Lavinia stepped into the toy bedroom and quietly closed the door behind her. With a smile at the flower-wall-papered walls, she whispered, "I'm alone." Sweet silence all around, except for the crickets.

Theo lay quiet in bed. Maybe asleep, already. For the last two nights he had attempted to stay awake all night to protect her. Lavinia knew that. Pa was gone, it was dark all around. Not enough kerosene to burn the lantern all night. Not sure how far they were from other people... and help. Trying to take Pa's place... had Theo been.

She gently turned back the sheet. Nice clean sheet, like back in Kentucky with Ma. Slipping into her wrinkled nightie (maybe I can wash it tomorrow) and laying her head on the feather pillow. Hair smoothed out. Smelling cleanly of lye soap. Like when she was in Kentucky. Ma, things ain't so bad. If I couldn't stay with you, I'll like this little toy house.

She was awake with the first rooster crow, startlingly at the strange surroundings. Memory flooded in with the warm sweetness of buttered honey on a warm rock. Energy began to arouse. Today she would learn what she had to do to get to stay in this toy house forever.

The sun was coming up when she woke her brother. He would be embarrassed to be oversleeping today... of all days.

After breakfast John asked, "Theodore, which name do you prefer, Theo or Theodore?"

"Either, Sir. Whichever you have time to say. I even answer to 'hey, you.' After I milk the cows, do I start to work?"

"You do, indeed." After getting him started, with bucket and all, John Markham went to the door with the big sign MARKHAM'S PHARMACY and entered. It had taken a lot of thought, but the boy obviously wanted to work. Why not try something he had thought of several times. He had already determined that Theo had cleared the sixth grade which was the highest grade offered, and that he had made "tolerably" good grades.

He looked at the shelves down each wall and an island of shelves in the middle of the large room. His business had just grown by itself, and he knew where everything was, but no one else did. If he was going to have help, that would have to change, and he had spoken the honest truth when he said he considered taking on a young boy for help.

A pencil, a ruler, and a pile of sheets. There first had to be a paper plan, so that would be the place to start. Making a sketch of one bank of shelves, he marked off spaces and set it aside. The boy finished the milking, donned overalls (fairly clean) and a shirt (wrinkled), and he wore carefully slicked down hair. Good start.

"Theo, I've decided where we start. I eventually want preparations of each type shelved together, and then we need to mark the shelf with the name, so that if someone comes while I'm not here, you will know where to find it.

"First off, look around at everything. Take all day if you want, and tomorrow we will start placing it. If you have a question, ask and don't hesitate. This is an important job, and I'm thinking you will be very good at it."

With that, he disappeared into the back room to get out of his way. A bright young fellow would not want someone looking over his shoulder. It wouldn't take long to discover his ability and extent of education.

With a small smile, he left the building and ambled across the street to the Livery Stable. He liked to check in every few days, just to see what the gossip was. Most men of the small town of River Bend checked in with the Livery fairly often... or at least they wanted to.

John Markham had hardly come within hearing distance until it was shouted toward him. "Well, John, how're you getting' along with them hillbillies?"

"What hillbillies?"

"Them youngens from Kaintuck. Bound to be hillbillies what got lost on their way to nowhere."

The pharmacist did not honor the stupidity with a response. Then Ed, the manager of the livery wondered, "How'd that horse do... the bay with the sprain?"

"Lookin' good. The boy treated him and this morning I saw him walk the animal around the barn after he finished the milking. Slight limp, but a body'd have to expect that. Thinkin' he'll be right as rain by tomorrow. The kid knew what to do. Seems to know his way around horseflesh."

Allen Upchurch, who had originally tipped John off to the problem, commented, "Strange set of circumstances around those two. Did you find out where they was headed?"

"Not yet. It's seemin' like they're not ready to talk. Easy to understand that. Got the boy over there now, inventorying some of the stock." The pharmacist just couldn't resist countering the hillbilly claim.

"Inventoryin'? Hmmm, well, reckon he'll know what he's doin'?

"Wouldn't see why not? Him havin' completed the sixth grade and havin' a pa who gave him good trainin'. Sure glad to have 'im,

Gonna give me a chance to come over and jaw with you fellows from time to time."

Theo looked at the sheets of paper, and then toward the shelves. Bottles. Hundreds of them. See, there was cold medicine in the back of the quinine. Nobody would see that if they didn't know it was there. And the bandages down on the bottom shelf. And more bandages on the second shelf.

Yeah, well, if this was his job, he could handle that. Next, it was hard to see those tiny bottles of the top shelf. If the bandage cotton boxes were put up there, and those bottles of peroxide that were easy to see…. How would that be? And…

He looked them over. Some, actually most, of them were unfamiliar to him, and he wasn't sure there was time to read the labels today. He could, however, gather everything that was alike into its own little space. He'd write down the name of them, and then the man would only have to tell him one time what they were and where they went.

Grouping the items on one bank of shelves, he moved on to the next one. So engrossed he was that he did not hear the door open when John came back from the livery.

The pharmacist watched as the tiny mercurochrome bottles were set together, and all of the medicated petroleum jelly together. And the ear-ache oil…miniature bottles that so easily tipped over… were now setting together in a cardboard box lid. Good idea.

As he gathered like items into groups, Theo cut a small strip of tape and pasted it on the shelf edge. With the pencil, he copied the name on the bottle.

Quietly, the man eased past and disappeared in his office room. Hmmm, could it be? Don't get your hopes up, John. That boy is not yours, and he may be gone tomorrow….

But he wasn't.

Later, at the supper table, John decided to compliment him in front of his sister. "Good job you did, Theo. You got a really good start on a big job."

The boy shrugged, but grinned. "Shucks, that didn't hardly seem like a job." Then after a few bites, "You aimin' to let me go on doin' it? I think there's gonna be more room left over, the way I see it. We got somethin' else that goes there?"

John forced himself to keep from smiling at the "we." Don't think about it, John. He could be gone in the night.

It was in the afternoon that Lavinia faced Lily with the question of her future. "Miss… uh, would you tell me what my job will be so's I can be doin' it?"

"I have a question, Lavinia. Do you like staying in the toy house for a while?"

Brisk nod.

"Then it means we'll see each other a lot, and you need something to call me. I think you might have aunts that you liked, and if you wanted to, you could call me Aunt Lily. You think about it, and if you have an idea of another name, we'll talk about it. And that job. I know you went to school. Which grade did you reach?"

The girl was silent but quickly raised four fingers. That would be about right. Then she added, "Almost." So she'd been taken out of school.

"Well, we have a very good school here and a smart teacher. Your job will be to get yourself ready for school every morning and be there on time. If you need help with something, I'm right here. One other thing. I don't want you to wash the breakfast dishes. You may have homework to finish, or you can take extra time getting ready. You can wash the supper dishes unless I tell you not to."

She nodded. "And what is the job for me to do?"

"School. For a girl who is ten years old, school is the best job she can have. I think you'll like it. Several girls there are about your age, and I'm thinking you'll like them. I'm certain they'll like you."

She was still concerned. "That means I don't have a job? But I can still live in the toy house?"

"Honey, you can live in that toy house until you're 99 years old if you want to." Finally something brought a smile to the girl's face.

Then came a Monday, and the girl prepared for school. She graciously allowed Lily to tie the red bow in her shiny black hair. Red, to match the red checked jumper she wore over her freshly-laundered white blouse. She had refused offers of help with the sad-iron on the wrinkles. Always did it herself, she insisted.

Lavinia's mother was obviously a good hand with the needle, as her clothes were all well-made and well kept... as soon as they had a chance to go through the wash water, that is. Hard to keep clean on the road, for a fact.

The girl turned down company to walk her to school the first day. She knew where the school was, she said, "'cause she saw it out back'a the livery." She even refused the company of her brother, "'cause he's got a job to do and I know the way."

There were things to be admired in such fierce independence, if it just didn't go too far.

The most descriptive statement she made when asked about her first day was, "...that teacher's a fellow! Did you know that?" Of course Lily had known that, but it didn't seem unusual, as the town insisted on male teachers. Females got themselves married off and then weren't allowed to continue.

The only other manifestation of the change that school made in her life was the list of spelling words she pinned to the kitchen curtain so she could study them while she washed the dishes.

4

Then Tuesday rolled around. That was when all the River Bend ladies, who could possibly make it, converged upon the church for the Tuesday Sewing Circle, a routine begun over a generation ago.

This activity consisted of attaching a colorful 'quilt top' which had been pieced in a variety of designs, to a 'bottom' often pieced together from the better parts of a worn out sheet. The center was filled with something called a 'batting' which was often a worn blanket, or maybe a roll of cotton made for the purpose but was considered 'frightfully expensive.'

The attaching of these pieces together was called 'quilting' and consisted of stitches through all layers, and spaced not fewer than five to the inch. Six to eight stitches to the inch was preferable.

There were some less skillful hands that could not manage that, and a few who were forced, by lack of time, to bring personal sewing to be done there. It was important to have this time of weekly visiting, of general conversation and of catching up on the community news.

Not gossip, certainly. That might be frowned on, and possibly be sinful. It was just that one had to know what was going on, because they might be in position to help a neighbor.

If one of the ladies was not 'a good hand at sewin' quilts' there would be a polite way to let her know, and she would then be relegated to tea preparation, and maybe threading the needles for those whose eyes were too dim for the job. It was secretly thought, by some, that certain ladies could do it, but messed up on purpose, so they could just sit and enjoy the tea and cookies that came with the event.

As usual, Lily Markham took herself to the church and occupied her accustomed position, knowing the ladies were consumed with curiosity.

"So you got yourself a little girl, huh?" Maisie opened the subject. Maisie, herself, loved the Sewing Circle. In fact, she had once come knowing she was in labor and produced her twins in one of the children's teaching rooms.

Other ladies joined in, encouraging Lily, the childless, to expound. "What's her age? About ten they was sayin',"

"Sorta come on sudden like, didn't they? Just the boy and the girl?"

"How're you doin' with her?"

Lily waited for the first round of questions to appear, then she began, "I'm not so sure she's mine. Pretty well takes care'a herself."

"I speck so, livin' in that wagon out in the rough. No place for a girl, I'd say."

"Folks does what they can. Now, Lizzie, if'n you had a girl and a trip to make, what'd you do with 'er, pack 'er in a crate and ship 'er on the Mississippi Central?"

Lizzie Cantrell let that remark pass. "What was the meanin' of the the trip, anyway. What was wrong with Kaintuck?"

Before Lily could answer that, they didn't yet know for sure, Dollie shared what she'd heard from the conversation at the Livery, the next best location for media exchange. "They was a'sayin' that the family had taken to movin' west, and the youngen's folks was aimin' to follow."

"Who was the folks? They couldn't'a been from River Bend."

"Jacksonville, most likely. Could'a been Little Rock."

"Reckon we'll not know, less'n the youngens get to rememberin' somethin' that was said."

Finally Lily had a chance to get in a word. "That girl's mother was a fine hand to sew. To look at the stitches on her clothes, her mother could'a made the eight stitches to the inch with no trouble." That was a degree of skill that all would recognize.

"Reckon she had time to teach the girl?"

Dollie again took over. "Now, Lizzie, she ain't been here even a week, so how'd Lily know?"

Lily thought it was a good answer, but she added, "Chance she stays here, there'll likely be school dresses to be made for next year. She seems a bit small for ten, but she's bound to grow."

"Yep. They all do."

Then Eva Owens. "My Orville stopped over for a bottle'a cough syrup, and he saw that boy a'movin' bottles around and studyin' the labels. You don't reckon he's got mischief in mind, do you?"

This created interest. Lizzie had a comment, "Wouldn't be a chance of him a'mixin' things up so'a we'd get the wrong thing?"

But Dollie was there to help. "'Course not, Lizzie. They all got labels on 'em. "Sides, John wouldn't let that happen, knowin' we count on 'im."

Lily decided to let that one go, as well. Dollie just about covered it. And the grilling continued for the most of the morning. Lily had lived her life in River Bend and knew that some things just had to run their course, and then a new subject would come around. She had no criticism, as it was always entertaining, and that's what they had come for. Entertainment.

While down the road at the Livery Stable, information exchange did not wait for Tuesdays, but was fairly continuous, forcing the men to arrange their work carefully to be able to check in regularly.

"Saw that little hillbilly girl pass by goin' to the school. All by herself. All spiffed up, she was, with ribbons and shiny shoes."

"Sorta heard that girl carries a gun. Don't know how well she aims, but that could be dangerous… for a girl."

"How'd you hear all that?"

"It was the boy. Him sayin' he'd'a shot that black cat, but his pa had the shotgun and the sister's gun wouldn't'a done 'im in. Likely only made 'im mad."

"Strange about how they come on in here, late in the day, like."

"Not so strange. They was alone in a strange country and was lookin' for help. Natural thing to do was look for a road and foller it. Sooner or later they'd find people. Bein' so late in the day was 'cause they had so far to come... seems to me."

"How far away did that cat jump their Pa?"

"Boy couldn't say. Them a'travelin' down that right-a-way cut by the Mississippi Central, over the stumps and rocks, they'd'a not knowd how far they come."

"Interestin' thing about that girl and that gun, though."

At this point, a newcomer pointed out, "Chances are you fellows ain't been to Kentucky. They's places there where vines and trees are so thick, it'd be hard to raise up an Enfield to get a shot in. A Smith and Wesson handgun'd be as necessary as a compass, in them woods."

Mulling over the words of an expert who had actually been there, most of the men were ready to let it go... the fact that an undersized girl child had a gun. At least, they'd let it go for now. Something to reserve an opinion on until more facts were known.

It was up into November that Lily mentioned as they were eating their spiced cake with whipped cream topping. "Just thought I'd mention, with it getting cold, you two might be warmer in an upstairs room, and there's three of them empty. It'd be no problem at all." Enough said. They would do what they wanted to do, and Lily was certain of that. Still and all, she'd like to get that girl into the house. Maybe, in time...

It was amazing about the boy and the pharmacy. It seemed to intrigue him greatly, and he read all the labels, the hand-outs sent by salesmen and consumed every one of the government pamphlets. John watched, but like Lily, he was careful what he said. Even if he'd like to help, that boy didn't need much of it.

A self-starter, he was. John would have to be careful to keep him from being a 'self-starter' somewhere else. In three or four years, there were a dozen places over in Jacksonville that would snap him up like a rat in a store-bought trap.

It gave a fellow thought.

5

It was still warm enough to be working on the railway right-of-way, and Ezra Sutter was camping out by the week, coming home on weekends. That left Estelle by herself with David, age 7, Maggie, age 3, and a new little someone else due to come on sometime in the spring.

He hated to be gone, but cash money was hard to turn down, and him with a growing family. He had his Pa's farm, a nice hillside acreage up back of the church, but sooner or later, it took cash money. School shoes just didn't grow in a garden.

Young David had just come home from school and was in sight of the house when he was met by a terrified mother pulling a wagon with Maggie stretched out on a quilt. A lot of blood on Maggie's face told him a lot.

"Davie, you turn around and run to the Markham's and tell 'im we're a'comin' in. Maggie got herself kicked in the face by a mule, and we're needin' whatever he can do."

Without a hesitation, David turned on his heel and ran, the first part of the trip was down hill, so he made good time. His seven-year-old feet were still making good time when he burst through the door of the Pharmacy. Fortunately, John was there.

"Mr. Markham, my ma sent me on to say our Maggie got herself kicked in the face by a mule. Ma was needin' help."

That got the immediate attention of the pharmacist. "How bad is she, Davie?"

"I ain't knowin' fer sure. Didn't look too close, but there was a spate'a blood all over, and Ma's a'pullin' her in the toy wagon."

Huge frightened eyes stared up at him. John forced his mind to click into gear. It didn't sound like something he could take care of with his minimal medical training. He was, after all, just a licensed dispenser of medicine with only first aid training.

It seemed clear from David's description that this was a case to go to the hospital at Jacksonville, 12 miles away. And it was late afternoon. He could hardly leave to take the child there, and Ezra was out of reach. Not only that, Estelle was heavily pregnant. And Davie was terrified.

Think fast. "Davie, your ma and Maggie are going to have to go to the hospital in Jacksonville. As soon as you say goodbye to your mother, you must go down to the preacher's house and say what you told me and that I wanted you to stay there. Tell him I'll be down to see him as soon as I can.

"Theodore, I want you to head on down east and try to meet Davie's ma, and help bring the wagon on in. She'll be give out by then. Someone is going to have to take her to Jacksonville, and I'll go hitch up the buggy."

Theo stood poised for flight toward the east, but had a word of advice. "If'n you was to need speed, it oughtta be Buck and Blue. They're fast when they have to be." Then he was gone.

What the boy said made sense. The Kentucky animals were hardened to the road. He pulled his two seated buggy from the shed and backed the willing animals into position. Forcing his fingers to be efficient, he attended to the straps and buckles and had moved the buggy to the road. His only option seemed to be to step over to the Livery and see if there was someone available for the trip that would have taken them far into the night to return.

Looking to the east, he saw Theo with his arms full of blanket and child, and Estelle a few yards behind hurrying on with an empty wagon.

Breathless explanation, "I was thinkin that jouncin' and bumpin' in the wagon wasn't doin the baby no good. Shall I put 'em... Sir... uh, Uncle John, was you thinkin' on makin' the trip? 'Cause I could make it faster, them animals bein' used to me a'yellin' at 'em. Seems like I couldn't get lost with this road leadin' there."

John looked at the serious black eyes trained on him, and the lock of black hair plastered across his sweating forehead. He was obviously accustomed to making instant decisions. This was his observation and his best answer.

"Theo, run in the house and get your heaviest coat and a cap, grab up whatever you see to eat, and come on out here." The boy held out the blanketed bundle. John took the silent child and placed her across the rear buggy seat. Still breathing. There was a chance.

With hardly a turn around, the boy was back. "Stay here with the girl, Theo, I've got to give her ma something." Taking the distraught woman by the arm, he propelled her into the pharmacy. Pouring a few pills into a bottle, he handed it to her and took one more pill. Holding a cup of water, he insisted she drink. "It'll help, and don't worry about Davie. I'll see to him."

The pill was gone in a gulp, but her terror continued. "You ain't lettin' that strange boy take that buggy, are you Mr. Markham?"

"Estelle, that boy is not strange, and he's the fastest we have to get you to Jacksonville. You're as safe with him as if you were at your own house. Maybe safer. Trust me. Now, I'll help you climb in, and you try to lean back and maybe get some rest. It'll be a long night for the both'a you."

With the patients in the back, he turned to Theo. Handing him a small bag with coins, he told him. "Go fast, but careful. Look for the sign at the edge's town pointing to the hospital. You can't miss it. Then you put the horses in the hospital stable, and someone will find you a bed for the night. Now go."

"Thank you, Uncle John. You ain't gonna be sorry you let me do this." With a meaningful stare into the man's eyes, he slid himself into the driver's seat.

John Markham watched the disappearing buggy as it stirred up its own small dust cloud. He certainly hoped he was not sorry, but he was confident on this decision. Very seldom did his snap judgement turn out to be wrong. Especially impressed he was, at the boy's parting words... meant to ease concern.

Theo had no watch to tell him the time, so he did not know he made the three hour trip in slightly over two hours. Darkness had settled in, so he stopped the buggy to study the sign. He couldn't afford to make a mistake. The exhausted animals hung their heads low, heaving and panting, steam rising off their sweaty bodies in the cool November air.

Clicking them on, he promised them, "Only another minute, fellows. You done a good job."

At the hospital door, he yelled at the animals to WHOA, and, knowing them to be obedient, he jumped from the seat and pounded on the hospital door. "HELP! HELP! SOMEBODY HELP ME!"

Somebody did. The door opened and the woman in white was met with, "GOT A REALLY BAD HURT BABY HERE." She turned on her heel, yelled something, and was back in seconds.

Theo stood by the buggy until the door closed behind them. He had done all he could for the baby, so now, the horses. Rubbing their noses, he promised. "Good supper for you, tonight, fellows and no more runnin'. We'll take it slow going home."

In the hospital Livery, he was able to rub down his sweaty animals and was given a blanket to cover them until they dried. Sweaty animals that stopped still in the cold were just inviting all kinds of mischief... from colic, to tangled guts, to stiff legs. He was really glad to get the blankets for them. Also the quarts of corn which he paid for. Hay to nibble on came free.

Now, for himself. He wasn't for certain what was in the lunch sack. He hadn't stopped to look. Whatever it was, it was going to be gratefully eaten. Then he took the blanket he'd been instructed to get and wrapped up in it, stretching out as much as possible on the buggy seat. He was intent on being close enough to hear his animals if they made a sound.

After a somewhat restless, sometimes wakeful, night, morning finally came. He could smell food being prepared and tracked it down in the hospital kitchen. Asking to buy a bowl of oatmeal and maybe a biscuit, he was placed at a table and fed ham and eggs... no charge.

He bought another quart of corn and divided it between Blue and Buck, and they scrounged up every grain from the feed bucket. He asked about the baby and was told the doctors worked through the night, and she was still breathing. They'd make no promises. That was the best they could tell him.

With that, he clicked the team into action but let them set their own pace. Of course the folks back in River Bend were eager to hear, but they could just wait a little longer. Those wonderful horses had outdone themselves yesterday. A slow walk or maybe a period of trotting would be good for them… better than standing in the hospital Livery for the day.

He did a lot of thinking on the way home. He had been so busy during the last four months, he hardly had time to take stock on his present circumstances. By the time he saw the silver bridge ahead, the one over the Tuscalara River right where the rambunctious War Eagle River joined in, the one that defined the entrance to River Bend… by the time he got there, he had summed it up all together. "Pa, I sure wished you hadn't'a had to leave us, but I gotta say this, you shore left us in a good place."

And right on the heels of that thought was another one. Pa would never have let him leave for such an errand without the shotgun. He might have needed it for his own protection… then again, he might have a chance to bring down a small deer, or maybe a brace of rabbits. It was too late in the year for bringing down a couple of geese. They had all flown over last month.

"That's alright, Pa. This is not the wilds of Kentucky or even the danger of the Mississippi River. This here is River Bend, and I'm thinkin' it'd be about a safe as anywhere." There was a lot more that he would be telling his Pa, but that would be later, sprinkled out over the next years.

It was coming on noon when he passed Bascom's Boarding House, just a half a mile from the Pharmacy. He'd like to have had better news, but at least the little girl was still breathing… at least she was when he had left Jacksonville.

Someone had saddled up and found Ezra, working up closer to Calhoun. He was checking out from the railway and would go on over to the hospital now, as he knew that if his Davie was with John Markham or Preacher McCrey, he would be fine.

The River Bend residents were told the medium good news, and nodded. It was the best they would have expected, and the Good Lord's will be done. They had done all they could.

6

It had been washday, and the clothing was carried in from the clothesline. Lavinia sorted out her dresses and sprinkled them for ironing, rolling them tightly together while the sadirons heated.

Lily hung around but was sure she would not be permitted to help. That girl was determined to be as little trouble as possible, not realizing that Aunt Lily would actually enjoy a little trouble. Begging for it... fact be known.

Lily commented, "Your mother was certainly handy with the needle. All your dresses are so pretty and well made, it's a shame they won't grow with you. It looks like you will need some new things before school next year."

Lavinia changed out the iron that was getting cool for a hotter one on the stove. She nodded, "Ma was goin' to teach me, but we never got to it. I got money to buy dress goods, but I think I may need help to cut them out."

Lily paused and thought of the words she heard. Is this the right time to assert... or what? After another moment of consideration, she decided. If not now... when? So she plunged in.

"No, Lavinia, that's not what will happen."

The startled girl turned her face toward Lily. Totally white-faced frightened.

Lily continued. "You are now living in my toy house, and doing things to earn your way. Of course, I know you want to spend your money, but you are not going to be permitted to do that. Part of your job is to let me have the pleasure of buying your dress material and helping you cut out the dresses. But you, of course, shall pick out the colors you like and decide how you want them made." There! Had she said too much?

Lavinia walked back to the stove and set the sadiron back over the heat. Returning to the table she sat down, buried her head in her arms and sobbed. Lily had a moment of regret, but it was a thing that had to be done. Something had to tell the little girl she was wanted, and not just taken care of. Or put up with.

Waiting a couple of minutes, Lily pulled a chair up beside her and put her arm around the heaving shoulders. Gently pulling her closer, she broke the independence just a little bit. "Honey, I know I sounded cranky, but I couldn't help it. I just love doing things for the girl who sleeps in my toy house, and I decided it was my turn to insist. I have never had a little girl, and I could be doing things all wrong with you, but we might just have to forgive each other sometimes."

Tear stained face. Red weepy eyes. "No, Aunt Lily. It was that for a minute there, you sounded just like Ma. When I went too far in my thinkin', she brought me back with words. Like sayin' I was give to her by the Good Lord, and she had to do the best for me, even if I didn't like it." Sniffles and hiccoughs. "I'd be right grateful for you to buy my dresses and help me sew. It's really hard to be without a Ma, when I had such a good one for so long. It sounded good to hear you sound like her."

Oh, dear Lord in heaven, thank you!

Lavinia, the strong minded, stood, wiped her eyes with her sleeve and again picked up the hot, metal, smoothing iron and proceeded to remove the wrinkles from her dress, carefully and skillfully tucking the point of the iron into the ruffles at the hem.

Just a stray sniffle occasionally. Lily said nothing, but she knew a turning point had been reached. From this point, she would not have continue to treat her words with such concerned hesitancy. If she could occasionally sound like the girl's beloved mother, so much the better.

It took the town a whole year to accept that Theodore Brownfield knew a few things at the pharmacy and could be trusted in his words. He would not know it, but he had passed the test in an incredibly short time, considering the attitude of the mountain village. At his age, it could have taken five years before he was totally thought of by the townspeople as being one of them. The rush trip with the little girl had boosted the time up a bit, as well.

He was most often seen behind the counter dispensing whatever was called for, if the buyer knew the name of it. Otherwise, the pharmacist was called. That new, inexpensive thing called aspirin, he knew well. Boiling willow bark tea was no longer necessary to treat pain. Of course, the tiny white pill had been on the market for a lot longer time, but the cost had been practically prohibitive. Until now. And now, everyone could afford the little tin holding a dozen of the white tablets, and maybe even the bottle of fifty. The time of the Aspirin had arrived.

Also, candy sold well. Most of the town's candy was sold down the street at the Mercantile, but the Pharmacy had the huge glass jars with heavy glass lids, and they held a rainbow of colors and flavors that could be had ten for a penny. The sale of candy had begun when John first opened up for business, after being sent by his father to Little Rock to Pharmacy School. The same school taught Barbering, and was thought to be the best place for learning… it certainly cost enough, but John's parents could afford it.

The new young pharmacist had noted that a lot of his very young customers came for relief for a minor injury, a bad case of sniffles or an ear ache. A piece of brightly colored, individually wrapped sweet (that they had chosen) seemed to help the feeling, if not the current malady. The availability of the candy seemed so popular that it was continued… and was offered for sale priced at cost.

The subject of the Kentucky orphans was of continued interest, both in the Sewing Circle (where careful words were chosen) and at the Livery Stable where John Markham was not often present (and anything could be, and was, discussed… ad infinitum).

"Big thing about that boy makin' that fast trip to the city. No longer'n he was here, Markham took a risk. That kid could'a took that rig and barreled off to who knows where."

Obviously the speaker, Spike Morton, had not thought this through, and a number of heads turned his way.

"With that hurt baby in the back?"

"And leavin' his sister behind?"

"Ya remember how he had no time to think out a theft, if'n he'd ever wanted to…?"

Spike attempted to defend his hastily taken position. "But that there buggy'a John's, that's a ritzy rig. Worth a bit'a cash."

"Yeah, but them horses were worth a lot more, and they belonged to the boy all ready. I can't see how…."

"Did you notice how there was hardly a word 'tween John and the youngen 'afore he took off?"

"Yep, and that means there was a lot'a trust goin' on."

"Could be the boy's smart enough to see he has a good thing a'goin'."

"Well, for one thing, that youngen is smart, else John wouldn't have 'im behind the counter handin' out medicine the way he does."

"The way I hear it, the youngen slept in the buggy in the barn, 'stead'a takin' a hospital bed. That'd mean he was lookin' out for that buggy and his own animals… seems to me."

"You know… the way I see it, losing' a pa was bad, but that could work out good for John and the kid, both. Him with no youngen and the kid with no pa. Like syrup on the hotcakes or cream in the coffee. Some things just naturally goes together, and could be the same with folks."

And at the Sewing Circle.

"Lily, how's that little girl comin' on with her sewin'?"

"Yeah… is she gonna make a quilter for us, some day?"

"A body'd thought she be already getting herself taught by her ma, and her ten years old, goin' on eleven."

Here's where Lily decided to jump into the discussion. "You ladies might recall, she was ten when she got here, but she wasn't quite eight when she left Kentucky, and there'd be a time the trip was planned, and her mother would have other things to think on ahead of teachin' sewin'."

Small silence, then, "But how's she comin on with your teachin'?"

"Lavinia is a strong minded girl, and when she starts something, she stays with it. She wants pretty dresses, and she knows what to do to get them. She's also learning to crochet. I see her lamp light on when she likely should be sleepin', but I don't say anything. Mostly she knows what she's doin', and her school grades are very good."

Figuring she had said enough to allow the subject to change, she helped herself to a cookie and warmed up her mug of tea. She was wrong.

"What about that gun? The men folks think a girl shouldn't oughtta be carryin' a gun."

Lily stopped amid step and set down her mug of tea. "Think about what you just said. Do the 'men folks' think a girl's hand is any different from a boy's hand, and don't they start their sons with the BB guns at five and six… soon as their arms reach? Do you think that girl has had someone with her all the time to protect her, and do you think her brother had nothin' to do but follow her and take care of her? That Theo is a really smart young fellow, accordin' to John, and he's mighty glad to have the help. He's had good trainin' by his pa.

"'Nuther thing. I hear it was rough country over on the Virginia-Kentucky border, along by the Cumberland Gap. Good chance that girl would'a met up with a critter of some kind, two legs… four legs… or no legs at all. Could be she's still alive on account'a that gun. Calls it a 'snake gun' and it'd take good aim to hit a snake, skinny as they are, and the way they wiggle.

"Besides that, I don't recall anyone sayin' that she's pointed it at anyone, and guns don't do that all by themselves. What I hear bein' said about it would mean the girl was not bein' trusted. Nothin's been said about her brother with a shotgun, that'd blow a human into the next life. I haven't asked, 'cause I don't care, but I'd guess that boy wasn't more'n eight when he was bein' taught. Wonder if his neighbors wondered about that. He's a good strong build, and he could'a handled one of those Enfield Rifles by then… maybe.

"Leastwise, when she goes up the bluff to pick greens for a meal, the way she likes to do, I feel better that she has that dinky little gun in her apron pocket. Her pa told her when she was out like that, she needed to make a noise like singin' or sayin' her ABC's. The fact bein' that most snakes would slither on away if they had a chance. Don't too many try to attack, at least that I've heard of. From around here, anyway."

At this point Lily Markham paused for breath and heaved a lengthy sigh. Picking up her tea mug, she sat down in her place and finished the sugar cookie in her hand.

Silence for a full fifty seconds. Then, "I'm sorry, Lily. I wasn't meanin' nothin'. Just passin' along what was bein' said."

"Yeah, we wasn't sayin' you wasn't good…" But she couldn't complete her sentence.

Lily placed her tea mug on the bench beside her and looked around. These were all her friends and neighbors, and they all came to the Pharmacy for their needs. She had been rather rough on them and needed to make amends. At least attempt something.

"The thing is, ladies. Times we just repeat what the fellows say, not thinkin' about whether it had been thought out. Most times, it just makes good conversation that we all like, but that little girl and her brother sometimes get more than their share of words. Could be we could speak about other children, sometimes, and what they do. I know I haven't been around a little girl on an all-day basis very long, and it could be that I'm over-sensitive. Lavinia doesn't take the gun to school or anywhere around people, but I wouldn't be a bit afraid if she did. From where my thinkin' comes from, if that gun saved her life sometime, then the world is better off for it. Same would be said about your children."

Silence, and then from another voice... "You know, I'd'a thought the wind-fall pears would'a all hit the ground after that blow outta the west over the weekend, but I still see some up there, ready to fall."

And a response. "Fer a fact, I noticed the same thing, but I was more'n glad some stayed up there. I got my hands full'a the fall butcherin'."

"Speakin'a butcherin', anybody know where there's a fed-out hog for sale? I checked the board at the livery and at the pharmacy, and nothin' was posted."

"Hmmm, you might check with..." and the conversation picked up again in a safer vein. The ladies made a mental note to watch their tongues around Lily Markham. Gentle, ladylike, and soft spoken, but when that little girl was discussed, her words could be sharp as a butcher knife. Fact is, though, she was right that no one felt free to discuss other children, so why should the Kentucky orphans be fair game for criticism? Why, indeed?

And that very evening when she came in from school, Lavinia commented, while donning her apron with the deep pockets, "Didn't have no homework so I thought to go pick greens for supper."

Tucking her small Smith and Wesson in her pocket, she picked up a knife and a pail and left, humming the tune to the old song from the war between the states. "...thistledown... thistledown... riding the winds that blow. Where they will... come down to earth... only God will know...."

Lily wondered whether she perhaps should be ashamed, but shook her head... decidedly. She realized she was not in the least bothered and a small smile crossed her lips. Lavinia's Pa had told her to sing, and that was what she was doing, and there was every chance she would come back with a bucket of fresh mixed greens that the children loved so well when wilted in a skillet with bacon grease.

And the girl would come back alive.

7

YEAR 1720, England

The Earle of Macomber had five healthy sons, but his estate was not particularly large. As was the English custom, the entire estate was passed on to the oldest son, while duties were assigned to the others, and they were entitled to live on the estate for life.... working for their keep, so to speak.

With a resigned sigh, the later-born sons often bowed to what seemed to be an inequity of birth and did as they were told by their brother. But not always.

Many times the younger sons turned into 'black sheep' sons, causing trouble trying to get what they thought was their share of family importance. Some simply took their leave and headed to the continent or down to India, and some went to sea. There were those, however, who boarded a ship to the colonies.

Westley Macomber boarded the Viking ship called Dragon's Breath. He signed in as Lesley Comber and none were the wiser as to his linage. By the same token, none would care if they knew, and the Earle, when he learned of the departure, considered one small problem to be sailing away.

He'd known that young Westley could turn out to be trouble. Clever lad and mischievous, two traits not always valued by the English in later sons. Acquiescence and obedience were preferred. So his absence was not only accepted, but financed to a small degree.

The boy disembarked at Jamestown Virginia but didn't stay long. He had it in his head to strike out to the big river and maybe farther and as soon as he was suitably re-provisioned, and, armed with a hand-drawn map of the best place to cross those impossible mountains just west of Virginia, he was on his way.

Age nineteen was a wonderful age to be. A boy like Westley was certain he knew all the answers to the world's problems, and, as yet, none had fallen on him so how could he not believe his feelings? Some people just seem to live a charmed existence.

Following his map, more or less, he came to the gap in the mountains that was not so much a gap, as it was a saddle among mammoth peaks of the mountain range. Nice country. Lots of wild game… be no way a fellow would go hungry there, as long as he had ammo for his weapons.

He looked around, rested, ate heartily, slept when weary and was in no hurry to leave. In fact, the lay of the land was just about as near heaven as that lad had ever expected to get.

It seemed that this gap in the mountains was well known, and there was an interesting lot of traffic that came down the trail near Westley's camp.

He was very well provisioned, and the natives liked him. He wasn't trying to change them or steal from them. There were others, however, who were not nearly so well provisioned as Westley (who for humorous, private reasons of his own, became known as Earle Cumber). There was no one to object, and no one knew his father was an English Earle, whatever that was. Nor did they care. His name was Earle, and that was as good a name as anyone else had.

Of those who were ill provisioned, most had realized by now that their supply of ammo could (and should) have been greater, such was the need to provide food and safety along the way. They were now open for a trade. Would Earle Cumber have extra shot for their weapon? And would he sell?

Westley, now Earle, was glad to oblige. When he ran low, he just commissioned a clever native to head back to civilization and bring him more. He would pay them well.

It didn't take long for the news to get around (how this happened was a puzzle to many), but the gap became a map-marked stopover for re-supply. Why burden yourself with ammo, heavy as it was, when it could be purchased at Cumber's land, located right there in the gap where they were going anyway.

Small trail markers strangely appeared pointing out the correct path to take to Cumberland's Gap. Then later, the location became a landmark during the war between the states, and Cumberland Gap appeared in many of their nostalgic songs of home... along with song, Thistledown.

In due time, Earle Cumber finished his days and passed on to whatever future awaited him, and was laid to rest with sadness. He left behind, however, a number of sons and enterprising natives who were happy to carry on his work, having been trained well by the Earle, himself.

The legacy he left behind was ten times greater, and more... than that left by the Earle of Macomber of the old country. There was no one around who knew this, or would care if they did, but Wesley (Earle) left behind him a well-known name, though, in truth it was never his name to begin with.

The settlements around the Gap grew, and as young men are often restless, there was a big country to move into. In those days large families contained many sons, and there were always those, like Westley (Earle) who were shorted on an inheritance at home, so they went elsewhere. And elsewhere mostly meant due west.

It seemed clear that Earle McComber's 'royal' blood line (whatever that was) was sprinkled and distributed liberally from the Gap to the Rockies.

Now we drop backward to the Arkansas town of River Bend and more about this later.

In two years, at age twelve, Lavinia Brownfield completed her years at Mr. Wilson's school. Her grades were nothing to be bashful about, nor were they thought of as anything special. No one would have thought of anything else from the 'daughter' of Lily Markham.

Lily must have been an excellent teacher of needlecraft because Miss Lavinia was always outfitted in the best fitting, most attractively designed fabric that was available. It was expected that when she acquired a shape other than little-girl slimness, the styles would continue to be appropriate.

She became clever at making small changes that the pattern maker might have done if he had been more artistic. Just little things here and there in the placement of tucks and the method of creating gathers.

It was first mentioned at the Sewing Circle.

"Lily, that girl'a yours sure has come along on her sewin'. I been wishin' I had time to get my Mae and my Ella started."

And...

"You know, I noticed that. I especially liked that white dress that was trimmed with all white in three different patterns of lace. Sure liked that lace, too, and I was certain the girl made it herself."

Lily said nothing. She was no dummy. When her side was winning, what could she add? And why would she try?

'It was good the Mercantile took to stockin' dress goods. I'm hopin' Mr. Jenkins'll get in more of a variety. I like runnin' over to Jacksonville, but it takes a whole day, there and back. I can't afford that too often."

"That little girl sure learned quick. Could'a been partly natural passed down from her other ma."

"Hmmm, well, that'd be a strange thing to pass on in the blood. Anyway, she wouldn't'a needed it with Lily to teach her. Her havin' enough time, and all."

Then, striking at the meat of the conversation, Maisie wondered, "That girl wouldn't have time to be showin' my girls a thing or two. Would she?"

Lily hesitated for an unforgivable length of time. "Oh, well, I hadn't really thought of it. You'd have to ask her, though. I don't speak for her, and she knows what she wants."

"What'd ya expect that she'd want for doin' it? That is, if she agreed?"

"I couldn't say. You'd have to ask her."

But it was later that day that Lily passed on the news. "My dear, don't be surprised if some of the ladies approach you about teaching their little girls how to sew and change patterns the way you do."

Somewhat startled, Lavinia stared at Lily.

"Just wanted to mention it ahead of time, because they asked me what you would charge, and I said that IF you wanted to do it, you would set the price. Now I don't know, or actually care, whether it's something you'd like do or not, but it would be a nice gift to a few busy mothers. I'm thinking you would likely say you would do it for nothing, but you might think about this. I realize money is scarce, and you might do it for nothing, but if you charged a small amount, they would value it more than something given for free."

Lavinia looked at Lily with eyes crinkled with amusement. "You know something? That's exactly what my Ma would have said, and I can just hear her saying it. She would have said to give a gift for free it might have no value, but if someone offers money, that means they expect to receive something worth that amount of money."

"Wise mother you had, my dear. You were very fortunate."

The girl nodded. "Yes, I was fortunate. I still am."

With that she slipped on her apron and dropped the small weapon into the pocket. Picking up her bucket and knife, she left singing, "Thistledown... thistledown... riding the winds that..."

And she was soon out of hearing distance. Lily settled back in her chair by the table and sighed with total contentment.

In was two days later that she, hearing a sound on the second floor of the house, went to the stairway to listen. Soft footsteps... moving back and forth among the three rooms. Soft voice.... Thistledown... thistledown...

Smiling broadly to herself, Lily tiptoed away from the stair. It could be that the girl was investigating the possibility of moving from the toy house to one of the upstairs bedrooms. This would be a huge victory, knowing how she loved the toy house. Maybe....

It was a week later that she commented, while soaping her hair, "That bedroom on the back has a lot bigger bed than the one in the toy house."

"You're right. The toy house bed was picked out for old Miz Markham, and she was a tiny person. The bed seemed to fit her the same way as the house." Lily would like to have said more, but she had learned that more was to be gained by patience. And sometimes silence.

She only had to be patient for two days. She did say, however, that with the toy house bedroom being empty, Theo could move down there.

Lavinia chuckled and reported, "That's what I told him, and he told me 'not on my life.' He likes that attic because he said that no matter how he rolled, he never fell out of the bed. I wasn't surprised. He'd wanted that one from the first."

"That's fine… as long as he's happy. Of course there's the other two bedrooms upstairs."

The girl shook her head. "That won't happen no time soon. He won't mind if it's cold. He never fired up the little stove, anyway. I don't think he'll ever leave that room till he gets married… or somethin'"

8

YEAR 1860

Not that it affected Central Arkansas so much, but it was a thing to talk about. News filtered through, mostly by word of mouth, hearsay, or from the outdated newspapers brought back from the city.

In those days of limited printed material, the newspapers served a unique purpose for the young of the state. This certainly included the children of small community of River Bend, consisting of a couple dozen farms sprinkled around the War Eagle River Valley.

A newspaper, even weeks old, contained printed words in the English language, which was still somewhat difficult for recent immigrants. It provided good practice for the young.

It was also a fount of correct spellings, punctuation, and sentence structure, which made them a good example of grammar for children of third grade and up. It was instinctively known that just seeing and reading correct usage was valuable training.

Then there was the other purpose for the paper before it made its way to the privy behind the house. (Where it was greatly preferred above the catalog with its slick textures.) That third purpose was served by children of second and third grades and up. These were those who, when they could barely puzzle out jumble of symbols that made up the English language, were required to read to their parents who had received no education at all.

This activity served to give the child practice, and to educate the adults as to the outside world. It reinforced the appreciation on the education the students were getting. It also gave the fellows talking material in the Livery Stable, and items were occasionally mentioned in the Sewing Circle.

One visitor to the Livery Stable commented, "Folks over to the east seem right up tight about slaves. I thought they was referrin' to us, till I heard that some was kept and made to work, and even bein' bought and sold."

"Yeah, and a thing like that's gonna stir up a war, just you wait and see."

"There's that fellow, Lincoln... they got him so dithered he don't seem to know which way to go."

"If he'd come out here, we'd show him how work gets done, and then he could maybe make up his mind better."

Wise observations such as these gave way to the abundance of mud-catfish that were occupying the Fishing Lake up on Five Mile Hill. If a body wanted to go to the trouble of drying them, a couple days' stay at the lake provided a valued variety in the meals for a month. Maybe all winter.

Teenage boys were usually the ones to do this because it was a long-wished-for vacation from the plow.

The dried fish could be pounded into a heap of shreds, mixed with eggs, cornmeal and salt, and deep fried in hog lard. With a heap of those hush puppies and a pile of stewed greens on the side, they landed on the dinner table. On a meal like that a fellow could plow at least half the south forty.

But there was still that strange upheaval on the coast. Surely it wouldn't reach as far as the big river... but it did. When it really got started, the war between the states not only spilled into Arkansas, it involved Oklahoma and Kansas as well.

Those from Tennessee, Kentucky and the state of Mississippi, who had plans other than donning a uniform and wielding an Infield, began to filter into the mountains and valleys, and into the practically hidden valley of River Bend, as well as Piney and Calhoun. It was a way to keep from being conscripted. Even Gideon's Crossing began to fill up with those wishing to be farmers rather than soldiers.

A young fellow named Hampton Tuttle brought his bride with him and built her a cabin back up toward Dogwood Bluff. The 'cabin' grew into a mansion of a house with two floors and a total of nine rooms. Absolutely unheard of. He must be expecting to have a dozen youngens.

The thing was, he didn't seem to have any. He hadn't been here a year till he took his bride back to Virginia, and they bought fancy uptown furniture to ship back into the mountains. He also brought back his wife's young sister.

The story about that sister was that she had had a sickness of some kind that caused a fever. Like Starlet Fever or something. When the fever left, it took along with it some of her 'head' sense, it was said, and that she had times when she wasn't all in her head.

The married sister kept her close, and the town didn't see a lot of her, times her sister was not around. The big sister was called Malinda, and the afflicted one was Ollie. Short for Olivia.

It was just the three of them up on the mountain, and they kept rather much to themselves. There were those from the settlement who attempted to visit and were treated cordially, but without enthusiasm. After a while there was not a lot of thought about them, either way. They did what they did, and caused harm to no one. So they were left alone and out of mind.

Then it was rumored that the fellow was killed, no details about how, and the two women were left on the hill. Anyone who trespassed too close would be favored by the whine of a bullet that grazed by their head. That was the mark of a crack shot… to manage to miss a critical spot. As it would have been easier to sight in on a whole person, and make certain he never bothered again. It took skill to graze… and then miss.

Because of this, friendliness and visitation were discouraged, and it was no problem to anyone in the valley as there was plenty to do in the little town… just trying to keep body and soul together. By the turn of the century, the two ladies were getting up in years, but still asked nothing of the town. Occasional trips into Jacksonville seemed to satisfy their needs.

Back to the Kentucky orphans in the year of 1900.

Theodore Brownfield had turned fifteen, and he had spent a lot of time in the Pharmacy, arranging stock, cleaning dust and reading the flood of pamphlets the government sent along outlining new medical preparations meant to heal just about any ailment.

There came the day that John called him into the office, and that was not an unusual occurrence. It was usually to discus a minor change or an update in this or that. Nothing unusual.

The boy settled himself across the desk and waited for the new assignment.

"Theodore," John began with a solid, no nonsense voice. "We're about to make a change here, and it's going to be a big one. I'm dreading it in a way, but in another way I glad the decision is here to be made. The worst part of it is that I'm really going to miss you."

The relaxed, eager expression instantly changed to one of amazed horror. "What did I...? I mean did I forget...."

He didn't get to complete his sentence. John smiled a slight smile, and continued, "Now that I have your attention, I have a very small story to tell. I have always lived in River Bend. My parents came here shortly after they were married, thinking that this small town would be a perfect place to grow the family they would have. They were exactly right, it was a good place, but the family did not come. All they got was me.

"My father did well with his cattle business, which was very important at the time, and when there seemed to be no more sons to require the money, they decided to spend it on me. I really had no choice in the matter, but would likely have chosen the same as they did, if I had been given the opportunity.

"It was decided that, since they could not give the town their sons, they would give it a Pharmacy. I would be sent to Little Rock to the Pharmacy School, which was a two year course. The Barber school was at the same place, and it took only one year, but it was actually possible to cut hair without much knowledge. There were some who simply placed the correct size bowl on the youngen's hair and trimed around it. It worked on hair, but there was no doctor with medicine for the sick.

The best they could do was send me to learn the small amount of medicine that was part of the pharmacy course, and I was put on the list to receive any other information that came available. You are aware of that, because it still comes and you have read most of it. The information might not be particularly helpful, but at least it doesn't harm anyone... at least not that we know of."

By now he had Theo's full attention. Becoming engrossed in the story, it almost slipped his mind to be concerned that he would not be here.

"So my parents used the money to pay my way to school and to stock the business. My pa opened it by selling a few items and telling everyone I would be back in two years with my head full on knowledge. He didn't make any money, but then again, he didn't lose any. Losing money was not something that my Pa would knowingly do. As it happened Pa did the right thing, though I might have liked to have made the choice for myself.

"Now here's where the change comes in. By fall, you will be the same age I was when I was sent to Little Rock. I would like to do the same with you, though I don't know what I will do without you. I may have to beg the services of your sister behind the counter.

"The big difference is, you have a choice. Even if you were my blood son, which would be a blessing to me, I would still give you a choice. I am certain you know your own mind. You have the summer to think about it, and if it is something you absolutely do not want to do, I will find someone else, and you can continue doing what you do now."

Theo stared at his 'Uncle John' as though his eyes could not get their fill of him. "Sir… Uncle John, I don't need all summer. I would love to go to the school, but even if I didn't, I would go anyway. It is an opportunity I would never have thought of ever having."

He heard the stupid rhetoric coming from his mouth and was embarrassed. The words he said in no way expressed what he felt. He would do better, later. Now, he could only lean forward with his face in his hands and further embarrass himself.

He really would do better, later. He promised himself that. But just now he was totally overcome with… emotion…? Speechlessness, anyway.

Lavinia swung her bucket as she climbed the steep side of Dogwood Bluff. The mountain seemed to reach all the way into the sky. This was something that she dearly loved to do, and many tunes came to her mind. The ABC's took their turn, but she always came back to the haunting tune of her childhood. Among them the old tunes from the war between the states …Thistledown… thistledown…"

She saw movement in a clump of wild miscanthia. She stopped statue still, and her hand felt her pocket for her gun. Looking closely she saw the slender green head and the waving tongue, seeking to learn what he should do. Young snake. This year's baby with the multiple green stripes of a grass snake.

Lavinia reached down and picked up a small stick, pitching it in the direction of the reptile. Like a vapor of steam, the little fellow was gone. If she had been a coyote, skink or raccoon, he would not have had the chance to hide. As it was, she had shooed him away to do what he was meant to do… consume insects. He couldn't have bitten her if he had tried. Neither could his parents.

The she picked up the refrain, "…thistledown… fly on…"

Back into the past again.

9

YEAR 1825

Cumberland Gap was a wonderful place to settle. High and windswept. Healthy air, good food, lots of exercise. Log cabins sprang up everywhere. Large families followed. Lots of sons.

Families with lots of sons most always produce a few sons who are prone to wander. Mostly, when they wandered, they went west. The Brownfield's were one of them. They carried with them the interesting origin of their name, and laughingly wondered where were the Whitecotton's.

At the time of the great migration, the small ships often took a hundred days to make the voyage to the new world, and for young people of an adventurous nature, one hundred days were long enough to meet, get acquainted and marry, and to be well onto producing the next generation. Such was the event of Eldon Cotton when he married Isabel White.

The ship's Captain would be glad to marry two couples at once if they had the right amount of coppers. Two for the price of two. That was when Bennington Brown told Marietta Field that they just as well get married at the same time, because he wasn't going to leave her alone until she agreed.

By the end of the day, there were two new couples, Eldon and Isabel Whitecotton and Bennington and Marietta Brownfield. As it happened, these two couples headed west and got as far as central Kentucky when Isabel decided she had experienced enough of having nothing and caught the first defectors who would take her back to the civilization of the coast.

The Brownfield's were more durable and proceeded on until the war with Britton was declared, and then they moved farther to the big river. It seemed safer, somehow, and it was decided that if it seemed that Bennington was in danger of being conscripted for the army, he could just jump aboard a packet boat plying the Mississippi and hide until the danger was over.

Eldon Cotton, now single, joined the rebel forces and was issued a brand new Enfield rifle. Eldon knew what to do with an Enfield, and he fought until he got tired of it and was ready to move on. Colonel Jackson came along and conscripted him into the famous battle of New Orleans where he hid behind the cotton bales and fired potshots at the unfortunate British soldiers who were trained to fight like gentlemen.

Those rapscallion colonists had no idea of the way a war should be fought. They fired off their cannon balls when it was not even their turn, and those Enfield rifles were more irritating than the mosquitoes of the Louisiana swamps.

Eldon was a big man, and it was a good thing because it took a big chest to display all the ribbons he accumulated. History told of the exploits of Colonel Cotton and his great deeds, and some of them were actually true. History lost track of Isabel.

The movement was still toward the west, and the Brownfield's at the Mississippi were joined by other family members, fifth cousins three times removed, and such, and among them was toddler Theodore Brownfield and infant Lavinia. They survived for almost seven years, but then the family was down to three.

That was when Pa took his family and headed out toward the city of Jacksonville, Arkansas, where, the last he had heard, he had fourth cousins, twice removed. How would he have known that the cousins got tired of the 'Brown' and became 'Fields.'

A pair of them still lived up on a bench-land farm on Five Mile Hill just north of the little town of River Bend. They raised and broke horses for the cavalry over in Oklahoma. The Rock Island Line shipped the horses by the boxcar load. Good business for the hard working brothers. Jeremiah and Ezekiel were good business men.

One of the brothers. Ezekiel Fields, had chanced to stop in at the Livery just to see what was new, and got in on the fact that his near neighbor had heard the yowl of a big cat somewhere up near Fish Fin Butts. Those upraised sheets of ancient lava could hide a person or a cat as well as any forest of trees.

"Speck that was the same critter that attack them youngens' Pa. Don't know just where that happened, the boy not rememberin' but a tomcat panther would have 'im a wide huntin' range."

A sigh of concern. "Sure do hope that varmint ain't got 'im a ladylove anywhere near about. Them little bobcats of our hillside cause mischief enough."

It became more serious. "Might come down to havin' to round up a posse and head up into the timber. Can't be lettin' 'im feel a welcome hereabouts."

"I heard tell that when one of them cats tastes human blood, they don't go back to cattle."

"I recall the problem'a getting' rid of that pack'a wolves, but them fellows'll tell ya where they are. Can't keep from nosin' into the air and howlin'. Cats don't do that."

There were nods as the other men remembered.

Then, "The thing of it is, them cats sneak around quiet as a breath'a air less'n they're a'lookin' for a mate, and if that tom's howlin', he's got his mind on courtin'."

Another caution, "We'd do well to remind each other to stay outta the woods and don't pass under a tree th'out lookin' up."

Zeke Fields had listened with interest. They had a lot of horses, including a good crop of foals, and it'd be nothing to one of them critters to take on a month-old baby, and there'd likely be a pair of them if they were hunting.

Later, Ezekiel took his leave, leaped astride his stallion, and galloped down the street, across the bridge and disappeared into the trail up to his farm. About the best thing he'd like to have right now was a dead cat to dismember and spread around their corrals. That was a lot better than putting out poison, as there was no use killing other animals trying to get the panther.

As he took the well-worn short cut through the timber, he let the stallion find his own path while he stared up in the trees. Time to get used to being careful.

Back a few years to the year 1901.

Miz Malinda Tuttle from the mansion on the hill, was facing her eightieth birthday. It was something of a milestone, as she and her sister had existed alone on the hillside for the last 25 years. Managing for fire wood, and an occasional butchered animal, tending the kitchen garden and harvesting the produce occupied their days. Of course, there had been occasional spots of dis-repair in the lovely mansion that had been built for her, but nothing that was a present concern. One day followed the next, and so on.

It was that looming birthday that got her attention. Her little sister, Ollie was nearing seventy, herself, and her mind was no more clear than it ever had been. Since coming to the mountains there had been less stress, and she had more periods of time that she seemed normal. Couldn't count on it, though.

Miss Malinda's own failing health had brought to mind that her sister, being well kept and younger, might well live after her, and something must be done. That took a trip into Jacksonville. She hoped it would be her last, as it was becoming such a drudge to attend to hitching the animal to the buggy.

She managed, somehow, and they were off. It would be a two day trip, and they would check into the new hotel for the night. Old Lawyer Olsen was gone, but his son had taken over the business. It was time to see him about the land.

Of course, when her man had been killed, the land had gone to her, but with no children, she must now designate an heir. Their house and land was in a most beautiful spot, and when the leaves were off, there was a clear view of the whole War Eagle River Valley all the way from Applegate's Mill to the Church bell-tower.

She had given a lot of thought to this document and was sure that it was the best she could do. She had a brother back at the Gap, and he would be the one to decide what to do with the property, and arrange to come for Ollie who, of course, could not travel alone.

She did not communicate often with the brother, as they had grown so far apart over the years, but she now carried a letter to mail to him telling her plans. She also had placed a letter in the house in a special place in the kitchen with instructions for her sister to hand to someone, should something happen with her.

Olivia was to take the letter to the nearest neighbor and ask to be to be taken to the preacher down in the town. It would likely be Old Mister Sisco, but if not, it would be someone. When the preacher read the letter, he would know what to do.

Business taken care of at the lawyer's office, she and her sister walked around and saw the sights of the growing town until they were exhausted, and then spent a night in the new hotel. Very luxurious. Then they headed home with new shoes and new, warm robes to replace those worn to tatters from use.

Malinda's mind was now light and free. She had done her best and would legally pass the property back into Cumber hands. It seemed to be a family crave, to own the land where they lived. Perhaps someone of the family would be ready to move on west, and Arkansas was such a lovely place to live.

The Tuesday Sewing Circle took on the subject of the howling black panther.

"The fellows are thinkin' maybe that cat that took down them Kentucky youngens pa is the same one as was heard howling up by Fish Fin Butte. That's a scary thing."

Short silence. It was indeed scary. "My Oscar, he's been cuttin' wood up on the hill, and we decided to send Edward out with 'im, 'stead'a doin' the fall plowin'. We was thinkin' four eyes'd be better than two when it comes to spottin' the cats in the trees."

"Yeah, the cat couldn't likely take on two humans, and that'd turn 'em off."

Doubtful, but hopeful. "A body'd think so."

Then, "Just thought'a somethin'. Wasn't them two old women livin' up there near where that cat is? Wonder if someone thought to tell them."

"It'd have to be that older sister. That other'n ain't got but a half a mind, they say."

"Yeah, and they've done a good job of it, bein' up there alone. How'd you suppose they manage it?"

"And how old are they? Must be getting' on up in years. I'd think it'd weigh heavy to have an afflicted person like that in the family."

"Reckon they didn't have no choice in the matter. Did you think to bring on that cookie recipe from the paper… the one you used last week? Thought those'd be good for a change."

With an agreeable nod, "Good anytime, for a fact."

Lily Markham couldn't get past being thankful that she didn't have someone cutting wood up on the mountain… and maybe forgetting to look up. Sneaky things were those cats.

Lavinia had taken to checking the toy house regularly to straighten it up, but now that Theo was gone to school, it just didn't get dirty. She spent a little bit of time in the pharmacy when she was needed, but there didn't really seem to be enough to do. Maybe on the next trip to Jacksonville, she'd try to get books from the library.

Or maybe she'd try to write some herself! That brought on a chuckle, but the fact was, someone wrote every book that was ever printed. Books didn't write themselves. That gave her an interesting thought as she picked up the pail to gather greens. Winter was coming on, and they would soon be gone.

10

YEAR 1903

This would be the last year for Theo, and he would miss his school and its challenges, but it would be good to be home and working in the Pharmacy again. He had learned all sorts of new things, and he had whole folders of information that he could catalog and put into the reference books.

Seventeen years old. Pa, I'd give a lot to get to talk to you and thank you for bein' so hard on me to learn about everything I saw. It sort of got to be a habit, and it helped me a lot. Its spring now, and I'll soon be a licensed Pharmacist. Think on that! I know you'd be proud of me, and ...

Well, there were so many things he'd say...

Spring was coming on, and Lavinia was restless. Fifteen years old was an unwieldy age. Too young for this and too old for that and an active mind that needed stimulation.

An old favorite activity was collecting table greens, and that adventure could wrap around so many others. The tall mountain that backed up to the town of River Bend held a lot of options. There were paths and trails that were obviously made by animals, and there were rock ledges and caves. There was also danger, but the small Smith and Wesson in an apron pocket made a difference. And the requirement to make warning sounds, assured that most of the four legged danges would just as soon move on and not be confronted. The legless dangers also responded to human sound and even the vibration of footsteps.

She could hear Pa now. "Make noise. Sing, talk or recite your ABCs. Tramp, break twigs and make some kind of sound. Give the critters a warning."

The trail she chose today took her to the patch of land just below the hilltop house belonging to the Tuttle's. Interesting house, though it could use a little help on repairs, but it was not too bad, actually. Mostly, she saw no signs of life, but that was not unusual for a pair of elderly ladies.

The most notable thing about the hilltop house was that it was so large. Nine rooms, it was said. Who would ever need that much space, even with a big family, and the two old ladies likely rattled around in half the rooms trying not to get lost.

Making her own sounds and listening for others, she worked her way through the trees, ducked under the vines and peeked into the mouths of caves. There were actually very few edible greens in the woodland, but she'd gather them on her way back to the town.

Singing as she went, the sound of "...thistledown... thistledown... float away on the breeze...". Another sound competed with the song, and it was most unusual for the woodland.

"Baa... aaa... aaa." She stopped... stalk still... and listened. Sounds of dry leaves and moving brush, and then a human (?) voice wailing "Oh-h-h-h !", followed by a clear and distinct "Baa... aaa... baa."

She moved, carefully parting the limbs and tiptoeing forward, while scanning both ways. Finally she heard the human voice call, "Singin' angel? You out there?"

Singing Angel? What would that be? Maybe a special bird... the trees were full of them making every imaginable call. Working her way forward, she heard the human voice again, thin and whiny it called, "Singin' Angel, if you be out there, I could use help."

Lavinia sped up her steps, unmindful of legless varmints and halted just before reaching the source of the noise. Another bit of enforced advice from Pa... "...don't be rushin' headlong into the fight. First off, you stay back a tad and see what you got a'goin' on. Could be you'd be knowin' you needed to think of racin' t'other way...."

Gently pulling aside the vegetation, she saw the source of the sound. It was a human, truly, but she was no bigger than a healthy ten year and had hair as white as the rolls of cotton Uncle John sold to sop up blood.

She seemed to be wound up in some kind of a vine, likely muscadine grape, and there were tendrils and whirls almost hiding her. Something was in the tangle with her... some kind of ... animal... ? Seemed to be hairy and white, and it was tangled in the same vines and squirming most dangerously against the tiny woman. Then there was the high, whiney voice of a baby animal, like an "Aa.. aa.. aa.." and it was answered by a motherly "Baa... baa... baa."

Ah! A goat! A mama and a baby, obviously, and all three of them were somehow tied together. The mama goat was chewing with vigor on one of the larger vines, seeming to try to chew her way out of whatever it was that had them bound up.

The little fellow was wiggling and squirming under his mama's feet and in a fair place of getting hurt if she tried to jump or tear her way through the vines. Lavinia had a quick thought that she had never seen vines so tightly bound together, but she passed it off. Obviously these three were desperate to get loose.

She took a step, but stopped suddenly. Pa had said, "…girl, you always look up and then look down 'afore you point that iron baby in your hand and shoot…"

She looked down, and the ground was clear of reptiles. No self-respecting snake would stay around with all this confusion going on. She looked up into the darkness of the trees. Heavily leaved, and full of twisting vines. Dark. Too dark!

Moved slightly for a better view. The creature was as still as a the stones around her, and she would never have seen it if there had not been a pinpoint glitter of light on its eyes and on the shine of the white, stiletto-sharp teeth.

The girl knew instantly what was poised in the tree, sizing up the best place to pounce on the prey that was obviously bound together and waiting for her. Keeping her gaze on the animal, she sought for the chest of the animal, and it was behind a thick limb. Knowing the second best target to be the face, she stared, unblinkingly at its face while her hand moved slowly into her pocket.

Raising it just as slowly, she leveled the small weapon toward the face of the animal, and clearly saw that there would be no ground damage, and that the animal would leap free at the first sound. It was the best she could expect, as she knew her gun to be grossly underpowered for her position.

Her best plan would be to fire once… allow the animal to leap away, and follow with another shot at its retreating body. That would give her enough time to free the woman and the goats and get them into protection.

Her first shot elicited a howl of anger and a flurry of movement on the limb. The next shot was aimed at the retreating rear and lashing tail of the totally black cat before it reached the ground. Then there was the crackle of dry leaves as it scurried away.

Lavinia had known from the first glance what the cat was… but this time there was no big brother to push her down behind the protection of a loaded wagon. There came a time when your protection was in your own hands, and she had been warned about that from the time she could understand.

"I hit it, Pa", she heard herself say aloud, "I was scared spitless, but I know what you said. Thank you, Pa..."

Then the thin, trembly voice of the old woman. "Honey, was it you singin' the angel song?"

Taking in a deep breath and squaring her shoulders, she answered, "I was singin', Ma'am, but it was about thistles. Now I'm going to help you out of that tangle."

On closer inspection, it was not just a vine. The big trouble was a spiral of wound up wire with barbs, and the wild grape vine had circled and twisted within it, creating a knot tighter and more complicated than the thread of a crocheted collar.

With her cutting knife, she severed vine after vine, concentrating on the smaller ones. The goat seemed to be trying to help, with her continuous bleating, and the tiny kid was actively searching for something to eat. He knew where it was, but couldn't get through the tangle of feet to get it... his ma's and those of the two humans. He was noisily registering his own displeasure.

The old woman stood patiently as the vines were being snipped away. The fifteen-year-old girl stood almost a head taller than the snowy hair of the woman, whose hands were thin and bony with skin that seemed almost translucent. Her clothing had snags and rips from the barbs on the wire, and when Lavinia reached low to release her feet from the tangles, her hand was suddenly covered with blood.

Startled, she jerked her hand toward her face. The old woman exclaimed with horror, "Oh, honey, you cut yourself."

Lavinia knew that had not happened, but she didn't know how serious was the wound that had actually caused the bleeding. She hurried. Likely time had become an important element. What were those things... arteries?... that bled until they were stopped?

Then, in a conspiratorial whisper, the old woman confided, "I was seein' that big cat in the tree, but I had to save the goat. She just come fresh. My sister was sayin' we'd be needin' the milk. I was chasin' that cat away."

Oh, this had to be the woman who was… what did they call it? Wasn't always in her whole mind? She couldn't be in her mind and think she could chase away a panther just by yelling at it!

As the last few tangling strands fell away, and the wires were bent back, the baby found its dinner, mama stopped struggling, and the woman stood free. Lavinia stooped to examine the source of the blood. It had streamed down her stocking and into her shoe. Lifting the skirt, she saw the problem was much higher, so she knew she needed to be in the house.

"Miss… uh, Cumber? We gotta take you back to the house so we can stop this blood." Why wasn't she screaming with pain? Whatever the cut was, it had to hurt terribly. Uncle John should be seeing this, but he was at least a mile away.

The woman had a little trouble with the two steps up to the porch, but all in all, she moved along fairly well. Inside the house, Lavinia called out… "Hello? Anybody hear me?"

Silence, with faint echo. Rooms were almost empty of furniture. She called a little louder, "HELLO?"

Then she met the faded blue of the old woman's eyes. "She ain't gonna hear you. She's asleep upstairs."

"Oh. Then I'll just step up there and call her. She needs to be here."

"Won't do no good. I been callin', and she can't hear. She was very tired on the kitchen floor. That wasn't no place for her, so I took her upstairs."

The girl looked at the tiny, frail looking woman. It would seem to be a struggle for her to carry a newborn baby up the stair, let alone, a full grown woman.

"How did you get her up there?"

Miss Ollie Cumber sighed and shook her head. "Weren't easy. Caused a mite'a concern, but I rolled her in a quilt and tied a rope onto the quilt end. I must'a done right cause she didn't even wake up bein' pulled up the stairs."

Hmm, this was getting to be a lot more than Lavinia expected. Or wanted. Well, back to the blood. It had seemed to stop flowing, and was coagulating on her stockings. Lavinia sat her down, and lifted her skirt. There it was… a gash just above her knee… and her tight elastic garter might be stopping the blood.

She found water and cleaned away the blood, then changed the soiled stocking. The old woman seemed not to feel the two inch snag the barb on the wire had dug into her thin, stringy thigh muscle.

"Miss Cumber, I think I'll just step up stairs and check on your sister. She might need somethin'."

The woman was agreeable, but warned, "Won't do no good. She'd been too tired to eat, so I quit takin' somethin' to her. Step quiet will you and don't bother her. I'll fix for her when she wakes up."

Heart pounding, Lavinia found the stairs and started up. Near the top, it became painfully clear what the problem was with the other Miss Cumber. The smell was overpowering, but she continued on. She needed to know what all to tell Uncle John.

Sure enough, there was a tea cup with dried tea stains. Plate with petrified food, and the crust and crumbs on the bed stand, along with mouse debris, where a small rodent had helped himself to the toasted bread.

There was the quilt in a heap on the foot of the bed. The sister was covered over with a thin sheet, over all but her face. It was a face that would not be recognized by anyone ever again. There were the coils of rope that had undoubtedly been used to pull her up the steps. There must be a lot of strength left in those thin arms on her sister to have accomplished that.

And that was not the whole of it.

The whole upstairs was crammed with furniture. Stools and chests were setting around, small tables turned upside down on chest tops and chairs pushed in wherever there was room. Boxes full of miscellaneous items with no relation to each other.

Lavinia stared around her, puzzled over her next move. Someone had to be told, and it would, of course, be Uncle John, and he would, of course, inform Preacher McCrey. But how was she going to do it? Would the old woman be all right while she was gone? Then, again, what else could she do?

Coming down stairs, she faced Miss Ollie. "Still sleepin', wasn't she? I knew she would be. I got a question."

"What would that be?"

"Are you the singin' angel I been hearin' time and again? There was times I thought to go find it, but then the singin' was gone, and I didn't know where to go."

The girl nodded. "Maybe you'd say I was the angel. Sometimes I sing. But, Miss Cumber, I gotta leave for a little while, but I'll be back to check on you later. Please don't go outside until I get back."

The old face smiled, her wrinkles framing her bony face. "I won't go outside. The goat knows where to go with the baby."

Lavinia nodded and closed the door behind her. Sure, that goat knew where to go, and so did the painter. Only they called it a black panther, here. Clearing the house, she broke into a run on the leafy path that was surely the old buggy road.

Lily glanced occasionally up the road. The girl was often gone for a while, but this seemed longer than usual. Something could have happened. At least she knew the direction she went, the girl was good about telling her that.

"John, I'm gettin' worried. I wonder if you'd...?"

John knew if Lily was worried, very likely he should also be worried. "I could toss a saddle on and head out. I suspect she went up the hill?"

And the pharmacist was on the way. About half way up the hill, he met her coming down. "Uncle John! One of those women up there is dead. I was comin' to get you. She's upstairs dead in bed. What do I do?"

"Slip on up behind me, and we'll go back to town and sort this thing out."

"But I told 'er I'd be right back!"

"Do you want to? You won't be scared? The word is she's not..."

"Uncle John, one of 'em is dead, and the other'n ain't much bigger'n I was when we pulled our wagon in to town. Don't actually see nothin' here to be scared of."

Reason told her this was no time to bring up the fact that she had been scared, less than an hour ago. Fact was, no need for anyone to ever know. She had handled the problem and if Aunt Lily knew about the cat, her new mom'd worry herself sick every time she stepped out the door. Then there'd be no more walks.

The man hesitated a moment, then decided she had outlined the situation rather well. He couldn't resist a word of parting advice. "Things get out of hand, you'll know what to do." He wheeled the horse around and disappeared down the hill.

Lavinia turned back. Now… if she could just figure out what to do until help came.

First, she took a puzzled tour of the downstairs five rooms. Almost empty. The parlor was totally bare, but the sofa had only made it into the drawing room. Likely too big for Miss Ollie to move any farther.

That was another part of the puzzle. How did she get the other items of furniture to the crowded second floor… and why?

The why was easy. With a smile, the old woman told her, "Them things was all belongin' to my sister, Linda. They was give to her by our papa. I wasn't wantin' no one to steal 'em while she was asleep, so I took 'em up to where she was. That way, she could tell 'em to leave her things alone."

"How did you get everything upstairs? Weren't they too heavy?"

"They was heavy but I had the stairs. Pulled 'em on up. Took a day… or three days… or? I don't know how they got there. I just looked and they was all in that back room. Figgered that was where Linda said to have 'em put." A smile and a nod of the head as though that explained everything."

"Have you eaten anything?"

"I was a'waitin' on my sister to come down. Yesterday I ate eggs. Now we can have milk 'cause Shaggy had her baby. I was helpin' her to get untangled. Are you the singin' angel?"

"Maybe. Why don't I fix something for you to eat?"

"Oh, I should'a give you tea. Linda'd be 'shamed of me. She'd think I didn't listen when… has she woke up yet? I could tell her about Shaggy. I think a big cat was fixin' to get her baby. Did you have blood on your hand? I remember blood. Linda's my sister that takes care'a me all the time."

Suddenly she stopped and cupped her hand behind her ear. "You ever hear singin' that come out'a nowhere? It'd have to be an angel, don't you think. Do you hear it now? It was singin' a song my mama liked about a girl bein' careful who she married. Linda was. She was real careful. She kept Hamp a'waitin' a sight'a time."

Lavinia cut into the tirade. "Miss Ollie, let me see if I can find some eggs. I'll make you some food."

"Eggs ain't hard to find, course I don't know about angels. I'd go to the henhouse for eggs. Do angels like eggs?"

"Thanks, Miss Ollie. I'll go look in the henhouse." In moments she was back with a pocket full of eggs. Seemingly, the old woman obviously just brought in what she wanted right then. No telling which of these were good... or what?

As she opened the door, she met Miss Ollie on her way out. "I was thinkin' to go listen for the angel. There are some days I hear it, and sometimes it isn't there. Try not to wake my sister. She'll come downstairs when she's hungry."

"Wait, Miss Ollie. I'm going to make us some food. I can make biscuits and eggs, and maybe something else."

Miss Ollie shrugged her shoulders and argued, "I'm goin' to listen for the angel."

With a sigh, Lavinia began singing "... Thistledown... thistle down... float away on the breeze. Many's the time that a young girl in love..."

With a squeal of surprise, Miss Ollie clapped her bony hands gleefully. "You're the angel! I was wantin' to see the angel. I heard it when I went to chase away the cat. Our mama never let cats stay around."

While the girl set the wood in the firebox of the cook stove and lit a blaze, she stirred a batter for drop biscuits, and broke eggs one at a time in a saucer first. Ma always said to do that if there was a doubt.

During that time she sang, "The sun is going down, Lorena. The snow is on the ground again..." And, "Just before the battle, mother, I am thinking most of you..." Followed with "John Brown's body lies a moldering in the grave, but the troops go marching on..."

Miss Ollie sat at the table with her hands folded in her lap, listening. The girl raked her memory for every old fashioned song she could think of... those her mama used to sing. The biscuits browned, the tea was steeped, and the eggs scrambled in the skillet.

Then she explained that angels had to eat, and Miss Ollie needed to eat with the angel, or there wouldn't be any more songs. Eventually she was persuaded to butter a biscuit and eat. It was taking Uncle John forever to get back.

Then they were there. Team and wagon, Preacher McCray, Uncle John's buggy, and two more men who were at the Livery. The next problem would be getting the body out of the upstairs.

Miss Ollie wasn't sure those men should be working around outside, but when Lavinia kept singing she was quiet. When the body was loaded, the wagon left and the next problem was to get Miss Ollie to go.

"NO", she yelled with anger. "I can't leave till my sister wakes up. I'll go wake her and see if she wants me to go."

Lavinia resorted to the truth. "But she's already gone. You can go and see for yourself. I'm supposed to bring you."

The old white haired woman wagged her head from side to side when she saw the empty bed. "I have to wait for her to get back."

With great persuasion and with the preacher and Uncle John on both sides, she let herself be walked to the buggy and helped into the rear seat. Lavinia climbed in beside her, humming the song of the Thistledown.

Theo still being in school, the toy house was empty, and was considered the best (and only) place for the old woman. Aunt Lily had tea (with sedative) all ready and in time the faded blue eyes were droopy, and she permitted herself to be put in the bed 'just for a minute to rest.'

She did not wake until morning, but she woke up screaming and beating on the door to be let out. Her sister would need her to make the tea because she made it so well. Lavinia had been sleeping upstairs, just to watch and be handy, and she came down the narrow stairway just as Miss Ollie managed to open the bedroom door.

The deranged woman rushed to the stairs and climbed up, carefully holding to the protective railing. As soon as she saw the triangular attic room and the feather pad on the floor, she screamed again.

"They stole it away. All my sister's things and they even got the whole upstairs. They took it away. I wasn't to let anything be taken, and I did wrong! Everyone gonna be mad with me. I tried so hard. Oh, I tried!"

Lavinia climbed the stairs and coaxed her down. "No, your sister had to go away for a while. She wanted you to stay here where there were folks who wanted to take care of you."

The old woman was not convinced, but she was not allowed to get out of sight. She was only reasonably calm when her private 'angel' sang, and Lavinia was getting just a bit tired. There had to be another way.

The funeral was held as soon as possible, and those who could get away from work, attended out of respect, and to have someone for the preacher to speak his words to.

"Friends and Neighbors, we're here to say goodbye to one of our neighbors. There is a lot to be said for this lady. She was not born here, but she lived here for near onto five decades among us and cared for her sister. Such a sacrifice will be remembered in her favor in the next life…."

With relief, the box was lowered, and there was no family to signal final farewell, so the custom was adeptly ignored, and the ground was smoothed over. The attendees walked away, each grateful that they had not been called on to make so great a sacrifice of their lives.

It was later that day that Zeke Fields came cantering down Main Street on a beautiful red-gold filly, and stopped in to the Livery Stable to allow the assembled men to admire the animal before he let it go. It was sold to a young fellow over toward Calhoun, and Zeke was giving it a last bit of schooling.

He had another purpose for stopping by, however, and from his saddle pack, he took a large, soft bag… actually a faded pillowcase. Making sure of a suitable assemblage, he drew out of his pillowcase a folded pile of black fur, its pelt hair sleek and smooth. He stretched the skin over a saddle tree and stroked the hair into place.

Every pair of eyes in the stable knew exactly and instantly what fur it was. Eyes were wide and admiring.

"So you got that old fellow that attacked those youngens' pa, huh?"

"Right big one. I can see how a pair'a them wouldn't have no trouble with a grown man."

"Did he come callin', or was you huntin' 'im?"

"That'll be a relief to a lot'a folks, once we spread the word it's been caught."

"What're ya aimin' to do with it… hang it on the wall?"

When the questions died away, Zeke told them, "Was thinkin' I might hang it in the shed for a while, and I'd like to say I was the one to bring 'er down. This here's a lady cat, and she was down in the woods, the dogs sniffin' her out and them bein' way ahead'a me. When I got there, they was circlin' and barkin' somethin' fierce, knowin' she couldn't attack.

"She'd been hurt, and was tryin' to birth the kits and them not due yet. Groanin' and carryin' on, drivin' them dogs crazy. I put'er out'a her misery, and then looked 'er over. She'd been hit with small shot, grazed through one eye, and sprayed shot dust in the other'n. Got infected and…"

"You sayin' she was blind? That someone shot 'er in the face?"

"Shore am. The shot still there, stuck in the flesh on 'er neck See, right here." He indicated a damaged place where the bullet had slid through the skin and lodged."

"You got the actual shot… fer a fact?"

"Yep, and here it is." With that, he fished around in the depth of his overall pocket and took out a bullet shell less than an inch long and barely bigger around than a go-fer match. "Thought you fellows might know what kind'a shot it was."

The group gathered closer, each hoping to be the first to have the answer. It wasn't the most common sort of ammo most of them counted on.

"Been a while since I saw somethin' like that. Wouldn't be too much call for it, I'd think."

Another man, head shaking, "I can say for positive, that didn't come from the Mercantile. Jenkins wouldn't mess with somethin'a that size."

Just at that time, Preacher Joe McCray walked in.

"Hey, preacher, come over here and look at his. Remember seein' something like this?"

Joe McCray picked up the small lead object, turning it over in his fingers. "You know, fellows, happens I do. Back when I was in the seminary, we were given a tad of training in self defense, and it was this here ammo we used because it was cheaper. Fits a baby Smith and Wesson, and maybe others, and that 'baby' bein' so small, it could ride in our Bible satchels."

"You was taught killin'…? In the seminary…?"

"Sure were. Some of the fellows were going into wild wooded areas, not safe places like River Bend. The seminary was thinking a dead preacher was a waste of their money. Dead preachers don't preach."

"Hmmm, well that's interestin' to know, and I can tell you somethin; more. That there looks like what would'a come outta that little weapon belongin' to that Kentucky girl. I got a glimpse, the evening they rolled in. It was a Baby S&W, sure as I'm standin' here."

"You sayin' it'd be that girl that shot that cat? She didn't say nothin' about it."

"Got it right in the face. Up close, too."

"She should'a let us know, so we'd be on the look out for it."

"You gonna ask her about it, preacher?"

Joe McCray had been thinking. "I could likely guess one reason why she didn't mention it. The injury might have been the day she was trying to pacify Miss Ollie, after her sister died. The girl had her hands pretty nigh full that day. Still does.

"Could be another reason for her not sayin' nothin'. Those youngens had parents that gave 'em good trainin' and likely she was to shoot and scare the cat away, maybe from Miss Ollie, herself. Bein' successful, there'd be no reason to say anything at all. At least, right then."

"Hmmm, and her a girl! And there was words said about lettin' her carry a gun around with her while she went walkin' in the woods. That'd give a fellow thought about his own girls, them needin' help of a fellow when they were out and about."

A small pause, and the subject had been rather well talked out. Then, "What'll they be doin with that big house up there?"

All eyes turned to Preacher Joe as he would have the best information available at the time, when John Markham was not around. "Don't really know for sure. I know they fired off a letter to folks at the Gap. Would'a pecked a message out on the Marconi, but there didn't seem no need for speed. Way I hear, young Lawyer Olsen over in Jackson is handling it."

As Zeke Fields returned his interesting black pelt to the pillowcase and cantered away, someone observed. "Well, one good thing. That was a female and the litter was got rid of. If she was the only one, that male oughtta be leavin' soon.

"Yeah, he'll not stick around without a mate."

The next Tuesday came around. Lily Markham had made a platter of divinity candy for the Sewing Circle ladies. The snow white fudge was a wonderful use of extra eggs. It took a lot of the egg whites, and the yolks made wonderful pound cake. The cake, however, was saved for the table. It was John's favorite, with lots of butter slathered on top.

As Lily tucked in the loose strands of her graying hair, she smiled to herself in the mirror. This was one time that she was going to enjoy the conversation to the absolute fullest. She knew the women, and was certain what subject would be covered. And to what depth.

She was right. She put the platter of divinity fudge next to the assembled cookies and took her place at the quilting frame. Needle threaded, and point inserted, she deftly rippled the thick fabric and withdrew her needle. Seven perfect stitches. Neatness and consistency were Lily's strong points.

Maisie, who had a long way of come to the meetings, helped herself to the fudge. "I just love this stuff," she advised, her mouth full. But she followed on with, "I sure am glad that black panther got hisself done in."

Immediate response. "It was better than that. It wasn't a male, is what the fellows are saying. It was a mama full of babies. Got 'er with one shot."

"Yeah, right in the face. Blinded her, seems like."

"What I like is that it was Lily's girl that done it. Didn't even tell no one till she was asked by the preacher."

"Yeah, and it was just 'cause she happened to be in the right place. The fellows was sayin' that old Miss Ollie was all tied up with her goat and the new kid in a mess'a vines. That old barbed fence is vicious when it gets busted and rolled in with the vines. I've had my own slashes."

"That girl took Miss Ollie in the house. We all knowd there was somethin' missin' in her, but a body'd think she'd know she couldn't chase away a panther."

"Likely she didn't know it was a panther. Thought it was a big, black pussy cat. Maybe."

There were several who agreed with her. It was logical, actually, as the old woman had not often been out and around by herself.

Ina Mae McCann left her place at the quilt and brought over the tea pot, warming the cups that cooled so quickly.

"You know, that's a thing that's been in my mind before. Folks hereabouts trainin' their little boys to defend themselves, and their sisters, too. That seems it'd be a strain on the boys havin' to be responsible for the girls, and it's takin' away the responsibility for the girl.

"Then there's them like me, that's only got one little girl. 'Course she ain't walkin' yet, but I decided she'd gonna be like Lily's girl. No reason why she can't do what her boy cousins do. I already made up my mind, almost, and then when I heard about that panther, I knew it for sure. I'm plannin' for Marcel to locate one of them guns they was sayin' were 'baby' guns. Way I see it, that baby was enough to save the life'a Lily's girl, and who knows how many others when those kits didn't get to grow up."

It was a long speech for Ina Mae, who, after years of wanting, now had a baby girl to rock and sing to. Instead of seating herself back at the quilt, she picked up a block of the white fudge and walked to a window, staring out at nothing. Those who knew Ina Mae, would have bet the farm that Marcel McCann would be looking for whatever that was she wanted for that baby, and he'd find it, too.

Old Granny Nelson brought Ina Mae back to attention. "Ina Mae, honey? Would you come thread this needle for me? Seems that the eye in these needles gets littler and littler every day."

Ina Mae turned from the window and threaded the needle, and also her own, and settled herself at her usual position. Needle inserted, cloth rippled, needle pulled, and thread showed eight perfect stitches to the inch.

Her fingers knew what to do, but her mind was still working toward the safety of her precious daughter. It might be Ina Mae more than any of the others who knew exactly how Lily felt about the little girl from Kentucky who came into her life by means other than her birth canal. Years of waiting and wishing put a high value on what they finally got.

Next was Laura Ella Conners. "Reckon there'd be a chance to ask Mr. Jenkins to stock those guns at the Mercantile? There'd be a few of us interested."

Then, "Good idea. Mr. Jenkins'd stock anything he could get if there was a sale for it. He'd likely offer elephants and zebras if there was someone to buy 'em."

Every one of the ladies around the quilt knew, for an actual fact, that Mr. Jenkins would be informed of their conversation, and if it was possible to get the weapons, he would. It would then be up to the ladies to get the fellows to go along with it, and he would be betting on the ladies. Every time.

The conversation could now go on to other subjects. "Was thinkin' we'd maybe get new neighbors on that mansion up the hill. That young fellow that moved in don't seem to be in a hurry, though."

"It's a lot'a house up there. Crowded as it gets at my place, that'd seem like a palace, to me. 'Course, we couldn't afford to buy the doorknobs, likely, and youngens grow up so fast. When they're gone, what we got is all I'd want. That house does seem a far piece from town for most folks."

Lily had been quietly listening, smiling to herself. Purely interesting to see how the idea of a girl with a gun could change as soon as it meant something to the mothers, personally. Lavinia had killed the mama panther and babies, and likely saved a number of lives at the same time. Gave those ladies something to think about… it did for a fact.

She, herself, had something to think about. She had been noticing with sadness the way the young fellows were looking at her little girl, now a fresh and beautiful fifteen. Someone would get her but… please Lord… let it not be right away.

Then that dashing young fellow in the hill top house came out of nowhere and would go back as soon as he accomplished what he came for. Not only that, he had almost unlimited access to Lavinia's company as she was the only one who seemed able to keep the old woman from going completely out of her head.

Seemed clear to Lily that the young fellow should stop fussing with that house and take the old woman back to... wherever... and then maybe come back and do what he had to do. It would have to happen sooner or later. Better to be sooner.

The worse part of it was that he came from Kentucky. He was from over near to the Virginia border, and Lavinia was born nearer to eastern Tennessee, but it was Kentucky, nevertheless.

True... Lavinia did not seem to be taken by the handsome fellow, but she was not indifferent, either. But then, she was always nice to everyone... the way her ma trained her. Smiling and soft-spoken, as a rule.

It wasn't so noticeable when she was ten and her dresses were just below her knees, but now that they were lengthened to nine inches above her shoe tops... and she often twisted her hair into a roll up to the top of her head... Lily watched her lovely daughter with fear in her heart. She mustn't leave with that fellow. She really mustn't....

And Lawyer Olsen had really wanted to send a wire on the Marconi, but the law that had been called out to look things over had refused. No use creating an expense on the town as the old woman was already dead, and the other one was being took in by John Markham.

The letter reached the Cumberland Gap in due time, and was read and re-read by old George Washington Cumber. Hmmm, he had always liked his sister Malinda, and it was a wonderful thing for her to take over little Ollie, and her not all in there all the time. The thinking had been that she would never get better and nothing in the letter said so, one way or the other. It only said that the younger Miss Cumber was being sheltered by one of the local families, and would appreciate a family member to come quickly and settle her and the house.

Old GW had reached his seventh decade of life, and was rather well spent in his legs. For a fact, he could not make the trip alone...

back into the middle of Arkansas to take care of the matter, but he certainly knew who could.

Years ago, he and his wife had produced a family of daughters, good girls everyone of them. They were married and were producing grandchildren at an alarming rate. Then when he had been well past fifty, his wife had produced a son. He had bragged with pride that he now had a son, though this circumstance was sometimes referred to as a 'fall crop' but more usually a 'surprise baby'.

There he was, his son, carrying the revered name of Abraham Lincoln Cumber, most commonly known as 'Linc.'

Now Linc, like other twenty year olds, had his eye on every girl he saw, and had been asking when pa would furnish him with his own place, as he had for all his daughters. So far, Pa had held off. Figured the lad could use a little more maturity, and it wasn't too good for a man to give in to a youngen too quick. Then they'd be wanting something else.

The bad part of it was that most of the girls had their eye on him, as well, knowing that sooner or later he would come into his own with the family money and prestige.

GW must now make his decision about the Arkansas property. It became clear to old GW that this might be a good deal, all the way around. That boy needed to see another part of the world, and he needed to be able to conduct a bit of business. Getting experience, and all that.

The way he heard it, the house in Arkansas was something spectacular and was considered top of the line in the little town. Certainly it had been enough to keep his picky sisters happy for decades. This was made to order for young Linc. When GW was clear in his mind, he would put it into action.

As there was actually a time element involved, it became clear in GW's mind during the night. Come morning, he called the young man into his office and sat him down.

"Son, it is time for you to do a bit of business for me. As my only son, I need you right now, and I have a plan that will see you well paid. There is the house in Arkansas that must be disposed of. There is a partially demented aunt who must be returned to the Gap. All that, you know.

"Here is the next part. I am having papers prepared that will permit you to act in my stead. The house is prime and worth a good deal of money, and you are to decide how much and handle the sale of it. You are becoming anxious to have your own place, and the Arkansas house is yours to sell.

"I will pay for the trip there and back, and for passage of Aunt Ollie, but the money for the sale of the house and lands is yours to turn into whatever you want, back here in the gap. The more money you are able to get for the Arkansas house, the more you will have for yourself when you get home."

"But Pa, that Aunt Ollie, isn't she… sort of…?"

"Yes, Son. She is not only 'sort of'… she is 'totally', and it will be your duty to get her here safe and sound. You will get ready immediately to board the locomotive that runs down through the center of Arkansas and passes through the capitol city called Little Rock. From there you will be on your own. You will have a letter of introduction to the lawyer who is handling the will, and I believe he is in someplace nearby called Jacksonville."

Young Abraham Lincoln Cumber sat on the edge of the chair, stunned into silence. "But Pa…"

"Son, you haven't much time. Also you are now of age to make up your own mind, and in addition to that, you want money from me and I have just assigned you a way to get it. Don't be wasting time arguing. You may get new clothes, and I will give you a handgun. Other than that, you are on your own." In spite of himself, he felt sorry for the lad. He was a stunned statue of fear and fright, and was actually pale.

GW had one more thing to say. "The next words I want to hear from you are, 'Good Bye, Pa.' Now git."

Linc Cumber 'got.' He stood and walked out the door. He felt the inborn 'Cumber Confidence' welling up within him. If he must do this, he could. He was a Cumber, for goodness sake!

11

The town of Jacksonville, Arkansas was up-to-date enough to have a Marconi Telegraph Office. The next communication between father and son went as follows:

"PA stop GOT HERE stop"

By return airwaves, a message came. "SON stop NO SURPRISE stop FIGGERED YOU WOULD GET THERE stop"

He had not yet reached River Bend and his Aunt Ollie

Miss Olivia Cumber was most unhappy and confused. Her house, that she had lived in for so long, and so happily, had suddenly changed. It was smaller, and all the furniture she had so dutifully saved and managed to pull up the stairs had actually been stolen after all, and that was what she had tried to avoid. The singing angel was always around, and that was good. The angel helped her to know what to do. That was important. Still the question. Whatever happened to her sister who could not wake up, and the big house that had suddenly become small?

Life had always been confusing, and now it had become much more so. The best things she had was her evening cup of tea. So tasty and relaxing, and it helped her to sleep and not be confused.

There was the young fellow who came to look at her, and it was strange. She didn't like him, and then he went away. She had no way to know the feeling was mutual.

After the first visit with his aunt, young Linc Cumber decided he would very well be earning the money for the house before this assignment was done. Aunt Ollie was tiny and white haired, bony and wrinkled, and there was a look in her eyes that scared him all the way down into his expensive, brand new boots. In fact, that look turned his knees to jelly.

At least the girl (hey, wasn't she a looker!) agreed to keep Aunt Ollie until the house was sold, and he was ready to go. Then he'd have to come up with some way to get her home. There was likely a law that said he could not bind her with ropes for the trip.

For a solid and truthful fact, he could not do this job alone. He would have to hire help from some woman, maybe two women, to help him get her back to the Gap and into Pa's care. Maybe that girl would consent to help. Auntie seemed to like her, and he could pay her way back home to Arkansas after Auntie was deposited.

He had talked with the lawyer about the sale of the house and was not exactly happy with the conversation. There seemed to be something called 'being over-built.' It seemed that the house was just built in the wrong place. People who wanted to live on the mountainside could not afford the price, and those who could afford the price did not like the mountainside. If it had been in Little Rock or Jacksonville, it would bring a fabulous price.

Back to the Marconi. "PA stop TOO MUCH HOUSE WRONG PLACE stop"

The response shot back. "SON stop DID NOT SAY IT WAS EASY stop"

As it was, it might be hard to sell at any price, due to the history of the other aunt's undiscovered death. How could a house have a reputation? It seemed this one did, and that was bad news for him. Oh well, it was a nice place to stay while trying to figure it out.

He rode his newly-acquired horse down to the little town of River Bend. Quaint and interesting, and there was a lot to see. The place called the Livery Stable always had men who were willing to talk and tell him whatever he wanted to know. They knew about everything except where to find a buyer for the house.

He thought he should keep his pa informed. "PA stop HAVE TO DROP PRICE stop"

Quick response. "SON stop LOWER PRICE AS MUCH AS YOU THINK NECESSARY stop IT IS YOUR MONEY stop"

Well, put that way, he'd just hang around a while longer and see what could be done.

And he came often to look in on his aunt. She still didn't like him, and he was still scared of her, but that girl who took care of her was something else again. Beautiful, black hair and a bewitching smile. Not amazing, truly, that it was she who could calm down the witches that seemed to live in his aunt's head.

The old woman obviously did not understand death. She was sure her sister was somewhere, and people were just trying to keep her hidden to torment her. Then she would seem all right, but in a minute she would say something that proved she wasn't.

Lincoln toured the house again. If he was going to be stuck here a while, he could perhaps make it more comfortable. So far, he had been sleeping on the sofa that had been dragged into the parlor. So he toured the upstairs rooms, weaving his way in among the array of furniture. It was evident even to his young eyes that the furniture was expensive… likely some that was designed in a special way and expected to cost a lot.

There was that bedroom with the messed up bedding, and he didn't really want to go in there. He carefully and silently closed the door, feeling relief at the resounding click as the catch worked. Not even a breeze through the window would open that door.

There was, however, another room with bed and chest. It had only a few light-weight items which he moved out. He pulled back the curtain at the window and was amazed that the whole town of River Bend seemed stretched out before him in a panoramic view. He barely saw the cross on the church, but it was definitely there, and at the other end was the Silver Bridge, obviously new, that crossed that roaring river after it had been joined by the river that virtually fell out of the mountain. What a view!

"PA stop FROM UPSTAIRS WINDOW CAN SEE HALF THE WORLD stop FANTASTIC HOUSE stop."

"SON stop FORGET FANTASTIC PRICE stop DO SOMETHING AND COME HOME stop."

Sure, he'd do something. Saddling up the horse he had bought to come out to River Bend on, he rode down the carriage road noting that overgrown limbs and sprouts had come up in the road. If he got an ax and a hatchet, he could clear some of this out. Then it might be more attractive to a buyer. Pa was seeming to run out of patience with the delay. Never did have too much, anyway.

At the Livery Stable, he was greeted with interest. The fellows had talked out most of their subjects and were ready for something new.

"How's things goin' for you?"

"About like usual. Beginnin' to look like no one wants that house back up the hill."

"Ain't really that, son. They's a lot'a folks'd like it. Just ain't got the silver it'd take to get it."

Then, "Say, you ever considered movin' in and stayin…?"

Lincoln Cumber grinned his handsome grin, causing a slight dimple to form in his left cheek. "Fact is, fellows, I have thought that. I've thought it ever since yesterday when I moved into that room on the south and opened back those velvet drapes. That dim, musty old room was suddenly a bright tower that looked out all over town. Would you believe I could even see part'a this here stable? I think. A body can see half way up Rock Mountain, and the morning sun shines on the river like a blazing fire."

A bit taken back by the vivid description, the accumulated group in the stable drew back, thoughts active. This fellow talked like an educated fellow when he got to going. Talked mighty like the way the preacher did.

"Was there horses back up there when you moved in? I know you bought that bay over in Jacksonville. The ladies up there had 'em a pair they used to run over to Jacksonville about once a year, and come done here to the Mercantile now and agin."

"Still there," was the short answer, followed up with, "I was gonna ask about that. I got a mare, stallion pair and a couple'a fillies. The truth of it is, there's more'n I need, and whatever I do, I need to let the fillies go. Didn't really plan to be here very long, and… well… My pa's gettin' antsy for me to get back and bring the old lady. Don't really know how I'm gonna do that, and I know it won't be without help. No bigger'n she is, she'd still be a fiery handful."

"That's what I heard. What about the goat?"

"Haven't decided. I need 'er till I go. Gotta eat somethin', you know, and milk is the easiest thing there is up there."

"You said the fillies were up for grabs. If you was serious to do it now, you could put up a notice here. Everyone does, and everyone looks at it, sooner or later."

Lincoln looked up with interest.

Another bit of information, "Fact is, right up there on the hill next to you is the Fields brothers, Jeremiah and Ezekiel. They're about the best horse trainers around here and raise some'a their own. Could be they're lookin' for a couple'a brood mares. They'll be down here in a day or two, and we'll point out the note to 'em."

"Thanks, fellow. Right now I gotta find a choppin' ax to get some of the brush cleared out'a the road. Growed up till a body'd have trouble gettin' up there in a buggy if he was to be interested in buyin'. Does the fellow over to the Mercantile carry tools?"

"Yeah, some things. What you'd want would more likely to be at the lumber yard. If he ain't got it, he'll order it. Take a couple'a days to get here."

With a nod of thanks, he turned toward the horse. "Guess I'll go over and see about that," and he rode away. He did not go directly, though, as the Main Street Café was right there in the way, and the aroma of ham and beans was strong for a quarter of a mile each way. Likely even floated across the river.

A comment from the Livery, "Seems like that choppin' ax is gonna have to wait. Them ham and beans have pulled him in by the nose."

"Don't doubt it. Cookin' their own vitals don't appeal to young fellows like him."

Old man Crosley looked up from the whittler's bench and, with poised knife, stated, "Don't appeal to old fellows, neither."

Old George Washington Cumber fidgeted on his bench under the low limbs of the liveoak tree. It was not often that he had regrets over a decision, quick or otherwise, but this had the ability to be one of those times.

A fellow in his old age who finds himself with an unexpected son, shouldn't ought to let him get a couple of states away, much less do the sending of him. It had seemed to fit so well, send him out there, give him experience in selling and develop an appreciation for money, bring back the demented sister, and settle him down with one of those beauties who couldn't seem to take their eyes off him.

And now, here it was going on a month, and he was still there. Old G.W. had sent a Marconi message, but likely the young rascal hadn't been in to Jacksonville to get it. How far was it, anyway, to go into a decent town? The maps of the mid states were still a bit sketchy. Towns and roads were mostly there, but the miles didn't always work out.

Now that he thought on it a little deeper, he should have turned it over to that lawyer... Olsen, was it? He'd know the ends and outs of the place. He could send another Marconi message, but who knew if it would get picked up.

So he fidgeted and squirmed. He really didn't like having to re-judge his own actions and disagree with them. Whatever was happening over there was not worth the loss of his son.

While at the lumber yard, Lincoln picked up a sharp-looking ax and a shiny hatchet. The limb loppers looked so attractive, he got them, too. Turning to leave, he suddenly knew why so many of the horseback riders carried saddle bags behind them. Turned out he had to leave the ax and to poke the hatchet handle and the limb lopper handles into the back of his belt. He could get a lot done with these and come back for the ax.

He did, too. The smaller saplings from the road, and the lopped-off low hanging branches were heaped alongside the trail. Standing back to survey his efforts, he decided he liked it. Removing some of the big limbs would make it look even better.

He had made a list of a few things he needed and decided he really needed to make a trip into the city. Pa would be wanting an update, but Lincoln was not sure he was going to like the one he was going to get.

The thing to do would be to take the buggy. There was that road across the hill top and over to the river called War Eagle. He could follow it down. It might be steep, but couldn't be no steeper than the one he stood on. For a fact, he'd have to take the buggy to bring back the things he needed.

A thought flitted momentarily through his mind, that it would be a much more pleasant trip into the city and back if he had that black haired young lady beside him in the buggy. Maybe she'd let him buy her… a… hmmm, what was there in the city, anyway? Something a girl would like? He'd go early and look around. It would be nice to have something in mind… just in case he got the chance…

Trudging back up to the house with the hatchet and loppers, he thought about all that furniture. He could pull that sofa back to the parlor and bring down the two matching chairs from the other bedroom. There was that side table that could go in the drawing room where the books were, and likely there was an overstuffed chair upstairs somewhere. Someone with that many books should want a comfortable place to read them. There were small tables a plenty, packed boxes everywhere, and wasn't that a rug that was rolled up and tied? Looked like a large one, too.

Then, for the two dozenth time, he wondered how that tiny scrap of a lady could do the moving she did. He might think she found help, but her personality just didn't match that solution. She could act like a little spitfire cat, and it was an unmistakable fact that she didn't like him. Or likely, even the ground he walked on.

First off, he went to the Rock Island terminal where the locomotive turned around and pushed the railcars back to Little Rock. The Marconi terminal was there, and so were three messages. All of them wondering why it took so long, and stating that 'it is time to cut your losses, son, and get on back with the aunt. We'd talk about it when you get here.'

Lincoln Cumber could be as stubborn as the next fellow. He sat down at the table with the composition form. "PA stop THIS IS GOING TO TAKE A WHILE stop I WILL FIX UP SOME THINGS AND PLACE THE FURNITURE stop I PROMISED TO DO WHAT YOU TOLD ME TO DO AND I AM. stop I REALLY LIKE IT HERE AND HAVE SOME THINKING TO DO stop."

He read the three messages from his pa again, and then re-read his own. Pa wasn't going to like it at all, but he deserved to know it. If he wanted to get mad, this way he could get a head start on it. He read his own message a third time trying to determine if it sounded hateful, but it didn't. It just sounded firm.

He did, however, change the last words so it read "...TO DO AND HERE IS A GOOD PLACE TO DO IT stop." A sigh and a nod. Now it was really going to make him mad, but better to get it over with. It was the truth. In spite of Aunt Ollie, he was liking it here, and it was better than a vacation. All the fellows at the livery were friendly, and gave him needed advice. He even cleaned up and went to the little church on Sunday, but Lavinia wasn't there. He knew where she was, and he was beginning to feel guilty about it. Being the 'singing angel' was quite confining.

The time was getting close to decide if he should hire someone to help him take auntie to the gap now and then return? Or should he just give up the house, and eventually termites would settle the matter? Which way to go…?

Miss Ollie was having a lot of silent spells. She stared into space and conversed with nods and head shakes. She ate what was handed her, and drank when she had to. She made her trips out to the privy with the angel coming along. The angel stood protectively by the door until she was ready to come out. She knew the angel was taking care of her, and she was grateful. Otherwise she would be really scared.

It seemed that nothing was right anymore. It all happened when her house shrunk up so little, and the wide stairway got so small it was almost as narrow as she was. There were times that she felt bad because she had let her sister's things be taken away, but she had done everything she knew to do, and what else could one do?

But then, in a few minutes, she knew that she had been in the little house forever, and the big house was a dream. Maybe she had never had a sister, either. Everything in life was confusing.

It was beginning to get dark, and the other person came with a teapot. Her usual evening tea. Somehow she just wasn't quiet ready for it, and it sat on the table until it was cool. Weariness flowed over her, and the angel said she could lie down if she was tired. So she did. Under the quilt, she relaxed and didn't wonder about anything anymore.

It was near midnight, and she heard the howl. It wasn't really close, but she must do something anyway. She sat up on the bed, and the howl came again. Going to the window, she looked out. A fear crept over her as she knew there was something she should do, and she just couldn't hold onto the idea of what it was.

The moon was huge and round and the yard outside the window was almost as bright as daytime. There was something about the yard that reminded her of what she should do. It was something outside, so she lifted the window and leaned out. The ground was very close, not like in her room at the bigger house. Sitting on the sill, she drew up her legs and pushed them through the window. They almost touched the ground.

The howl again. Oh, it was the goat! The goat was all twisted up in the wire and vines, and there was that big cat. That's what she had to do.

Dropping to the ground, she walked on her bare feet toward the sound. There would be a path here somewhere, and it would take her to the goat. Malinda said the goat was valuable for food. Miss Ollie knew her sister would want her to shoo away the cat.

As she started up the path, the gray and yellow striped bobcat leaped from his tree and scampered away. He had just thought he'd call out to see if he could attract a lady friend, but it wasn't worth it if the two-leg animals were stomping about. They didn't usually bother at night, but here one came. Best he leave... so he did.

The grass was damp with dew and felt cold to her bare feet, but Miss Ollie had never had things easy so she pressed on. A thread of memory told her that going uphill meant safety, so she climbed. She couldn't seem to find the wide road, but that didn't stop her. Her thin nightie hung loosely around her bony shoulders, so she hugged the garment close with her arms.

The moon was full, and only scattered clouds covered it. When a cloud covered the moon, she stopped and waited, shivering. When she could see the trees again, she walked on. Walking warmed her slightly, and her frightened mind pulled her onward.

But why was she alone? She was never left alone, so where was the person who should be with her? She kept glancing about. Surely the singing angel would appear and guide her home to safety. She had surely done something wrong, or she would not be here. Alone.

A flowing branch of a brier vine reached out to her, clutching her gown. When it pulled against her, she jerked it loose and walked on. She had not been able to find the road, and the rocks were continually in her way, and must be gone around. She knew she was not doing well.

When she finally had to stop and rest on the big, flat rock, a thick cloud came over the moon, and the mountainside became totally dark. Obviously, she could not go on, so she lay back on the rock and dozed... totally exhausted.

Even the brisk shower of rain did not wake her, and when the first rays of the sun appeared, she shivered herself awake. Wet. Somehow her gown had become wet, so she must find the house so she could change. For the first hour she climbed upward, then stopped, puzzled, because the answer should have come by then.

Struggling with the thought, she remembered that if she didn't go up, then she must go down... so she turned around. Going down was harder, because of the depth of the dead leaves under the trees. Time after time, she slid down and wearily pulled herself up, until the time came that she could not make her muscles work. She laid back on the leaves and curled into fetal position. Warmer that way. Her eyes were so heavy, and she would have gone to sleep sooner, but her feet hurt so bad...!

She had not bothered to examine her feet. There should be someone to take care of whatever the problem was, so her feet would feel better. Even if she had seen the blood from the cuts and scrapes, it would have meant nothing.

She slept soundly under the calls of the birds, the skittering of the creatures in the leaves, and even when the possum stopped to examine her, she was totally unaware.

The female possum had only passing interest. She had feasted well on the crickets that had gathered after the rain, and was leaded back to her hollow log. It was her time, and she needed shelter while her litter transferred themselves from the warmth of her womb to the softness of her marsupial pocket. It was an event she would sleep through.

She did, however, stop and give a moment to the strange object before her. She did recognize the smell of human, and she also recognized the smell of blood. Somehow, the two did not go together. A quick lash of the tongue against the drying blood was not satisfying after her huge meal, so she passed on by.

12

When morning came in the toy house, Miss Ollie's bedroom door remained closed, and that was something of a relief. Lavinia could perhaps enjoy her breakfast before her duty as an angel was resumed. But as the sun arose in the sky, she was suddenly aware that this was not normal. Backing up that feeling was the cold cup of tea... the tea that was intended as a bedtime relaxant.

Tapping lightly on the door, and turning the knob, she peeked in into the room, and her eyes widened at the sight of the wide open window. Miss Ollie never… ever… wanted the window open. It was not safe, she always insisted.

Rushing in, she leaned out and looked both ways. No sign of the white hair under the ruffled night cap. She stepped through the window and down to the yard, scanning every direction. If there were footprints, the rain would have washed them away. Time to get help!

Within minutes the residents of the small town had scattered like leaves before a gale wind, searching every nook, cave and cavern. A person like her… well, there was no end to the places she could be, and she'd certainly not know where she was.

Preacher McCrey galloped his saddle horse up the two mile trail to the hilltop house and pounded on the door. Lincoln Cumber was settled at the dining room table enjoying a breakfast of eggs and flapjacks. He had become justifiably proud of his miniscule culinary accomplishment.

"Come on in, Preacher," he greeted, cheerily. "Pour yourself a cup'a tea and sit a spell."

Preacher McCrey did not sit a spell. He accompanied the owner of the house as every room was searched. There seemed to be an outside chance that she had found her way home to the house where she had spent almost six decades of her life.

The third bedroom was searched carefully, though it should be easy to see a human among the stacked furniture. Nothing. She could not have been in the bedroom where he slept, or he would have heard her.

The room where her sister had been found had not been touched since that awful day, and the ruffled covers were just as they had been left. She was definitely not there.

Together, the men searched the downstairs, the goat shed, the carriage shed where the buggy was kept, and every bush or shrub nearby. Absolutely nothing, so the search was taken back to the town.

After Miss Ollie had slept, she woke up with a renewed urge to somehow manage to get home. Find someone who would help her. There was always someone to tell her what to do, and she must find that person. Or the angel. Confusion settled as a mist around her, but she climbed higher and higher on her bruised, bare feet, though they no longer hurt.

What hurt the most was the effort to clear the confusion. She had obviously done wrong and must find someone to help her make amends. It was late afternoon that she finally met with success.

Her heart beat furiously within her chest when she saw the gate to the picket fence, and the familiar porch columns. Relief swelled within her chest because the house had once more become itself. It had grown back to the one she almost remembered, and she immediately felt at home.

Here would be someone to tell her what to do, and she crossed the porch, opened the door and came in to the room she knew so well. Seeing the wide stair stretched before her inviting her toward somewhere that she knew she would find rest.

At the top of the stair, she looked into a room that had furniture piled everywhere, and she could not see her bed. Perhaps she had made a mistake so she opened the next door. Ah! Success! Just as she had remembered, and Malinda would be near.

She sat on the bed, pulling her slashed and bruised feet after her, she snuggled into the quilts, drawing them up against her chin. Instant peace settled around her, and the pounding pain in her chest quieted.

Just before she dozed into sleep, a sharp pain engulfed her whole body, but that was all right, because she could see her sister coming through the door.

Malinda was smiling her wide, comforting smile and was coming toward her. Her sister was crinkling her eyes with pleasure as she did when she was proud of her little sister's accomplishments. So now, Miss Ollie knew she had done the right things, regardless of how confusing they were, because her sister always had such a beautiful smile when she managed to do something right.

Her sister was humming the tune to the thistledown song that she had sung to her so many times when she was tiny. Now she was singing again, and Miss Ollie sighed and felt no more pain.

The town of River Bend searched for the better part of the day, then decided to alert the authorities in Jacksonville. By evening of the second full day, the message came back that the law would take over, and true to their word, a dozen uniformed men appeared at dawn.

The men thoroughly searched every square yard of the town… exactly as the town residents had done, and with no better success. At the end of the third day that she had been gone, they gave up, stating that if she could not be found in three days, she must have been met by a wild animal. The woodland, after all, was full of them. Bones and all would be consumed. So that was the way it was written up.

Lavinia was torn between the feeling of relief that her ordeal was over, and guilt because she had not checked the lock on the window. No number of people to tell her that Miss Ollie would have known how to work the lock seemed to relieve her.

Down at the livery stable it was discussed thoroughly every day.

"If that ain't the beatenist thing about that old lady. Can't see why she'd try to get away when she was bein' treated so good."

"Now, J.W., you gotta recall that the old lady didn't have half her senses."

"Yeah, but she could do some things."

"That's the reason. She could do some things but not everything. Folks gotta know everything to be in their whole minds."

"Still nothin' showin' up, huh?"

"You know there wasn't nothin' or we'd'a heard."

"Not even a scrap of clothes… nor nothin'." It was not a question, just an exclamation of incredulity. Things didn't just disappear.

Old man Whitner summed it up. "It seems like she was just spirited away to another planet."Could be he was right.

John and Lily Markham stayed close to their home, being weary of discussing the puzzle even once again.

Young Lincoln Cumber finally took himself to Jacksonville and sat at the table in the Marconi office of the Rock Island Spur. How could he tell pa that he had lost Aunt Ollie?

He had been given an assignment, and he had failed. He'd already decided he'd never go back to the Gap, but would find something to do here in Arkansas. If he went back the failure would be held against him for the rest of his life.

With a sigh, he attacked the problem. "PA stop TROUBLE stop AUNT OLLIE SNEAKED OUT WINDOW AT NIGHT stop TOWN AND LAW SEARCHED THREE DAYS stop SAID LIKELY WILD ANIMALS stop REGRETFUL stop."

Response came immediately. "..SON stop FORGET HOUSE COME HOME stop SOME THINGS GOT NO ANSWER stop I WANT YOU HOME stop."

Mixed relief. Pa was not mad at him, seemingly, but still, he had failed in what he had been assigned to do. He was definitely not going home to the Gap until he had thought things through. Maybe take a month. Everyone in the town was so sympathetic and seemed to want to help him feel better. He'd stay here a while and help them help him.

He spent hours looking out his bedroom window toward the town. Some great view he had. When all those separate trees turned their leaves to color, and they were beginning to turn, that was going to be a scene, for certain. What if he just decided to stay a year? There was nothing back at the Gap that was beckoning? What was one year in the space of a lifetime?

Such a wonderful silence, almost like hanging in the clouds. Then there was a sound. The tripping, pattering of tiny feet in a hurry. Familiar sound. Needed to set traps. There would be traps somewhere, and he assumed they were in the shed. He'd go look, and he had just opened the door as the tiny creature scuttled down the hall and disappeared under the closed door of the first bedroom.

Good. Now he knew where to place the traps as soon as he found them. And he had guessed right. The traps had been cleaned, and were hanging on a nail in the carriage shed.

Armed with two traps that were baited with a bit of raw bacon, he opened the door to the first bedroom, and was assailed with an overpowering stench. Backing out the door, he closed it behind him, but the stench had spread out into the hall.

Dead mice? Couldn't be. The one he saw was certainly alive, and a dozen dead ones would not create that stench. Putting the traps on the floor, he eased open the door and let himself into the room.

The covers had been pulled up but there on the pillow was the bush of snow white hair among the ruffles of her night cap. He stood staring for several minutes. Puzzle about Aunt Ollie solved, now what...?

Heart pounding, and in a semi daze, he left the house and walked out in the pasture to the saddle horse. Leaping astride, he headed down the trail to the town. The Livery Stable? Uh, well…

Maybe Uncle John. He'd certainly be glad of the puzzle being solved, but Lincoln somehow did not feel ready for that.

Reaching Main Street, the horse turned east, and just ahead, the young man saw the church. Preacher McCrey! Of course! He was the one who had helped search the house, so he should be the one to tell. And there he was, just going into the church. Preachers had to listen to these things, didn't they? Whether they wanted to… or not…? Wasn't that a requirement that God put on them…?

The words came out all in a rush. "The thing is, Preacher, I just can't figure how she did it. I'd have heard her come in. And we looked. We even went in and looked. I'm glad you were there, or I'd doubt my own words. She climbed that hill on bare feet in the dark, and it rained that first night. She couldn't have done that, but she did."

Preacher Joe nodded, and let him talk it out. Finally, "Some things just have no answer."

Lincoln nodded. "That's the same words pa used. Fact is, I was gone several times, and all day in Jacksonville that third day. That must have been when she came back. What do we do now? Have a funeral?"

"Yes, most certainly there'll be a funeral. Those people who spent more than a day of valuable time to look for her, they deserve a funeral so it can be put by."

"And then we have to… tell the law?"

Small sigh, "Yes, son. But nothing says we have to tell them right away. It might be a week or two before someone will have time to go in to Jacksonville. Nothing can be changed now, and likely the law will be glad to have it over. Then they can correct their books."

"And I have to tell pa."

Preacher Joe said nothing. What was there to be said at this late date?

At the Marconi office, he wrote "..PA stop SHE SNEAKED HOME TO DIE IN BED stop FUNERAL OVER stop PUZZLE SOLVED stop."

The young man walked away and found himself in the Ice Cream Store. "Vanilla, please," and he sat at the tiny table and licked the sweetness, his thoughts whirling. Then he returned to the Marconi office.

"SON stop REPEAT stop LEAVE HOUSE COME HOME stop YOUR DUTY DONE."

But Lincoln had no hesitation, and wired back. "PA stop NOT READY TO COME HOME stop MAYBE NEXT SPRING ".

Immediate reply. Pa must be waiting in the Marconi office, too. "SON stop GIRL KEEPING YOU THERE stop GOT GIRLS HERE"

"PA stop NO GIRL stop BEAUTIFUL HOUSE."

"SON stop DO NOT BELIEVE YOU stop IF YOU CAN NOT LEAVE GIRL, BRING HER ALONG stop GAP CAN ALWAYS USE ONE MORE."

"PA stop THANKS stop WHEN I FIND HER WILL BRING stop HOUSE TOO BIG TO BRING stop HAVE TO STAY HERE WITH IT stop."

"SON stop LISTEN TO ME stop GET YOURSELF HOME."

The young man studied the reply. Pa was being his old stubborn self, and it was Pa's fault he was here. When talking didn't work, he commanded. Well, not this time.

The Marconi faithfully carried the final reply. "PA stop NO stop."

He waited around for an hour, but there was no reply. Pretty much what he had expected, so he picked up his horse at the livery and headed east. In another month he would be twenty one years old, and he was feeling good. It was time for him to become his own man, and this was the place to do it. This was a place where a man could be whatever he was big enough to be.

As he jogged along, the words of the funeral played through his mind.

"....and so, neighbors, we have come to bury our little sister. We will disregard the seventy years because we are dealing with just a few of them. When you think over the actions of these last few days, just feel a relief that you did the best you could for her.

"By the same token, she did the best she could, and she acted as a little child would when lost and afraid. She tried to return to safety and loved ones, just as we would. She did the best that she, a child, could do...."

And there was the rest of the sentence "...best that she, a child, could do, and she is now rewarded with eternal bliss and no more pain or confusion..."

Then he, Lincoln, as a relative, was required to permit the grave closing. Somehow, that had also closed the confusion her ordeal had created in his own mind, and he had buried it with the lowering of the box into the Arkansas soil where she had lived her tormented years.

Aunt Ollie would now be with her sister and at peace. What could be better for a tormented mind that was aware only enough to know that she was not aware all the time? Preacher Joe had been a big help.

13

A letter was now appropriate, as speed was not necessary. It was time to get with it. "....and so, Pa, that was the way it was. She had to have slipped into the house while we were all out looking for her. Pa, the whole town dropped whatever they were doing and spent most of a day and a half searching every crevasse of these hills. They'd have kept on, except it was certain she was no longer alive and the law would have to be called in, anyway. Can you just imagine folks like that?

"It was said they kept to themselves, mostly, and here I am, only been here a month. Good people, huh? So, Pa, I wanted to explain everything so you would know we did everything we could, and she did everything she could. The final papers said she died of "an apparent heart seizure due to climbing the mountain at her age".

"Anyway, as I saw it, the climb up the mountain got her to where she wanted to be... with Aunt Malinda......"

He sealed the letter and would drop it off over at the Land Office where the mail boxes were. Then he'd go over to the Livery Stable and chat. He was becoming at loose ends, and the condition of the paint on the house was beginning to annoy him. He'd talk with the fellows about where to get a tall ladder.

"Son, you sit down and take advice from the old fellows. Understandable, you wantin' to fix up the place. Seems like you're aimin' to stick around a while, but you take look at how tall that house is. You gotta have help. Don't you know not to be climbin' two story ladders without someone around? Too easy to get hurt.

"The thing to do is find someone needin' what you can do and team up. Work together. That's the way of it here, and there's only one house hereabouts with a ladder that tall. The Owen's over to Calhoun got one. You'd need to see about borrowin' and then get some help."

More puzzles. He looked from one to the other of the men, and sighed a frustrated sigh. "How's the best way to go about that?"

"Easy. Thought we told you. Anything you want, you just post a note. If it's here about anywhere, someone'll know someone that'll have a answer. All the folks around here like to help."

Well, yes, he'd been told that, just like he'd been told to post the fact of the two fillies he would sell. Just hadn't got around to it. Note posted, he bought ten cans of Pork and Beans from the Mercantile, another box of matches, ten pounds of flour and a half a dozen candy bars.

Three days later, as he was staring up at the height of his second story wall, a fellow galloped up, pulled the horse to a 'whoa' lifting a small cloud of dust.

"Hey, neighbor. Name's Zeke Fields, and I'm over to the west'a you. Fellows at the Livery said you was aimin' to sell a couple'a fillies. I'm thinkin' I may know which ones. Could be the ones that touch noses with my stud over the fence, and get his hopes up. You set a price on 'em, yet?"

"Uh, well, no. Don't really know what they're worth, to tell the truth. Hadn't been in a hurry to let 'em go, but I'll certainly not need 'em."

Zeke nodded. He'd figured as much. "Tell you what. I know what I'd pay over at the auction, and I'd lose a day to do it. Now, I'd say twenty dollars and the price of my day would add two more to it.

Thing is, if you took 'em over, you'd loose a day, so that brings it back down to twenty dollars each. How'd that do to you?"

Hmmm, well, why not. Here was a neighbor, and neighbors were valuable. He set the price, so it must seem fair to him. "It's a deal. You want 'em now?"

"Uh, no. That brings up another thing. My brother and me, we find ourselves short of space, and we've got a dozen broke animals we have to ship off just to make room. If we got us a deal made, we'd like to leave them fillies where they are for a little while. In fact, we wondered how you'd feel to rent us a little space?"

"Rent? Where'd it be? Truth be told, I ain't quite sure what I got here that'd be enclosed and rentable."

"We figgered that. Now, you got land a mile and a quarter to the west, with no cross fences. If we was to rent something, we could just let the horses run in your pasture, or we could put up a wire if we needed to. We're backed up together and sharin' a fence for a half a mile, like I said, and we'd like a place for the mares that're bred, to keep 'em away from the others.

"Quick as we get animals broke to the saddle and obeyin' orders, we send 'em off on the Rock Island Spur to the army in the Oklahoma Territory. You can see, we're always movin' animals from here to there and back. With a part'a your pasture, that'd cut down on a lot of the movin'."

Lincoln had listened fast while his neighbor was talking. Needed to learn everything as fast as he could. So his land went for a mile and a quarter across the top of the hill to the west, and about a half a mile to the east. Bigger than he had imagined. Set his mind to figuring, and that was one of the best things a Cumber does. Neighbor…land he did not know what he had… chance to do a favor… close enough to swap help… why not?

"Neighbor… Zeke, was it? How about this. I got no current use for that land, and I'm thinkin' it'd support more than them two fillies. Why don't you just count on usin' whatever you want of the land till we decide somethin' different. Be no reason for a cross-fence, as far as I'm concerned. At least for a while."

Zeke brightened. One small duty lessened. "How much'd you want for the rent of that whole pasture, all the way up to your corral fence?"

Another quick thought. Give a favor! You may need one at any time. "Tell you what, neighbor. If you'd make the gate that I know you'd need, why not just turn' em in. We can talk money later, if it comes to me needin' the space."

"Thanks a lot, pardner!" So Ezekiel Fields peeled off eight five dollar bills from the wad in his pocket, and wheeled the horse around. "Got to run. Got things stackin' up on me, but I'll consider those fillies ours, and we'll build the gate. Take care'a the papers later. I've got to run. Come over sometime!" In a whirl of dust and flying horse tail, he was gone.

The height of his outside walls being far from his mind, at the moment, he stepped back into his kitchen, picked up a can of pork and beans, cut away the top with a sharp knife and picked up a fork. Starting to sit down at the table, he changed his mind and stepped out on his front porch. Seating himself on the edge, he proceeded to have his lunch. Wonderful things, these canned beans. Did a good job of filling the stomach and didn't taste half bad while they were at it.

Sound of hoof beats, and a blue roan with rider burst around the bend and pulled up to a halt in front of the porch. "Howdy, neighbor! Name's Spike Westfall. Note at livery says you need a paintin' buddy. This here the house?"

Lincoln swallowed hastily, and nodded.

Spike looked the house up and down and continued, "Don't look too bad to me. Make you a deal. You buy the paint for both places, yours and mine, and I'll go to Calhoun and haul back the ladder. Don't need it on my place, but we'd have to have it here. Tricky thing to haul, that ladder, but I got a log wagon, and I'll be havin' to take a load'a trees to Jacksonville Lumber, and I can swing back around and put it on the trailer."

'Uh... sure man. What color paint you want and how much?"

Spike was ready with the answer. "Take about six gallons, maybe seven, and I ain't too particular about the color. White, tan, yeller... anything but red. My Daisy wouldn't like red."

"I wouldn't either. I'll pick up 7 gallons for you, and how much you think it'd take for mine?" When information was being passed out, any good Cumber man would take what he could get.

Spike slid down from the horse and walked to the corner of the house. "I'd say about fifteen. If you was to get eighteen, there'd be enough for the carriage shed, along with it."

"Good enough. How do I go about paying for the use of the ladder?"

"You don't. That fellow needs my log wagon, now and again, so, me and him, we got a deal. Swappin's the way to go, man. Later..."

With a whirl and a clatter of hooves on the hard-packed ground, Spike was gone. Lincoln followed with his eyes until there was nothing but bushy trees at the bend of the drive. Seating himself again, he picked up the half eaten can of beans.

Grinning with satisfaction, he told the noisy mockingbird, "Bird... this place is pure fun. A body couldn't buy fun like this. Better'n that cinema troupe that comes through the Gap every spring."

Well, it seemed he'd be making a trip into Jacksonville to get the paint. River Bend Lumber sold paint but certainly not twenty five gallon cans of the same color. Besides that, there were a few other things he needed. Ought to write out a list.

Taking the can back to the kitchen, he happened to glance toward a letter clothes-pegged to a nail. Hmmm, well, the letter was sealed, but everything here was his, and that included the letter.

Slitting it open, he found eight one hundred dollar bills in his hand, along with a letter. It read:

"For whom it may concern: My name is Olivia Cumber, and I need help. I may not be able to explain it, but I have been left alone. My sister, Malinda Cumber, is gone, and I need to see Lawyer Olsen in Jacksonville. I have money to pay my expenses, and what is left, give to Lawyer Olsen so he can get me back to my brother in Cumberland Gap. My brother is George Washington Cumber.

I want to thank you very kindly for your help to me, and take enough money to cover your time. I won't be able to answer any questions, but Mr. Olsen will explain and take care of everything.

Thank you very much."

He read the note again. Slowly. Then looked at the huge amount of money in his hand. Clearly, Aunt Malinda had made the best arrangement she could imagine in the event of her death, but Aunt Ollie had not been able to accept it. Possibly it was not really the best of plans, but what else could she have done that would made her sister safe, except to commit her while she was still alive. Of course, she couldn't do that. That would be tantamount to killing her, outright. Looking up, he whispered, you did your best, Aunt Malinda.

It was also apparent that Lawyer Olsen did not know what all had happened, naturally assuming that she had been taken away as he had instructed in the letter to Pa. Well, that was also a reason to make the trip to Jacksonville. Mr. Olsen should be notified, so he could clear out the case.

Finally heading east toward River Bend with paint cans in the boot and in the floorboard of the buggy (he should have taken the wagon, he realized as he was loading them.) And feeling the bulk of the envelope in his shirt pocket, he had more to think about. Lawyer Olsen was surprised, but not puzzled. Things like this happened so often, and death just did not give a warning when it was going to strike.

He remembered Aunt Malinda well. The perfect model of a southern gentlelady, clear in speech with well thought out plans. It had occurred to her that Ollie would not be able to do what she asked, though she had instructed her many times, and her sister had said she understood. She knew, however, that a problem involving her would eventually come to Lawyer Olsen, or he would be able to determine who else it would be. Estate settlement was his specialty.

Aunt had given him the final five hundred dollars to settle the sale and the deed to the hilltop land, and the lawyer handed them to the new owner. He had smiled and shook his hand as Lincoln prepared to leave. "So glad to have this in your hand, son. Now if you have any work of this sort to require help, I'll be glad to do it. I suspect, however, it would be my son who would do the work. He's about your age... perhaps a few years older. So goodbye, and the best of luck."

It had been an eventful and fulfilling day, and Lincoln Cumber wrapped the reins around the resting hook and settled back in the comfortable seat. The animals knew where to go, and there were no choices along the road until they reached the mill on the War Eagle where they would turn to head up the long, long hill. To home. Strange how comforting the word already was.

Among the thoughts that turned over in his head was the wonderful people who had helped him… a stranger. Would there be some way to repay them? He certainly had the money, now, but something told him that was not the thing to do. The same thing that told him that, also told him that this was not a question to ask the fellows at the livery. They were all among the volunteers who helped.

But what? And who?

When he saw the silver bridge up ahead that signaled the War Eagle River road, he made an instant decision. Two choices. He would go through town, right down Main Street, and make a decision. The only persons ruled out for asking help was the Pharmacist and the Preacher. The Pharmacy came before the church.

He stepped inside to be met by a wide smile and a head of shiny black hair, piled on her head and secured with combs. Could that be Lavinia? Or… of course it was! It was the hair. Wasn't it? She looked so grown up, and he knew she was sixteen.

When he found his tongue, he asked, stupidly, "All alone?"

A toss of the head. "No. Uncle John in right through the door. Shall I call him?"

"If he isn't too busy, I'd like a minute."

And there he was. "You had a question? Why not come in my office and have a seat."

It was a simple question, but Uncle John looked doubtful. "Son, you've come to the right place, but you got the wrong person. Lavinia, go see if Aunt Lily is available."

She was, and Lincoln found himself seated at the kitchen table with tea and cookies. She listened thoughtfully, and took a moment to answer.

"There is a way. I'm not sure you can work it out, but paying money would be most inappropriate, as you thought. This town operates on the 'swap.' The people knew they did you a great favor, but it was what they would do for anyone. And they would never ask for pay. If they accepted money for something that did not cost them money, it would seem that you had hired them and they are very proud.

"I'm picturing that lovely house up on the hill. In the winter when there are no leaves, we can see it from Main Street. Your aunts were lovely ladies, but they did not blend well with the town, and did not come to the Tuesday Sewing, so they were not well acquainted.

"A fact is, the ladies would love to see the inside of the house, and get a look at the unusual furniture they think is there. Also, no matter how much they wanted to see it, they would never have asked.

"Now, if they had a chance to go through the house freely, they would most certainly love to look at everything. Not as though they were visiting, but more like a party… or perhaps a tour."

Lincoln watched as she smiled, an attractive crinkle formed around her eyes. He had never met his mother, but wondered if she might be that attractive. "But Aunt Lily, the sad thing is, the whole place is a mess. It was that way when I got there, and I haven't helped at all. I don't think I could…"

Lily breathed deeply, sipped her tea and pushed the cookies nearer to Lincoln. "Give me a moment, and I think I have an idea. If there is anything the River Bend ladies understand it's that one can't have company with a messy house. One of the other things they understand is that they know what to do about it. And this is something I could help with.

"I could select about six or seven ladies who would dearly love to go through that house from top to bottom and do a 'spring turn-out' they call it. Cleaning, airing, curtain washing, cabinet cleaning and totally mouse-proofing. And I know what they would like in return. It would be an even swap and wouldn't cost you a thing."

He reached for another cookie, and brightened. "What do I have to swap for a 'spring turn-out'?"

Lily smiled again, with crinkle lines beside her eyes. "I seem to recall that when that house was build, the builder… your uncle?… ordered blossoming shrubs to be put all around the outside. Those bushes have multiplied, and though I haven't seen it recently, I know there will be dozens of rooted cuttings around the parent plant.

"I could pick ladies who I know would love the bushes, and they would dig the bushes themselves. If they were to be given... say, ten rooted cuttings each, of whichever plant they chose, they would love it. These ladies share and trade plants all the time, but they do not have the althea, crepe and bridal wreath that you have.

Cookie gone, he stared at his hostess. "All those bushes... they bloom? I bought a hatchet and an ax and was going to chop them out of the way! Can you believe it! I guess if I didn't get it done till spring, I would have found it out, huh?"

The minute hand on the wall clock made a couple of rounds. "You think the ladies would do all that, just for a few bushes? I couldn't help at all with the cleaning. But I could dig bushes. You really think they'd do that?"

'I know they would. Most of the ladies could go through their yard and say, 'I got this from so and so,' and 'this was where that house burned.' 'And this was for my birthday.' 'Come fall, I'm giving so and so a start of this.' That way, their plants take on importance, being tied to friends or occasions.

"There's another thing. These same ladies would help you give a house-party so everyone could see the whole house. You could invite the town, and they would be there. You can bet on that."

"Hmmm, what could I... I mean, wouldn't there have to be food or something...?"

"Easy. Just ask the ladies what you should buy to give a really nice party for the whole town. They would have such fun deciding, and then cooking. Then they would insist on serving it."

"I have one more question. Why would they do that and me a stranger?"

Lily nodded understanding. "But remember, it isn't for you, totally. It's for themselves. Life is very routine here in River Bend. Safe but not exciting. Parties make a day something special to be looked forward to, and be planned for. A lot of it would be for them. I could pick the ladies who would have the time, and they would talk about it. Others would help them make plans. They're the same way about weddings. The town loves for occasions to be important.

"Take my word as truth. This would work, and your expense would be the food and drink, and every lady would create her own specialty… one that has been proven in previous parties. If you decided to let them roast a pig in the back yard, they'd take care of that, too."

Mouth full of cookie, he nodded his head. Then, "I know I want to do this. You just tell me how. Actually, though, I'm not sure I could be trusted to pick up the food ingredients. That's an unknown territory for me."

Lily's smile again. "Give me a few days, and then stop in again. I may have more ideas." Dropping the rest of the cookies in a convenient sack, she handed them to him. "You go, now, and think about this. Just don't worry. This will be no problem for me."

She stood, dismissing him to digest what she had told him… as well as the cookies he'd been enjoying. Cookies in hand, he climbed aboard the expensive buggy, actually a carriage. The horses had a wonderful rest, and now they could pull this load of paint up the hill. All in all, this had been an exceptionally wonderful day.

Something he remembered from being a little fellow and riding with Pa. When something good happened, be sure to look up, because that had to be where it came from. From the tilt of the buggy and the steepness of the hill, if he looked through the windshield, he would be pretty much looking up. So he did.

14

And he would finish the day with another thing that was good. He'd write to Pa and catch him up on the news. He was painting the house, and giving a party. 'Pa, I want to thank you again for this trip and this house. You couldn't have given me a better present.'

In one of his Marconi messages, Pa had heatedly suggested if a girl was keeping him here, just bring her on home with him.

"Well, Pa, when I find that girl, I will bring her for a visit if she will agree to come, but then I will bring her back to our home.

"Another thing, Pa, I've looked around a bit, and I know for a fact that one of these girls is mine. She just doesn't know it yet, and I'm not sure which… but I'm thinking I may have a preference. Pa, how old was Ma when you married her? ……"

Lincoln Cumber was kept fairly busy for the next two weeks. What with his massive house, and then Spike's house, all he could think of was paint and his sore right arm, as well as the blisters on his palm. A body would have to admit, though, that the fresh paint made that house shine like diamond.

That he was busy did not, however, keep him from thinking. It wasn't so much a 'pay back' for a favor as it was an appreciation gift that he wanted to give. That the town ladies would enjoy examining his house and furniture was a puzzle and a surprise.

He had not ever thought that he understood women… or girls. And now he was totally and unassailably certain that he did not, and like a lot of other fellows, he was not certain that even women understood women. They did, however, seem to have a better understand than he did, and for that reason, he was humbly and gratefully appreciative of Aunt Lily's help.

If she said it would work, then who was he to second guess? She also wanted a little while to give thought to how it was to be done, and for that he was also grateful. For right now, it was enough to dip the brush and slather the paint. Climb down the ladder on aching knees and refill his bucket. Climb up again on calf muscles that seemed to be on fire.

Lily Markham was a neatly dressed, quiet spoken lady, but that was only on the outside. Inside, she was a watcher and a thinker. She was careful to examine all angles and study a problem from various positions. This had been her habit of a lifetime, but had become more pronounced after Miss Lavinia Brownfield had ridden into town with her brother.

At that time, her thought and views had become colored by how they would affect the girl. Never attempting to be a mother, as such, she considered the girl a gift that was handed into her care. For a while.

It was that 'for a while' that was most disturbing to her. Girls married and then maybe they stayed around… or maybe they were gone. It mostly depended on the fellow, and young men were often unpredictable. It seemed to take a few more years for them to become settled into what they would eventually be.

She had begun noticing the young men who were friends of Theo. It was likely from these that Lavinia would make her choice. Admittedly, the knowledge was often scary to her. But what could she do?

For one certain thing she was truly grateful. The girl was a lovely child, but she was not beautiful. Grouped with other girls, she held her own well, but no one would have immediately singled her out as 'a beauty.' Thank you, Lord. This would likely give her a chance to be herself instead of the constant center of attention.

On the other hand, the time would come when a choice would be made. Was it a mother's place to guide her daughter? How much 'guidance' could be given before it became 'bossiness'? And what if the person who cared most was not actually the girl's mother? A lot to think on, but that was what Lily Markham did best.

She had not given much thought to young Lincoln Cumber, as he was here to sell his house, take his aunt and go. But then things began to change quickly, and he was still here. It was clear to her that the boy's father would be trying to coax him home, but, so far, he had resisted. Stubbornness was often a plus.

That was a point to remember, but from Lily's position, was that a plus or a minus? Was it a mark of stubbornness or a fact of knowing his own mind? Then when the trouble occurred with Miss Ollie, and she had to be taken away, he was solicitous and caring toward her, though she was afraid of him, and he had never known her. He seemed to know his duty to her, and was thankful to Lavinia as the only person who could manage the poor, demented old lady.

Then came the wish to repay the town for the help, and he seemed to know where the best advice would come from. That was very flattering, but often young men of substance were taught to use flattery to get their own way. Somehow, that didn't quite fit the fellow from Kentucky as he tried to fit himself into the Arkansas town.

He was quick to agree with Lily's first suggestions, but was that just to get the matter of 'repayment' over with? That also did not seem to fit, and then when he frankly admitted he did not know the bushes around his house were expensive and beautiful shrubs, she was again surprised. He also did not realize the local value of them to the ladies who would value a 'gift' of a shrub greater than one they had purchased from the mail order house. They instinctively knew that gifts tied friends together, and one could never have too many friends.

All of these words and incidents were logged into her mind, and to the plus side, Lily added in the fact that he had performed unaccustomed labor for two weeks just to get the house painted, when he knew for certain that the paint would not help it to sell. That was definitely on the plus side. One did not paint a two story house just because he had nothing to do.

It was beginning to turn out that she knew more about the handsome, black haired newcomer than any other young man in the town. At this point, being perfectly honest, her plusses and minuses were just about even. It seemed that whatever he did, it could be judged two ways.

No matter how much she thought, she always came back to the irrefutable fact that it was from the local young men that Lavinia would make her choice.

It was then with apprehensive relief that she decided to make a step in the direction of guidance. Seeing the young man in the Mercantile puzzling over the tall cans of salmon verses the little flat cans of sardines, being a new item in the store. Finally, he picked up one of each and turned to come face to face with her.

As she passed by, she whispered, "Stop in when you have a chance' and then she was gone. He stared after her with interest. Did she have another answer for his attempt to integrate into the town?

Hardly an hour later, he was again at the kitchen table with tea and cookies. Through the window he could see Lavinia with her hair tied up in a scarf, and the breeze fluffing out her apron as she stirred. From the steam coming up, he thought it might be from the soap pot. He was right.

Though the girl loved the fragrant soap bars that come wrapped individually in their own papers… they were for hands, face, and body. For her hair, there would be the lye soap her ma had said was healthy. She did not look around and would not know he was in the room.

Lily Markham's eyes missed nothing. The young man definitely enjoyed the sight of her though she did not know to what degree. She began, "I've given some thought to what you said about not being able to shop for the party ingredients."

Now she had his whole attention. He had turned away from the window and reached for another cookie.

She continued, "I'm certain Lavinia would be knowin' where to get everything and she…"

His eyes widened, and he cut in, "But I couldn't take…"

Lily lifted a hand to stop him. Her whole being leaped with pleasure at those four little words spoken so quickly, but she would now finish the sentence. "…and she could take along a friend, who would certainly know. Most of the girls her age are well acquainted with party foods. But I thought of something more. Next week her brother will be home for a vacation break, and I'm sure he would like to go along. He might be helpful in locating certain stores."

She paused. She knew for certain that Lincoln would have had no difficulty in finding stores, and she knew that HE knew that she knew. She was just using the 'southern lady' way of making an important suggestion.

Lincoln Cumber knew how to field this one. "Oh, are you sure he wouldn't mind? I know he would be a big help." A foursome. Girls along. Safety. He had been taught early that girls had that strange thing called a reputation, and that fellows had an obligation to see that it was protected. Even before they were quite sure what it was.

His eyes drifted momentarily back to the window. She was carefully dipping and pouring the scalding gravy-like substance into the forming trays to harden before cutting into squares.

Then he was back with his full attention on his hostess. Lily added, with a smile crinkling around her eyes in a conspiratorial way. "If you were to stop over at the ice cream store with them, it would be a lovely party, and I'm certain Theo would love to go along. I think he's about two years younger than you, but he'd rather not be reminded of that. We did notice, however, that eating is his favorite pastime, and eating ice cream tops everything else."

Deciding that she had said enough, she stood and again filled a sack with the remaining cookies. "Take these along with you. Lavinia loves making cookies, and now she'll get to make more."

And he was gone. His purchases and the cookies in his saddle bags (like he had noticed the other fellows used) he headed up the steep trail, his head whirling with thoughts of every kind. Aunt Lily must have decided that he was going to stay in River Bend and had decided to help him fit in. That part of the 'fitting' would include her daughter and son, was a huge plus to him.

Nearing the top of the trail, he gave a bit of attention to the bushes that he had been about to slaughter with his new ax. Hmmm, well, it did seem that they had small ones coming up all around. If he was to lift some of those and set them back beside the trail in the skips, he could eventually have the whole trail lined with them… all the way down to Main Street.Something to think on, anyway.

Lily Markham sat at her table and reviewed the conversation in her mind. The boy would surely never know what it meant for him to have blurted out so quickly that he could not expect to take Lavinia in his buggy for the day… alone. She could still hear those four beautiful words… "But I couldn't take…" It was obvious there was not a doubt in his mind about that that.

If she was to again line up the plusses and minuses, the conversation she just had would stack up on the plusses side, for certain. There was a long way to go, however. She looked out the window just as her pride and joy was scraping the last of the gooey substance into the forming trays. True, she was not beautiful, but so, so lovely, and she moved with grace and confidence. Lily's heart ached with love for this gift that had been given her, and wondered if mothers of blood daughters had these sudden attacks of gratefulness.

Then on to the next step in her plan. She had early decided that if the party became a reality, she would choose Edna Rollins to spearhead the project. She was a fanatic on cleanliness and efficiency, and she was a natural 'take charge' kind of person. She instinctively knew how to accomplish without hurting feelings. And, naturally, Edna would choose those she wanted to work with.

Edna was quick to plan, and almost instantly decreed there would be three partial days of cleaning, and maybe four, and then the men with shovels would arrive to claim the ornamental bushes. It was a wonderful swap both ways. Then, as Lily had said, the party would be for the whole town.

As for the food preparation, Edna, herself, decided that any lady who wished, could help. That insured that there would be no hurt feelings.

Theo was happy to make the trip. Very close behind his love for Ice Cream came his pleasure in the sight of Susannah Leverage, his sister's closest friend. The girls sat in the back of the fancy buggy and chatted, giggling and teasing the fellows. The fellows rode ahead enjoying every syllable of the sound they pretended not to hear.

The huge boot of the buggy was packed high, and other items were stashed around the girls' feet. It was to be a 'disregarding the expense' party, and Lincoln was positive he was getting his money's worth.

It was on the way home that he commented on the song Lavinia had used to pacify Aunt Ollie. That one about the Thistledown. He thought he had heard it, but had never quite figured what it was about.

Lavinia was quick with the explanation. "It was a war song. Our ma said it was about the soldiers comin' and goin' and lookin' good to the girls who was left behind when their fellows got conscripted. There was those other songs at the same time, like 'The sun in going down, Lorena,' and 'The girl I left behind,' and 'Tenting tonight on the old Camp ground.' And there was that one, 'Just before the battle, Mother, I am thinking most of you.'

"Those were written for the fellows and the way they felt, but 'Thistledown' was for girls, warning' 'em about the way the fellows was likely feelin'. Turned out the song had a tune folks liked, so they kept singin' it after the war was over."

About a quarter of a mile of silence followed, and then Lincoln wondered, "Would you mind singin' it? I never did hear all the words."

Lavinia cut her eyes quickly toward her brother, who nodded. "If you think you want me to, I'll sing it. I learned the words from our ma, and I think they might be right.

"Thistledown… thistledown… float on the air.
Where you come down, there is no one to care
But God and the thistle seed always know where."

Then she explained, "That's the chorus and it was mostly what I sang to Miss Ollie, but this is the verses:
"Now, lassie remember the words that I say,
Hold tight to your heart and don't give it away.
A long happy life on these words will depend,
Before you're a lover, you must be a friend.
"A friend is a diamond to wear in your heart.
A lie and the thistledown, all are a part
They'll leave you to grieve, and ride off on the wind.
Before you're a lover, you must be a friend.
There's laughing and singing and sweet words to say,
And the sound of the bugle will take them away.
There's no way to know how the battle will end,
Before you're a lover, you must be a friend."

The sound died away, and there was another quarter mile of silence. The message was painfully clear. There had been a lot of stories around the Gap… about the soldiers… the dead… and the battles that went first this way and then that.

Finally Theo rescued the conversation. "From the stuff we got here in buggy, this party'll be enough for the whole county. Likely gonna have folks from Calhoun and Piney linin' up for a share."

Then Susannah. "I like gettin' all that coconut. Miz Edna makes a fruit bar outta apples and raisins and a lotta coconut that're really good. I hope she makes some."

Lincoln found his tongue long enough to answer, "Then we'll ask her to do that. That will be your job, Susannah."

Then Lavinia, "What's my job?"

Her brother was quick with, "You can keep the flies shooed off."

"Aw, it's too cold for flies. Well, maybe not. It'll have to be out on the porch 'cause that kitchen ain't big enough for the whole town."

Back to Lincoln, "Only one thing. I'm truly glad it ain't me havin' to figure it all out."

Susannah giggled. "Miz Edna wouldn't let you come close. Gettin' to do this here is like getting' a Christmas present, for her."

And then the conversation took off again, chattering and giggling all the way to the silver bridge.

Miz Edna was ecstatically pleased with the party ingredients and assigned them to the hand of each who would be part of the preparation. Through some sleight-of-hand magic, she had converted the young billy goat into piles of sausage stuffed into tubing and pinched off like a string of rosy red beads. The little fellow was young and tender and was actually the one saved from being cat food by Lavinia's apron pocket weapon.

The sausages would be displayed on the massive tray she found in the Lincoln's kitchen... solid silver and appeared to have never been used. A bit of silver polish and a lot of elbow grease promoted it to its intended shine. One table would furnish an endless supply of the spicy tubes of meat and surrounded with every known variety of pickled vegetable... the only way, actually, that goat sausage should be served.Everyone knew that.

The heaps of sausage would stave off starvation while the fish were being fried. The fish were local river cats seined up from the ponds of Cal Boudreau, to be cleaned and filleted by a few drafted husbands. The Frenchman who grew the fish, raised them on the mineral water from the springs spouting up from Rock Mountain. They were locally known to be the absolute best... just ask the household cooks from Jacksonville, where the fish were mostly sold.

Along with a couple of bushels of baked potatoes, the whole town could be easily fed, and leftovers were sent home by those who consented to take them.

The big attraction, though, was the massive house with the huge rooms, and the fancy, up-town furniture. Few houses were ever examined to the extent Lincoln's was, and it would provide conversational topics for the next couple of years.

The view from the upstairs bedrooms was marveled after, and they viewed with silence, the furniture of the room where the Cumber sisters had each been taken from this life.

All in all, it made a long day. Lily Markham attended with interest. She was by nature a watcher... the way a farmer watches the clouds for rain... the way a stockman examines the metal shoes of his horses. She watched the way a cook attends the cake batter, and fisherman watches for the jiggle of the cork, indicating a fish was taking the bait.

Lily watched the young women… the teenage friends of Lavinia. She noted their wide eyed enthusiasm with the pictures on the wall, the depth of the parlor carpet and the design of the cut glass in the door panel. Behind the excitement in their eyes, was a look of longing. Lily watched… and wondered.

During this time, her daughter was enveloped in an apron and outfitted with a slotted spoon for dipping the browned fillets of fish from the smoking fat to the platter.

Lily watched Lincoln Cumber as he moved comfortably among the groups, answering questions when he could, and shrugging off those he couldn't, or wouldn't, with silence and a grin.

It must be said in Miz Edna's favor that she insisted on coming back the day after the party to 'tidy up' which took most of a day.

The planned foursome trip to Jacksonville for supplies had been an open door for others. When Theo was available, and he had been making a point of being home on weekends, there would seem to be a thing or two to go to the city for.

When Theo was not available, it was easy to recruit another friend, and Lincoln was put in position of chauffeur for the three young ladies… not a bad position, actually. Especially when it promoted Lavinia to the front seat of the buggy beside him.

Of course, it was normal for young people to look for something to do while they were sorting themselves out, and a buggy trip, with ice cream involved, seemed to fill the bill rather well. At times they included their driver in the fun, but often the girls tossed their conversation back and forth as though he was not there.

This put Lincoln in the enviable position of being able to study and watch, to listen and learn. Susannah Leverage was an unmistakable beauty. Her conversation animated, eyes that sparkled, hair softly brown and shining. She was very easy to watch.

Elsie Mae, daughter to Miz Edna, the organizer, was often the fill-in rider. Elsie Mae was handsome, as a thoroughbred filly was handsome. Miz Edna would do no less than bring up a sensible daughter. Olive skin and rosy coloring, dark liquid brown eyes trimmed in dark lashes. Infectious laugh, and marvelous sense of humor. Elsie Mae was a welcome addition to any group, and one of Lavinia's favorite friends.

Lily, the watcher, noted all of this. Lavinia was friends with the most beautiful of the young ladies of the town and she was sure that the young man was not blind. Neither would he wait around forever, but was that bad...? Or good...?

Lavinia would pick someone, somewhere, sometime, and she turned seventeen burying herself among the other girls. Somehow, though, Lincoln seemed to have no problem with it. Was he some kind of a pushover... who would let girls push him around? She had heard there were fellows like that, and if they were not pushed around, they were not happy...? So she sighed and turned to other thoughts and duties.

Lincoln, on the other hand, seemed to have the talent of being the recipient of gifts thrust at him. Recently the Fields brothers, Jeremiah and Ezekiel, had left their duties and took a ride over to his house. With a proposition.

Their handyman and groom, who was hired to care for the horses that were not currently being 'broke' to the harness and saddle, sincerely wanted to help with the breaking, rather than caring for the mares and foals, and keeping the breeding charts. Or taking extra animals to the auction when they did not fit the strength and confirmation of the customers in the Oklahoma Territory.

The two fillies they had bought from Lincoln had finally given them the idea. What the brothers really needed was another partner who could match them in contributions to the partnership, and his huge pasture would just about do it. If they could take him on as a third partner, it would free up the hired hand who was not actually adept at record keeping, and they were sure Lincoln was... if he would just agree.

They had also decided that he would need to furnish a large shelter, or possible several smaller ones for general care of the young animals for the first couple of years while it was decided if they were 'keepers.' There was also a need to keep record of the brood mares, and they would need shelter at times.

The crowning asset owned by Lincoln was the hilltop pasture equaling a half a square mile of grassland. It was worth a half day of shutting down their own activities to persuade him, or at least, get him to think about it.

They gathered around the kitchen table and talked. Lincoln listened to one, then the other, and began to place himself in their plan. He did not, however, have any particular experience. It would take some book study and a lot of on hand experience. He had been knowing that he would be looking for something profitable to do, and what could be better than to work with someone who wanted and needed him?

While they continued to talk, he had decided that he would not be able to be worth one third of the profit, as they were talking of, but his mind was figuring and putting skill against profit, and came up with his own offer.

"Here's what I can do, fellows. I really like the idea, and I want to try it, but I have so much to learn, it would have to be like this. The first year, I would take one fifth interest rather than a third. If things work out for the three of us, the next year I would take one fourth. Then, if I was not worth one third on the third year, I'd go find something else to do. Could you go with that deal?"

The brothers looked at each other, then at him, and before they could speak, he added, "I think four sheds would be about right, and they could be put about half way from your place to mine, or maybe a bit farther your way, wherever we find a place flat enough for sheds and corral fencing."

A short silence. "And one more thing. I don't ever have to put a saddle on one of those ornery stallions or actually get on their backs. I ride only on educated horses or four wheels." That drew a relieved smile from the horse trainers.

It seemed to be a deal, and a handshake seemed to be enough to seal it. So Lincoln had a job and permanence. He would also be taking animals to the Jacksonville animal auction, a time consuming chore the brothers did not like.

15

Lavinia had moved into an attractive seventeen and found things to do. She still liked to wander the mountain to collect greens.

She still taught beginner sewing to young girls whose mother was too busy. It was not a job she sought, and she taught only when specifically asked.

She sewed her own clothing, from the skin out, and sometimes made a new shirt for her brother. She went to the Tuesday Sewing Circle occasionally with Lily, but it was not a regular thing for her.

Lily watched, and as her daughter moved into a lovely, ladylike seventeen, the handsome fellow on the hill turned twenty two, and Lily was sure there was talk of what was going on. Amazing that he had not already selected one of River Bend's attractive young ladies.

The ladies tended to watch their words after the situation with the gun and the black panther, but a fellow like that one would naturally attract the attention of mothers of marriage age daughters.

They would never admit to others that their gentle and friendly attempts to lure him to Sunday dinners had been skillfully turned aside for this or that reason. Surprising that the young man had things to do with the horses on a Sunday, but that was the way it was, and discussions continued. He was, they agreed, a most unusual young man.

There was the lovely spring Sunday afternoon that the fancy buggy came down to town and picked up three attractive young ladies for a drive out to see the dogwood trees in bloom on Dogwood Bluff. Admittedly, the trees were a spectacular sight, and the new grass in the pastures and the shiny Black Angus cattle who grazed there were also a sight. The road wound around up the bluff and then down, with masses of the white blossoms on every side.

The girls often left the buggy and walked around under the trees, even picking bouquets to take home. Their patient driver spent his Sunday with that little chore, and smilingly drove them to their respective homes. Lavinia was last.

She still wore her Sunday dress of pink ruffles and lace and was somewhat hidden behind the mass of blossoms she had picked. He was not invited in, today, but he did have an unusual request from her.

Would there be a day in the next week that he would be able to get away, and if so, would he come on the saddle horse and not the buggy? There was something she would like to do.

As he climbed the hill, he reasoned that if she had wanted him to know the plan, she would have told him, so obviously he was not to know. No problem. Maybe there was something to do with the horses, not that he would be much help. He did know that they had a couple of animals to go to the auction but no arrangements had been made. The team that had brought the brother and sister had produced regularly, and it was actually possible for the town people to become horse poor if they didn't sell a few ever so often. That was likely it. Anyway... it didn't matter.

But when he arrived, he saw her little single seated buggy harnessed and ready to go, and he could drop off his horse back in the corral, please. She'd meet him in the buggy.

Hmmm. Alone? Totally alone? Well, she was looking at eighteen soon, so perhaps... well, he'd see. There was no Susannah to come along. She and Theo had firm plans that included only each other.

Somehow, this seemed to be an item of interest to pass around. Theo was bearing up well to the teasing, however, and was busily at work in the Pharmacy. There were a lot of new things since John had gone to school, and a lot of new products were offered. Theo took care of those.

Lincoln stepped up into the little buggy that was occasionally referred to as a 'courtin' buggy' and clicked the team into action. She'd tell him what was going on when she wanted him to know. He could imagine his pa in this situation. "Girl," he would demand, "tell me what's going on with you and me, or these wheels don't roll."

With a slight inward grin he thought of that, and how different he was from his pa. There was the other thing, also. He would never be as successful as his pa, but that didn't seem to be a problem to him either. Every time he thought of that, another thought that was more interesting crawled in and scooted that one out of the way. Like so much waste of time.

There was not nearly so much conversation going on as usual. With Elsie May and Susannah along, there was hardly a completed sentence. Chatter like a flock of geese going overhead. Not that he cared, of course, he didn't hear half what was said, and it seemed that was the way it was meant to be. Mostly, he could have been a paid teamster... so much a mile for his services.

Lavinia relaxed against the corner of the seat and looked around. Pleasantly inactive. And quiet. Was he expected to start a conversation? If so, where did one start? If he was given a list of possible and acceptable subjects that would be of interest, without doubt he could hold his own. Still silence ruled.

They passed the silver bridge, the gravel of the road making a conversational crunch amid the faint jingle of harness rings, with the clap and slip of the pony's hooves keeping time. Sweet riding little buggy this was. Good springs.

The Dogwoods were still blooming on Dogwood Bluff. There were several with pink blossoms instead of white, and they were a little bit later than the white. There were spots of pink around one of the houses on the hillside.

No comment from his passenger. They had gone at least two miles in silence, then she commented, "Couldn't ask for a better day for a trip."

"Sure couldn't," he stupidly replied. *Lincoln, say something important. This is a chance of a lifetime so don't blow it. Hmmm.*

She was first. "How are you getting along with the horses? I'll bet they're keepin' you really busy."

Did she mean was he too busy to come to see her? Or did she mean he couldn't do the job in a shorter time? Uhhhhh. Think of something.

Finally, "Oh, I'll be fine just as soon as I learn to speak horse. I find myself talking Appaloosa to the Roans and Roan to the Paints. But I'm working on it."

About a hundred yards of silence while he beat himself over the head. Such stupid nonsense, Lincoln. Couldn't' you do better than…

And at that moment she began to giggle. Slipping a handkerchief from her bag, she covered her face to hide her laughter. When she could speak, she told him, "When I was little, I kept thinking one of our horses was named Haw and one was Gee, but pa just couldn't remember which was which. I didn't mention it to him because I didn't want to embarrass him."

Relieved, he chimed in, "My favorite word is 'Whoa.' The mares have already decided I'm a pushover. My partners say it takes time. One thing about it, those animals love my pasture. It hasn't had anyone grazing on it for... years? Maybe...?"

Now that it was going, the conversation lasted for at least four miles then died away... a natural death. There was a long spell of silence during which she made no attempt at conversation. Then, when Jacksonville was dimly in view, she discussed their itinerary.

"If you have something you need to do, I'll be all right at the shoe store. It takes me a long time to get my size right... and then I need some sewing supplies. That store is right next door. I'll be fine until you get back."

Hmmm, is she saying she wants me out of the way for a while? Or that surely I have some business in town. Or that I don't have to stay with her and be bored? Which...?

Be brave, Lincoln. Dive right in. "Miss Lavinia, here's a little secret. What I'd really like to do is walk about a step and a half behind you and carry your packages while you look at everything you want to see."

She turned to him, full face. "Is that the truth? You want to carry the packages?"

Deep breath of relief. "Sure do. Or maybe take them to the buggy and lock them in the boot. Then come back for more."

Which is exactly what he did. Young Mr. Lincoln Cumber learned more about women's things that afternoon than in his whole twenty two years of breathing. He learned how yard goods was measured, that needles had a dozen different sizes, that thread came in about a million colors....

He learned that perfume came in tiny, tiny bottles, and must be sniffed carefully. He learned it had to be sprayed directly on skin to REALLY tell what it smelled like, and he was amazed to learn that when the lady ran out of available skin on which to spray scent, she had a right to use the back of the hand of her escort (and buggy driver). After sniffing each perfumed spot several times, she settled on one she liked best and bought it.

He learned that patterns for clothing were purchased from a picture book on a tall counter. They sat on high stools and turned pages. Apparently there was a need for the interesting items that go under a dress and are not usually seen by the public, to remain secret.

Anyway, she chose a couple of styles and was handed an envelope, which she paid for.

He noticed that stockings came in fifteen shades of brown and tan, and they must be studied closely to get the exact right one, though only about four to six inches of them were ever visible to the naked eye. There was eventual success, though, and she bought two pairs.

Then they looked at mirrors. Small ones with a handle to look at the back of the head. Strange, he had never thought of that. Girl's hair always looked good in the back... or else it was messed up all over like they just woke up. The bad part was, after all the examining and inspecting of mirrors, none were just right, so she didn't buy any.

Then the shoe store. He sat in a nice chair and wondered if he should get a pair for himself, but decided against it. He likely had a bit to learn just by watching. True enough, she was hard to fit. It might be that, in the future, if that salesman saw her coming through the door, he might decide to take the rest of the day off.

Rejects were stacked eight and ten boxes high, and the poor fellow was up and down the ladder at least fifty times. He finally got it right, though, and she bought two pairs. She paid and he picked up the packages. Not enough yet to make a trip to the buggy boot, but they were piling up. What was next?

Seemed like there was a little store that sold spices and fancy tea, but she had a note in her bag with the kinds needed. Apparently this was for Aunt Lily. Only took a few minutes to buy, but another few minutes for her to examine a few other products which she didn't buy.

Then turning face to face with him, she said, "Ice cream?"

"Sure thing, if you're sure you're ready. We're not in a hurry, you know."

"I'm ready. We'll go right by the buggy and get rid of that load. I always like strawberry."

"Huh...?"

"Strawberry ice cream. I wasn't sure you remembered, so I told you before we got in there."

"Miss Lavinia, I knew exactly what kind you liked. I remember everything about you that I've ever known, and I will never forget." He grinned at her amazement and took the key she handed him. The packages hardly made a dint in the size of the boot.

The last several trips to the ice cream store had found him sitting at the tiny foursome tables with the three young ladies, as Theo was often busy. He remembered hearing chatter… the same as a flock of black birds echo-locating before as they gathered to migrate.

Today, they sat across from each other, and she concentrated on the cone in her hand, the pink ice cream contrasting nicely with her creamy-tan skin and black, black hair. As he ate, he took note of the brown checks of her dress sprigged with yellow and orange flowers in tiny clusters with green ferns. Tan collar with the same flower clusters embroidered on each side.

Many things escaped his notice, but girl's dresses were not one of them. He wondered momentarily if the decoration on the collar was furnished with the fabric, or had she created it. He noted the slight gathers at the shoulder and the elbow, creating a slim silhouette. Was that the way the pattern came, or did she sculpt it herself for effect? Delicate lace on the cuffs and around the collar. It would have to have been handmade in order to match so well.

He was aware that she often taught beginners (mostly little girls) the basics of stitching. She had to be good at it, or the ladies of the town would not hire her. Pennies were well counted in most households… but then, so was time and the value of a skill. So the ladies must think they got their money's worth.

Down to the last of the ice cream, and the little pointed end of the cone was popped into her mouth. She looked up with a smile and raised eyebrows. He was sure that meant she was ready to go. She had said not one word during the time in the shop.

He nodded, and she picked up her bag and they left. The trip home was about the same. Restful silence as she rode along, short conversations or observations. A three hour trip of relaxed contentment, as near as he could see. He was not particularly pleased to see the silver bridge ahead.

They passed Bosom's Boarding House, the Land Office, the Livery and Annabelle's Hat Shop. At the Pharmacy, he turned in and guided the pony to the corral.

"Lincoln?"

He turned toward her. "Yes?"

"Thank you."

"Uh… well…" He purely hated to be caught off guard.

A wide smile and a twinkle of her dark eyes. "Thank you for being a friend."

"A friend…?"

"Yes. The sewing ladies said it wasn't done. That fellows would not do what you did today?"

"What I…?" There was a puzzle in here somewhere, if he could just figure it out. Then he'd know the answer.

"Fellows are not supposed to be patient and carry packages and ride along quietly. They have to tell ladies how things have to be, and what to do. I just wondered if what they said was true."

A full two minutes of looking into her face, and the amused twinkle in her eye. A sigh as it became clear. "So I was being tested, is that it?"

A smile was the only answer he got. Well, he could give as well as get.

"Let me tell you something, young lady. The time comes that I don't want to walk behind you and carry packages, and admire the way you walk, and the way your hair shines, that'll be the day I'm dead. The time I don't like to watch the shoe salesman sweat and groan looking for the shoes for your very attractive feet is the day they can bury me. And for that matter, watching you eat pink ice cream is a heap sight more fun that watching that wicked stallion munch hay by the bale."

Still no answer. Just a smile.

So he concluded, "Just so you know it, Miss Lavinia, I'm tough. I don't know about other fellows, though I hear a lot at the livery. I do know that today was clearly one of the best days of my entire life, and any time you want to do it again, you know how to find me." A meaningful pause, then, "So there!"

The back door opened and Aunt Lily's voice, "All right, you two, get on in here and get washed. Food is going on the table."

They obeyed.

But it was when he was in the saddle headed up Five Mile Hill to his house that he mulled over the last conversation in the buggy.

Thank you for being my friend. Friend…? Wasn't he always a friend? Somehow he didn't think the word was used by accident.

And it was later as he stretched out in his upstairs bedroom and pulled up the covers that the strains of her Thistledown song re-played through his memory. 'Before you're a lover, you must be a friend.'

Of course! She was telling him she was open for single dating and maybe discussing something permanent. She made it as plain as a lady politely could.

He had a lot of thinking to do, now. At this point, he must NOT do the wrong thing. How could he tell her how he felt? There was sure to be a good way to tell her. One that was as smooth and natural as she had told him.

Then, again, why was he attracted to this particular girl? There were girls who were clearly prettier than Lavinia. There were the chatty, friendly ones so valued by fellows who had trouble thinking up the right thing to say. There were girls who seemed much easier to understand… who were clearly open to friendship, and it was somewhat of a puzzle to figure where Lavinia was… or was not.

So his thought whirled in a dizzying pattern as he climbed the hill. But wherever his whirling thoughts landed, they were forced to admit to a relaxing and enjoyable day. But was that what he really wanted… forever?

The roosters crowed him awake at dawn to the remembrance of a new chore for today. It amazed him at the amount of paperwork and record keeping that was required by a horse breeder/trainer to do business. Not that he minded… record keeping was something he had a lot of experience in. He rather liked the solid, black-and-whiteness of record books, furnishing instant knowledge of profit and loss. He had done a lot of it for his Pa, with all his small businesses and real estate holdings back at the gap.

This was, of course, quite different as he was dealing with live animals that ate, jumped fences and got the colic. Horses' bodies looked so solid, it was hard to believe that their innards could be delicate at times.

And today's duty would be to move Emperor into the corral with the seven mares who were ready to breed… to keep him from tormenting the young fillies and colts. Who were not. Small chore, actually.

After breakfast, morning milking and feeding, he was on his way to the breeding pen a good half a mile away. He was comfortably saddled on Lazy Lady who loved to amble along but would trot if her rider insisted. Lincoln decided to insist, just to keep her in practice of taking orders.

The huge black stallion was waiting at the gate. At least, Lincoln didn't have to track him down. The size of the horse was a bit daunting to one not accustomed to actually handling the animals. Most of his experience had been in guiding a saddled animal or steering a buggy or wagon. Pa usually had things for him to do that were not with the animals.

So be it. He was ready to learn. He guided Lazy Lady up to the gate where the locking-bail was put over the locking post for extra security. It was amazing how clever some horses could be at opening enclosures meant to keep them in. Or out.

He lifted the metal bale and laid it back over the locking post, and the gate began to swing open. Emperor was not in a mood to wait for the gate to swing open enough for his well-fleshed body, so he gave it a shove with his shoulder… and pushed on through.

Lazy Lady saw she was in position to be bumped by the swinging gate, so she reared her front hooves and whirled. Spinning her rider off her back, she landed her feet in the handiest spot, part of which was the upper part of Lincoln's foot.

At his scream, she instantly stepped off and bent her head around to see what was his trouble.

Jagged pains shot in every direction as Lincoln told himself he would not… nay, could not… afford to pass out from the pain. He fought to pull his wits together for a decision. Somehow he had to get back on that horse as it was much too far to walk for help. Lazy Lady was agreeable and stood with head hanging down as if apologizing.

There was no way he could leap into the saddle with one foot, so he hopped, agonizingly, back to the gate and its metal bars. Securing the locking bale over the gate, he pulled himself up to the second bar, making himself a foot closer to the saddle. Lazy Lady stood quietly, watching his efforts.

The pain was too great to lift his left foot, and too injured to hold his weight so he could lift the right foot. There was only one way to board and that was to lean over the saddle belly down, dead-man style, and trust the animal to know what to do. He did. And she did.

At his 'get up' she ambled back toward the barn. The injured man was grateful that the mare did not like to trot… for that would have been frightfully painful, and his hold to the saddle was precarious.

In due time, the animal got to the barn and stopped, waiting for orders, or for someone to open the gate to the coral.

It was still early spring, and the mountaintop was covered with a dozen shades of green as everything leafed out. Lavinia had washed a tub of unmentionables and pegged them to the drying line. Deep breath. The air smelled like spring and reminded her of the hills in Kentucky. Good day for a walk.

Even better… it was a good day to collect some of the various edible greens, now a few inches high and just begging to be gathered. Pail in hand and snake gun in pocket, she headed up the hill.

Young, spring rabbits everywhere, but she was not hunting rabbits today. A rotund mama skunk waddled across her path followed by three roly-poly babies, likely engaged in their first outing. She wisely stopped to let them pass as Mama skunk knew she would.

A mountain rattler, not long from the birth ball, was nestling in the leaves, and raised his head, flicking his tongue to test the surroundings. He shouldn't have done that.

Lavinia moved her hand slowly into the apron pocket and closed on the gun. Such a harmless little reptile, hardly a foot and a half in length, but she well knew that a mountain rattler was born with poison fangs, and there was talk that the very young ones had more poison than they would have later, because it helped in securing food. Clearly, he had to go.

BANG! The light weight ammo for the small gun was enough to separate the rattler into two pieces. She dropped the weapon back in her pocket and kept climbing. Beetles and ants would make the rattler carcass disappear before sundown.

The man on the horse, in such an undignified position, heard the shot. Hunters! He had not always been glad to have hunters on his land, but this time he was instantly grateful.

"HELP! Anybody hear me? I need HELP!"

Lavinia stopped, motionless for an instant, then ran. Lincoln's house would be hardly a quarter of a mile on up the hill, and that seemed to be the direction the voice came from, and the voice sounded eerily like his.

When she reached him, he had lowered himself to the ground on one foot, and was leaning heavily against the saddle. He left foot was suspended a few inches off the ground, and blood dripped freely from the toe of his shoe.

"LAVINIA! Can you help me get this shoe off?"

She shouted back. "NO! Leave that shoe on! Don't take it off!"

The girl's thoughts raced through her head as she ran the last few feet, then sat on the ground yanking off one of her own shoes. Stripping the stocking from her leg, she wrapped it snuggly around his lower calf and secured it with a knot.

She waved aside his attempted explanations and dashed to the corral. Hitching a horse to a buggy was second nature to her, but she knew Lazy Lady. Nearest to the barn was Dasher, a young paint. If they ever needed to 'dash' this would be the time, and he allowed himself to be led by the mane into the buggy shafts.

The young animal galloped as fast as the steepness of the hill would permit, and no words between the two in the buggy seemed adequate. At least, the blood was no longer dripping.

"Whoa" brought the paint to standstill amid the skid of gravel under the wheels. Lavinia leaped from the buggy and yelled into the Pharmacy. "THEO! We've got a broken foot. Hurry."

He hurried. Between Theo's broad shoulders and Uncle John's helping arms, the injured was conducted into the nearest thing to a doctor's office that River Bend had.

Leaving the tourniquet in place, the young pharmacist cut away the shoe. Flesh scraped away to the bone on the upper part of his foot, and one toe broken. The middle one.

Theo, surveying the damage, commented, "Only good thing is that it ain't the big toe that's broke. Takes longer to heal, and make it harder to walk. If the ground hadn't been so soft, you could'a lost all of your toes."

Even after the pain medication, his foot still throbbed. Of course, Theo would be right, but it was hard to see any good in all this. Especially when he replayed the accident through his mind. Of course the waiting stallion would be eager to get through the gate, so he should have dismounted, left Lazy Lady standing a bit apart, and let the horse through. It was his own fault, no doubt about it, and that did not bring any comfort, either.

Fortunately, neighbor Spike was ready to fill in on his chores. He was always ready for a swap, and he already knew what he wanted. He would do the milking and feeding for the next couple of weeks and also check in with Jeremiah and Zeke to see it there was something else urgent to be done.

What he wanted in return was a pair of Lincoln's guinea hens so he could raise a setting of eggs for his wife. She had always known that guineas were better watchdogs than watchdogs were. They stayed near their home property, and they saw everything that went on, setting up a quacking-squawking racket when they did.

His wife also knew that a flock of adult fowls would not stay on a new place so it was useless to try to buy a start. Spike had decided, however, that if he could get a rooster and a hen, maybe two hens, he would keep them in a tight pen until chicks hatched, and the chicks would be attuned to his own place. He had that plan already in his mind because he was sure the outlander on the hilltop would need more help, sooner or later.

So now it was sooner, and he had the capture pen all ready. Likely the adults would set up a quacking howl for a month or two, but so be it... sometime down the road, he would have his own guineas, something that his wife so greatly wanted.

Lincoln hardly batted an eye over his speedily offered plan. It was very much like Spike to have an agreeable plan, and it was necessary to stay on the good side of such good help.

"Tell you what, Spike, old man. You take all of them squawking fowls you can catch. If you get too many, I hear they are all dark meat that is more flavorful than the tenderest breast meat." Actually, it was marvelous that he had such a wealth of swap-out material just scratching and clucking around. And the fact also was, Spike'd never catch them all.

He spent a wakeful night in the lower bed of the toy house. Theo went home to his wife and left the injured to think over his mistakes. But that was not before the eventful evening meal.

Theo's wife, Susannah, had been invited, and the six of them passed through several topics of conversation, and came, naturally, to the incident on the hill. The injured man was truthful, sparing not his own stupidity. Theo was heartless.

"Man, don't you know anything about horses?"

"I do now."

"But you, at your age…?"

"I know. You'd think I knew better, but my pa kept me busy at other things. He had grandsons to take care of the animals."

With a shake of the head, Theo commented. "Man, oh man! That was really stupid. I'm thinking you need a keeper."

A slight pause as the humble recipient of the harsh words, shrugged and turned dispiritedly toward the girl beside him. "I reckon so. Do you want the job?"

He was as surprised as the other five at the table at what words had just come from his mouth. A painful quiet settled around the heaped dishes of food and silent silverware.

But Susannah, who had been picking delicately at her plate, insisted on an answer. "Well? Answer the man. Do you want the job?"

With a half smile, Lavinia shrugged, and replied, "Actually, I wouldn't mind."

And the thing is, proposals of marriage are strange things. Some are stated in so many words, and others just seem to be timely words spoken at the moment. The latter instance had rescued many young men from days… nay, weeks and months… of agonized thought, and are most often spoken from the depth of truth. It almost seems as though guardian angels who have charge of humans have pity and arrange those appropriate 'slips of the tongue' that are not slips at all

Either way, Lincoln's mind might be whirling yet, while he over-analyzed his feelings. As it was, he had apparently proposed marriage and was accepted, and escaped the whole ordeal of asking the scary question. Not only that, there were witnesses.

Theo had a slight snarl of disgust that his friend, and likely future family member, should get off so lightly.

Susannah, who actually had prompted the decision, was inordinately pleased. Now her friend would be available again for foursome entertainment, and if it happened to be at the hill top house, so much the better.

16

A proposal over a plate of food, prompted by an injury caused by stupidity.

Uncle John was still trying to figure out what happened, and Aunt Lily signed a breath of relief. Step one had been taken, so when the next step, the wedding, was over, her daughter's future would be assured. If only he did not decide to take her back to her homeland... and his. She did not expect that to happen, because Lavinia had a solid anchor to the valley... her pharmacist brother. Another anchor was the unsalable house.

Lavinia was calmly spreading butter on her bread. Nothing had happened that she had not planned to happen... it just happened a bit unexpectedly soon though not unwelcome.

It was three days after the eventful meal that Lavinia had ridden up the hill to check on his well-being. And, it was after two days of intense thought by Linc about what to do for an engagement present for her.

Would she like to be taken to Jacksonville, or even Little Rock, to pick out a gift? Would she prefer a surprise? One problem with a silent girl, it was hard to know what she wanted until she told him.

It was when he had gone into the aunt's room to check his traps for rodents, that he chanced to open a bureau drawer that he had locked during the open house. The reason? Jewelry! Lots of jewelry... the kind that girls and women seemed to instinctively know which part of their attire should be adorned.

Bright and sparkly, and just lying there in the dark drawer. Why? Certainly he had no use for it, but… WHAT in the world was the matter with him? Surely, he must actually need a keeper, as Theo had suggested.

Lavinia would know exactly what to do with it. It would eventually be hers… his mind had not yet gone so far as to visualize the wedding. That was not a 'fellow thing,' anyway. Girls took care of that… didn't they?

Anyway, she should have whatever she wanted of it, and he'd tell her the next time he saw her… which happened about an hour and a quarter later.

"Whoa!" and the grind of wheels on gravel ceased. Lavinia approached with a covered dish. Food, no doubt.

She made fresh tea and sliced the golden pound cake. Spread on a liberal topping of strawberry jam, and set it before him.

After the snack, he maneuvered the crutch under his arm and prepared to stand. But Lavinia was quick with, "Wait. What do you need and I'll get it."

He shook his head, and balanced himself against the chair back. "No, my dear, you cannot do that this time, but you can come with me."

Puzzled, she followed him to the aunt's bedroom and waited while he struggled with the match to light the lamp. Then he drew aside the shade from the wide window, and led her to the bureau.

The entire top of the glossy old walnut of the bureau was spread with glitter. Fitted together, their jeweled edges touching, were necklaces, bracelets, breast pins and rings. A few small sparkling cases for storing this and that and a pair of glittering bags of a sort that ladies sometimes carried when attending special functions.

Lavinia stared at the array, and then at him.

"Lavinia, I love you, and I want to marry you. Just now, I want you to take what you like from this stuff, and if it isn't right for you, we can take it to Little Rock and a jeweler will surely have something you like in trade.'

If he had been expecting a girlish squeal of pleasure at the sight of such finery, he would have been disappointed. By now, he knew her better, and expected quiet acceptance.

She looked from one end of the display to the other, and picked up a ring with a light blue sparkle... much like the water of Sycamore Fishing Lake. Then she selected a small pin in the shape of a lily.

He waited, but she was through. "Only two pieces? Isn't there something more you'd like to take now?"

"Only one, for now," she told him, showing him the ring on her finger. "This lily is for the only mother I have."

Lincoln felt his heard pounding against his chest as thought tumbled around inside his ribs. Did he, one time, manage to do the right thing?

Thinking further, he picked up one of the smaller jeweled cases. "If it is to be a gift, would it be right to put it in a case... maybe like this one?"

She took the case and set the lily inside, smiling.

And now, there was this other things he had to tell her. He needed to leave for a few days, and he was missing her already.

"It's for my pa, really. He sent me out here to do a job and was expecting me back. It's not really right to treat him that way. I need to catch the train and make a trip back. He knows about you, and he deserves to be told about the wedding... face to face. You understand, don't you?"

She was silent, so he continued.

"That catfish dinner party you suggested... would there be time for it now? It would make a nice engagement party for all your... I mean, our, friends. And that fellow, Boudreau, with the fish ponds, he wouldn't have any trouble providing the fish? And your girl friend's mother, she..."

"Wait. You must go ahead and see your pa. He deserves that. Then you'll be back, and we can have the party. That way the town'll have time to look forward to it."

So it was arranged. Theo and Susannah went along in Lincoln's big fancy buggy. Velvet tufted seats and rubber treads on the wheels.

Built for the streets of Boston and not the hills and gravel roads of River Bend.

Lincoln was getting better at maneuvering his crutch and avoiding being tripped by the plaster cast holding the broken bones in place. It would be an uncomfortable trick to relax in the train seats, but what had to be, just had to be.

It was a Monday morning, and the train pulled out at noon from the Rock Island Spur. A layover in Little Rock, and another in Fort Smith. An all-night ride to St. Louis, Missouri. After that a whole day until he could go on to the Gap.

There was no train close to his pa's place. They were still laying tracks, and it was slow going through the mountains. Digging and blasting and occasionally tunneling. Very slow going.

He had not arranged to be met, because it would mean a long trip, and lost time for someone, so he'd just hire a carriage if there was not one going that way. Sometimes there would be a motorbus, but they were very irregular. Those mountain roads were precarious, and no place to have trouble with finicky auto engines.

Anyway, no one was expecting him, and he and his crutch would just do the best they could. Theo had handed him some of the newest pain relievers, but warned they would make him sleepy. Good! That would be something to help pass the hours. Sleep.

So it was in a medicated daze that he passed through Missouri and pulled into the station at St. Louis. Rain. Steamy fog off the Mississippi and heavy, moisture-laden air.

Folks scurried when they could and huddled under slickers or umbrellas when they couldn't. Lincoln was hampered by the crutch and stood as close to the boarding area as possible. He certainly didn't want to miss his connection because he was too slow.

Daylight had barely dawned, and the rain had backed off to a mild drizzle as he waited by the tracks. He watched the cars go by as the brakes pulled to a stop. Dark windows. Passengers looking out at their destination.

Someone waved, and if he had been able to lift a hand, he would have instinctively waved back, and then grinned at his reflex action. Where he came from, you waved when being waved to, whether you knew the person or not. It was just the thing to do, but in this case, the person was just swiping the fog from inside the window. Sure to be.

He was pretty well soaked from the mist when he finally got aboard, but the train car was warm. And his foot ached abominably. He'd get settled and food would be ready, then he'd take another pill. With the stops through Kentucky, he'd be all day just crossing the state.

That done, he settled himself into the comfortable seats. It was the right thing to do, of course. Pa had a right to a visit and a chance to hear more about his new daughter in law. He spent a few miles wishing he had taken her to one of the new photo shops so he would have a picture, but pa wouldn't care. Looks were not that important to him. Anyway...

Then, when he drowsed awake, he found himself still in the St. Louis terminal. He grimly reminded himself that he had been thoughtful in not asking to be met. No telling when he'd get there.

At the closest stopping point to the Gap, he hired a young man with a buggy. Jobs for young men were not so easy to get, and the buggy driver was happy for the chance. Though it would be all day over the mountain trails that masqueraded as roads.

17

Back at the St. Louis station, the pair, a young man and an older gentleman with a cane, settled themselves into the comfortable seats of the car. The food had been good, the dessert perfect (how did they do all that in a moving kitchen?), and they had been moved out of the diner for the next group of hungry passengers.

The younger man restlessly stared out the window. "I really think...."

The older man impatiently chided him. "Let it go. What could you see through a steamy window?"

"It wasn't steamy after I wiped it off. I just know...."

"It couldn't be. He's somewhere up in the Arkansas hills. Now, Wilson, just keep quiet and let me take a nap."

Wilson knew grandpa's voice well enough to know he meant what he said. That was all right, though, because it wouldn't matter. If he saw what he thought he saw, it would be evident soon enough. He had picked up a newspaper in the station, and now would be the time to read it.

The tired horses pulling the buggy had huffed themselves up the last little hill, and it would be level across the top of the mountain for the last half mile before it settled into the gap. Lincoln had been on the back seat of the buggy, his injured foot stretched out on the bench beside him. It seemed to ache less if was elevated.

The young driver. "Mister, would there be a place where I can sleep a little and rest my horses 'afore I go back. The hayloft would be fine, and if I could turn the horses out on the grass…?"

Horses and a bed were the least of Lincoln's worries. "Say no more. I knew you'd need to stay over, and there's beds aplenty. And the horses will be fed. Someone will take care of it, and you can sleep. This happens a lot."

"Say! Thanks, mister."

But within moments young Abraham Lincoln Cumber was met with amazed eyes of cousin Andrew Jackson Cumber. 'What're you doin' here?"

"Came to see pa for a few days. Can you take care of these…"

"But, Linc… Grandpa's done gone to Arkansas to see you. We didn't get no message you was a'comin'."

"Pa's done what…?"

"He took off two days ago with Wilson. Should be there by now, but we ain't heard nothin' back."

Lincoln felt his weary shoulders droop with discouragement. He should have checked… he knew that. Sudden changes of plans often went this way, but the injured foot had pushed him into recklessness. Who would have thought that his old pa… well, it just didn't seem like something he would do. Surprises were just not his thing.

To cousin Andrew, "Take care'a this fellow, will you? We'll both of us be a'headin' back out at first light." Planting his crutch firmly on his home soil, he hoisted his drooping body to a standing position and moved toward the house. Toward a bed. Toward decent food. To a place to do some serious thinking.

As it so happened, the serious thinking was postponed. The familiar softness of his childhood bed claimed him and would not let go until morning. There was the wonderful comfort of being at home and not being in charge of every decision. So different from the big house on the Arkansas mountain.

Relief? No, not really. The challenge of making his own decisions as against taking orders (however kindly) had been an interesting stimulation to his mind. Well, he'd soon be back to it, and with that comforting thought, he passed into the oblivion of sleep.

The old man had waited at the Jacksonville depot of the Rock Island Spur while the younger man, totally without orders or direction, disappeared to locate appropriate transportation. That was the way he liked it. The young should be grateful to serve the old, in view of what the old could make available to them. Only made sense.

Wilson Cumber, with the experience of almost two years, quickly located a buggy and horse for hire, and assisted the older man onto the seat. He had also procured the specific direction to the town of River Bend. "Just go east till you can go no farther without crossing the river. You'll see it on both sides'a the road." Seemed easy enough to follow.

The wide eyed greeting the two received in River Bend was almost as astonishing as the one Lincoln received at the Gap. Stopping at the Livery Stable had been the logical thing to do.

"John Markham? Well, you're pretty nigh there, stranger. Lookie down the road a piece and you'll…."

Before he could complete his sentence, another voice demanded, "You wouldn't be the kin of the new fellow up in the big house, would you?"

Before Wilson could answer, another voice advised, "I gotta say, you shore made good time."

Wilson glanced from one to the other. "Good time…? Well, we…"

"You wasn't expected till Lincoln told us when."

Impatient voice from the buggy demanded, "How do we find Lincoln?"

Glances flitted from one to the other of the townsmen. Finally, "Mister, if'n you ain't got 'im with you, then you passed 'im on the road somewheres."

Another voice. "That's a fact, fellow. He was headed out to tell you about his upcoming marryin'. We don't know the set date, though."

Whereupon Wilson Cumber turned to his grandfather with a burning gaze and silence. His eyes said, 'I told you I saw Linc in St. Louis.'

Ed, the manager of the Livery, took over, as was his due. "Mister…? Sir…? What you need to do is go down to John Markham's place, and they'll fill you in. That where his intended lives."

With the proper amount of thanks, Wilson again took his seat in the buggy, and without a word, proceeded to the indicated destination, the local pharmacy.

In the parlor of the Markham's home, the journeying pair were again met with the same wide-eyed astonishment. They soon realized, however, that such an unusual set of circumstances deserved a unique set of plans. Consequently, within hours the preparations began to take place.

It was decided by the best figuring and knowledge of the participants, that Lincoln would immediately make plans to return and that would be at first light on the first morning after his arrival. Then he would… or world not… reach the nearest railway station in time for the next available locomotive.

If he reached it, he would be in Jacksonville in three days, if not, then it would be a day later. In either case, he would arrive at 4:00 am and be met by the dray wagon from River Bend who was there to pick up the mail and freight for River Bend and a couple of other small towns nearby.

He would then come out on the dray wagon and be at River Bend in three and a half to four hours later. Allowing for delays, he would likely reach the Livery Stable by 10:00 am, the perfect time of day to begin a period of festivities.

Their first night in the small town found the travelers occupying the toy house, and the next day they were taken to the big house on the hill.

Lily and Lavinia accompanied them for the first day, but then set about arranging for the homeowners 'welcome.'

Fish would be the best. Fast cooked and more easily kept fresh. A gigantic fish fry with the whole town invited. Everyone must be notified to be ready to attend in either three... or maybe four... days. There was the problem. And there was the trip that Lavinia must make to Jacksonville to pick up a very important document and convince officials to let her have it.

That would be a good job for Wilson, and the buggy he had hired could be towed along and returned.

Meanwhile, Miz Edna's services would be procured for the day, either three... or four... days hence. In her capable hands, it would just take a little bit of planning. That was no problem for the hardy and flexible residents of the small town, who were always ready for a celebration of something. All they needed to know was when, and what part they could play.

After delivering Lavinia back in town, Wilson would return to Jacksonville with a fast horse and wait for the arrival of the "human" baggage. Meeting every train. If he didn't come in three days, he would, for certain, come the next day.

All the town residents had to do was watch for the signal. The fast horse with one rider could make the trip between the two towns in two hours... maybe a few minutes less, and the dray would be at least another hour and a half behind him. A lot could be done in an hour and a half when the ladies set their heads to it.

The deep-fry kettles of fat could be set simmering, small children who would be stationed at the Livery to watch for Wilson's return and run home with the message that this was the day. An hour and a half was time for the catfish that were already caught, to be brought in their holding tubs, kept alive and swimming to be totally fresh. There was time for a half a dozen skillful people to have them de-scaled, de-boned, filleted and ready for the batter.

There would be time for the various pickles to be opened from their Mason jars, and for the garden vegetables to be shredded and steeped in their sweet/spicy vinegar... for what was a fish fry without slaw and pickles?

There would, indeed, be plenty of time to be ready, though bets were taken that it would be four days instead of three, and in that case, there would be no hurry at all. There would, of course, be Wilson who would gallop in and spread the word, but in any case all would be ready.

18

Lincoln Cumber waited for 20 exhausting hours for the train that followed the one he just missed by less than an hour. As he and his driver cleared the last Kentucky hilltop, they saw the plume of black smoke threading through the valley as the locomotive pulled its cars along.

Not that Lincoln was surprised. The way his last few days had gone, this sight fit the pattern. Not only that, his broken foot ached abdominally from his activity.

Dismissing the driver and buggy, he settled himself in the depot to wait and promptly fell asleep. The grind of the gears and huffs of exhaust, as well as the clanging of shifting cars and cargo failed to wake him for the next ten hours as he lay prone on a leather covered bench in the waiting room.

Then it was more hours of waiting, breathing exhaust smoke and thinking. There was a lot of thinking going on. One thought tended to drown out the other thoughts as he thought of his hilltop house. The more the thought, the more it seemed to be his castle, and the quicker he installed the queen of it, the quicker things would become normal. He'd attend to it at the very first opportunity, and as his pa was already there, it could be soon.

When the next locomotive huffed its way into the roundhouse, he waited by the rails... leaning on his crutch. He would not miss it. It would not leave for at least two hours, but that did not matter. He would not be able to rest until he was safely aboard.

Thinking continued, and plans solidified as the locomotive pulled him toward the west. In St. Louis he changed locomotives and headed south.

By that time, the frazzled young man was so exhausted, he fell asleep with his cast-enclosed foot draped over the seat next to him. He did not wake up until Little Rock, Arkansas, and then he was less than an hour from Jacksonville. After that, three and a half hours would bring him into River Bend unless the dray was slow getting loaded.

The town of River Bend had held its breath, but now it could breathe. When the rider did not appear on the third day, then it would, for certain, be the fourth. No one would need to be notified.

The tubs of catfish were delivered. Miz Edna took charge of the backyard and the sawhorse tables. Lavinia and her friends were opening Mason jars of pickles and chopping cabbage. And giggling and laughing all the while.

Lavinia made trips to the little third bedroom to see for sure her billowy white dress was still hanging where it should be, and that the crisp white shirt and pin-striped suit were in the second bedroom.

When Preacher Joe McCrey came in his buggy, all seemed to fall into place. Wilson Cumber trotted in on his horse… there had been no reason for the poor horse to gallop twelve miles to deliver the message everyone knew.

The weary animal reached the top of the hill about a half an hour ahead of the dray wagon, just in time to notify Lavinia to take the small buggy down to meet the weary, crippled traveler.

Lincoln had decided he would beg the use of the toy house for a day as he could not face going to the huge empty house… not just yet. The sight of Lavinia and the buggy was an unexpected gift.

The friendship with her had been such a natural, quiet thing that had grown so unexpectedly… like his love for the hilltop house and the little Arkansas town. It didn't seem to need words.

He settled back against the right side of the buggy bench, so he could better watch her as her quiet hands held the lines that directed the pony. She had not even suggested that he drive.

Lavinia was seething with thoughts… they were tumbling all over themselves and twisting into knots. It was a big scary thing she had planned, and there was still time to call it off. He had, after all, promised she could have a Fish Fry party with her friends. She could say this was it.

As it was, she had about a mile of road in which to be sure.

Lavinia did not often talk with her departed mom… not like just after she had been so ill that she had to leave. But now, she could hear her mother's voice humming the tune to "Thistledown," the old war time song.

"Mother," her mind said, "he is truly a friend, just like you said the special man would be. I just thought you would want to know that."

From the corner of her eye, she watched him as he lounged against the leather-padded upholstery of the expensive small buggy. She felt his eyes studying her… just as hers had studied him for the last couple of years. If he had found her lacking in any way, he had not made it known.

He had gone with her and done things with her without showing impatience. She had never seen him joke or flirt with other girls who she knew were much prettier than she. Likely more witty, as well. He had always been there when she asked him to be.

He already treated Theo like a brother, and she knew he loved Aunt Lily.

He had never acted as though it was a great thing that he lived in the big house on the hill and from the size of the gathering now surrounding the house, it was obvious the whole town accepted him as one of theirs.

He had tried, though sometimes unsuccessfully, to do jobs that the local men were expected to do. Even though he had no experience, he was determined to learn.

As she guided the pony around the curves of the uphill road, she saw the stakes along the way where he would eventually move crepe myrtle bushes. All she had done was mention that, as he had so many young plants… still… they would make a good border for the road.

He had spread out his aunt's jewelry as though it was nothing for her to make a choice. He treated it with no more importance than asking she which flavor of ice cream she wanted today.

He had watched as one after another of her pretty, vivacious friends were picked off and married, and still he patiently spent time with her. Doing what she wanted to do.

"Mother," her mind asked, "is that enough? Is that what makes a friend?"

Her mother answered this time, and that was unusual. "If this is the one, Viney, my darling, you will know." Lavinia remembered other times her mother had said this same thing about other questions. "When the time comes, you will know."

"Thanks, Mother."

As they rounded the last curve, the first sight of the wide porch was a blaze of color with every spring flower competing with every other flower to be the brightest.

Porch posts were entwined; windows were draped, while massive bouquets lined the porch. At first glance, Lincoln wondered if this was usual for a fish fry with friends... but he did not wonder for long.

When he saw Preacher Joe in his Sunday suit, he drew in a breath. Was the mountain air making him dizzy... or did this actually look like a wedding? He turned to Lavinia and was met with one of her quiet smiles, but her eyes danced with excitement.

She nodded, and whispered, "You remember you promised that I could plan my party? Well, I did. Your suit is hanging in your bedroom, and we'll all wait for you to be properly dressed."

But as she halted the pony by the porch, she admonished, "Just don't be too long! We mustn't let the first batch of fish be overcooked!" There were priorities... naturally.

The nuptial event now being put in its proper place... right behind the fish fry, they moved on. The future bridegroom grinned, shrugged, and manipulated his crutch and clumsy cast slowly up the flower-lined walk.

When he returned to the decorated porch, Lavinia stood waiting. Snow white from head to slippers, she stood like a lone glistening candle among the flower garden of her friends.

Lincoln took his indicated place between Theo and Wilson, with Pa leaning on his cane and looking on. A fleeting thought passed through his head that he might still be on the night train speeding through the black hills under the starry sky. From everything he had heard, weddings did not happen like this... but then, there was only one Lavinia.

With Preacher Joe's first words, he came into reality.

"Friends and neighbors, we are gathered here on this hilltop where we will be joining two of our town's residents together. We are honored to have the father of the groom present for this occasion."

All of the proper words followed, ending with "...I now pronounce you man and wife."

On that queue, the bouquets of her friends were tossed high, and loose blossoms showered over the heads of the bridal party.

Slight pause, and the deep, authoritative voice of Miz Edna rang out. "Come and get it while it's hot! Gotta make room for the next batch of fish in the pot!"

Pa and grandson, Wilson, stayed in town for almost a week until Pa began to be itching to get back to the gap. Seemed like the older folks got, the less they wanted to be away from home, but there had been a wonderful time of catching up with Lincoln... examining the big house... learning all the gossip and getting acquainting with the family of his bride.

Lincoln even found time to apologize to his nephew. "Wilson, old man, I regret to have left you stuck with the job of nursemaid to Pa. I had no idea I would be staying here and..."

"Say no more, Linc. I love this job. Easiest one I ever had, and it was time I moved up and let Andrew have the job in the stables. You know how Grandpa has to be right all the time? Well, I pulled one over on him. I saw you at the St. Louis depot just as we pulled out, and he wouldn't believe it. He still won't talk about it."

Wilson grinned his handsome grin and winked. "I have him now! Anytime he gives me an argument, I'll just remind him that he can be wrong. And, hey, I love this job. Easiest one I ever had!"

Lavinia was hugged and congratulated, and was finally permitted to fill a plate with the smoking hot catfish, freshly seined from the catchment pond of Cal Boudreau over on Rock Creek Road.

She looked out over the War Eagle River Valley toward the rocky peaks of Rock Mountain and then looked up. "Ma, I'm so glad you were here today. You met my wonderful Aunt Lily, so you won't have to be worried about me no more."

By afternoon of the wedding day, Pa was becoming restless. "Abraham, son, I've sorta got things goin' with these fellows from the Livery. Been thinkin' I'll take Wilson and go on down for maybe a couple of days. I rather liked the toy house."

Wilson, with a sly wink at his young uncle, assisted Pa into the buggy and they were gone.

Preacher Joe bade best wishes and turned to go, signaling it was time for the crowd to disperse. It was necessary, actually, because it would be time for evening chores by the time most of them got home.

Miz Edna disposed of the well-used frying oil and tossed scraps to the pigs. Wiping the well-used kettle clean, she waved her farewell and proceeded down the hill.

One last hug from Aunt Lily, and a hand shake from Uncle John… and they were gone. The bride and groom watched from the porch until they disappeared down the trail.

A small, quibbling gaggle of crows descended to the area of the party to scratch among the grass clumps and clean up the last of the dropped goodies. Spike, the caretaking neighbor, galloped past, waved and headed on to the barn to fulfill his promise and collect the last of his guinea hens. As per the swap.

One last look around, and the castle on the hill was quiet. The king of the hill had returned and the queen had been installed. Nothing else mattered.

Fall weather was definitely on the way. The sumac and wild berry vines had colored leaves and the last of the wild pecans were dropping.

A breeze veered up and over Rock Mountain, flowing through a patch of Scottish Thistle. The ripe seeds arose in a cloud of silver umbrellas against a cloudless, blue sky. They grouped and scattered, then grouped again as they sailed over Dogwood Bluff and past the house on the hill. Truly…

"…. thistles fly as south wind blows, and where they rest, only God and the thistle plant knows…"

THE SHELTERING STONES
HISTORICAL FICTION SERIES FOR ADULTS

BOOK 3

THE MAKING
OF A TOWN

A Novel of Historical Fiction

THE MAKING
OF A TOWN

I n was in the year of 1898 that Francine Canfield's life began to fall into place. Francine had always known this would happen, she just didn't know when... or exactly how. The thing she had known, however, from the age of four was that at some moment she would know, without a doubt, what she wanted for the rest of her life.

At age four, she had sat with her older sister and three-year-old brother in a moving covered wagon headed to where she did not know... nor care. She was busily admiring the many doll dresses received as a gift from the same grandmother who provided her future inheritance and chatting with the brother who was busily admiring the set of animals and farm equipment from the same grandmother.

Young Francine knew, at that moment, that she would someday have many beautiful dresses, and they would be for something special that she would later learn about.

It was during two years at the PRAIRIE ACADEMY that Francine had learned in detail what she would do with her life. She would teach school in the Territory to children who had no other school. She didn't know where, but that was not a problem. She would be ready when the place became available, and that was why she was making the ten outfits of clothing. These beautiful new dresses would give her the dignity and confidence she thought she needed to impress small boys into obedience and be a role model to inspire small girls... the way that Miss Josie had inspired her. Her career would begin in the neighboring town of Shady Ridge.

If a teacher for Shady Ridge had been available from the fledgling Board of Education, the salary would have been $376.00 a year for one who was Certification Qualified.

A Shady Ridge parent wondered, "What kind of a teacher would we git for that kinda money?"

Answer, "Whoever was willin'. It'd be someone that was likely turned down by the school board of any big community, if they was to be able to get someone better. She, or he, could be anywhere from 14 years old to still breathin'. They's places that are letting a 11-year-old girl teach' cause they can't do no better. They call 'em 'teachers in training'. Sometimes they call 'em 'parlor schools'."

"But there's them New York trained girls Gray Eagle told us about.... What about them?"

"Well, the question now is, can we get one of them girls. It'd cost money for one thing. I can say $1.50 a month'd strain me a bit, but I'd manage. Some way. You speck we could figger a way to get one of 'em girls?"

"Wouldn't know till we tried. We could count noses'a them that's interested, and have ourselves another meetin' in a week or two."

"How long you thinkin' it'd take to get the buildin' up, John?"

As it happened, the folks at Shady Ridge had a mind to work. By the last of March, the building material was on site and shaped into a large cabin that literally grew up out of the prairie soil, liberally fertilized by the sweat of concerned fathers. It turned out to be 40 feet long and 20 feet wide... totally adequate, everyone agreed. There would be a classroom of 20 by 30 and a private room for the teacher measuring 20 by 10.

In due time the offer was made to Miss Francine Canfield to be the teacher of the Shady Ridge children.

It was later that day that Sam Canfield watched his life's partner as she struggled with her thoughts. Maybe he could help her... at least he should try.

"Julie? Let's talk on this. I don't like it tearin' you to pieces this a'way."

The girl's mother was having a pang at losing her younger daughter, not yet 14 years old, but her father put it another way, and pointed out, "I know. But think on it. Shady Ridge, that's a heap sight closer'n Oklahoma City... or even Argyle, for that matter. And here's the thing that'll comfort us... those ladies from Shady Ridge said the community'd be happy if she was to marry someone close and maybe stay on. That'd never happen if she was to take a job with the Board of Learnin' in the city. If she went to Shady Ridge, she'd pretty nearly be the boss'a herself, and you know how our Francine is. She knows how she wants things to be, and she's mostly right in her ideas. Seems like them folks want her so bad they'd do 'most anything to get her, and they come here a'beggin', almost. Think on it… beggin' for our little girl to come and do what she wants to do already."

And that is the way it happened to cause Francine to shine up her worn shoes and put on new dress number three. She had just completed dress number seven and was looking forward to the next three, which would be skirt and blouse combinations. Mrs. O'Grady had encouraged her in that direction, explaining that skirts grew with young girls as they became taller, and that shirtwaists could be made to expand in selected areas. When that could not be done, they could be replaced much more easily than an entire dress. Francine had listened carefully, and within her own mind could see that styles for shirtwaists changed more often, as well.

So it was that she and her parents traveled the three miles to the west for a visit. They were treated to coffee and cake and given a tour of the new schoolhouse in Shady Ridge. It was a cheerful thing to see the freshly painted sign bravely stating: SHADY RIDGE ACADEMY.

The almost 14-year-old girl glanced about the classroom still smelling of new lumber, checked out the size of the closet, and examined the small stove.

Annabelle Martin offered, "Now, Miss Francine, we can put in a bed…'

Whereupon Francine reassured them, "No, thank you. I'll bring the one from my room. What about school books?"

On learning none had yet been purchased, Francine nodded agreeably. "That's all right. Don't bother about books, I'll bring them when I move in. Next August." Which was what she wanted to do, anyway.

The Canfields left two happy ladies with wide grins of satisfaction. Success! Wasn't it wonderful, after all their work and talking and planning? They had a teacher! A real New York trained teacher!

On the journey home, Francine's mother hesitantly asked her, "Honey, how're you feelin' now?"

After her usual hesitation, the girl calmly answered, "Pretty much how I expected to feel. I know I'm ready."

Such confidence was scary to her mother. The girl sounded so much like her father had sounded when he had announced that he planned to make a run for property in the Territory. She had asked him, "Do you think you can?"

The answer had been, "I feel very confident. I know I'm ready." And he had been.

It would be necessary for Francine to have transportation home for weekends, so her father purchased for her a lady's buggy, a small one made for a couple of friends to shop with or take an outing. The abbreviated cab was so narrow that two large persons would not have fitted well, and even two smaller persons would need to be good friends. It was perfect for Francine.

The horse was also perfect. He was a Connemara from the breeding stock of Jefferson Wilson, Miss Josie's cousin. The horse's only problem had been that he was not born with a coat of dark gray displaying the signature charcoal face and feet. The fact was, the animal did not match any pattern that Jeff was working for. He aimed for the matched carriage horses that would bring a high price. Francine bought the animal at the first sight of him.

Francine's choice of a horse had been born an offshoot of the northern animals introduced into the Irish stock by the Vikings, and his color was a medium chocolate. Also instead of smooth coat, his was somewhat shaggy in a texture which, along with the color, was deemed by the northern newcomers to Ireland to be more adaptable to the cold dampness of the climate. It showed his true Viking heritage.

In the case of Francine's horse, the animal was the winner. The girl took one look at the dark animal and knew he was the one she wanted. The buggy was duly found by her father and painted the same shade of chocolate as the horse's slightly shaggy coat. The horse and buggy pair cut into Francine's inheritance money a bit, but there were still funds to buy the necessary books for the library and enough slates for every student to have at least two for their assignments. With some left over.

The animal, whose name was reduced from "Chocolate" to "Chock," amiably trotted between the double trees of the buggy, answering her commands with no objection.

Into the small buggy seat, on the floorboard and into the small boot at the back were the books, chalk boxes, slates, and more. Later on, the students would be required to furnish their own… and a few rulers. There were a number of other things for her own desk. Also, there were her clothes, extra bedding, and kitchen items that would come later.

She had hardly pulled into the yard before a girl of about eleven and a half came running to meet her. She recognized the girl as Isabel Brown, oldest daughter of her host family.

"Oh, Miss Francine! My ma said I could help you carry things in if I wouldn't get in the way! I got to come over yesterday and put the coverlet on the bed. I smoothed the mattress and felt how soft and fluffy the feathers were, and I plumped up the pillows. I brought the three boxes to slide under the bed for other things like ma said you'd need. Can I help?"

With a smile of greeting, Francine called her to the buggy. "See all these books? I suspect you can guess where they go?"

"I can! I can! Let me carry them all!" insisted the excited child. Well, that was Francine's best offer of help for the day until a boy came racing across the road. "I'm Troy Cameron from over there." An elbow pointed to the house across the street. "My ma said I could be the one to take care'a your pony if it was all right with you. I can do as well as anybody else, and I know how to brush their coats to dry 'em out when they get sweaty. Do you want me to take him now?"

"Not today, Troy, and I would be very glad to have you take care of Chock. Later, I'll tell you about special things I want done for him and for the buggy. I just came to deliver things today."

"Then can I help you carry something?"

"I believe you'd have to ask Isabel. She thinks it's her job."

The two children worked together on the loads of books, Troy carrying and Isabel arranging them on the bookshelves that had been constructed all the way along the side of the classroom. In due time, Troy was called home, and Isabel looked for things to do to get to stay. On impulse, Francine asked the girl, "How are you at reading?"

A hesitation. "I can read. Some."

Selecting a book of about second level, she opened to a page and handed it to her. "Let's see how you do."

The girl took the book and began with a bit of hesitation. Most of the words she knew, but she had no confidence and read in a monotone. When she came to the word 'cabin,' she substituted the word 'house'. Francine nodded to herself. The girl was looking at the illustration of a house, and the word 'cabin' was the one used in the text.

If Isabel, being one of the oldest, stumbled on that word, it indicated a strong need for phonics... the sounding of each of the letters. She had imagined, actually, that the whole group could be introduced to sounds at one time, and the younger ones would learn as well by listening.

In time, Isabel was called home, leaving Francine alone. The long, long bookcase was over half filled leaving space for the future. The tables and benches were arranged. Her desk was stocked, and she stood, looking around in all directions. Alone.

Her chest became heavy, and her breath labored. Her eyes filled, and she could not stop the sobs. Sitting at her desk, she buried her face in her arms and the tears flowed. A depression settled upon her like a sudden spring shower, weighing her down. Soggy and dripping. There was no way she could conduct a classroom like Miss Josie did. Why did she come here? She didn't have to do this!

Her shoulders heaved, and her stomach tightened. She had to get out of here somehow. She was only fourteen years old! What had given her the idea she could teach this class?

A deep breath. "FRANCINE," she shouted at herself. "STOP IT, THIS INSTANT! WHAT DO YOU THINK YOU'RE DOING? YOU'RE SCARING YOURSELF!"

Squaring her shoulders, she reached in into her carpet bag and brought out a large, efficient handkerchief. This was no job for a tiny lace hanky! She had more to say to herself, now that she had her own attention.

"Francine, you big baby, don't you ever do this to me again! You can do what you learned how to do. You taught lessons when Miss Josie was not in the room. You were so busy you didn't notice when she went in and out.

"Why do you think I worked so hard these past three years, studying, teaching, and sewing for you? Do you remember when I sat at the table with Rosie and Raymond, and we studied for two hours after supper. Sometimes three hours, and there was more the next morning while we ate breakfast. Why do you think I did that? Maybe you thought it was so you could bawl like a baby. If you thought that was it, you were WRONG! WRONG! WRONG! Don't you ever let another tear fall about teaching. You can cry about other things, maybe, if we got the time, but not about teaching."

At this point she stood, lifted her head, and sniffed loudly. She crammed the cloth of the handkerchief into her eyes, blotting them dry. Her tight stomach began to relax and produce a couple of final hiccoughs.

Stepping back into her tiny living quarters, a room ten feet by twenty feet, she surveyed it critically. The narrow bed fit perfectly against the left wall. The closet was at the foot of the bed, and there was just enough room to open the doors without bumping the bed. Near the foot of the bed was the slipper stool.

She sat down on the stool and pulled out one of the boxes from under the bed. Roomy and sanded smooth, they were, and about a foot deep and two feet square. Perfect. Handy for so many things. Near her pillow was the tiny stand with a place for shoes below, and it had a small drawer above. Hardly more than a foot square. A kerosene lamp she had brought was placed there. Cut glass and as sparkly as pond ice. It was one she had ordered from Aunt Sharon in New York because she liked Miss Josie's lamps.

The table was a hinged shelf that let down when not in use. Saved space. Francine had planned to have her meals at her desk in the classroom when she didn't want to eat with the family so she might not need the shelf.

On the right-hand side of the room was the kitchen. Tiny cabinet with a few dishes. Two small kettles hanging on the wall. A washstand with a water pitcher and wash bowl and under the stand was soap and a space for other things. Next to the cabinet was another small stand holding the miniature kerosene stove, with extra heating oil on a shelf under it. A match container hung on the wall. A small chest of drawers would serve well as a dressing table. She only needed a mirror.

The far wall contained a door and a small porch with a roof over it. Everything looked good. Perfect for her. She was not particularly interested in engaging in food preparation. There was a small tea pot, and she'd likely get herself a coffee pot. Maybe in a week or two. She had taken a liking to that expensive brew while she was at the Academy. Miss Josie really liked it. Smiling at the thought, she told herself perhaps she'd teach like Miss Josie if she drank enough coffee.

Whatever she had forgotten to bring, she would be home every weekend, at least until bad weather. If she needed something bought quickly, her pa would see to it.

Next trip, she would bring her clothing, quilts, and slippers. Certainly a mirror, comb, and brush. A fluffy rug for when the floor was cold. Maybe she could buy a wolf skin rug from Mrs. Gray Owl. The ones the old woman brought to the Academy were handy and cozy, and shook clean so easily.

A shelf high on the wall held a candle in a tin pan holder. Safety factor. If she should go to sleep with the candle lit, it would eventually put itself out. She would use her lamp to read by, and she must bring the huge poem book Miss Josie gave her. No one else ever checked it out, and Miss Josie said it had been ordered especially for her, anyway.

And she'd need composition books to put in the tiny drawer of the nightstand. She never really knew when a poem would happen, but when it did, she had to write it down or it would keep bothering her until she did.

At first she was a bit embarrassed that she liked writing about common things like snow, turtles, cats, or whatever. Miss Josie showed her in the poem book that a poet in England even wrote about a field mouse he'd turned over with the plow. Also, about a louse that crawled on a woman's bonnet in church.

Her teacher had insisted that she MUST write down every poem that came to her, and that she, Miss Josie, wanted a copy of every one. Strange! Very flattering, though! It seemed to Francine that it was normal to think in poetry... she used to think to that everyone did, but it didn't seem to be that way.

With a sigh, she took a last look at the tiny living quarters, turned back to the classroom, and saw the tear-soggy cloth on her desk. She snatched it up with disgust and crammed it into her carpet bag. Whatever had gotten into her? Anyway, she had gotten it over with, and she didn't expect to have time to go through that again.

She heard a jingle of harness as Chock fidgeted and tossed impatiently at the stinging flies. Time to go. She locked the schoolroom door with the key they had given her and stepped aboard the buggy. She just loved the buggy her pa had picked out. It fit her just right, and she dearly loved things to be just right. Pa was a good shopper.

A click of the tongue turned the animal toward home, and he trotted along with no further direction. He knew where he was headed. She set herself to thinking about Troy and what she would have him do. Curry Chock several times a week. Keep straw for him to sleep on. She wanted to get linseed oil and have Troy oil the leather of the small bench in the buggy and the leather harness lines. She wanted the buggy to last for a long time. Maybe she'd have him oil the wheel axels occasionally.

The Cameron's had suggested they keep the buggy in their barn. It was so small, it would take up very little room they'd said. That should be worth a dime every week for the ten year old. Maybe a bit extra when she wanted something special done.

With a sharp turn and a quick stop, the small horse had brought her home. Twenty minutes later, she had him out of his harness and turned into the pasture. A sigh of accomplishment. One more trip to take the last things, and another for the welcoming party the Shady Ridge parents wanted to give her... the one where she could make a speech if she wanted to. Should she make notes on what she should say? Or maybe just see what she felt like saying? Well, that was next week, and she had plenty of time.

But the time passed quickly. Hot! It was hot! Just as it usually was at the end of August. The classroom would be crowded with the eight or nine families of the new students. Then there was her own family, along with classmate, Carmelita, who said there was no way she would not be there. And Miss Josie and her husband, of course.

What would she wear...? well... The royal blue broadcloth skirt with the "prairie point" trim on the hem and waistband. It flashed through her mind that she had made the extra solid seam in the waistband. It wouldn't do to have a fabric separation because a child had perhaps tugged at her skirt for attention.

Then the white shirtwaist that had been treated to lye soap bubbles until it glistened... as did all her white shirtwaists. Crocheted collar and sleeve trim. Short sleeved, reaching barely to her elbows. That would be about as cool as anything she had.

Not... a hat...? Hmmm... no, she was not going to town. But this WAS a party! And it was being held where she would teach these parents' children. A bow. That would be best. There was the white velvet bow with the very secure clasp... simple and attractive. If she twisted her long, heavy mane of dark hair up from the neckline to the crown, and pin it securely, then the bow would fit well and the clasp would hold solidly for the evening. Yes. And her white, pearl button shoes, as there would not be many times to wear them after she went to work. Black would be best in the classroom.

That taken care of, she thought of her... speech...? She would for certain be asked to say something. She could make notes, or she could wait and see what seemed right. Which...? This being her first experience at this, she had no idea which way was right, but her knowledge of herself said for her to wait. So often, the exact right thing came to her at the moment she needed it, and then she would know what should come next. Yes. She would wait.

The Shady Ridge schoolyard was a seethe of activity. The half-grown pig had been butchered yesterday. It was much too hot in August to butcher any animal that could not be immediately consumed, but that would not be a concern at this time. The rise of community excitement promised the ladies of town that every crumb of every food product was sure to be gobbled up.

Egg salad, potato salad, pickles (cucumber and beet), heaps of sliced onions. Biscuits and cornbread. Angel food cake and fruit cookies sweetened by persimmon sugar and crammed full of toasted pecan and hazelnut kernels. There were even sacks of store-bought marshmallows for the children to toast on sticks over the coals.

The pig on the spit turned slowly, juices and fat oozing as it turned… dripping onto the coals. A tormentingly fragrant smoke floated into the surrounding trees. Older boys were drafted to turn the spit handle slowly and evenly, creating a flavorful crust on all portions.

Tables were created on the sawhorses used in the building of the classroom. White sheets covered the boards giving them a festive look. Older girls were drafted to keep flies from the table as it was being loaded with food.

Francine smiled to herself as she remembered her decision on words to say. NO ONE would want to hear very many words with the aroma of this treat waiting just outside the building! They would be thinking of what would be waiting under the covering bed sheets, placed there to protect the food from insects while words were being said.

Francine sat with her family and watched as they approached the schoolhouse. A numbness settled over her, as though she was having a dream and she knew the events would happen totally without her. It seemed amazing, though, that her inner self realized that she, Francine, had made this possible.

Not that she was surprised, but more a sense of satisfaction that she saw events happening as she had expected they would. Like climbing a ladder, one step followed the last one, and nearer the top, there might be apprehensions, but her apprehensions were not so strong as the knowledge that she WOULD reach the top and that there was a solid place for her feet when she got there.

Folding chairs and benches filled the classroom, and she was directed to her reserved place by John William Brown. Her own family and Miss Josie were settled around her.

Stretched across the end of the room on the wall above her desk, a sign proclaimed, "Welcome to Miss Francine." Words were said, and an applause spread through the group, but the words were lost on the fourteen-year-old girl who was the center of the celebration.

Then she was standing before them. Smiles! Nods of heads! These people wanted her to be here, and they were proud of themselves because they had secured her. She was acutely aware of that. A small shiver of thankfulness flowed from the nape of her neck down her arms. Hers! These were her people, and she would make them proud!

"Thank you so much, everyone. You will never know how excited and pleased I am to be here, and so thankful to you for asking me. I promise that I will try to be all you are expecting.

"I do have a few small things to say, and I'll speak fast because of the aroma coming in through the windows." A chuckle sprinkled through the grownups, and a few giggles and restless movements passed through the younger children.

She continued, "The discussion of the tuition was made and set without consulting me, and I feel I must make a change." Profound silence met these words. "The amount of $2.00 per child per month is very flattering to me, and I appreciate it, but this is what it will actually be. The amount of $2.00 will be for the first child of any family, and the rest of the children will attend free, except for the bushel of cow pats which will certainly be needed." A relieved twitter of surprise was the only sound.

"On to other things. Discipline. With a class of 20 children, there can be no willful disturbances by any child. The first instance of misbehavior will be discussed with the child. The second will be discussed with the parents. The third will be that the child no longer attends the school. No exceptions. It is clearly not fair to allow one child to take up the time of the children who want to learn and whose parents are paying for their education.

"Next thing. The lessons taught here will NOT be easy. Miss Josie, whom you see here, will agree with me on this. My brother and sister and I used a great quantity of kerosene every night at the kitchen table. We were expected to have our assigned lessons prepared, no matter how long it took. There were times that my sister and I took our outside reading to our beds and read by candle light. You see on your left the long bookcase someone so kindly built us, and it is stocked with books arranged by Miss Isabel Brown. These books are not here just because they look nice. Your children will read them. They will read so many that there will be times they will hate me, and you parents may not be really happy, either, but that is my requirement. I refuse to waste my time. I expect to be successful with every child. I just need for every parent to understand that at the beginning.

"Now, just one more thing. I see the nice shed that contains the bin for the cow pats, also the bench for the privy. It is very nice, but I have one concern. All children will have recess at the same time, and I expect their needs to be taken care of then, and the children will want a few minutes to play. For that reason, I ask that as soon as possible, another privy be constructed. That would be one for the girls, and the current one reserved for the boys, as they will also be responsible for storing the cow pats.

"I am so pleased that Miss Josie could be here. She is very important to me, and if she had not been forced by her family misfortune to be here in the Territory, then I would not be standing here tonight. It is because of her that my sister and I could make up four years of lost education in only one year. It is because of her that I had an additional year and a year of practice to be sure I could do this job. It is because of Miss Josie that I lost a lot of sleep, and that my parents bought a lot of kerosene. I might possibly have been mad at her, sometimes, if I had had time, but I was too busy working to even think of it."

Miss Josie seemed to be having trouble with her eyes. Smoke from the roasting spit…? One hand plunged into her bag to search for protection, but Mr. Brad was quicker. He thrust into her hand a more adequate item than she would have found in her bag. She dabbed against her eyes and sniffled a bit.

"Miss Josie, would you please stand for just a minute? I want everyone to see the person who made it possible for me to be here."

Josie Wheeler Cullen stood and looked around. Applause rippled and then thundered. She nodded her thanks and seated herself again.

"Thank you, Miss Josie. One more thing. My parents, Samuel and Julia Canfield did not expect any chores or other duties from myself or my brother and sister during the time we went to school. It was truly a sacrifice on their part. They made it their sacrifice for their children, and they never, even once, mentioned it to us. Please stand, pa and ma."

Sam Canfield turned beet red, and Julia hid her face in confusion, but they stood for a few seconds. More applause. Francine studied the faces of the adults. Did they really understand what would be required of them? Likely not.

"Last, just for the fun of it, I want my sister and my very good friend to stand. This is Carmelita Wilson, cousin of Miss Josie, and Rosalie Canfield, my sister. I'll leave you to decide which is which." A twitter that grew into a guffaw passed through the parents. A giggle from the two girls, their appearances so different. One of them leaned toward a mirror image of Francine, herself, and the other was a girl with tight, red-gold curls and a delicate pink tint highlighting the pale skin and dimpled features. The girls seated themselves giggling noisily and hiding their faces in their hands.

"Now, if there is anything else I need to say, I'll send a note home with your child." Guarded chuckles. Very likely this teacher meant it, and they might just as well be prepared. How did this 'child' speak with such authority... like she was at least fifty years old?

Francine again. "That's all. Let's go eat that wonderful food on the outside tables." Now a thunder of applause. Children raced through the door, and parents gathered around Francine. Smiles. Pats. Encouraging nods. And then it was over.

By the time she and her family had reached the laden tables, the trees had been festooned with lighted lanterns and two of the men were wielding sharp knives, stacking thick slices of meat onto platters to be set along the tables. The fourteen-year-old guest of honor didn't remember much after that. She had said what she wanted to say... intended to say... and now it was time to do what she intended to do.

In time they were headed home. In the rumble and jiggle of the wagon on the rutted roads as the family headed back east, Francine had the thrill and chill of emotion that so often happened after a recitation of poetry in Miss Josie's class... one that she had worked hard on. It was as though something flowed through her arms and body like...? What? Energy...? Excitement...? No, not really. But she remembered one special time that this feeling had happened.

There was the poem that someone had written about the voyage of Columbus, the time when his crew was begging him to go back because they had seen no land for many days. Surely, they would fall off the edge of the earth at any moment.

The second man in charge, called the mate, had pled with Columbus. The poem went, "The Good Mate said, 'Now we must pray, for Lo! The very stars are gone! Brave Admiral, speak! What shall I say?' But Columbus said, 'Why say, Sail on! Sail on! Sail on!"

Days later the Good Mate again pled, "My men grow mutinous day by day. My men grow ghastly, wan and weak." A salty spray blew over the deck, and he continued, "If we sight naught but seas at dawn?" Columbus answered, "Why, you shall say, at break of day, 'Sail on! Sail on! Sail on and on!'" Reciting the words in her mind, she again felt the thrill bumps of excitement raise on her arms.

And aboard Columbus' ship things had gotten worse. The mate argued. "Why now, not even God would know... Should I and all my men fall dead. These very winds forget their way, for God, from these dread seas, is gone. Now speak, Brave Admiral, speak and say!" But he had said, "Sail on, sail on!"

> They sailed. They sailed. Then spake the mate,
> "This mad sea shows his teeth tonight.
> He curls his lip, he lies in wait,
> He lifts his teeth as if to bite!
> Brave Admiral! Say but one good word
> What shall we do when hope is gone?"
> The words leaped like a leaping sword:
> 'Sail on! Sail on! Sail on and on!"
> Then even Columbus himself was seemingly discouraged. He
> walked the deck and looked in every direction.
> Then pale and worn, he paced his deck,
> And peered through darkness. Ah, that night
> Of all dark nights! And then a speck—
> A light! A light! At last a Light!
> It grew, a starlit flag unfurled!
> It grew to be times' burst of dawn!
> He gained a world! He GAVE that world
> Its grandest lesson! "On! Sail on!"

One hand held to the jiggling seat of the wagon, and the other reached to her eyes. Of course, she could never expect do anything like Columbus did. His voyage to America made it possible for the parents and grandparents of the people of Shady Ridge to be here. That was his part. And now it was up to her to play her part. The excited chill again raised goose flesh on her arms.

Columbus only did what was already inside himself to do. That's all anyone can do. Tonight, she felt a kinship with Columbus… now that it was her turn. She would be the best teacher that Shady Ridge would ever have because Miss Josie had brought her a dream. She swallowed hard against the lump in her throat.

The horses stopped at the barn, and the family walked through the familiar yard in darkness. Weariness. Tomorrow was another day. A day that work had to be done.

It was much later when they were finally in their bed, that Sam Canfield commented to his life's mate, "Julie, did you take note'a our girl bein' so quiet on the way home… after a party that was just for her?"

A hesitation. "I took note'a Francine bein' Francine. She was busy feelin' things, like when she practiced them poems Miss Josie assigned. She was livin' inside'a some other place and wasn't even in the wagon with us. She was bein' part'a the words and part'a her own thoughts, and that's what happened on the way home. I was lookin' at 'er on purpose."

Sam hesitated. "So you're thinkin' we did right by them youngens'a ours? Who'd'a thought she'd say what she did about us?"

Julia Canfield grinned to herself in the darkness. Such a clever daughter they had! "Yeah, well it weren't all for us. She was a'warnin' all them parents what she expected them to do for their youngens. We was just bein' part'a the lesson."

Sam Canfield reached across in the darkness and patted his wife's shoulder. Then he turned over to a cooler place on his pillow. Sleep. Get some rest. Tomorrow was another day.

Julia Canfield stared at the dark ceiling. Thoughts rolled about in her head. If the evening had been for Rosalie, it would have gone so much differently. She and her friend, Carmelita, would have chatted and giggled the whole way home. They would still have been wrapped up in the festivities of the evening, discussing what was served and what was said, and how people looked. So different her girls were for all the fact that they would almost pass for twins if Francine had not been a bit taller. So very different, but inside each of them was the same determination. Rock hard and permanent.

The girls could both be hard as nails when they made up their minds, but the paths they took were so different. If Francine had taken the job at the rock ledge school, she would have been hard to work with because she KNEW what she wanted and she would get it done. By herself. If Rosalie had taken the Shady Ridge job, she would have been uneasy and apprehensive at first, and lonely for a coworker later on… someone to share decisions and successes.

Life was interesting. Their son, Raymond was next, and he would likely go in yet another direction. She turned her face to a cooler place on the pillow and shut her eyes. Sleep. Tomorrow was another day.

Francine opened the window higher to capture every breeze possible. The night was as dark as the ink in the bottle in her desk drawer. She, too, was full of thoughts and possibilities. She stared into the darkness. She felt she was standing on a bridge. Tonight and tomorrow night would be her last times to sleep in this bed before she moved.

Sunday afternoon she would take Chock and her darling chocolate colored buggy to Shady Ridge, and she would spend the night on the narrow bed in the schoolroom. A new life. She smiled with satisfaction, turned her face to a cooler spot on her pillow. Sleep. There were things to do before she left, and tomorrow was another day.

Miss Josie Wheeler Cullen was silent as she prepared for bed. Brad was understanding and also kept silent. The night breeze moved over the bed as she stretched out. Thoughts crowded together.

Francine had spoken very much as Josie had expected. Friendly, businesslike and to the point. She left no wiggle room for slackers or discipline problems. The first few months might be a bit scary for the students and their parents, but Josie would bet the farm and her Cinderella carriage, that before Christmas the parents would be singing her praises. Cutting back on the tuition was a thoughtful move. They would not forget that.

She nodded to the darkness. Francine was a teacher. Teachers were not made, they were born. Training made a teacher a better teacher, but it could not make a teacher from one who was not a teacher. Josie was comfortable in her assignment, because she, herself, was not a teacher and she knew it. She had never thought for a moment that she was.

She stretched back against the cool sheets with a bit of selfish satisfaction. She was not a teacher, but her gift to the Territory was the creation of teachers. So far, there had been four. Her cousin Carmelita, Rosalie and Francine Canfield, and Eve Adams who now taught in a classroom three miles south. If she did nothing more, she would feel satisfied that she had done what was handed her to do.

Francine's praise of her had been unexpected. Not that she did not know Francine was thankful, but that she expressed it so well, also using the praise as a warning to the parents of what they could expect. Very clever. And being only fourteen, Francine would only get better in the next few years.

Another nod of satisfaction. Francine may marry and have a family, but it will not keep her from her dream. If she had taken a public-school job, that would not be possible. Just another tiny little thing that she, Josie, could pass on. She had been so favored in having a private tutor, she knew that the gifts of ability that she could give were very important. There was a lot more to think about over the next months and years.

She sighed a relaxed sigh and turned her face on her pillow. Tomorrow was another day.

Mr. John William Brown was silent as he prepared for sleep. The lanterns had been taken from the trees and the scraps of leftover food retrieved by the preparers. Tomorrow, he would again store the saw horse tables. Now that the school was started, there would be other times for the saw horses to be used.

Elsie was also silent, but not for long. "John William, you comprehend the words comin' outta the mouth'a that child? You'd'a thought she was fifty years old! She spoke like no fourteen-year-old girl I ever saw." John William was silent, knowing there were more words to come.

"Can you even think on all the words that'll be tossed around Shady Ridge for the next weeks? I'm figgerin' the youngens are going to get a word'a warnin' about puttin' their heads down to learn. I don't think our Isabel took her eyes off that teacher to even blink. I can see her thinkin' on copyin' her in talkin' and walkin' and maybe even dressin'." A hesitation as John William raised the window a bit higher and sat on the bed. Elsie stretched out on the cool sheets, and he laid down beside her.

"What'd'ya think, Elsie, that we may'a prayed for a shower and got us a toad strangler flood?"

A sigh "No. More like we set a trap for a wren and caught ourselves a bird'a'paradise. You reckon Shady Ridge is ready for a bird'a'paradise?"

John William thought for the best answer. He knew Elsie was looking for comfort. "Elsie, honey, if we ain't quite ready for a bird'a'paradise, give that girl a year or two, and she'll get us ready. Top'a that, we'll be glad she did. That's what I'm thinkin'."

"Then I'll think that, too. We been worried, some of us women, that she'd not be up to the discipline, but I changed my mind on that. Still yet, it'll be good to have another grownup there for accidents or such." Then she added, "'Course, I'll be here just a yell away."

John William knew there would be a lot more words said, but they would come in the next few days. Just now he was plum wore out, so he turned his face toward the open window. Sleep. Tomorrow was another day.

Someone else was awake after the party. Margie Van Pelt, fifteen, tall and slim, sunshiny yellow hair braided into a thick crown around her head (hair a gift from her Dutch mother). Pale, pale complexion that required constant protection from the prairie sun and a smile that set off her chin dimple and her pronounced cheek bones. She had gone to the party with her brother's family because his two little girls, five and six, would be going to the school.

Margie slipped into her nightdress and blew out her lamp. There was nothing she needed light for, so she looked out the window at the stars. Thoughts raced themselves around in her head, and ideas tried to form and themselves together, whirling around like clouds in the wind, just out of reach. She had the feeling that she was nearing something, but it needed more thought. Seating herself on the floor below the window, she prepared to spend another sleepless night.

Margie had a problem. One of her feet was perfectly normal. The other was not. Her left foot required trimmed and reshaped shoes to accommodate an ankle that was totally turned in. This caused Margie to walk with only a slight limp, but caused a weakness that kept her from so many of the duties that the territory required. Heavy lifting, extensive walking as well as extreme sun-sensivity created a multiple problem.

Family disasters had decreed that she migrate west when her brother won land in the run. Somewhere in the circle of family problems, health problems, and scarcity of schools, it had left Margie with no education. She felt the lack severely. Not that her brother had much schooling, but his was more than hers, and it was different for healthy men... they could DO things. Her sister-in-law could read... almost. She could not help Margie with more than a few words. But she had a husband to make up the lack. Margie had only herself.

Now, Margie knew about the new teacher who was coming. She also knew that the teacher would need help in the form of another person, just in case of accident or something unforeseen. She listened to the teacher speak, and excitement played up and down the nerves in her arms. Somehow...? She just must try...!

She'd talk with her sister-in-law and brother. If someone had to be at the school, how could the busy women of the town manage it? There was so much for them to do, especially in the mornings. Margie, herself, had very little to do in the mornings. The girls dressed themselves, the new baby was at least six months away, and the breakfast dishes could be done when she came home.

Now, if she could just sit at school until noon, there would be a lot of words said, and she would learn a lot just by listening to the lessons. She was actually very quick to learn. She was certain of that. If she needed to be home by noon, then one of the other ladies could take the afternoons, and that would give them mornings to do the things all farm women had to do... cooking, taking care of the milk, putting on the beans, picking and canning garden produce. In short, here was the question. Would there be a way to put it to her brother and others that would make it seem to be a help to them if she got to be in the classroom where reading was taught?

When would be the best time to suggest it, and would maybe one or the other of them need to go with her? Who would make the decision as to whether she was capable enough? Would the beautiful girl who was to be the teacher… care… if she just sat and listened in?

Where she had sat in the classroom at the party, she had been so close to the bookcase that she could have reached out and touched the books. She didn't, though. Instead, she had stared at them, feeling a grain of an idea forming in her head. The idea was still growing, and it was certainly past midnight.

Stretching out on her bed, the thoughts continued. Around and around they raced, looking for a place to break out. Ideas! She was still chasing the BIG IDEA when the first rooster sounded off in the barnyard.

During the morning meal and on into the Saturday, her thoughts continued to chase themselves. Here she was, fifteen years old, and nothing had happened. Her memory was dim when she thought of the place called New York City. Smells and smoke, of course, but they were normal. She had stayed in the house with the neighbors. Their big girl, Annetje was fun to play with, and Margie's other brother Hendrick carried something called "new papers." Then he got sick with something, and he was gone. Her other brother worked until dark, then he came for her and took her home to Ma and Pa. Nobody played. Too tired. Pa leaned into his plate to eat… too tired to sit up straight, she guessed. Ma spread oil on her red, raw hands. Hands rubbed raw by the cloth she sewed. Her eyes were red and weepy. Every day. Nothing different.

They talked the other language they didn't want her to hear. Sometimes Ma cried, and Pa hugged her, shaking his head. Every day.

Clearer was the memory of leaving town. Her biggest brother, Jakob, and Annetje moved her into a wagon with a roof and they took a long trip. She missed Pa and Ma but so much happened. Food cooked beside the road. Being wrapped in a blanket and put to sleep under the wagon seat. And she would drift off to sleep with the breathing sounds of her brother and Annetje (who she was now supposed to call 'Anita'.)

New things to see along the way. Anita had held the straps that guided the pair of horses, and Jakob (Jacob) rode the really big horse alongside.

Sometimes she was allowed on the ground to walk alongside the wagon, and she could run... but not very fast. She didn't know why she had a different kind of foot, but she didn't think of it very long. When she got tired, she climbed into the wagon... or sometimes were special, and she got to ride on the big horse with Jacob.

She knew they were supposed to speak with the new words that were hard to say. She didn't know why, but she DID know that it was important. Her brother and sister-in-law had a lot to say to each other in the evenings while she played about. After supper, they mostly sat close together talking low, struggling with the new words while they held cups of hot tea. Sitting close to the fire with their cups held like they wanted to warm their hands... even though it wasn't cold. That was years ago.

On her fifteenth birthday, a few months ago, Margie realized she was the exact age of her sister-in-law when Anita had decided to leave her family and go with seventeen-year-old Jacob to the Big River. Such a terribly brave thing for her to do! And here she, Margie, was. And she had never done anything brave in her life. She helped with the housework and spent a lot of time with Edith and Susan, born in the same year. Diapers to change and wash. Food to cook while Anita was working with Jacob. Teaching the girls to walk. Singing them to sleep, always with the new words.

But now? Her lungs seemed to swell out at the thought, and excitement popped out in thrill bumps along her arms. She would... somehow... figure on how to spend some time at the schoolhouse. These thoughts occupied her through the whole day.

Jacob and Anita Van Pelt also spent a sleepless night and a thoughtful day.

Anita first. In the darkness of the bedroom, she touched his arm. "Jacob, that girl at the school... she wasn't even as old as Margie, but did you notice her words? We're even luckier than we thought that the girls get to go listen to her."

Jacob had not been asleep, either. "Yeah, it'll take a chunk'a time to get 'em over there and back. Mile and half, that'd be too far for 'em at barely six. I was thinkin'a ridin' 'em double on the horse, but that'll make a slow start in the work here. No way to help it, though, and like you said, we're really lucky. It'll be easier for them to say their words in American if they get to listen to that girl. Miss Francine, did they say?"

"I can take the girls," Anita insisted, bravely.

"No." Jacob's voice was firm. "You're sick in the mornin's, and we ain't takin' no chances after losin' the other one. I'll figure a way. Maybe Margie? Could hitch up the cart. 'Course that'd take her away for over an hour… two times a day."

Anita then. "We'd manage. I wish it'd be so she could stay there. She'd likely be a help, and we already thought she'd have to go in my place when it came my turn go. That girl don't hardly get anything fun, and the way she is…"

Yes, the way she was. That doubled over foot had gotten no better, as they had hoped would happen as she got older. She just learned how to manage it. She was slower, but she got a lot done. Ironing. Darning socks and sewing up rips. Cleaning the floor. Never complained, but Jacob had noticed her silence and her yearning look during the party. Reminded him of someone looking through the window of a candy store, knowing they could never go in.

"Days she stays, she'll have to leave the horse hooked onto the cart. Not good for an animal, but I don't see no other way. Don't reckon she could ride on a saddle…?"

"I don't think so. She's a girl, remember. Almost a lady and it wouldn't be proper ridin' straddle in a skirt." Anita sighed, wearily. "Gotta keep thinkin'."

"Well, listen here. There's a way for women to ride. It's called a side saddle but I don't know what that is. I'm wonderin', no farther than it is, could she sit with one leg around the saddle horn to be steady? Old Plodder, he's so slow…" He paused for Anita's response. It was slow in coming.

"That'd be for her to decide. It'd take a burden off both of us if she could. And here's this, if she could go one day when it was my turn, why couldn't she go more days if she liked it. It'd do her good to hear the American words, and if she's ever to have a husband, he'd surely be American. And you remember that she missed school entirely, and she might pick up readin'… or somethin'…?"

Jacob wisely remembered that another day would be coming. "Let's go to sleep and talk tomorrow. Could be we'd get a good idea… or something'."

It was after the evening meal that Margie pulled together enough courage to put forth her idea. "Anita, you and Jacob got time to listen for a minute? I keep thinkin' on that party last night. That teacher, Miss Francine, she had words like I never heard anyone say. I could'a listened all night. I remembered how they said someone would need to be at the schoolhouse in case of an accident… or somethin'?

"I'm thinkin' I could walk that far of a morning, takin' my time, and you'd not have to bother with it. At least, till the weather gets bad. If I could do that every day, and stay till they had lunch, the other ladies could have their mornings at home. Everyone's got so much to do in the mornin'." She hesitated, watching their faces to see the reaction. All she saw was interest, so she proceeded. They could always tell her if she was on the wrong kind of thinking.

"I was thinkin' the girls was big enough to walk that far. The way they skip and run, that'd be no trick for them." She saw her brother look toward her sister-in-law, with a meaningful expression, so she waited.

"Margie, sis, we been thinkin', too. If you'd be brave, could be I got an idea. We think we got somethin' that'd work."

Margie sucked in a sudden breath of surprise and pleasure. "Oh, do you think so! And I'd make up the time I was gone. The ironin' I can do in the afternoon, and the cleanin'. And I'd take darnin' along with me, or whatever needed doin'. That'd be such a pleasure to listen to Miss Francine talk to the classes! I thought I'd look for a stick to carry, maybe helpin' me walk faster. I can be really brave but it's not even two miles to the school, and I'd take care'a the girls, like always! It didn't seem from the talks that whoever stayed had to know somethin' special. They just had to be there." She caught her breath and suddenly ran out of words.

Then Jacob. "Margie, sis, that wasn't the brave I meant. I'll go take care of somethin', and then I'll call you outside." With that, he was gone.

Margie looked at Anita to supply an answer, but she just smiled and shook her head. "This here's your brother's idea."

Later, as she stood in the yard and looked up at the saddled horse, Margie began to think it might, indeed, take some bravery. There the massive animal stood beside a sturdy box.

"Can you step up on the box and turn your back to the horse?"

She did and watched her brother's face, wondering.

"Now, reach back and see if you can pull yourself up into the saddle. Don't be concerned as how you're sitting. Reach back and hold to the saddle horn. If this works, I'll make you something better."

She was not particularly athletic, her foot being what it was, but she managed to pull herself up into the saddle, her skirt bundling about her legs. The old horse bent his head around and looked her with a puzzled expression, but he stood patiently.

"Now, sis, I know it's shakey up there, but here's what I want you to do. Your right leg, there, bend at the knee and hook your leg over the saddle horn. Easy now, Old Plodder'll get used to it."

Careful to hold to her dress and protect her modesty, she did as she was instructed. She saw the look of concern in Anita's eyes.

"But, Jacob, that'll make her foot go to sleep, won't it?"

"Not on a two mile trip, I don't think. It won't take more'n fifteen or twenty minutes to get there. And see here, there's room for the girls on behind. I'll lift 'em up today, but I can make it so they can climb up by themselves."

First one giggling girl, then the other, snugging up against Margie's back. "Now, Edith, you hold tight to Margie, and Susan, you hold to Edith. I'm going to walk around the yard and see how it works." The old horse responded to the lead line and ploded calmly behind his master, seeming to disregard the strange load on his back and the squealing and giggling of the small humans.

Following a wide circle and returning, he asked, "How did it go, sis?" A smile and an energetic series of nods was his answer. "And you, Anita?" He knew without looking at her that he had her answer. He lifted his daughters to the ground and turned his attention to his sister.

"Now we get down to work. Margie, you are going to have to learn to guide this fellow, at least for the first week or so. Then he'll know what he's supposed to do. Say 'Come on' and try to sound like me. At the same time, kick your heel against his ribs and jiggle the reins."

The old horse took another look behind him, then a glance at his master, finally lifting his feet into a solid plod. Around the circle of the yard, he went.

"All right, Margie, I want you to ride him around until it begins to bother your leg. I'll step into the barn and do a few things, but you just yell if you need me." With a reassuring smile, he left her. He heard her encouraging voice, "Come on, Plodder."

When she called, almost an hour later, he helped her down and reassured her, "For the first day or two, I'll ride along, to see if everything works out all right. You know, Sis, if you can go alone with the girls like this, it'll really take a burden off Anita and me. It's so important that the little girls go where they talk American words and not the way we say them. They're going to live here, just like you are, and they need to know, just as you do. Thanks for being brave."

As she returned to the house, Margie told herself, "HE was thanking ME? He's sounding like I can do this every day! Not just on Anita's day." She felt so energetic, she thought she could burst from the excitement of it. Books! Children! American words from the teacher! Words she so sorely needed. Pronounced so beautifully and musically!

As Jacob Van Pelt went about his work, his thoughts traveled over the last twelve years.

Back to the ship. He was not yet clear in his mind why they must leave Holland. It seemed his mother was the driving force and that there were good and important reasons for the voyage, most of them centering around himself and his brother, Henrick.

Crowded ship! Hardly room to sneeze with families jammed up together just looking for a dry place to sleep. It was summer, but for some reason the ship was always cold. Waves blew salt spray over the rails and into the hold where the passengers huddled.

Anita's family was pushed up against his family, and the children of all families became very well acquainted. They had to. The proximity forced them into each other's private conversations as though they were in the same room.

Riddles, string games, puzzles. That was all the children had to amuse themselves during the weeks on the ship. Grownups had their fears to occupy their thoughts, and the faint hope of a better life. Food was scanty and poor, and better food was available for those with gold coins, but most of the travelers, if they had coins, were certainly not going to spend them here. They would just suffer, and if hunger made them a bit more miserable, so be it.

Jacob's family was no different, and he remembered cold, hungry, and worried faces of his parents. He was almost ten, and his brother was three years younger. Anita (then Annetje Buijs) was eight. When cholera hit, Anita's two younger brothers were victims and were buried at sea, along with many other children and a few grownups.

They came ashore, the two families, easily carrying all their possessions. Their first home was one room in a huge house. Anita's family had an adjoining room. The privy was three floors down and in the alley. Water came from a faucet protruding from the ground in the front yard and must be carried up. They knew they were lucky to get the room after spending only one night on the street.

Mrs. Buijs was again expecting. Very bad timing. But what could one do? Children came when they came. The men were put to work immediately digging at the excavation to widen the channel of the river. More water was needed in the city. It was dangerous, but it paid coins.

Jacob's mother went to work in a factory, leaving Henrick with the Buijs' between his paper routes. As soon as Henrick could read American numbers, he had been set to work, and he was lucky to get the job. Older boys would have liked the job. Jacob, himself, was even more fortunate. He went to work in a stable where dozens of horses were kept for city work. He carried feed and water and mucked out the wastes. He hated it because of the smell that arose from the hot buildings, but he was glad to have the job. It paid coins and many others, including men with families, would love to have had the chance to smell the wastes.

The smell stuck to his clothes, and the waste gummed up his only shoes. Later he was able to buy rubber boots. Then the two families were able to get an apartment with water in the room. They shared the kitchen but had three rooms to each family. So much better. Unbelievably wonderful, actually.

They stayed there for years. He remembered the times his mother hopefully asked, could they, somehow, finally go west to the big river? Things would be better there. Pa agreed, but insisted the time was not right. He and Mr. Buijs would know when, and then they would go. It would need to be early spring, but not THIS spring.

The factory where his mother worked sewed heavy fabric into work pants, jackets and sometimes bags. There was no way to wear gloves, and the rough fabric fairly took the skin from her fingers. Blood! But she couldn't even be permitted to bleed, as it would ruin the item she was sewing. Deep creases of resignation settled into her face, and her coughs grew worse. Lint from the fabric, she insisted. Just one of the many things to be endured.

Jacob learned everything there was to know about horses. At times, after he was thirteen and fourteen, he was permitted to drive someone somewhere, and sometimes he even got a few extra coins for doing it.

He often wondered what jobs there would be at the Big River to the west. He thought there would come a time to go, but Pa could never agree that it was right. Pa was becoming stooped and haggard. He was not cut out for heavy digging. In the old country he was a carpenter, doing finish work inside houses, and building sturdy, classic furniture in a shop, but there did not seem to be that kind of work for him here. Perhaps it would be better at the Big River, but if Ma couldn't talk him into making the move, certainly his son couldn't.

Little brother Henrick got older, but he was of a small, slender build. The weight of the papers and the hurrying it took to deliver on time were about more than he could do. He seemed too tired to talk when he got home, and only wanted to curl up by the fire and doze.

Thinking back later, Jacob wondered if his brother had not already given up and was too tired to go on. His parents seemed not have noticed, but their son's problems may have gotten drowned within the problems of food, clothing and coal for the stove. Then a man appeared at the door carrying Henrick in his arms. He seemed to have no trouble carrying the frail body that still held breath, but the blood that soaked his clothing told the future. No one could lose that much blood and live… and he hadn't.

The driver of the carriage wept when he told of there being no way he could avoid the 'child who walked calmly into the path of his four-in-hand teams.' Sixteen horse hoofs had done the damage, and it was a miracle that the boy was recognizable. He blessedly never regained consciousness.

Then his mother was pregnant with Margie. Very poor timing, but what could one do? Children came when they came. The cough became worse, and she wanted to go west to the Big River, but Pa seemed unable to tear himself away from the grave of his son, though he had no time or strength to visit it. One more year, he promised, and there would be enough money, and the baby would be born.

The baby was born, and Ma went back to the sewing factory, leaving Margie with Anita's family. Silent and haggard, she dragged herself to work, coughing. Coughing. Gagging and coughing. It was more than the lint from the fabric. In was the dull and dingy rooms, filthy streets, noise and germs, and no sunshine.

Margie was four when the end came. Ma had called him to her bed, privately. "Son… you're my last hope." Her voice was now a whisper, and her coughs brought up flecks of blood. "You will promise me one thing. I will be gone, but…" and Jacob had stopped her words. "No, Ma, you'll get well!"

"Don't stop me. I may not have much time. Under the mattress I have stored the winter coats and my heavy blue cape. Today, I want you to lift up the mattress and take out the cape. Sewn in the cape is a number of gold coins and a few pieces of jewelry. You till keep it a secret even from Pa, but you will persuade your Pa to take you and your sister to the Big River. When you get there, you'll know what to do."

"But, Ma… I can't keep a secret from Pa… can I?"

"You must. You must finish my dream for you. I KNOW we should go to the Big River, but your Pa is stubborn and afraid. If he knew about the coins, he would spend them to make life better for us here, and it will never be better until we leave. Don't open the seams of the cape until you have made plans to go. I haven't kept it all the way from the old country to lose it now before my dream comes true."

"But, Ma, I'm only sixteen. What can I do to make Pa hear me?"

"Jacob, my son, you are only sixteen on the outside. Inside you are older than your Pa. There is money in the jar at the bottom of the flour barrel. You know that. There is enough money to take you to the Big River, and you keep the blue cape with you all the time. It is warm and heavy and will wrap around your sister in the winter. Don't let it get away. Don't wait till spring. Make your plans now..." Her words were cut away by the coughing that shook her shoulders and produced blood on the cloth.

Now, in the hot September Saturday on his own place in the Oklahoma Territory, the strong, young Hollander shook as with a chill. His height clearing six foot four, broad shouldered and filled out, a head full of yellow hair and a curly beard of reddish gold, he seemed not one to cry, but his memories didn't know that. Laying down his pitchfork, he hid his face in his shirt sleeve and wept.

That had been the last day of seeing his mother alive. It was in the night that Pa woke him up and wept on his shoulder. It was also then that Jacob sincerely hoped that he was older than sixteen on the inside, because his father's strength seemed to have turned to water.

His mother was put into the New York soil near her son, and Pa silently picked up his shovel and headed for the excavation. Jacob lifted the mattress and took out the blue cape. It was heavy, made of wool fabric and lined with fur. So many times he had seen it on his mother, and even now it carried the smell of her. He would like to have cried, but he hadn't the time.

Reaching to the bottom of the flour barrel he took out the family's banking jar. Heavy. A lot of coins, though he did not know how many it would take to get to the Big River, it was time to make plans. His mother had given him instructions, and he had always obeyed.

Wagon and a team. A solid wagon with a canvas cover to protect the people and possessions from the weather and furnish a bit of privacy. He paid for them and left them in storage where he worked.

His greatest pain was leaving Anita as they had become fast friends. They had talked of marriage… sometime. Jacob nodded in agreement with himself, as he knew the 'sometime' had come and he must, somehow, persuade her to come with him. She was only fifteen, but like his mother had said of him, she, also, was older than fifteen on the inside.

His worst problem would be Pa. He would find it terribly hard to leave the graves, but Jacob would persuade him. He would finally threaten to take little Margie and go without him. He was considerably bigger than Pa, and a lot stronger. But when Pa dragged himself home each night, Jacob found he hardly had the heart. How could he badger the old and weak person that was his Pa? And each day followed its yesterday.

His mother had been in the ground for six weeks when the rain came in a downpour that seemed determined to wash away the entire city. The muddy streets were practically impassible, and trash and filth floated down toward the river.

Still Pa went to work. Dangerous. The river raged and the metal equipment was water logged and sunken into the soft river banks. Finally the soaked ground could hold no more water and turned into a moving morass of soggy dirt. Water slamming against the machine that operated the drag-line… it lifted the wheels, turning the whole piece of equipment over. Two men were under it, and the first one was not breathing when he was dug out. The other one had a leg crushed, and he had passed out from pain, though he was still breathing.

Jacob was rushed to the hospital just as the surgeons were about to amputate. He leaned down to his father's ears. "Pa! You'll be fine. The doctors are here…."

- END OF EXCERPT -

ADDITIONAL BOOK SERIES BY JOANN KLUSMEYER

The Great I Am Bible Story Series for Kids
6 books

The Young Pioneers Adventure Series for Kids
5 books

The Wentworth Triplets Mystery Series for Young Teens
3 books

Footsteps in the Canyon Adventure Series for Young Teens
4 books

Burnt Tree Junction Historical Fiction Series for Adults
6 books

Ozark Mountains Historical Fiction Series for Adults
7 books

Taming the Wilderness Historical Fiction Series for Adults
4 books

The Sheltering Stones Historical Fiction Series for Adults
5 books

The Trilogy of Wishbone Hollow Historicial Fiction Series for Adults
3 books

www.ingramcontent.com/pod-product-compliance
Lightning Source LLC
Chambersburg PA
CBHW070851250626
47159CB00003B/1026